Critics are screaming for the novels of Michael Slade

"Will raise hackles, eyebrows, and blood pressure everywhere. . . . Gives you real shock value for the money."—Robert Bloch, author of *Psycho*

"Would make de Sade wince."—*Kirkus Reviews*

"There is no safety for a reader in a Michael Slade book."—*Vancouver* Magazine

"Slade runs a three-ring circus of suspense."
—*Booklist*

"A thin line separates crime and horror, and in Michael Slade's thrillers the demarcation vanishes all together."—*Time Out*

"The kind of roller coaster fright fans can't wait to ride."—*West Coast Review of Books*

"Bloodthirsty, scandalous, and gory."
—*Publishers Weekly*

"To put it bluntly [Slade] is not for wimps."
—*Fangoria* Magazine

"Well written, very well researched. A gripper."
—*London Daily Mail*

BURNT BONES

Michael Slade

A SIGNET BOOK

SIGNET
Published by New American Library, a division of
Penguin Putnam Inc., 375 Hudson Street,
New York, New York 10014, U.S.A.
Penguin Books Ltd, 27 Wrights Lane,
London W8 5TZ, England
Penguin Books Australia Ltd, Ringwood,
Victoria, Australia
Penguin Books Canada Ltd, 10 Alcorn Avenue,
Toronto, Ontario, Canada M4V 3B2
Penguin Books (N.Z.) Ltd, 182–190 Wairau Road,
Auckland 10, New Zealand

Penguin Books Ltd, Registered Offices:
Harmondsworth, Middlesex, England

Published by Signet, an imprint of New American Library,
a division of Penguin Putnam Inc.
Previously published in a Viking edition by Penguin Canada.

First Signet Printing, March 2000
10 9 8 7 6 5 4 3 2 1

REGISTERED TRADEMARK—MARCA REGISTRADA

Printed in the United States of America

PUBLISHER'S NOTE
This is a work of fiction. Names, characters, places, and incidents either are
the product of the author's imagination or are used fictitiously, and any
resemblance to actual persons, living or dead, business establishments, events,
or locales is entirely coincidental.

For the Islomaniacs

PART I

Question

Here's to it!
The fighting sheen of it,
The yellow, the green of it,
The white, the blue of it,
The swing, the hue of it,
The dark, the red of it,
Every thread of it!

The fair have sighed for it,
The brave have died for it,
Foemen sought for it,
Heroes fought for it.
Honor the name of it,
Drink to the fame of it—
The TARTAN!

—Murdoch Maclean

Cold, Cold Ground

By the light of a harvest moon four days short of full, the Druids of Shipwreck Island fashioned a Wicker Man. Clothed in black robes with pointed cowls, they sat in the Stone Circle hidden in an oak grove above a rocky cove and wove sapling branches into human form. Like black fingers clawing from a premature grave, moonbeams cast long shadows behind the upright monoliths ringed around them. The Wicker Man was large enough to cage a captive inside, with an octagon head on a square body flanked by stubby arms tipped with finger-like sticks. The stiff legs were angled to support the finished figure once it was erected, at which time the earth around would be piled with kindling. Now the earth around was strewn with autumn leaves, and beneath four feet of cold, cold ground, a groggy man drugged with sodium pentothal came out of unconsciousness to find he was buried alive.

Fitzroy Campbell freaked.

First he feared he was in a trench in the First World War, just after an artillery shell exploded nearby, throwing up a wave of earth that crashed down on him, flattening the hapless soldier supine at the bottom of a filled-in ditch. That's why no coffin encased his flesh and moist, worm-riddled soil packed him down, paralyzing his limbs like a quadriplegic's so he couldn't move a muscle. Then he recalled that he was born too late to suffer this fate in that war, and he remembered his uncle recounting the dread as his own.

Plus he could breathe.

The freak-out that seized him was fostered by the overwrought prose of Edgar Allan Poe, for he had delved into "The Premature Burial" too early as an impressionable boy. *It may be asserted, without hesitation, that* no *event is so terribly well adapted to inspire the supremeness of bodily and of mental distress, as is burial before death. The unendurable oppression of the lungs—* the ground above Fitzroy pressed down on him, forcing Campbell to heave his chest against the weight for air— *the stifling fumes of the damp earth*—even though his mouth and nose were sheathed in some kind of mask, he could smell the decay of animals and plants in the dirt—*the clinging to the death garments*—his wet clothes would be his shroud—*the rigid embrace of the narrow house*—claustrophobia!—*the blackness of absolute Night*— not a thing to be seen—*the silence like a sea that overwhelms*—not a thing to be heard, except whispers in one ear?—*the unseen but palpable presence of the Conqueror Worm*—Jesus, he could feel such worms squirming on his cheeks, and imagined a grisly image of them making him a meal, burrowing into his body to suck and chew on organs inside—*these things, with thoughts of the air and grass above, with memory of dear friends who would fly to save us if but informed of our fate, and with consciousness that of this fate they can never be informed—that our hopeless position is that of the really dead—these considerations, I say, carry into the heart, which still palpitates, a degree of appalling and intolerable horror from which the most daring imagination must recoil.*

Fitzroy Campbell shrieked.

The shriek was caught by the microphone within the oxygen mask over his mouth and nose, and carried up the wire to a transmitter above. So loud was it, the scream reverberated through the ground to the overhead circle, where it curled smirks on the faces of the cultists in the hoods. The mind of the underground man was gripped by a powerful drug, a barbiturate used as anesthetic to knock him out, then—now—as a truth serum after he came to. Pentothal induced in him the urge to talk, for it was a tool of psychotherapy or interrogation applied to glean repressed or consciously withheld information. With no one to talk to, Fitzroy shrieked instead, as he was overwhelmed by a heightened state of suggestibility, also drug-induced.

Night fright squeezed him.

While he relived it . . .

Hooded demons lurked behind the trees of his Orcas Island estate, waylaying him as he carried veggies from the garden to his home for dinner, one of them wielding a sap that slammed his head. The phone in the house was ringing as they dragged him to the dock—was that his son in Atlanta, calling with news that a grandchild was born?—blood drops from his scalp being smeared by trailing legs. They shoved him onto a launch and powered out to sea. One of the demons bent over him, blocking the glow of the moon. Then a needle winked in a hand approaching his arm, and he felt it bite deep into an exposed vein. Blackness closed in from the borders of the starry sky, and the last sight his mind took in before night became absolute was of pagan eyes in flesh painted blue glaring from the hood.

Deep, deep and forever, he slept the sleep of the dead, only to awake from blissful slumber to this, such terror that it surged the blood from his brain in a torrent back to his heart, which was pounding in the cage of his chest in a frantic bid to escape, as he, too, struggled against the cold ground to burst free, writhing, squirming and twisting to no avail, for he was held as rigidly as if frozen in ice. The concrete overcoat of gangsters was no worse than this. A long, wild, continuous scream issued from his throat. Life shrank down to an obsessive need to move, if only to push back the rigid embrace of the grave by a single inch. Oh God, how long must he suffer like this? A day? A week? Eternity? Until he starved to death? Another minute locked in here and he'd be stark raving mad. . . .

Then a voice . . .

In his ear . . .

From an earplug . . .

Words down the wire from the transmitter above . . .

A chilling voice . . .

Heartless . . .

"Where's the Hoard, Campbell?"

Gibbering from the premature grave was transmitted by the microphone in the mask to the upper floor of the Victorian mansion high on the bluff that overlooked the Stone Circle in the woods. Speakers that usually blared Wagner's *Götterdämmerung* or Highland bagpipe wails into the lunar observatory under the peaked roof now brought Fitzroy Campbell's shrieks of dread to Mephisto's ears. As the antiquary listened to his prisoner's despair, no emotion touched his heart. A greenhouse stocked with an array of carnivorous plants was built into the southern slant of the roof. The cold, gray eyes of the psychopath stared through the glass at the moonlit confines of his charnel garden. Dishes of meat rotted within the silver gloom of the hothouse, breeding insects. Halos of flies swarmed around plants on cedar shelves, drawn by nectar sweetening the traps. Like miniature hands with curling fingers hinged at the wrist, Venus flytraps sprang shut with the clap of death when trigger hairs were brushed. Globs of glue stickier than household cement glistened the tips of spines jutting from pincushion-like sundews. Flies caught by dozens of both species of hungry plants were *buzzing buzzing buzzing* uselessly to get free. The gaping mouths of pitcher plants lined the tiled floor, open maws with spiked, downward-bent bristles a one-way staircase forcing creepy-crawlers to plunge into acidic wells. The hoods of cobra plants hunched above. Flat on the ground among them were butterworts, flypaper traps exuding adhesive if touched by insect legs, holding the prey as oval leaves rolled up like cigars. There was an aquarium of bladderworts, submerged sacs with trap doors triggered by hairs, the inward rush of water sucking in aquatic insects.

Moonlight mirrored the ghost of the watcher on the glass. His black hair was slicked back with every strand in place. His sunken eyes were black pits, like those of a skull in this dark room. His Vandyke beard narrowed to a perfect V, in which his sadistic mouth was a slash of cruelty. Mephisto was the name he assumed back when he sold his soul to the Devil in exchange for knowledge and power. With the clinical fascination of a scientist vivisecting a rat, he watched eelworms squirm through a growth of fungus to reach wheat sprouts. Fungus stalks grew straight up from the pot, then bent, branches down, to fasten near the roots. As one manicured hand stroked the V of Mephisto's beard, he watched an eelworm stick its head into one noose. The loop tightened instantly around the worm, tighter and tighter the more it tried to retreat. As Fitzroy's screams rose to a fevered pitch, Mephisto crossed to his telescope.

A microphone was clamped near the eyepiece.

Into it, Mephisto asked, "Where's the Hoard, Campbell?"

The antiquary was dressed in garments of the past. He wore the tartan of his clan, for such was the symbol of kinship. The Gaelic word for tartan is *breacan,* which means "checkered," so the checks on a belted plaid slung over one shoulder and draped down to his knees as a kilt were green and blue with white and yellow stitching. A brooch at the shoulder pinned it to his vest. Below the belt and dirk at his waist hung a leather sporran. Hose of a tartan pattern rose from silver-buckled shoes to garters above the calf, and tucked in the righthand stocking was his *sgian-dubh*. In dress, if not in manner, Mephisto was a perfect Highland gentleman.

His war cry was *"Cruachan!"*

Eye to the eyepiece, he gazed up at the moon. When Mephisto marveled at the pocked surface every night, he saw not the ruined wonder of today, the lifeless chunk of dust and rock on which Neil Armstrong planted that supposed "giant leap for mankind," but the moon of ages past that ruled every life. The phases of the moon were carefully charted in almanacs of old, for only if the moon was out could people travel safely at night on rough roads with no artificial illumination on vehicles or the way. The moon was said to wax—grow—as that's what watchers believed it did. In vague shadows across the disk, the imaginative saw the Man in the Moon, the Madonna and Child, the Crab and other moon lore. The changing size of it held the moonstruck in awe. Why was the moon larger some nights than others? Why did a full moon shrink as it rose from the horizon? When it was a narrow crescent, why was the faint outline of the full moon, the so-called old moon in the new moon's arms, seen? Hunter's moons and harvest moons governed gathering food. The lunar eclipse was a sign of foreboding. Predictable phases of the moon led to their use as a calendar, and before there was writing to record them, such movements were set in stone.

And would be again.

If Mephisto was right.

The screams from the speakers went suddenly hoarse as something in Fitzroy Campbell's voice box tore. The antiquary nodded. On this, too, was he right? No phobia is worse than claustrophobia?

As a boy, he'd walked the dusty streets of Pompeii with his father, the eerie ghost town taking possession of his hyper imagination while the archeologist painted a vivid verbal picture of Mount Vesuvius erupting on a hot summer day in 79 A.D. "With a blast like a horrific cannon, the lava plug in the crater of the volcano blew sky-high. Molten rock hurled a mile into the air cooled to rain down as pumice stones. Poisonous gas hissed out of the fissure to kill birds in flight. Daylight turned to darkness when a black cloud of ashes torn by sheets of flame and zigzag flashes roiled down to smother this doomed city. Pushed by earth tremors, the Bay of Naples rolled back on itself. Pliny the Younger, who witnessed the calamity, heard cries of women, wails of children, shouts of men. Some called to parents, some to bairns, some to husbands and wives. Convinced this was the end of the world, most raised helpless hands to Roman gods. Fountains of steam from the crater mixed with sea spray to pour scorching cloudbursts down on Vesuvius, surging an avalanche of boiling mud and lava down the mountain to cover Pompeii. Overcome by fumes, or buried beneath a deep layer of pumice and ash, or entombed by lava in sealed-up rooms, two thousand Romans perished in this volcanic catastrophe."

The lost city, his father explained, was uncovered sixteen centuries later, in the 1700s. First a source of treasure, later it was systematically dug up to see how Romans had lived, and then, from 1860 on, how they had died. For that was the year Giuseppe Fiorelli took over the dig, and he soon noticed that cavities in the pumice seemed to have human shape. He filled them with liquid plaster and let it dry, then chipped away the rock molds to see what was inside, and found that he had resurrected the dead of Pompeii. The bodies of those covered by what vomited from the volcano had been preserved in perfect casts before they rotted away. Wandering among such grim tableaux of wretches buried alive, the boy felt his morbid fascination spawn obsession.

Here was the Temple of Isis, complete with animals to sacrifice. And mourners at a funeral feast gassed to death at the table. And a man entombed with a dog that must have outlived him, for it died gnawing at his leg. And criminals forgotten in their cells. And gladiators locked in their barracks, one of whom, best of all, was trying to escape. He had loosened a stone from the wall of his room, behind which a narrow passage sloped down an incline. The tunnel constricted to a hole just large enough for him, forcing the gladiator to snake along on his belly, arms stretched in front of him to claw with his fingers, legs stretched behind him to push with his toes. Sunlight or moonlight on the wall of a bend ahead promised freedom. So steep and gripping was the incline that he could never go back, but that didn't overwhelm him until he wormed around the angle to find the tunnel sealed by an iron grate.

How long he was confined in there is a matter for conjecture, but when ash and pumice buried him it must have seemed a blessing.

Claustrophobia!

What terrors seize the mind?

How long until a man snaps and goes mad if buried alive?

Like many mysteries that hooked him as a boy, a need to know obsessed Mephisto still. No more could he shake this compulsion to prove claustrophobia the worst dread of all than he could shed this maddening compulsion to find the Hoard.

Interring Fitzroy Campbell alive had scratched one itch.

Now if only it would scratch the other.

With an eye on the moon through his telescope, Mephisto spoke to the microphone.

"Answer and I'll release you. Where's the Hoard, Campbell?"

Kidnapped

"Hey, Mom. I found one."

Six-year-old Becky stood at the edge of the potato patch with a brown lump in her hand and dirt on her cheeks and forehead from where she had brushed back from her impish face wayward strands of russet hair rumpled by a playful breeze off Rosario Strait. Stalks of corn in the patch beyond stood like green footmen waiting to convey this Cinderella to the upcoming fall fair in one of the orange pumpkins plumping nearby. Come Halloween, ghoulish grins would line the porch.

"Take it to Gram, honey. That in the pot will give us enough for stew."

"Texas pot roast?"

"If you like."

"Goody," Becky enthused.

For better or worse—better for keeping his memory alive, but worse for the ache it brought to her heart—Jenna could not face her daughter without remembering Becky's father. With the fox face and slender chin arched by unruly hair, the sly, mischievous eyes stalking her every move, waiting for an opening to crack a joke on her, Becky was the mirror image of Don. To live with the pea was to live with the pod, and that was to live with a prankster.

"See that old man over there?"

Her memory went back to the bistro in Seattle that final night. Beyond the glass beside their window table a cranky old bugger berated an old Chinese for spitting on the sidewalk.

"Which one? They both look eighty."

"The white guy who went to the doctor today."

Jenna rolled her eyes. "Is this one off-color?"

"Not unless you hate old-man jokes."

"Okay," she said, playing along. "Why did he go to the doc?"

"Plumbing problems. His wife took him. The doc did a physical and explained, 'For tests I'll need urine, stool and semen samples.'

" 'Ehh?' said the old man, cupping his ear." A squeak in Don's voice mimicked the geezer's. "He turned to his wife and said, 'What'd he say?'

" 'He needs your underpants,' she yelled in hubby's ear."

The punchline caught Jenna by surprise. For jokes with lists, he usually went through them one by one. This snappy kicker got a laugh from her.

To listen to Don, you'd think a day at the DEA was a joke-telling session. Every night he came home with a zinger and found a way to feed it into chitchat before dinner. The Suits at the Bureau rarely told jokes, for their white collars were starchier than the blue denim at the Drug Enforcement Administration. The emphasis was on *Special* at the FBI.

Special Agent Jenna Bond.

La-di-da.

"Something's up, Jen. Got a meet tonight. May be a lead on the cartel."

"Spoil your birthday?"

"I won't be late."

"I'll wait up to celebrate."

"Lots to celebrate if this works out."

Which it didn't. And Don was gone. Never to return to her and never to be found. Just his voice on a tape that they wouldn't let her hear. Hours of torture some-where at the hands of the cartel. Sent to the DEA as a threat spawned by Colombian machismo. Voiceprint proved it was Don.

A week later, Jenna knew she was pregnant.

"Hey, Mom. What do you call a camel without any humps?"

Becky's question brought her back from seven years before. The child was on her hands and knees in the potato patch, the brown lump balanced precariously be-tween her shoulder blades.

"Got me, honey."

"Humphrey," Becky said, shrugging off the potato.

Jenna laughed.

"I got another one."

"I'm sure you do. But save it for dinner—which we won't have if you don't take that potato up to Gram for the pot."

She watched Becky climb the path from the patch to the farmhouse porch, unlatching and relatching the mesh deer fence. Deer were the munching marauders of Orcas Island. All the way up the stone steps to the pillared veranda, Becky juggled the potato from hand to hand, passing under the gabled room in which Jenna Bond had been born in 1962. That year, the film *Dr. No* had opened in Seattle, and Jenna's mom had heard island women talk of the sexy hero. Assuming that influenced her choice of given name for the girl—and who could have known how *lasting* the James Bond franchise would be?—in hindsight it wasn't a good moniker for a kid who would follow her father into law enforcement.

Oh, well, it could have been Valentine Hart.

Who was a freckled redhead at Becky's school.

The San Juan County sheriff was elected every four years. Hank Bond was returned to office twelve times in a row before he suffered a stroke at his desk and died with his boots on. In Friday Harbor on San Juan Island, the sheriff's office was a square, brown-brick building behind the red-brick courthouse. Displayed on the wall inside the main door were pictures of all sheriffs elected back to 1892. From handlebar mustaches then up to user-friendly smiles now, the face that seized attention was Hank Bond's. With his no-nonsense eyes in an angular face and the cropped hair of a Marine, only fools would fail to think twice about messing with him in his county. Which no doubt explained why Hank was elected again and again and again. Jack Palance as Wilson in *Shane* was Sheriff Hank Bond, yet no child could ask for a more loving dad at home than him.

Becky and Don.

Pea and pod.

Jenna and Hank were the same.

For she, too, had an angular face and cut her hair short. Androgynous—like Annie Lennox—was how others saw her. It wasn't that Jenna played down the fact she was female, or that she wasn't sexually oriented toward males, but she had always preferred the functional style of men to frivolous primping and fashion. Here on the farm she wore flannel shirts, jeans, overalls and gum boots. On the job she wore suits, no make-up and a shoulder holster. Sometimes she'd pause inside the door to face her father's photo. The glass would reflect her own features back at her, and superimpose her face over his. It pained her to think that not once would Don gaze at himself in Becky.

Like most island kids, Jenna found Orcas too small in her teens. The lure of the city drew her to college and Seattle's FBI. That seemed a giant step up from the life of a San Juan cop, but that illusion died when Don was kidnapped, tortured and killed. A single mom faced with the option of working and raising Becky alone amid urban grunge or going home to help her widowed mother maintain the Orcas farm, Jenna returned to island calm, breathing space and salt air. Hank's daughter became a deputy at the sheriff's office, and worked her way from uniform into plainclothes. Detective would be the final step before she ran for sheriff, and hopefully her face would join Dad's on the wall.

Islomania.

Jenna had caught the disease.

With her back to the farmhouse, she stood in the potato patch and squinted out to sea. Sunlight sparkled on the backs of waves whipped by the wind, while haze hid the horizon of the mainland east. Seen from the water, she was the farmer in *American Gothic*, lean and weathered in bib jeans with her hoe the painting's pitchfork. Past the rows of squash and beyond the deer fence, a lawn sloped toward a pebble cove, where a gangplank extending from shore was hinged to a float. As Jenna watched the *Islomania* ride the tide, the pager in her pocket called.

Friday Harbor.

Sighing, she followed Becky's tracks uphill to the house.

The yellow-and-white two-story boasted a new coat of paint, yellow brightening bay window walls and white defining trim. Autumn leaves shed by surrounding maples quilted the shake roof, which was gabled over dormers, and tumbled down on the breeze to carpet Jenna's way. After moving up the steps, along the porch, then past Gram and Becky, she entered the house her father had built to attract her mom as a wife. Varnished walls paneled with knotty pine. Braided rugs on blond fir floors. Ruffled curtains cinched back with bows. Rockers by a wood-burning stove and built-in window seats. Rustic Americana from Rockwell covers in picture frames spread throughout her home. Jenna picked up the phone on the end table by the plush easy chair and called dispatch.

"Trouble, Em?"

"Missing person, James."

"James" was a joke to him and a "Paine" in the ass for Jenna. Emmett Paine was the dispatcher at the sheriff's office, and just as M sent Bond out to save the world, so Em sent her around Island County. Not for the first time, Jenna thought, Time to change my name.

"Who's missing?"

"Fitzroy Campbell."

"He's almost a neighbor of mine."

"Why I called. You're so near. Ought to be you checks it out."

"His being a pioneer family and all?"

"It's good PR. In case you plan to run for sheriff someday soon."

"Hadn't crossed my mind."

"In case it does. Look bad if we dispatch from East-sound, what with you so near."

"Neighbor call it in?"

"Son in Atlanta. Trying to phone the old man since last night."

"Could be off-island."

"Fitz said he'd wait for the call. Grandchild born in Georgia is his first."

"Last night, huh?"

"Phone rung off the hook. Son tried the neighbors, but no luck."

"Today's Columbus Day. Could be at events."

"Speaking of which, why ain't you? Good PR, James. In case you plan to run'"

"I'll take a run to Doe Bay, Em, and call you from there."

It was doubtful her potato would make it to the pot, for by the time Jenna returned to the porch, Becky had fashioned it into Mr. Potato Head. Gram sat at her easel dabbing a watercolor.

"Why'd the leopard lose the race?" Becky asked her mother.

"Beats me."

"The other guy was a terrible cheetah."

"Ha ha," Jenna said, messing Becky's hair. "Friday Harbor, Mom. Spin in the boat. Fitzroy Campbell didn't answer an important call. I'll check on him and be home for dinner."

"Did Em call you James?"

"His running joke."

"Wish I'd named you Elspeth instead."

"I like my name."

"You could change it."

"Thought never crossed my mind," Jenna said.

"But you will change out of that? By plainclothes, they don't mean *that* plain."

Hank bought the *Islomania* secondhand, and with it came the previous captain's log. Stuck inside the front cover was a passage from Lawrence Durrell, the opening lines of *Reflections on a Marine Venus*. Zane Grey, Max Brand, Louis L'Amour: Hank read solely westerns when he read. But he liked the quote, kept it and passed it on in the log:

> Somewhere among the notebooks of Gideon I once found a list of diseases as yet unclassified by medical science, and among these there occurred the word *Islomania,* which was described as a rare but by no means unknown affliction of spirit. There are people, Gideon used to say, by way of explanation, who find islands somehow irresistible. The mere knowledge that they are on an island, a little world surrounded by the sea, fills them with an indescribable intoxication. These born "islomanes," he used to add, are the direct descendants of the Atlanteans, and it is towards the lost Atlantis that their subconscious yearns throughout their island life. . . .

A Cancer by birth and nature, Jenna felt an affinity to the sea, avoiding her car when she could take the boat. To her, she was the Marine Venus Durrell wrote about, a mermaid in her fantasy life as a child, a siren in her erotic dreams now. The woman inside wasn't the woman on the surface, and deep down her subconscious fathomed Atlantis was home.

Islomania.

Having made her way down from the house, Jenna walked the plank to the float on the cove. She climbed aboard the *Islomania* by the stern and opened the engine compartment under the deck. A hundred-watt bulb burned to circulate air. She used the manual bilge pump to empty the hull of water, checked the oil (as it was the life-blood of the engine), then turned on both batteries for juice. With this compartment shut, she ducked inside the cabin to activate the blower to suck any gas fumes from the bilge, then cranked the ignition and "lowered the leg" to sink the prop in the water. As the Leg Up light went out, Jenna returned to the float. She untied the boat, walked it back and gave the bow a tug to swing it around before she jumped back on and climbed to the bridge. Here she pulled the weather tarp off the captain's seat.

Twenty-four feet long, nine feet wide at the beam, the *Islomania* was a command bridge cruiser powered by a Volvo Penta 290. It could be steered from the bridge up top or the cabin below, but unless inclement conditions forced her inside, the bridge was the command station Jenna preferred. She took the captain's seat on the starboard side of the boat, shoved the black-handled transmission lever forward from neutral, then pushed the red-handled throttle to *Goooo.* . . .

The *Islomania* cruised out into Rosario Strait and turned north.

Back on the porch, Becky waved Mr. Potato Head.

Jenna threw her a salute.

The San Juan Islands were "discovered" by Spanish explorers in 1790 when Francisco Eliza sailed into the Strait of Juan de Fuca. This archipelago was named for the fifty-third viceroy of New Spain—now Mexico—Don Juan Vincente de Guemes Pacheco de Padilla H*orcasi*-

tees y Aguayo, Conde Revilla de Gigedo. That mouthful holds the tidbit of Orcas Island.

With wind wilding her sand-colored hair and tearing her cobalt eyes, Jenna rode the heaving waves up the inland shore of the island like a bucking bronc, spray spuming onto her as whitecaps cleaved. A square mile larger than San Juan Island two miles to the west, Orcas not only was the king of the county in size, but also reared up to its highest point, Mount Constitution. A cloud had lowered over the mass like a Portuguese man-of-war, a bladder-like mound adrift in the azure sea of the sky, trailing tendrils of mist down the slope to obscure the strait, through which, appearing and disappearing, came the *Islomania*.

Orcas Island had the shape of an inverted U, both south-pointing horseshoe prongs flanking the fjord of East Sound. The inlet endowed the island with waterfront property galore, fostering a tranquil retreat for escape-from-it-all homes. Jenna lived near the southern tip of the inland prong. The Campbell acreage was on the same strait, up by Doe Bay.

The acreage beyond the dock toward which Jenna now veered the boat.

The acreage where Fitzroy Campbell lived alone.

The cloudy man-of-war smothered Mount Constitution dead ahead. The Peapod Rocks, scattered up the strait to her right, fountained sea foam. Turning on the blower to suck fumes from the engine well before throttling back, Jenna powered down to maneuver the *Islomania* past small Doe Island offshore, approaching the dock from the port side. The Campbell acreage, hemmed in by towering cedars, was a grass green swath in a sea of forest green. What could be seen of the pioneer house was wrapped in gauzy mist, up where an orchard bordered primordial trees. No ax had felled the copse in which this Campbell clan had lived for fourteen decades. With the fenders already down on the port side, Jenna came in with just enough forward "way" to steer, bow about to nose the dock as she put the engine into reverse, turned the wheel hard to port and brought in the stern. Pushing the transmission into neutral, she left the bridge to scramble down a ladder to the deck, grabbing a line before she scaled the dock to secure the boat.

Then she saw it.

Blood.

Waves slapped the hull as it rocked back and forth on the surf. The fenders, squeezed between the boat and the dock, squeaked. A dive-bombing gull squawked and let go a splatter of white. Barnacles climbed creosote pilings to weathered planks above, planks on which drops of blood were smeared when someone—Fitzroy?—was dragged from the shore to here. Footprints on both sides scuffed through gull droppings.

Kidnapped? Jenna thought.

Too good a cop to disturb the dock until forensics were through, she returned to the *Islomania* to release the dinghy and row ashore to a path unlikely to have been used for the crime. It could be that the blood was from a perp helped away to sea, so she would check Fitzroy's home to make sure he wasn't injured, but in her mind—the blood was dry—she knew he was spirited away under cover of night.

For a moment Jenna stood at the stern to gaze left and right, up and down the strait between Orcas and the mainland. The San Juans have 375 miles of rugged shoreline, the most of any county in the United States. There are 457 islands, rocks and reefs visible at high tide. There are 768 visible at low tide. Of these, 175 have names. Jenna's jurisdiction was a kidnappers' paradise, so she ducked into the cabin of the *Islomania* to radio marine patrols from the sheriff's office and alert the U.S. Coast Guard.

Deep Blue Sea

A man on the cusp of old age, Gavin Campbell had
pissed himself. His incontinence didn't result from old-
age plumbing problems like those in the joke Don had
told Jenna on the night he vanished—the type of peeing
condition that sells Depends by the carton—but because
Gavin was scared shitless, pissless and spermless by
these three goons. Until he awoke in the stern of the
boat with his hands cuffed behind his back, head
throbbing from a sap blow and muddled with some sort
of drug, the last thing he recalled was chopping wood
on Mayne Island. Now here he was adrift on a foggy
rolling sea, the horns of other ships bellowing in nebulous white mist, clammy veils of vapor devouring him as
the trio of hooded pirates went about scuttling the boat.

His boat. Not theirs. Tied alongside.

The fog in his head was thicker than that swirling off
the sea, and it took him a moment to fathom what was
going down here, then Gavin realized what was going
down was *him!*

A captain and his ship.

SOS!

Dressed in waterproof gear not unlike their Stone Circle robes, blue faces buried deep in pointed plastic
hoods, slickers straightline to below their hips, these
Druids, who two days ago had buried Fitzroy Campbell

alive in the cold, cold ground, today focused their attention on the deep blue sea. The deep blue sea under the *Bounding Main*.

Unable to move because his feet were tied together and chained to a ring bolted on deck, and unable to try to reason with them because his head was encased in a diving helmet, all Gavin could do was piss his pants and watch them prepare.

Pants sheathed in a wetsuit living up to its name.

The goon nearest him hung over the side and used a depth sounder to measure the distance from the hull to a reef submerged below. He cut an equal length off a reel of waterproof coaxial cable, then wired one end to the microphone in Gavin's helmet, and the other end to a buoy fitted with a digital transmitter run by a lithium battery. As he linked this communications system to the headphone in the helmet, he gave Gavin a little wink through the plastic face mask.

Around his eyes were tattoos.

The goon beside them yanked wires from the bilge pump in the engine compartment astern, sabotaging it so brine leaking in would not be expelled. The third Druid ensured leaks by opening the seacock to the head in the cabin, thereby aligning the hole through the ball valve in the hull with the hose to the toilet, a hose he cut with a razor-sharp knife before exiting to also do this to the water intake that cooled the engine. As the boat began to fill like a huge bathtub, the Druids abandoned Gavin and his sinking ship for safety aboard their sea-tight craft. The last man off coiled the cable on deck out of Gavin's reach, and dropped the buoy in the water between as they cast off.

The boats drifted apart.

"Shrubby" is as good a word as any to describe an islander. Not your tourist or weekender or their ilk, but your islander-islander, who lives on-island year-round. Your *true* islander is overgrown and proud of the fact. Men get their hair cut a few times a year, whether they need it or not, and sometimes they shave, sometimes they don't. Make-up on island women makes them look like clowns. We're talking *real* people, folks. Not primped, powdered and puffed.

"Shrubby" was the word to describe Gavin Campbell. The Mayniac—that's how Mayne Islanders refer to themselves—sat on the transom at the stern of the *Bounding Main,* a trickle of piss running down his leg and blending with the incoming brine, while he struggled like Houdini to free his feet from the chain and his hands from the cuffs. The window in back of the cabin reflected him at him. A wild shock of white hair frizzed behind the mask, turning whiter by the second as fear of drowning took hold—an unfounded fear given the oxygen tank strapped to his back, for if it gave out he would suffocate, not breathe water.

Albert Einstein playing Jacques Cousteau, that was Gavin's reflection.

A continuous flow of deep blue sea gushed into the bilge as the waterline rose inexorably to engulf both man and boat. Hull timbers strained by the increasing internal weight creaked and groaned, as if tortured on the rack of a cruel sea. Water, water everywhere, while eyes behind the face mask darted frantically. Adrift at the outer edge of visibility, hazy, hooded goons watched the *Bounding Main* go down, pleased with their handiwork as water poured over the gunnels of the rapidly sinking ship. *AAAAH-wuh! AAAAH-wuh!* mourned foghorns behind the pale beyond.

First the deck, then the cabin, disappeared below. Gavin craned his neck as high as he could periscope it, but a moment later the face mask followed. The wretched man was swallowed by the sea, gulped *down,* more like it, as he sank sank sank. The plunging anchor of the chain fastened to the boat dragged him down to the bottom of the channel. Air compressed within the cabin escaped as clouds of bubbles like those of an Alka Seltzer tablet, fizzing up the coaxial cable unwinding off the deck to boil and burst among the heaving waves that bobbed the buoy above.

The keel of the boat came to rest on the reef of a liquid grave.

Gavin Campbell was buried alive at sea.

Like Fitzroy on Sunday night, the clansman freaked.

Shipwreck Island, Washington State

Atlantis, he thought.

Listening to the sounds of sinking carried up the coaxial cable from the submerged microphone to the buoy above, then transmitted digitally to the mansion on the bluff commanding the Stone Circle in the woods (the Wicker Man within the ring now complete), Mephisto stood in the greenhouse amid voracious carnivorous plants and thought back.

As a boy, he'd paced the rocky coast of Crete with his father, the Ancient World seizing possession of his morbid imagination while the archeologist told the tale of the sunken Eden. "First to write of Atlantis was the Greek philosopher Plato, around 355 B.C. The legend came from Egypt. He tells of an island situated to the west of the straits called the Pillars of Hercules. Atlantis was the island, and it was the heart of a great empire that ruled as far away as Northern Italy. The world's first civilization, it was destroyed by earthquakes and floods, and in a single day and night vanished into the depths of the sea."

In his mind's eye, the boy saw Atlantis sink.

The sky turned the color of dried blood and a mass of black clouds swept across. The earthquake, felt before it was heard, churned deep in the bowels of the island, rumbling as it shook the concentric rings of land and sea that were the Atlantean metropolis above. Roof tiles

shaken from the Temple of Poseidon clattered down into
the central courtyard of the city. Shock wave on shock
wave echoed out, tossing boats on the ring of the inner
harbor, toppling columns on the ring of the middle island, heaving waves from the ring of the middle harbor
over the ring of the outer island to the great harbor, the
wash swamping triremes before it found the open sea.
As hills around began to buckle and collapse, the
screams of those crushed by the shift were lost in the
ear-splitting din. People rushing from their houses
choked the streets, where panicking horses reared and
rolled their eyes in fright and dogs howled like hell-
hounds with each new quake. Those swarming the quay-
side found no safety there, for bedrock beneath the
ocean convulsed, too, crumbling the stone dock into the
swirling deep, dragging wailing thousands in. Those who
ran back to the now-flaming city were trampled by those
fleeing for the writhing shore. The turbulent sea threw
up tidal waves. Walls of water flooded the island as it
sank in on itself, swaying houses crashing into streams
that once were streets. The ground lost all solidity under
wading mothers holding their babies aloft. Death throes
from Atlantis' disembowelment took everyone down,
and the maelstrom left where land had been but no land
remained flushed those who managed to launch boats to
the bottom of the sea.

Coughing . . .

Sputtering . . .

Choking . . .

Regurgitating brine . . .

Down . . .

Down . . .

Down they went . . .

Into Atlantic darkness while sea water stung their
eyes . . .

Down . . .

Down . . .

Down . . .

While bubbles . . .

o

o

o

bubbled up.

"Aristotle," his father said, "thought Plato made Atlantis up, but the books of more than two thousand scholars disagree, and Plato flatly affirmed four times that the story was true. The myth of Atlantis came down to us as a golden age of mankind, a land of great observatories, libraries and laboratories that became the wellspring of human arts and sciences. Astronomy was at the center of their culture, for Atlanteans sought to discover the mystic force that powers the Cosmos. Harness such magic and there would be no end to human knowledge. Men would become gods.

"Skeptics likened Atlantis to Homer's tale of King Minos of Greece. According to myth, Minos was the king of a glittering civilization, which he ruled from a fabulous palace on Crete. Lurking in a dark labyrinth under his throne was the monstrous Minotaur, a hybrid human with the head of a bull. The ravenous beast was fed virgins and youths sent in tribute from Athens and left to wander lost in the maze until the creature culled them. Legend says Theseus ended this cycle of sacrifice. Unwinding a ball of string to guide him through twists and turns in the grisly labyrinth, the Greek hero stalked and killed the Minotaur."

The boy's imagination heard the monster roar.

What's it like to be eaten alive? Piece by piece? he wondered.

"For 2,800 years it was thought that Homer had weaved a dream. A fantasy with no more substance than the legend of lost Atlantis. Then, lo and behold, in 1902, the British archeologist Sir Arthur Evans unearthed the ruined city of Knossos here on Crete, with the Palace of King Minos at its heart."

The archeologist led his son up a dry, dusty slope to

the buff-colored complex that spread like honey over the mound of Kephala. The sacred summit of Mount Juktas to the southwest was where Zeus died each year once the harvest was in. Through a gap in the hills that cupped the palace and fell away to Crete's north coast, a blue Aegean Sea met blue Greek sky.

The honeycomb of the palace was truly a labyrinth. Without a guide, a visitor would quickly lose all sense of direction. They wandered through the baffling layout of multileveled corridors, colonnades, courts, shrines, halls, rooms and staircases sprawled over many acres. Each time an earthquake damaged the palace, Minoans had rebuilt and expanded the ruins.

"See how the myth of the labyrinth was born?" said his father.

The archeologist led his son through the palace to the Toreador Fresco. The wall painting depicted young acrobats—both men and women—grabbing the horns and doing somersaults over the back of a charging bull. The bull was revered as a symbol of power and fertility by Minoans. The chance of surviving this death-defying act of bull-leaping was about the same as exiting from the monster's labyrinth.

"See how the myth of the Minotaur was born?" said his father.

The boy's imagination heard an acrobat scream.

What's it like to be spiked alive on a bull's horns? he wondered.

Their last stop in the palace was the Throne Room. There, a gypsum chair sat backed against a wall painted with wingless griffins.

"Europe's oldest throne," the archeologist said to his son. "The ruins of Knossos tell us the facts behind Homer's story. Between 3000 and 1450 B.C., Minoan power and culture thrived on Crete, antedating Ancient Greece by many centuries. Knossos was large enough for a hundred thousand people. Minoan traders sailed the Mediterranean all the way to Egypt. But by the time of

Homer, all evidence of this society was erased. Soil covered the palace, and the only memory to survive was the myth about King Minos of Crete and his Minotaur."

The archeologist sat his son on the gypsum throne, then squatted so his Mephistophelian features faced the boy. Black hair greased back from a widow's peak so it hung in ringlets behind his head. Eyes like coal pits, and sunk as deep. Skin dark from too many years digging under a hellish sun.

"Wherever there's a legend, son, hunt and you will find. The legend of the Boy King lured Howard Carter to Tutankhamun's tomb. The legend of the Lost City of the Incas lured Hiram Bingham to Machu Picchu. The legends in Homer lured Heinrich Schliemann to Troy and Arthur Evans here.

"So," he said, leading the boy outside, "where do we find Atlantis? Seventy miles north of here"—his father pointed through the gap to the blue Aegean—"is the island of Santorini. Santorini is all that remains of the volcano Thera, which erupted and blasted apart around 1500 B.C. The only modern equivalent is Krakatoa exploding in the Pacific in 1883. That produced tidal waves that swamped neighboring islands, drowning forty thousand. So deafening was Krakatoa's eruption that it was heard in Australia, three thousand miles away, and it remains the loudest sound verified in history. But as cataclysmic as that was, Thera was four times worse.

"Waves three hundred feet high slammed Crete, and under them Minoan civilization drowned. No more trading ships went to Egypt, so the Egyptians may well have equated the flood that reached them with the sudden vanishing of the Minoans. Did that give rise to the myth of Atlantis heard by Plato, a rich and powerful island lost when it sank into the sea?"

"*This* is Atlantis?" The boy gazed around.

"The dates when Thera erupted and Minoan culture declined overlap. Atlantis may be an allegory born from what happened here, but I don't think so. The legend

of Atlantis came from Egypt, not Greece. According to
what Plato was told, the island sank *beyond* the Pillars
of Hercules, which we call the Strait of Gibraltar. Those
two promontories mark where the Mediterranean meets
the Atlantic, so Atlantis sank into the Atlantic Ocean. If
Atlantis was the world's *first* civilization, with its empire
stretching *east* to Northern Italy, the Egyptian legend
isn't about the Minoans, but has to be about the mythic
builders of the megaliths."

"Callanish?" said the boy.

"And the Ring of Brodgar."

"Newgrange?" said the boy.

"And Carnac in France."

"Stonehenge?" said the boy.

The archeologist nodded.

And that's when he told his son the legend of the
Hoard.

*"Wherever there's a legend, son, hunt and you will
find."*

So that's why Gavin Campbell was at the bottom of
the sea.

Atlantis!

Drowning!

What terrors seize the mind?

*How long until a man snaps and goes mad if buried
alive at sea?*

Like many mysteries that hooked him as a boy, a need
to know obsessed Mephisto still. No more could he
shake this compulsion to know if life passed before your
eyes than he could shed his maddening compulsion to
find the Hoard.

The Scotsman going down with the *Bounding Main*
had scratched one itch.

Now if only he would scratch the other.

Campbell was crying for his mother.

The pentothal had him babbling.

Beyond the glass of the greenhouse built into the
southern slant of the mansion's roof, fog crept through

the woods of Shipwreck Island, obscuring the Wicker
Man in the Druids' Stone Circle. Diffused daylight created a somber mood, befitting the carnage happening
around Mephisto. The breeding dishes of rotted meat
had been removed to stabilize the hordes of flies *buzz
buzz buzzing* within the glass prison. Overpopulation
swarmed the psychopath as he reviewed his array of carnivorous plants. Slowly but surely, the plants culled the
flies, for everywhere Mephisto looked traps had been
sprung or were springing. Lining the edges of the
shelves, brass plaques identified each species.

Ultricularia vulgaris.

The aquarium of bladderworts caught Mephisto's eye
first, as it was a visual metaphor for Gavin Campbell's
fate. Each submerged branch was tipped with translucent
green traps. Bladders full of water had sucked in prey,
and Mephisto watched the bugs within struggle to
wrench free.

"*HEEEEEEEEEELP!*" screamed Campbell.

He'd be struggling, too.

The aquarium gave Mephisto a diabolical idea, one he
told himself he must try in the future. Rather than sinking Campbell to the bottom of the sea, could he not
attain the same effect with an immersion tank and *watch*
the Scot freak out? Pumped full of pentothal to wag his
tongue, the unconscious man would be stripped naked
and cinched into a body harness, hands tied behind his
back and blindfolded before he was lowered to hang
suspended in a huge tank of water warmed to body temperature. The man would come to in darkness and not
know where he was or why, thrashing about in a medium
that wasn't air, as a regulator on a hose masking his
mouth fed oxygen to him.

Through the tank, Mephisto could watch every jerk,
twitch and death throe.

Sight *and* sound, while all he had here was sound.

Dionaea muscipula.

The ranks of Venus flytraps were having a feast as

snap snap snap they closed on landing flies. Jaws like sharks' teeth interlocked to swallow insects alive into makeshift stomachs. Crushing them slowly to digest them with enzymes, the snapped traps jiggled from prey panicking inside. Mephisto, crouching so light from outside backed some of these traps, watched the shadows within writhe and shudder their wings. The pincers of one trap held a fly half in and half out, so the psychopath pulled the *sgian-dubh* from the top of his tartan stocking to prod it all the way in.

The tip of the three-inch blade pricked the fly's eye.

Again the antiquary was dressed in garments of the past. Though not with the oldest Highland regiment, he wore the blue-and-green tartan of the Black Watch. What Mephisto fancied, Mephisto made his, for he saw himself as a chameleon worthy of any ancient role. The past was his and him. Claimed to be a Campbell tartan, the Black Watch was worn by the Duke of Argyll, and what was good enough for a duke was good enough for Mephisto.

He liked the pattern.

And the Campbell connection.

To subdue the Highland clans after their defeat at the Battle of Culloden in 1746, the English passed an act of Parliament disarming Scots and forbidding the wearing of tartan. Stripped of his two-handed claymore sword, musket, pistol, ten-inch dirk and targe shield, the clansman took to hiding a small knife, dubbed a *sgian-dubh,* in one stocking to defend his family. Tradition in the Black Watch regiment says that you never draw your *sgian-dubh,* unless you draw blood, so Mephisto nicked his knee before sheathing it.

How he loved tradition.

And hated modernity.

Though some technology, like digital communications, definitely helped.

"*PLEEEEEEEEEESE!*" screamed Campbell. "I'M GOING TO DROWN!"

From his sporran, Mephisto withdrew a portable mike like rock stars use. What he said was transmitted from here to the buoy bobbing in Boundary Pass, and down the coaxial cable to the headphone in Gavin's helmet.

"You won't drown. You'll smother to death. The air in the tank on your back is running out. If you want to live, answer my question. Otherwise, it's going, going, gone . . . for you."

Gasping.

Choking.

Rasping for air.

"Antigonus Severus. The Druid medallion," Mephisto prompted.

More gasping from the speakers.

"Where's the Hoard, Campbell?"

The Woodpile

Pender Island, British Columbia

Nick Craven was at the woodpile splitting rounds of fir when he heard a vehicle approaching down Dooley Road. Like Mephisto, Craven craved a return to the past, when life had deeper meaning, so recently he had pulled up roots in Vancouver to transplant himself here in the Gulf Islands, across Boundary Pass from the San Juans in the States. The first chore an islander has to learn is how to chop wood, for a wood-burning stove is the heart of his home when winter howls around. An honest cord is four feet by four feet by eight, the size of cord your grandpa knew, the *only* size of cord you could sell to Penderites, not the "face cord" or "metric cord" sharpies in the city sold to slickers with money to burn. At three cords a winter, that meant you swung the maul, ax and hatchet or froze. In a red plaid flannel shirt with cuffs turned up at the wrists, the muscles of his torso cinched in suspenders and jeans, noon sun bleaching his short hair and military mustache a lighter blond, sweat beading his forehead and streaking one cheek, as autumn leaves tumbled around him from the shedding trees, Nick confirmed Paul Bunyan had nothing on him. So adept had he become with these tools that now he could fracture a round of fir *within* its bark, storing the kindling as a bucked log until a blow from the flat of the maul freed instant firewood.

The woodpile as art.

Nick heard the car approaching almost half a mile away, winding along Dooley Road from Hope Bay, seaside estates on the left and rural spreads inland, past Hope Bay Bible Camp and donkeys in pasture corrals, until it reached his driveway and turned up. Raised in the city, Nick had tired of noise. That, the stench of gas fumes and kids flipping him the finger instead of waving when he patrolled, all made the grass greener on the Islands side. So peaceful was it here that now he caught *every* sound—his neighbor could fart three acres away and he would hear him pass wind—and soon could recognize the bark of each dog along the road and the engine rumbling of each local car, and when windows were indiscreetly left ajar on warm nights, he knew who felt the earth move prior to sleep.

General noise or particular noise: choice, but no escape.

Stranger on the farm, thought Nick.

He couldn't place this car.

The farm, if a farm it was, raised flowers instead of crops, milk or meat. From his woodpile, uphill near the farmhouse, Nick watched the vehicle come into view, slowly scaling the driveway past the Star Garden by the Dooley fence, where the last of the dahlias were drooping colorful heads; past the Pond Garden, which fed an irrigation pump in the hot months, each year a gamble as to whether water or summer would end first; then up between the greenhouse beyond the deer fence and the Gazebo Garden, still vivid with snapdragons within, to eventually round the Buddha Garden to park behind the house.

Ax in hand, Craven approached the car.

"Nicky!" Katt greeted, alighting from the driver's side of the Mercedes Benz to throw both arms skyward in a dramatic gesture befitting a ham onstage. "At last I have wheels!"

"And what wheels they are," said Nick, touring the car. He noted the yellow happy face and Jack In The Box giveaway topping both antennas, the fuzzy dice dangling from the rear-view mirror, the imitation black-and-white cowhide cover on the driver's seat, the steering wheel sheathed in fuzz to match the dice, the Esso tiger tail sticking out of the gas tank, the orange Garfield with suction-cup feet affixed to the rear window beside the Student Driver sign and—his eyebrows shot up—the bumper sticker!

"What a ride!" DeClercq said, emerging ashen-faced from the passenger door. "I thought it best to turn her loose on rural roads. She almost creamed a deer and put us in the ditch."

"You're the island cop, Nick. Why no deer-crossing signs?" groused Katt.

"You decked out the car like this?" he countered.

"Me and my friends. Imagine the shame in having to learn on this old-fogy-mobile. So we customized it with a little pizzazz."

Craven turned to DeClercq. "I have this right? You and Katt were seen off by her teenage friends, then you drove from the North Shore, across Vancouver, south on the freeway through Richmond and Delta, then west to the ferry at Tsawwassen, to sail across Georgia Strait to Galiano, then Mayne, then Pender Island, driving off at Otter Bay to reach my home—"

"We first went to the detachment, but you weren't there," said Katt.

"Great, so you left the RCMP office by way of the main road to travel this *very* conservative island known to vote Reform, a fifty-something man with a sweet young thing at the wheel—who, incidentally, doesn't look a bit like him—allowing her to drive his fancy automobile to my door, all the way flaunting your road philosophy on this bumper sticker."

"What bumper sticker?" said DeClercq.

"What bumper sticker?" echoed Katt.

"Your bumper sticker," said Craven, as they joined him at the rear.

Gas, Grass or Ass. Nobody Rides for Free.

Katt hid her face behind one splay-fingered hand. "I've been sabotaged!"

"Young woman," said DeClercq dryly. "Time to cull your friends. You want to be a Mountie, so solve this whodunit."

"Cool abode, Nick," Katt enthused, deftly segueing to another subject.

The farmhouse, if a farmhouse it was, befitted the novels of Tolkien. Rose canes arching the shake roof of the mud room at back would bloom yellow come spring. Up on the peak, a weather vane was crowned with a unicorn. Painted over the outer door was a rainbow, and scrolled on the inner door was Goddess Bless. The security decal in one window warned Protected by Angels. Nick left the ax outside as Katt led both men in and along a hall to the kitchen, passing an altar to the Earth Goddess in a nook off the hall from which a tunnel staircase rose to the upper floor. Calligraphy over the stairs prophesied Ultimate Abandon.

DeClercq glanced back at Nick.

"Don Juan," said Craven. " 'It does not matter what our specific fate is, as long as we face it with ultimate abandon'."

"Of course," said DeClercq. "I assume up there is your bedroom?"

"Oh, wow!" Katt exclaimed. "Get a load of this. It makes me want to burn our kitchen down and start again. Y'ever decide to sell this place, sell it to me, Nicky. Bob can finance it till I'm rich and famous."

"Good old Bob," sighed "Bob" DeClercq.

The just-turned-sixteen-year-old stood, arms out, in the center of the kitchen, spinning slowly like Julie Andrews in *The Sound of Music*. Hundreds of bouquets of dried flowers hung upside down from a lattice rack over her ash-blond hair. A three-tiered Bali umbrella strung from the ceiling seemed to whirl its colors around the walls: rooster red and sunflower yellow with blue-green wainscoting. Vines were hand-painted around windows

and the fridge door. Baskets of every description, suspended wherever there was space, overflowed harvest
cornucopias of garlic wreaths, Indian corn, artichokes,
beans and more flowers. Pioneer cooking tools hung
from the shade of a lamp over the stove. Shelves counter
to ceiling on both sides of the sink were lined with
apothecary jars filled with spices and herbs. There were
knick-knacks and candles and plants and plates and pots
displayed on one wall. There were tins of tea from
around the world and a teapot in a cozy. It was a hodge-
podge, but somehow it worked, this artistic clutter out
of Hansel and Gretel. From the smile on Katt's lips,
DeClercq knew Gretel had just dropped in.

"Don't sit there!" Nick snapped as Robert selected
a chair.

DeClercq jumped.

If it had been the electric chair, his shock would have
been no greater.

"Why?" he asked.

"That's the Queen Chair. No male's allowed to sit in
it. You'll curse the farm."

"What happens? A bolt of lightning zots in through
the roof?"

"She didn't say."

"Who didn't say?"

"The Flower Lady. A term of selling the farm to me
was that I couldn't mess with tradition."

"Have you lost your mind?"

"No, found it," said Craven.

"Shoo, shoo, Bob," Katt said, brushing him aside to
turn and wiggle her fanny and plump down with a sigh
of satisfaction. "Ah, yes, Nicky. At last a man who keeps
a liberated home."

Head lowered, DeClercq eyed his surrogate daughter
over specs he didn't wear. "Some of the male persuasion
might question that, Katt."

"Only sexists, Bob."

At times like this, he reminded himself that life wasn't

a film by Fellini. Crowned with sprigs of dried flowers and festooned with ribbons, the Queen Chair was crafted from branches and twigs harvested on the farm. Katt sat regally on this throne as if born to rule its New Age— or Old Age—realm. Maybe she was, for Katt was raised by Luna Darke, a practicing witch who had kidnapped her as a baby in Boston. They went undetected in Canada for fourteen years, until Luna murdered a private detective who had tracked them down and fled with Katt to a writers' retreat on Deadman's Island, where a psycho attempting to conjure Jack the Ripper flipped out. He killed a lot of writers, including Luna Darke, before Katt was saved by Craven and DeClercq. Robert was a cop with a tragic past. His first wife, Kate, and daughter, Jane, died at the hands of terrorists during the Quebec October Crisis of 1970. Twelve years later, he lost his second wife, Genny, to the Headhunter. Death had gouged giant holes in both their lives, leaving him with a house that was nothing more than shell and Katt on her own without a home, so he took her in and she salvaged his soul. Some kids are docile, some are off-the-wall. Living with Katt was to live with the most animated of all. Shakespeare penned "All the world's a stage" for her. With such a background, you might expect Katt to recoil from the Queen Chair of Earth Goddess Farm, but maybe the home of a white witch was the ideal sanctuary for this refugee from the black witch's realm.

The New Millennium.

Pagan times.

DeClercq turned to Craven. "I have this right?" he said. "You work your way up the ranks of the Mounted Police to get into Special X, a position sixteen thousand others would sell their souls to the Devil to attain. The world is now your oyster, with postings around the globe and your anchor in Vancouver, arguably the most beautiful city anywhere today, and I return from holidays to learn that you've quit your job with me to command one of the smallest rural detachments in B.C., selling the home in which you grew up to burn all bridges behind you. So out I come to see if anything's wrong, and find you holed up in a cottage sprinkled with fairy dust, alone with a chair you can't sit in!"

"I'm not alone. I brought Jinx, Mom's cat," said Nick. He nodded toward the living room beyond the Queen Chair. A black cat was curled up asleep on the floor by the wood-burning stove. Hand-painted flowers gussied up the planks.

"A witch's house. With a black cat." Robert rolled his eyes. "Asleep in a *pink* living room."

"Pink is peaceful."

"I know. They use it in prisons."

"That's what I said. 'A *pink* living room?' And the Flower Lady replied, 'You'll understand when the cherry trees bloom.' "

"Cool," said Katt.

"I'm listening," said DeClercq.

"Have you never wished you could escape to another time? H.G. Wells's *Time Machine.* Say you owned it. When in the past would you rather live?"

"London, 1880 to 1900. With antibiotics."

"Why?" asked Nick.

"New mysteries crept in from the Empire with every ship. Enchanting Edens beckoned if you sailed out. Life was exciting. Architecture was art. Artists crafted the chattels of everyday use. Theater, classical music, and opera reigned. Top hats, gaslight, fog and hansom cabs mixed. Sherlock Holmes, and *Dracula,* and *Dr. Jekyll and Mr. Hyde,* and Wells were hot off the press. Pageantry and politics were color and fire. And I'd have a chance to collar Jack the Ripper."

"I'd go back to the fifties," said Nick. "The last great decade before homogenization. You went somewhere, you found the place it was reputed to be. Not identical franchises strung coast to coast, so the main drag anywhere could be the main drag here. Doo-wop harmony and the birth of rock-and-roll. Music with melody, not too much angst and noise. Summer came and life slowed down to lazy hazy days. Not endless traffic jams and guys on cellphones exploding with road rage. Kids who were turned loose to play where they wanted returned if they were hungry. You went to the movies with a date to see Jimmy Stewart and Gary Cooper as heroes who stood for something. Not nihilistic apes ramming guns in people's mouths to yell, 'Suck on this!' as gangs of knuckle-draggers yelp, 'Yo, my man!' "

"You can't run away to the circus, Nick."

"Can't I?" said Craven. "You fear I'm verging on a breakdown, Chief. A mid-life crisis at best. You suspect that the one-two punch of me standing trial for the death of my mom and Gill dumping me as her lover has overwhelmed my reason. Incidentally, thanks for how you handled her coming on to you until we resolved it."

"The man who said all is fair in love and war had no ethics."

"Have you never wished you could shed your life to reinvent yourself? What those blows did was knock sense *into* me. They gave me a second chance to get it right, by severing all ties that bound the old Nick Craven to who he was."

He moved to the kitchen window, which overlooked the farm, and stood beneath the word *Awe* painted above. His hand motioned Robert and Katt to join him.

"Through that gap in the trees across Dooley Road you see Plumper Sound. Sometimes a pod of killer whales swims by. There's only one bald eagle in the sky above right now, but I've counted eleven. That deer outside the fence is Herbie. He sleeps beside the mud room in winter to keep warm. The ducks paddling on the pond are Jack and Jill. Depending on the season, owls, herons, kingfishers and hummingbirds are common. Each morning, I stand here with coffee and listen to Vancouver's traffic report before driving along that quiet road to work at the detachment, five minutes away. We've never had a murder, and no more than twentysome jailbirds pass through the cells in a year, mostly impaireds. My job is to keep the island so people don't lock their doors, not sit on the lid of a garbage can stinking up the city. Every building on the island is made to order. No franchises here. Community spirit abounds at the fall fair, barn dance and other get-togethers. What I have on Pender are all the things I crave from the fifties. And life has no resale value, Chief."

Robert nodded. Now he understood. "So all you need is a queen for the Queen Chair?"

"I'm working on it. That's why I bought this farm. You're looking at a fantasy in reality. The Flower Lady put fifty years into her work of art, and somewhere out there"—Nick swept an arm south along the sound toward the San Juans—"I know there's a woman of like mind to share it with me."

"Uh-oh, Nicky," Katt said. "Trouble in paradise." Behind them, pawing sleep from his eyes, Jinx sat on the Queen Chair.

"Don't panic," Robert said, playing it as straight as he could. "Are you sure the Flower Lady warned 'No male' and not 'No man'?"

" 'No male,' " confirmed Nick.

"Damn, scratch that loophole."

Katt protected her head against a zot through the roof.

The telephone rang.

"Does a male become an it if he's neutered?"

"Craven," Craven answered.

The call was a 10-72 from the constable on Mayne Island.

———

Mayne Island, British Columbia

If you're standing in Seattle looking north up Puget Sound, assuming you could see this far, the major San

Juan Islands, from west to east, are San Juan, Lopez and Orcas. Across the border of Boundary Pass farther north, the parallel west to east major Gulf Islands are Saltspring, Pender and Saturna. Saturna, however, is also the anchor for a north-south chain, so above it and still next to Pender is Mayne, and above Mayne are Galiano, Valdes and Gabriola, on up the inland strait between Vancouver Island and the Mainland of B.C.

The Pender detachment police boat—an antiquated twenty-foot Double Eagle—was moored across the island at Otter Bay. From Nick's farm, they drove to the dock in the farm truck, on which the Flower Lady had painted vines to match the house. DeClercq offered his car, but Craven declined. "My vines are less offensive than your bumper sticker."

"Where's the Force vehicle?"

"In the shop. Amies Road eats car suspensions for lunch."

To prove the point, *bumpity-bump,* they drove Amies Road.

Katt was hoping for action like on *Miami Vice,* but the only thing 13K 94099 had in common with cigarette boats was cigarette burnout. Tied to the first finger of the marina dock, the two-tone had a light blue cabin and deck over a white hull liveried with the RCMP bison crest. There was a searchlight in front, and horns, a loud-speaker and a hatch above. They took three of four back-to-back seats and set out to sea.

"Open her up," ordered Katt.

"Aye, aye, matey," Nick said, giving the boat more throttle. To *chug chug,* the launch—a euphemism—added another *chug.* "For the price of one of those cata-marans that the brass buy Marine, every coast detach-ment could have a s-p-e-e-d boat."

"Let's row," groaned Katt.

October is the month when fog rolls in, and banks of it to the south masked the San Juans. From Otter Bay, they entered Swanson Channel, sun adding sparkle to the whitecap waves, then angled up the west shore, past Port Washington on Grimmer Bay. Washington Grimmer, a Pender pioneer, settled on the island back in 1882, when rowing was how you got from here to there, there being Miners Bay village on Mayne. In 1885, he married sixteen-year-old Elizabeth Auchterlonie, and lived with her at Old Orchard Farm. When she went into labor with their first child, the only midwife was on Mayne, so Washington put her in the boat and rowed fast, but not fast enough to oar seven miles. Their son was born halfway across Navy Channel, a birth marked by the name given to the boy: Neptune "Navy" Grimmer, Nep to his friends. This trip to Miners Bay was less of an ordeal, with the *chug chug chug* of the engine replacing the sound of oars as the police boat bobbed across Navy Channel and up the west shore of Mayne, past Dinner Bay and Village Bay to Helen Point, rounding the Indian reserve to head east through Active Pass, between Mayne and Galiano. Miners Bay took a bite out of Mayne midway through the pass.

You might think Active Pass took its name from the volume of boat traffic, for this was the shortest route between the capital of Victoria, on Vancouver Island, and the city of Vancouver, at the mouth of the Fraser River on the Mainland, but no cigar. The big year around here was 1858. "GOLD!" was the shout along the Fraser River, word spreading south to miners going bust in California fields, luring them away to pan El Dorado north. Before you could say eureka, the Mainland Colony of British Columbia was born, and Captain Richards on HMS *Plumper* was charting this pass. Daniel Pender and Richard Mayne were members of his crew. Pender Island, Mayne Island and Plumper Pass were mapped, then Richards learned that the first ship to sail through the pass was USS *Active* in 1855, so he renamed the narrows Active Pass in honor of it. Active Pass by then was as active as could be. American miners by the thousands streamed up the coast to Victoria, where they launched a ragtag flotilla of sailboats, rowboats and canoes to reach the Fraser River by the shortest route, overnighting at Miners Bay to stock supplies and rest. The first land pre-emptions on Mayne Island date from then, one hundred acres each taken out by Christian Mayers, James Greavy and Ewen Campbell.

They didn't know it yet, but that's why the Mounties were here.

Those who cannot remember the past are condemned to repeat it.

George Santayana.

Wasn't he a rock musician?

Or did he besiege the Alamo?

With the bluffs of Galiano to the stern, jade green tidal currents surging by the hull and flocks of white birds skimming the waves, the Pender police boat angled into Miners Bay. The bay was a dip with rolling heights to either side, the hills yellow and orange, with a bit of red as autumn took hold, flanking a fertile valley that cleaved inland beyond. The seaside village retained its heritage, the streets and buildings much like they were in pioneer days, when this was the social center of the Islands. Back then, the Mayne Museum was the Islands' first jail. The first jailbird was Henry Freer, a con artist arrested for larceny on Galiano as he was gathering wild plants for his hair-growing and freckle-removing tonics. As Nick throttled down to approach the private dock on the east arc of the bay, two ferries in the pass behind seemed to go head to head in a nautical game of chicken.

The double wash rock-and-rolled the boat.

As corporal in charge of the Outer Gulf Islands Detachment, Craven commanded three local constables: one on Pender, one on Mayne, one on Galiano. The Mayne cop stood on the rocky beach beside the dock, waving the boat toward the float that served the neighboring property. He ran parallel to them along the shore, and caught the rope DeClercq tossed to moor the Double Eagle.

What had lured Chief Superintendent DeClercq to Mayne was a fax, received yesterday at Special X from the San Juan County sheriff, alerting the Mounties to the kidnapping of Fitzroy Campbell from his waterfront estate on Orcas Island, just in case those involved tried to hide across the border in Canada. When Craven related the 10–72 serious crime report from Mayne, DeClercq registered a possible U.S. connection.

His jurisdiction.

"Sir," said the constable, pleased to find Special X in his bailiwick. No doubt he thought Nick a fool for abandoning that for this. Special X—the Special External Section of the Royal Canadian Mounted Police—investigated crimes with links outside Canada.

The boaters disembarked.

"Constable Martin," DeClercq said, glancing at his name tag. "Meet soon-to-be Constable Katt."

"Where's the body?" Katt asked, hand shielding her eyes like Hiawatha.

"Sorry, only blood."

"You called me out in the middle of a rainy night for *only blood?*" said Katt dramatically, it being a sunny day.

"Constable Martin," DeClercq amended. "Meet soon-to-be *Commissioner* Katt."

All four shared an ice-breaking laugh, then Craven said, "Bring us up to speed."

"Greater speed than the boat, I hope," said Katt.

"Enough," said DeClercq.

The teenager zipped her motormouth. Seen but not heard, said her scowl.

"Gavin Campbell's a mainstay of Coast Watch," said Martin. "The DEA expects a mother ship to unload drugs at sea, and to smuggle the cargo in north and south of the line by small craft. Gavin keeps an eagle eye on boats in the pass, so when I couldn't reach him by telephone, I drove over. He's nowhere on his property. Come take a look at his woodpile."

From the float, they followed Martin up the adjoining

property on a so-called path of contamination, a route least likely to have been used by anyone involved, so therefore one that kept them from walking on forensic clues. They entered Campbell's acreage by an overgrown trail, and cut through the bush to a woodpile sheltered by trees close to his pioneer home. From the house, a swath of waterfront swept down to the dock on Miners Bay, with Active Pass beyond. Over the hill behind the homestead, green farmland spread up the valley cleaving Mayne.

Martin indicated the chopping block.

"Blood drops fan out from that point. Campbell was splitting rounds when he was attacked. Whoever bloodied him also ransacked his house. Floorboards pulled up and holes punched in walls. A thorough search for something hidden."

"How many?" DeClercq asked.

"Three," said Martin. "Their footprints are both in the house and around."

"Find what they wanted?"

"I doubt it, Chief. The search didn't finish until every nook was tossed."

"Ident called?"

"On their way. Best I could, I stayed clear of any forensic traces. But I had to make sure Campbell wasn't dying somewhere."

"Shallow grave in the woods?"

"None that I could find. Footprints climb from the dock to the woodpile, then walk *over* blood spatters to the house, then return to the woodpile and descend to the dock."

Katt unzipped her mouth. "Maybe he was chopped up and carried off in bags? Or run through a wood chipper, like in that *Fargo* movie?"

"Too little blood for that," Craven said. "I think it's more likely the spray fanned out from a blow to the head. Then whoever did it searched Campbell's house and land. Finally, they picked him up and trundled him down to the dock."

"How dull," Katt said, deflated.

No cigarette boat.

No dismemberment.

Modern sensibilities raised expectations.

Kidnapping was out of Robert Louis Stevenson.

Oatmeal, haggis and Highland clans.

"See a trail of blood to the dock?" DeClercq asked Martin.

"No, but I purposely stayed off the path."

"Campbell have a boat?"

"Shares it with a friend. Sometimes it's here. And sometimes around Georgina Point."

"Name?"

"The *Bounding Main*."

"Check it out?"

"Not yet, but I will. The three more likely docked and fled in their own boat."

Katt saw potential to salvage this crime.

"Could be drug smugglers taking revenge for his spying on them. Maybe Campbell cost them a load. If so, by now he'll be food for fishes at the bottom of the deep blue sea."

Blood Sport

The Scottish proclamation framed on the wall of Mephisto's observatory overlooking the Stone Circle was printed in 1782:

> ### LISTEN, MEN!
> This is bringing before all the Sons of the Gael that the King and Parliament of Britain have for ever abolished the Act against the Highland Dress that came down to the Clans from the beginning of the world to the year 1746. This must bring great joy to every Highland heart. You are no longer bound down to the unmanly dress of the Lowlander. This is declaring to every man, young and old, Commons and Gentles, that they may after this put on and wear the Trews, the Little Kilt, the Doublet and Hose, along with the Tartan Kilt, without fear of the Law of the Land or the jealousy of enemies.

His eyes focused on the words he had read so many times before in prelude to donning his garments of the past—this morning he dressed in a tartan once worn by Campbell of Glenlyon, who had commanded the government troops in the Massacre of Glencoe—while his ears listened to a tape recording of Gavin Campbell smothering yesterday at the bottom of the deep blue sea.

Gasping.

Choking.

Rasping for air.

"Antigonus Severus. The Druid medallion," Mephisto prompted.

More gasping from the speakers.

"Where's the Hoard, Campbell?"

As he listened to the final moments of the dying man, the antiquary recalled what his father, the archeologist, had told him that day decades ago on the Greek island of Crete about the myth of Atlantis and the legend of the Hoard.

In his imagination he traveled back to Ancient Rome.

Antigonus Severus.

The man behind the legend.

The origin of the Hoard . . .

Rome, 297 A.D.

Fight to the death.

Sine missione.

No thumbs-up from the mob in the tiers to reprieve the vanquished.

Only one man would walk off the scorching sands of the Colosseum.

Retiarius or *secutor.*

"Net man" or "pursuer."

Armed with a sword and a long, rectangular shield, the *secutor* stalked the *retiarius* across the arena, for the best defense of the latter was quickness of foot in flight. Circled by fifty thousand bloodthirsty spectators, the doomed man and his killer—betting furious up the rows as to which would end up which—were dark silhouettes on this dazzling 92-by-57-yard stretch of sand. Face hidden by the visor of the huge helmet he wore, sword arm sheathed in a leather sleeve with metal scales, red loincloth looped from his wide sword-belt and both lower legs protected by greaves, the *secutor,* sunlight flashing from armor, closed on the near-naked net man.

Trident in one hand, net in the other, Antigonus Severus turned to face his pursuer.

The mob up the tiers held its collective breath.

The Colosseum orchestra struck a dramatic note.

With his net swung in a circle overhead, Antigonus cast the meshes.

Before dawn, the mob had gathered in that ancient hollow where the Golden House of Nero once stood, with three of the Seven Hills of Rome around, the Velian, Caelian and Esquiline. Here, near the end of the first century, Emperor Vespasian, then Titus, then Domitian, had built—with the help of thirty thousand Jewish prisoners—the finest amphitheater of all time. Besieged by a clamorous crowd of the city's poor, who were impatient for opening so they could secure a seat up in the "gods," the Colosseum loomed in cruel isolation. The bloody sun had reddened the *velum,* bands of linen affixed to masts and manipulated by sailors to shade the tiers within from glare, before bleeding down the white façade of the oval arena—from Corinthian to Ionic to Doric columns, interspersed with arcades and embellished with statues twenty feet tall—until it washed over the rabble streaming through seventy-six doors. Non-citizens, slaves and women had to climb to the gods, where *vomitoria* spewed them out along the high tiers. Wearing dark mantles patched and clasped with cheap brooches, footwear gaping to expose coarse threads used in repair, they shoved and jostled for places with good views, where they would sit all day in the overpowering heat, eating, drinking and shouting above the emperor. Augustus had once sent a herald to suggest that the behavior of one man better suited his home. "Yes," said he, "but you don't risk losing your place."

A third of the way down the tiers, colors blanched to white. Here, a pillared wall divided plebeians above from patricians in togas, who were seated leisurely, for they had reservations. The right to enjoy Roman games was a perk of citizenship, assumed by dissolute tribunes, knights, magistrates and senators. Only those with puffy cheeks well-known to the public, sons of pimps or *lanistas* who traffic in gladiators, and gigolos who earn a fortune by the sure means of the vulvas of rich, old women applaud from these seats, wrote Juvenal. The front four tiers held the most corrupt. Backed by mosaics mounted on the marble wall thirteen feet up to protect them from African beasts released for arena hunts, the elite of Rome joined the emperor. Their wives, beehives dyed as blond as Germans', the jewels weighing them down hired for a day, arrived in litters carried by trotting Syrian slaves to sit with virgins who tended Vesta's flames. With scalps bald and beards grown to ape Stoics, the dignitaries jangled sesterce coins in greasy palms and wagered on which combatant's blood would stain the sand below. The emperor alone wore purple in this sea of white, for recently he had resurrected a tale of Caligula. His mad predecessor had offered games so he could sport the armor of Alexander the Great, robbed from the tomb for him. When a colored mantle drew the mob's attention away, Caligula had the offending king of Egypt executed there and then.

Now, as he cast the net, one hundred thousand eyes fixed on Antigonus Severus.

The net man's eyes locked on the pursuer.

He didn't hear the crowd hush as the meshes fanned out.

He didn't hear the orchestra's crescendo.

He didn't hear the roar of beasts under the arena, where five hundred lions, forty elephants, tigers, panthers and bears were caged.

All he heard was the dry rattle as the net slipped off the *secutor*'s helmet, smooth and without decoration so there was nothing for the confining meshes to catch. The pursuer ducked and raised his shield to just below his eyes, metal meeting metal to form a slick tortoise shell to thwart the enveloping net. Sword arm kept free to parry thrusts of the trident, the *secutor* counterattacked the moment the meshes fell away, before Antigonus could recover.

The mob tensed.

The *retiarius* was always the underdog. Except for the metal sleeve on his trident arm, and a shoulder piece protecting that side of his neck from lateral blows, he wore no armor. No helmet. No greaves. And no shield. So destitute of guard was he that often—though not today—he fought from a dais with sloping planks to equalize the odds. Caligula never spared the lives of *retiarii,* for the lack of a helmet meant he could watch death throes distort their faces.

Before Antigonus could recast the net, the *secutor* parried the thrust of the trident with his shield and slashed at the hand gripping the cord used to haul back the meshes. Blood gushed from his forearm as Antigonus dodged, and the razor-sharp sword severed the cord from his grasp.

The emperor smiled.

He, too, had placed bets.

Loss of the net dragged Antigonus a step closer to death. Apart from retreat, attack was his sole means of defense, and the net itself could determine the outcome of this fight. Not only did the cord recover the net if a cast failed, but, strung round the edge, it enabled him to cinch an opponent in a web of meshes and finish him off with the trident. Even when the net floated free on a *secutor*'s shoulders, a tug could jerk him off balance and expose a vital organ.

No net.

No cast.

No capture.

The theory behind *secutor* versus *retiarius* was that of the antithesis of fire and water. This *secutor*'s name, Flamma, suited him well, for like the irresistible force that fire symbolized, he was thick-set, broad-shouldered and muscular beneath the spherical helmet. Strength not speed was the threat he posed to Antigonus, despite the mobility implied in "pursuer." By contrast, the *retiarius,* armed with Neptune's trident and the now-lost net, a fish ornating his *galerus* shoulder piece, was tall, long-limbed and sinewy. With pure movement as elusive as trying to clutch water, Antigonus, a fisherman, turned the trident into his main offensive weapon.

To keep the swordsman at bay with its full length, he gripped the shaft with both hands, the left forward near the prongs and the right at the back end. Iron on iron, the fight became a test of heavy metal. The *secutor* parried jabs of the trident with his sword, afraid the powerful thrusts might slip in off his shield. With his feet planted wide apart for balance and his torso angled to narrow him as a target, Antigonus pumped the prongs horizontally. Then, as if to pin his opponent's foot to the sand, he jabbed the trident down in a feint to catch Flamma off guard, before reversing direction to ram the tines over top of the shield.

Clang! The spikes struck the visor before glancing off, only the helmet's eye slits offering something to hook.

Down plunged the trident, its direction reversing once more, but Flamma seized the opportunity of attack below to slam the bottom of his shield down on the shaft, his weight converting it from a defensive into an offensive weapon, the force snapping the wooden handle in two.

The slash of the sword that followed raked the net man's ribs.

Blood from his arm, blood from his chest, Antigonus stumbled.

"*Habet! Hoc habet!*"—He's had it!—shouted the mob. There might have been cries of "*Mitte!*"—Send him back!—had these been sporting games. The emperor would look to the tiers for guidance, thumbs-up in the throng for mercy, thumbs-down—*pollice verso*—for death. Had the loser fought well, he might be "sent back" to the Ludus Magnus barracks to wait for future games. Had he failed to entertain, he would be expected to die bravely: one knee on the ground as he held his executioner's thigh, avoiding any reflex to shrink away from the sword when the victor lifted his head and sank the blade into his throat.

Munera sine missione, "games without reprieve," offered no quarter.

They demanded a corpse on the sand.

Augustus had banned them, but he was long dead.

Antigonus, on hands and knees, did not have the option of pointing a finger of his left hand up the tiers to ask for mercy.

"*Jugula!*" cried the emperor.

Cut his throat.

Ut quis quem vicerit occidat, instructed a sign on the wall of the barracks, the Ludus Magnus, in which both gladiators were trained. *Kill the vanquished, whoever he may be.* With this in mind, Flamma raised his sword above the fallen man, who still gripped half the shaft of the sundered trident in his hand, along with the third weapon of the *retiarius*: a dagger.

As the blade came down to cleave his head—a sure crowd-pleaser—Antigonus grabbed the outer edge of the *secutor's* shield with his empty hand. Yanking it across to block the slash and throw the swordsman off balance, he pulled himself forward in a lunge and drove the sharp end of the shaft into the belly exposed by the shifting shield.

Flamma's bellow from shock and pain echoed within his helmet.

This brutal turn of fortune brought the mob to its feet.

Releasing the impaling rod so Flamma could crumple to wobbly knees, Antigonus cut off the *secutor's* cry by ramming his dagger under the helmet and into the doomed man's throat.

The mob roared.

It liked surprises.

The emperor frowned.

He disliked losing bets.

Piqued, he signaled the *editor,* who sat across from him on the minor axis of the Colosseum. As overseer of the games, the *editor* sent word down to the *lanista* responsible for the gladiators. Antigonus, drenched with blood on the scorching sand below, should have been given the palm of victory to wave at the mob as he circled the arena, followed by a sum of money or something precious. As he vanished, laden with rewards, two men in costume would claim Flamma. The Hermes Psychopomp would sear him with a hot iron to look for signs of life, then the Etruscan Charon, his nose like the beak of a bird of prey, would strike the corpse with a mallet to possess it for Hades according to ancient rites. A horse would drag the body by a hook in the flesh out the Porta Libitinaria at the opposite end of the main axis from the arch the gladiators used to enter.

Libitina, goddess of funerals.

But another roar from the tiers prompted Antigonus to turn. Running toward him, his body covered with armor, a round shield in one fist and a short *sica* saber curved like a scythe in the other, was a Thracian gladiator.

This was another way to whet the mob's insatiable appetite for blood.

Send for a *tertiarius.*

A *suppositicius.*

A fresh gladiator for the victor of the just-ended battle to fight at once.

Antigonus Severus reached for Flamma's sword.

Davy Jones's Locker

Boundary Pass, Washington State

The Atlantean in Jenna Bond was out in full force this morning. Wearing a diver's dry suit, with wind wild in her hair, she sat on the bridge of the *Islomania* and surfed it over the waves, left hand working trim tabs to level the hull, right hand adjusting the throttle to 3,400 rpms, so *boomph, boomph, boomph,* the boat plied north up the channel between San Juan Island and Orcas Island at twenty knots.

The fog of yesterday had lifted to become the sky. Slate gray, sullen, low-hanging clouds overshadowed the islands, which humped from the sea in green mounds like the spines of serpents. Tatters of mist drifted across the gray-green brine, beneath the salty swells of which lurked maritime hazards.

Danger Shoal . . .

Point Caution . . .

Shark Reef . . .

Halftide Rocks . . .

Shipwreck Island . . .

A sea of warning names dotted the navigation chart clipped beside the wheel that Jenna turned port or starboard to wend this nautical gauntlet. Not for nothing were the Strait of Juan de Fuca and its internal waterways known for centuries to wary sailors as "the graveyard of the Pacific."

Hank Bond had raised his daughter to be like the son

he never had. A tomboy she was then, and it still persisted today. He dressed Jenna in overalls, as Jenna did Becky now, and taught her to swim before she could walk and to fish before she was toilet trained. There wasn't an aspect of this boat she couldn't dismantle and put back together before she was in her teens, for when it came to ships and the sea, Hank had forged his daughter into an Atlantean.

At night, around the wood-burning stove with Jenna cuddled near, he told her tales of ships wrecked up and down the coast. The *Lark,* 1786. The *Resolution,* 1794. The *Boston,* 1803. The *Tonquin,* 1811. She still recalled their names.

"Breakers ahead!" Hank would yell, one hand cupped to his mouth. That all-too-common danger cry, shouted before a windjammer hit, wrecked and broke apart, meant it was storytime.

And what stories!

"The *Tonquin,*" Hank began, "was an American ship. We have the tale from Ten-Ta-Cloose, an Indian boy who lived near Active Pass in the Gulf Islands. Captured to be a slave by Vancouver Island Natives, he was on its West Coast when 'a great white ship' anchored in the bay. On deck were several strange-looking men with beards, who signaled the Indians to paddle out in canoes. When they did, the ship's crew insulted their chiefs and pushed them overboard."

Hank provided sound effects.

"War chanting filled the council house that night. Come morning, canoes piled with furs paddled out. Under the ruse of coming to trade, warriors swarmed onto the ship. Ten-Ta-Cloose heard 'the loud sounds of the white man's death weapons that spoke with fire and smoke,' and witnessed four sailors being killed as they tried to scramble up the masts. Five survived by locking themselves in a cabin.

"Next morning, a single crewman stood on deck. The other four had rowed to shore to hide in a cove. Indian canoes paddled out again. The tribesmen boarded without a fight, and that's when the *Tonquin* exploded—*BOOM!*—with a thundering roar."

Jenna jumped.

"The sailor sacrificed himself to ignite the gunpowder magazine. Chunks of the ship blew sky-high, then rained down to crush the women and children sitting in the canoes. When the smoke cleared, the white ship had disappeared from the sea, where the bodies of nearly one hundred Indians floated."

"Did the four escape?"

"No," said Hank. "The Indians found them hiding in the cove. Dragged back to the village, they were slowly tortured to death."

The wails of pain from her father became the wails of marine ghosts. No need for the Brothers Grimm in the Bond house.

Hank swept his arm toward the west.

"The *Tonquin* is out there, waiting to be found. It has been the object of a prolonged and persistent search since 1811. But where the wreck lies is a secret hidden in Davy Jones's locker."

I'll find it, Jenna thought, and from that moment on, the Atlantean in her was hooked on exploring sunken wrecks.

That's why she learned how to scuba dive.

Davy Jones was her siren.

It was shocking to see the tally of ships known to have met their fate in these waters, and more shocking to count the human casualties. The number of wrecks was in the thousands, and still climbing.

The Strait of Juan de Fuca is a deepwater channel flanked by soaring peaks and sandwiched between the tip of Vancouver Island and the Olympic Peninsula. Funneled in from the Pacific, sudden savage storms and banks of blinding fog ambush helmsmen trying to avoid a maze of submerged perils, like keel-gutting rocks and hidden reefs and foaming, churning shoals. A southeast gale of driving rain and low, scudding cloud will switch without warning to a howling westerly, as ebbing tidal currents abruptly turn to flow. Foolish is the captain who fails to keep a constant eye on weather and tides, so as she cruised north toward the Canadian border, Jenna monitored marine forecasts on VHF. Punch the red button on the radio and it would change to Channel 16, the West Coast emergency frequency.

Fire and logs.

The two surface hazards out on open water.

Fire was the hazard Jenna had faced last week. She was cruising home on a choppy change of tide when the smell of gas assailed her nose. Checking the aluminum tank in the engine well, she had spotted a welded seam that had cracked near its bottom. Gas had seeped into the bilge below, inviting a spark—*BOOM!*—to blast the *Islomania* as sky-high as the *Tonquin*.

Your novice sailor would have abandoned ship, getting the hell out of there before hell it became, which meant the tide would have sunk the boat on starboard rocks. But Jenna was an Atlantean, Marine Venus by name, so Jenna had pumped the gas out of the bilge, removed the hose from the fresh water tank, reattached it to the gas intake and pumped water into the gas tank. Gas is lighter than water and floats on top, so what seeped from the bottom crack was H_2O, allowing her to siphon off the gas above to power home.

Once there, she had welded the tank herself.

Hank had taught her well.

A log was the hazard this boater faced, and it remained to be seen if he was a novice or not. Angry as a speared shark, he stood in the stern of the sheriff's boat beside Deputy Irv Coutts and accusingly jabbed his finger at a buoy bobbing on the sea. The boat floating over the reef fifty feet below had the crest of the San Juan County sheriff on its hull: the bewigged noggin of George Washington with *The Seal of the State of Washington, 1889* ringing him, *Sheriff Dept., San Juan Co.*

encircling that, and a seven-point star spiked on the outside. Gray and black, it was a "clean, no-nonsense crest. One a steely SOB like your dad can wear with pride," Hank had always said. The angry man looked a bit like George himself, a frizz of hair tied back in a short ponytail, a black coat ruffled at the throat with a scarf. Jenna powered down to approach the sheriff's boat, and as soon as she pulled alongside, the clone zeroed in.

"You the detective?"

"Yes," she said.

"You the diver?"

"That's why I was called."

"I'm no novice. I know how to sail."

"Your name, sir?"

"George," he said.

Jenna blinked.

"George what?" she asked.

"George Waschke."

Jenna blinked again. And left it at that. She decided not to ask George if "Waschke" was short for something else.

"What happened, George?"

"My boat sank."

"You hit a log?"

"I hit *that* thing." He jabbed his finger once more at the buoy. "*Whack.* When it hit the bow, I feared I'd hit a log, so that's why I veered and struck the *actual* log, which tore the leg off the stern and ripped a hole in the transom. So down went my boat, ass-end first with me clinging to the bow. I might have drowned had Irv not come along."

"Plucked him off the jib, Jen," Coutts confirmed.

"What is that thing?" Jenna asked.

"Some kinda buoy. Linked to a cable and fixed with an antenna."

"I've cruised this way a thousand times and never seen it," said George. "What's a buoy doing out here in open water? I know insurance pricks. They'll blame poor me.

They'll say I was running at speed and not watching for logs. That's why I want a diver. To check this out. To back me up that I hit a buoy that shouldn't be here, and not the log I saw and hit only because I was ambushed by the buoy."

"I'll take a look," Bond said. And wondered if the log was a cherry tree.

With its depth sounder on, the *Islomania* separated from the sheriff's boat to zigzag back and forth along the reef. Readings of 100 feet, then 50 feet, then 100 feet again located the submerged ridge. Jenna jumped down on the foredeck to drop the Danforth anchor and its 32 feet of chain, feeding out an additional 30 feet of yellow rope to extend the anchor line. Returning to the bridge, she yanked the transmission handle from neutral to reverse, and backed the *Islomania* across the reef until the Danforth caught. Jenna made another jump to the foredeck after shutting down the engine so she could lengthen the rope by 30 feet (anchor efficiency increased by reducing the scope angle of the line), and she was ready to get wet.

Already suited up, the neoprene sheath hugging her lithe figure like a lover, Jenna pulled on a matching black hood to prevent heat loss through her uncovered head, then buckled on a weight belt to counter positive buoyancy. From this belt hung a combined unit pressure gauge, depth gauge and compass. As a tool and for protection, she strapped a dive knife to the inside of her calf, then pulled a pair of open-heel fins over diving booties. A Barbie she wasn't, but here she could pretend. Over Jenna's natural breasts, which never turned heads, she tugged a buoyancy compensator jacket with inflatable bladders, which turned her into a big-boobed babe fit for *Baywatch*. On her back went a single high-pressure tank, with a hose that ran to the regulator popped into her mouth. A dive slate for notes, an underwater torch and a wide-vision mask completed her equipment.

This was the year of El Niño.

And El Niño brought great whites.

So before the mask went on, Jenna took a last look around.

Haro Strait branched north from the Strait of Juan de Fuca to delineate the border between Vancouver Island and San Juan Island. Then it veered east across the mouth of this channel that separated San Juan from Orcas Island, Haro becoming Boundary Pass to draw the line between Canada's Gulf Islands and her beloved San Juans. Here in the far northwest corner of the States, a string of lesser islands ran west to east along the tops of San Juan and Orcas; beyond them you were in the Mounties' realm. These lesser islands were Stuart, Waldron, Madrona, Patos, Shipwreck and Matia. The reef under the *Islomania* was between Stuart and Waldron.

Land, sea or air, wherever Jenna cast her eyes, a wonder met her stare. Just above the waterline along a rocky shore, blubbery spotted harbor seals or sea lions with sagittal crests took a break from swimming. Around here was home year-round to the fiercest predator under the waves, the nine-ton, thirty-foot-long orca, or killer whale. To the north, toward the southern tip of Canada's Pender Island, Jenna caught sight of a resident pod of these black-and-white monsters swimming parallel to the shipping lane shared by both countries. Orca whales eat everything from salmon on up to other species of whale, hunting by echo-location, a sense similar to sonar. Soon a male breached right out of the brine, then crashed down by a spy-hopping female who seemed to sit, head out of water, to gaze around. High in the sky over these awesome mammals, two majestic bald eagles circled circled circled.

No wonder the bald eagle was America's symbol.

She wondered how many Americans lived their lives out and never saw one.

Cities! she thought.

Satisfied that no shark fins knifed the nearby waves—

survive a shark attack like she had and you could never be too careful—Jenna sat down on the port gunnel with her tank to the sea. After pulling down the mask, she held it firmly against her face with one hand, the regulator in her mouth held with the other, then rolled backward into the chuck.

The instant she entered the ocean, Jenna Bond gave way to Marine Venus. A mermaid of this primal womb, the Atlantean kicked her tail flippers to follow the yellow rope—called a rode by nautical types—down to the Oz of the reef.

An Oz it was.

This deep green fantasy.

Jenna felt as weightless as an astronaut. With a stream of bubbles trailing from her tank, she passed through a cloud of bubbles billowing below—air escaping from the cabin of Waschke's boat. Wavering like a heat mirage in the tidal current, the sunken reef was suddenly beneath her mask. An easy dive, the fifty-foot plunge took less than two minutes. What she saw was a ridge of rock that fell away as fathomless ravines on both sides, a seabed mosaic of eerie marine growths interlocking battlements and caves. Bunches of orange-and-white plumed anemones beat the water with their feelers in a ceaseless forage for food. Sinuous strands of bull kelp drifted by like loose giant's hair. Hordes of skeleton shrimp darted in and out of crevices. Sea lemons crawled around immobile blood stars and purple starfish. Dungeness and red rock crabs scuttled under sponge fans, a pile of their empty, cracked shells revealing an octopus lair with tentacles exposed. Brooding from a barnacled rock, a huge ling cod cast its permanent scowl. A wolf eel poked its head from a cave and bared its teeth. Ever-changing contours on the sea floor seemed to be in motion with the rhythm of the tide. The eye is selective underwater and things are missed, so that's why Jenna failed to glimpse death staring at her as she circled the boat and noted damage to its hull.

Then she caught it.

Motion to her left.

Something long whipped toward her from the edge of visibility.

Shark! she thought.

At the time of the last El Niño, Jenna was diving alone off Deadman Bay, exploring the wreck of the *Hornblower* in Haro Strait. The schooner was wedged against a ridge of honeycombed rock, the ribs of its belly exposed by a gash along its keel, all masts broken and rotting away. Few thrills equal groping about a haunted house buried beneath the sea, the ghosts of its crew seen in shadows at the corner of your mask, the gloomy silence absolute except for the hiss of your regulator. Like the sting of a red jellyfish, frissons shiver your spine. She was lost in the realm of Atlantean fantasy when a sudden current threw her against the hull.

Jenna cut her hand on an exposed nail.

Blood bled into the brine.

Again and again the current buffeted her, one wave so strong that it hurled her at a honeycomb cave and might have stuffed her into the funnel like a cork in a wine bottle had the backwash not sucked her out, a whiplash that launched her at an approaching blue shark drawn by her blood.

Never had she faced a maneater like this. The blue was an accidental tourist in from the unusually warm open seas and about to taste a local delicacy: *her!* It looked like your shark of nightmares, long, sleek and slender, all sharp teeth, strong jaws and menacing grin.

As Jenna shot toward it like an oncoming torpedo, the jaws snapped open to tear a chunk out of her, snout going up as the torch in her hand came down to bash its sensitive tip.

The blue turned tail and fled.

Because that incident was burned into her cerebral cortex, shark was the first paranoia that popped into her head—until the beam of the torch she swung around from Waschke's boat revealed the attacker coming at her to be . . .

Albert Einstein?

You never knew what you might find in Davy Jones's locker.

George Washington above, Albert Einstein here. She wondered if it was time to change breakfast cereal. Had those raisins in her bran fermented to wine, making her a morning drunk who didn't know it? Was ergot on the grain causing hallucinogens akin to LSD? Food these days . . . could be.

Schools of black bass and tube snouts followed her as Jenna kicked through the dismal green twilight zone, the beam of the torch knifing across the deep to unveil a puppet on a string jerking to and fro with the rhythm of the tide. The hair was Albert Einstein's, a shock of unkempt white, and the eyes behind the helmet mask were as wide as his must have been the moment he grasped the theory of relativity. The cheeks of the potbellied puppet were pinched concave by his desperate sucking for the last dregs of air in the now-empty tank.

Fitzroy Campbell? thought Bond.

The closer she swam, the weirder the set-up became. The feet of the corpse were chained to a ring fastened to the deck of a boat. The hands of the corpse were cuffed behind its back. The helmet was fitted with a microphone and a listening device, which were attached to a cable that ascended to the buoy bobbing on the surface waves. A buoy with an antenna. From the look of it, someone had put a lot of effort into squeezing this man.

Who? wondered Bond.

And why?

She circled the hull several times and could find no sign of damage. A good way to scuttle a boat was to sever a seacock hose, so Jenna shone the beam down into the open engine well to check if sabotage was the cause of this sinking, then she released the door to the cabin in a sudden burst of bubbles to examine the toilet hose in the head.

Suspicion confirmed.

Jenna used the diving slate to jot notes.

The registration number displayed on both sides of the bow began 13k.

A *K* meant a boat was registered in British Columbia. The prefix *13* meant Vancouver.

The name on the stern was *The Bounding Main*.

Hadrian's Wall

Shipwreck Island, Washington State

Again and again Mephisto played the tape through the speakers, savoring every nuance of Gavin Campbell's long, slow, agonizing death under the sea. As he listened, he watered his array of carnivorous plants.

Gasping.

Choking.

Rasping for air.

"Antigonus Severus. The Druid medallion," Mephisto prompted.

More gasping from the speakers.

"Where's the Hoard, Campbell?"

Obsessive-compulsive though the replaying was, in his imagination Mephisto didn't return to the Colosseum in Ancient Rome.

Instead, he traveled back to Ancient Britain.

Act Two in the evolution of the legend of the Hoard . . .

The Northern Frontier, Britannia
January 3, 306 A.D.

The winds of winter howled down from the north and banked swirling snow up the defensive face of the Roman wall. Running eighty Roman miles from Wallsend-on-Tyne west to Solway Firth, the fifteen-foot-high barrier of stone marked the northern boundary between Roman civilization and the territory of the barbarian Picts. Built by the legions but manned by fifteen thousand auxiliary troops, it was a composite obstacle of four linked parts: the stone wall, which had a V-shaped ditch in front, except where natural cliffs dropped away from it; a regular series of forts, milecastles and turrets to house the garrison; earthworks out back known as the Vallum; and a network of roads for movement of soldiers and supplies. So harsh was this winter that snow had filled in the ditch, leveling the first line of defense against the Picts. So cold was this winter that snow had turned to ice, layer on layer freezing up the Roman wall like steps. The worst wind of winter was the wind that blew tonight, hurling blurs of blinding white over the crusted parapet, where sentries numbing into snowmen shivered in hooded cloaks. Four men, two inside, manned this turret on the bleakest and most isolated length of the wall. With their wool *paenulae* clutched shut against the bitter cold, the two on guard squinted north at nothing but snow, snow, snow.

But the Picts who crept toward them saw more than the guards.

Their beacon was the glowing windows of the turret above.

Up the steps of ice and snow, they scaled the Roman Wall.

"Tali nocte velim Romae esse."

A night like this makes you wish you were in Rome.

"Non ego."

Not me, said Antigonus Severus, who once fought as a gladiator in Rome's Colosseum.

They were speaking Latin, the two auxiliary guards

inside the wall turret, but Latin was the mother tongue of neither man. Their cohort of eight hundred men—the Cohors I Tungrorum Milliaria—was originally recruited from the non-Roman Tungri tribe of Gallia Belgica, now known as Belgium, and was led by Tribunus Cohortis Primae Tungrorum Borcovicio. Tungrians had served the Roman army well in Britain, for when Julius Agricola invaded the Highlands of the north in 83 A.D. and fought a decisive battle with the Caledonians under Calgacus at Mons Graupius, it was this cohort that met the enemy. Some thirty thousand barbarians ranged up the mount, wild, tattooed heathens with faces painted blue, shouting as their chariots raced back and forth between the battle lines, their small shields and long, slashing swords waving in the air. The outnumbered Roman army was drawn up in front of them, Tungrians in the vanguard, legions kept back in reserve and cavalry on the flanks. The battle began with a hail of throwing spears, then Agricola ordered the Tungrians to march, a steady advance with swords stabbing and shields pushing back, closing in on unwieldy barbarian blades that cut but didn't thrust. When cavalry charged from both sides, the Caledonians fled.

Auxiliaries dead: 360.

Barbarians dead: 10,000.

And not one drop of Roman legion blood spilled.

Centuries had passed since then, and the cohort was still here. Caledonians had merged with other tribes to become the Picts. Hadrian had come to Britain in 122 A.D. to build this wall that honored that emperor's reign and acted as a barrier against Pictish raids. Now Cohors I Tungrorum Milliaria was camped at Vercovicium fort. If they served twenty-five years in the cohort, these two auxiliaries would be handed bronze diplomas, detailing their service and granting Roman citizenship, to hang about their necks.

The Latin they spoke was to practice for that far-off day.

If they survived the wall.

"Rumor at the fort is that you once fought in the Roman Colosseum."

"Many times, cohort."

"How many did you kill?"

"Enough," said Antigonus.

"They say the emperor himself granted you freedom. Is that so, cohort?"

"The mob forced him."

"How?" asked the curious guard.

"I became a slave of Rome for my part in a revolt. Because I was strong, they sent me to the Ludus Magnus. Beasts ate the other rebels. Tungrians are fishermen, so we are trained as net men: *retiarii.* I fought and killed a gladiator named Flamma. He seized my net and snapped my trident and brought me to my knees. The emperor ordered him to cut my throat, but I pulled the shield away from his gut and stabbed him with the sharp end of my broken trident."

"So you were freed?"

"No, I had to fight again. The emperor lost a bet on Flamma and called for a *tertiarius,* a fresh Thracian, to kill me. With saber and shield, he pursued me around the arena. As he closed in, I ran across my discarded net, then turned and yanked it from under him, which tumbled the Thracian to the sand. Before he recovered, I killed him with Flamma's sword."

"So you were freed?"

"If this is freedom. The mob was yelling for me to be given the *rudis,* the wooden sword that grants a man release from the arena. The emperor stood and addressed the crowd. The year was 297 and the Picts were threatening the Wall. So he freed me from slavery to fight with the cohort here."

"Is it true what they say about gladiators and the women of Rome?"

"What is that, cohort?"

"They spread their legs for scars."

"Yes, many love the sword. Even senators' wives. A woman named Eppia left her husband and children so she could follow a freed gladiator to adventure at sea. The less daring came to the *ludus* to visit celebrities, and donned their helmets and greaves for a go at the *palus* practice stake before lying down for swordplay of the cuckold kind."

"You should have used one of them to gain freedom, cohort."

Antigonus chuckled. "Like Faustina? Wife of Marcus Aurelius, past emperor of Rome? While watching gladiators go by one day, she fell so in love with one that passion made her ill. She confessed to her husband and begged him to free her love. He had the gladiator killed and drained of blood, then forced Faustina to bathe in it and go to bed with him. Their son, Commodus, also became emperor of Rome. So obsessed was he with gladiators that he had the palace turned into an arena, and fought them so he could shed blood in his own home. He never appeared in public without a sword, and unless he was covered with human blood."

" '*Ave, Caesar, morituri te salutant.*' Is that not what gladiators say on entering the arena?"

"Yes, cohort. 'Hail, Caesar, those who are about to die salute you.' "

The Picts were hunting silver.

The Picts were hunting heads.

Silver was the metal of choice for status in Pictland, and the only sources of silver were the Romans beyond the wall.

Roman heads were hoarded trophies in Pictland, and the nearest source of Roman heads was Hadrian's Wall.

Like all Celts, the Picts were a cult of the head. Wrote Diodorus Siculus:

When they kill enemies in battle, they cut off their
heads and attach them to the necks of their horses.
They nail such trophies to their houses, just as hunters
do when they have killed wild beasts. They embalm
the heads of their most illustrious enemies in cedar oil
and keep them carefully in a chest and show them off
to strangers, each priding himself that for one or other
of these heads either a forebear, or his father, or he
himself had refused to accept a large sum of money.

Not only was the human head a sign of war triumph,
but Picts believed the head to be a source of spiritual
power, so "brain balls" guarded headhunters from su-
pernatural harm.

These Picts were hunting silver.

These Picts were hunting heads.

These Picts who climbed the Roman wall with Bridei
Mak Morn.

The chief's red hair blew wildly in the wind, long locks
whipping his face, which was dyed the hue of blue that
was sacred to the goddess of the earth. Hate brimmed
in his eyes, which were circled by tattoos, and clenched
teeth were bared behind an unkempt mustache. The torc
around his neck was forged from Roman silver. His
cloak of wool, caked white with snow and clasped with
a silver brooch, hid his tunic of checked cloth, which
would evolve into tartan. For warmth against the bitter
cold, he wore leggings tied with thongs at both knees
and ankles, and footwear of hides. One hand gripped a
dagger that he stabbed into the ice like a climber's pick,
and the other held two throwing spears. Slung from a
chain across his back was a two-handed sword, which
would become the claymore of Highland clans.

The steps of ice and snow ended short of reaching
distance to the crenelated parapet above. To close this
gap, Bridei Mak Morn stood on the broad shoulders of
the Pict below and clawed his way up the stones as the
man climbed to the top step. The wind whistled around

the crenels and merlons of the wall's battlement like sharp gasps of breath through missing teeth. *Clink clink clink* passed the jangling armor of the Roman guard on the walkway above, then the Pict pulled himself up over the top.

The guard's back was to him, moving away.

Bridei Mak Morn stalked him along the parapet, then rammed a spear under the neck of his helmet so it burst out through his eye.

The Roman wall was a string of forts, milecastles and turrets. Each fort, a day's march apart, garrisoned a cohort. From there, patrols were dispatched to other barracks: milecastles set a mile apart along the wall, and turret towers set a third of a mile apart between those sub-forts. Each turret was twenty feet square and recessed into the wall. The ground floor had no windows facing north, but two in the sides behind the wall to release smoke from the cooking hearth. Here the auxiliaries that were not on guard hid from the cold, waiting their turn to brave the blizzard howling overhead. This room was the height of the parapet walk on the upper floor, access to which was by a stair landing supporting a ladder that rose to a trap door. The parapet walk along the wall ran through the upper room, two windows of which watched north for barbarians. So bitter was the cold that night that a fire blazed on this level, too, and that was the beacon that lured the raiding Picts. The guards had left the turret for their final march along the wall before relief, one going west, the other east. Having speared the guard to the west, Bridei Mak Morn, javelin raised, crept toward the turret, and one by one his followers crawled up onto the parapet.

Without a sound, the Pict passed through the upper room. Voices echoed from the room beneath the trapdoor. The storm tried to blow him off the eastern parapet as he hunted the other Roman guard.

Then he saw it.

An approaching ghost.

And he hurled the javelin as hard as he could at the snow-encrusted man.

The blood was black in all this white.

Voices below the trap door meant more brain balls, so Bridei Mak Morn unslung his sword and trudged toward the turret.

Drafts danced with the flames of the hearth as the soldiers armed for duty. Both wore belted red tunics to their knees, with red pants and leg warmers under that. Instead of the plated armor of a legionary, each donned a coat of mail made from laced metal scales. Protecting each head was a bronze helmet with ear guards extending down both sides like mutton chops, a ridge over the brow to shield the face and a piece jutting low at the back to cover the neck. The Roman *pilum* was replaced with a spear, and the rectangular shield with an oval one, but the two-foot-long, two-edged thrusting sword was a legionary *gladius*. Each tied a kerchief of red around his throat, and before he wrapped himself in his warm wool *paenula* cloak, Antigonus hung a silver medallion about his neck for luck.

The hearth light made it gleam.

A glint caught the eye of his cohort.

"Booty?" asked the soldier.

Antigonus nodded. "From a Druid I killed among the Stones west of Londinium."

The other man winced. "A Druid?" he said. He might fight for Rome, but he was a Celt, and even for one who questioned old ways, there were matters best left alone . . . just in case.

Like the Druids.

The Druids were the high priests of the ancient Celts. *Druid* was Celtic for "knowledge of the oak." The Druids were shamans who, through a trance, could gain access to the otherworld, and could represent both that and this world within the other. Their rituals were held in sacred oak groves or among the stone megaliths of the Ancient Ones, who were here before the Celts. Oaks and huge megaliths embodied spirits of the dead and the forces of nature. Sacrifice was central to their rituals. Druid augurs would kill a man with a sword stroke to the back, and glean omens in the way he fell, his convulsions and the flow of blood on the ground. The head held spiritual power, so Druids fomented headhunting. Sacrifice was essential to the smooth running of the universe, so Druids did not hesitate to sacrifice. Astronomy determined the ritual calendar, so failure to carry out the appropriate sacrifice when the time allotted arrived could lead to natural disaster of the worst kind. Caesar wrote, on encountering the Druids in Gaul, "They resort to execution even of the innocent, using figures of immense size, whose limbs, woven out of twigs, they fill with living men and set on fire, and the men perish in a sheet of flame."

Wicker Men.

A bad way to go.

So while the soldier doubted Druidic laws, killing a Druid was tempting fate. . . .

Just in case.

"Are those the Stones?"

"Have you not seen them, cohort?" Antigonus showed him the image engraved into the silver at the center of the medallion.

"The Stones are a temple?"

"A temple of the sky."

"Did Rome not annihilate the Druids in Britannia a long time ago?"

"Religions die hard. Druid cults survived. My ship no sooner docked than I was marched west to the ring of Stones to crush a Druid revival. We caught them at the Stones during an eclipse."

"What were they doing?"

"This," said Antigonus, circling his finger around the

disk to highlight the engravings that ringed the Stones at its center. When the ex-gladiator held the medallion out so he could see, the sentry noted that a silversmith had etched the new owner's name and cohort into its narrow edge:

Antigonus Severus
Cohors I Tungrorum Milliaria

"Druids raised the Stones?"

"No, the Ancient Ones. But Druids learned the secret of the Stones on this medallion."

"Druids are forbidden to write things down. Sacred texts are memorized."

"This isn't writing. This is sacred art."

"Do you not fear a curse, cohort?"

"I am a Christian. Christ saved me in Rome. Druids and their heathen ways will be forgotten. Christ is the future."

"You hope," said the guard.

As Antigonus swept his cloak about his shoulders like a cape, the cohort climbed five stairs to the raised landing and scaled a twelve-foot ladder to the trap door overhead. The room above was smaller than the room below, so shortening the ladder meant it could be hauled up and stored in case of trouble. Steam from the pot of soup on the hearth beside the landing—a welcome meal for the frozen sentries about to be relieved—followed the guard up the ladder to the trap door in the ceiling, which he pushed open.

A blast of winter from the north blew down through the hole.

Antigonus was halfway up the stairs to the landing when the cohort came tumbling down the ladder without a head, showering blood.

The ex-gladiator reacted on instinct, reaching for the sword held in a scabbard at his waist, which was hung from a strap across his chest.

The blade cleared the scabbard just as a Pict plummeted down from the trap door to land on the headless soldier. The Pict was a bloody Highlander with a battle-ax dripping red, into whose heart Antigonus sank his sword.

Another Pict plunged.

This arena was smaller, but what was at stake was the same, for the Roman gladiator knew this fight would be *sine missione,* with no thumbs-up from the mob in the tiers to reprieve the vanquished.

He leaped down beside the hearth as the pagan Pict descended, and hurled the pot of boiling soup up at the hairy face.

The Pict screamed.

And dropped his spear.

And screamed again as the sword ripped up from his groin.

No sooner had Antigonus stuck the scalded man than another Pict, and another Pict, and another Pict jumped down.

This arena was deadlier than the one in Rome, with *tertiarii* coming faster than he could deal with.

Antigonus cast his cloak like a *retiarius* net and stabbed.

Antigonus rammed his spear through the guts of two Picts in one skewering.

Antigonus used the tip of his sword to flick coals from the hearth to blind enemy eyes.

Antigonus stood by the landing and hacked the legs of jumpers, hamstringing them off balance for the fatal jab.

Antigonus ran to the door in a break-away attempt, but was unable to escape because pivot-hung Roman doors open out, and falling snow had banked against the rear of the turret.

Another Pict landed.

Antigonus heard feet hit the landing.

And turned to meet the barbarian with his two-foot blade.

But Bridei Mak Morn's two-handed sword was in full swing, a brutal cut that would evolve into the Highland charge, and the model for claymores to come sliced off a Roman brain ball.

The Pict picked up the severed head.

The Pict seized the silver medallion from the neck stump.

The Pict returned to the ladder and climbed to the upper floor.

The Roman below had killed so many Picts in the battle for his life that Bridei Mak Morn thought him an enemy of distinction.

His brain ball was worthy of the Hoard.

So back over the wall went the raiding Picts.

The Roman head and the Druid medallion were headed for the Highlands.

The Bounding Main

San Juan Island, Washington State

Back aboard the *Islomania* after diving down to the *Bounding Main*, Jenna radioed the U.S. Coast Guard, gave whoever answered the 13k number on the wreck's bow and asked him to find the registered owner through Canadian authorities. As Jenna cruised down the channel with San Juan on the starboard and Orcas on the port, moving toward the port of Friday Harbor on the starboard side, port being that side of the vessel traditionally moored to the dock, she frowned at the way your nautical types like to see landlubbers confused, so if you're all at sea on where the *Islomania* was heading, join the club. Meanwhile, the U.S. Coast Guard called Canada Customs in Vancouver, registration of boats being a tax matter up there (it seems *everything* is a tax matter these days), and before Jenna hit Friday Harbor to wantonly dock her *starboard* side against the pier, she had the answer.

The *Bounding Main* was registered to Gavin Campbell of Mayne Island, B.C.

Did that mean Fitzroy Campbell of Orcas Island was out of the soup?

"The Campbells are coming, O-ho, O-ho!" Bond sang in her mind.

The story of how Friday Harbor got its name is as hotly debated as the chicken and the egg conundrum. The Lummi Indians called it *Sta-l-quith,* meaning "Where the first-run sockeye salmon come." As for the English label, one local rumor is that the harbor was named for a reclusive Hawaiian shepherd who tended sheep for the Hudson's Bay Company before the San Juan Islands became part of the States. The English didn't want to use his Kanaka name, so the Hawaiian was renamed for the Polynesian valet in *The Life and Strange Surprising Adventures of Robinson Crusoe* by Daniel Defoe. Once the company quit San Juan Island, Joe Friday stayed on with his Indian wife; and Captain Richards, who also named Active Pass, named the harbor after him while surveying these waters. Another rumor is that the captain didn't step ashore, but instead yelled from the *Plumper*, "What bay is this?" The person who responded thought Richards had asked, "What day is this?" and yelled back the answer: "Friday!"

The imp in Jenna was tempted to launch a rumor of her own. While on vacation here, Jack Webb was told the story about Joe Friday, and that's what inspired him to create the police series "Dragnet." It was to be located on San Juan, where it would open:

Dum, da-dum-dum.
Dum, da-dum-dum-dummm . . .
"This is the island.
"San Juan, Washington.
"I work here.
"My name's Friday.
"I'm a cop . . ."

But L.A. being L.A., the network balked, so local legend Joe Friday was forced to relocate to the City of Angels, where he made good. . . .

The size of fish caught in the islands grows with each telling, and the best truths are born in the pubs just prior to closing. A grain of salt goes a long way here.

From the dock in Joe's mythic harbor, Jenna scaled a gangway mounted on pilings and made her way up to Front Street along the shore. Feeling grungy from her dive and craving a shower, she skirted Waterfront Park, which overlooked the marina that berthed forty thousand vessels a year (greeted by a town of less than two thousand people). Racing sloops rocked beside commercial seiners. At Spring Street, the main street, which was named for a freshwater spring, she turned inland and trudged up to the next terrace. All streets were lined with the funky shops you'd expect in a town with an economy based on three hundred thousand tourists annually.

The base used to be smuggling.

Jenna turned right on Second Street to shiver back across the upper harbor terrace to the sheriff's office behind the courthouse. Teeth chattering, she walked in the main door and paused a moment, as always, before the picture of Hank among the photos of sheriffs back to 1892. Jenna's image reflected off the glass and was superimposed over that of her dad. The black diving hood melded with Hank's cropped hair. The black dry suit merged with his dark uniform. Their lean facial features transmogrified into Sean Connery in *Dr. No.*

The name's Bond.

Jenna Bond, she said in her mind.

And laughed at herself, but had to admit a tuxedo would suit her well.

The office entrance mixed down-home nostalgia with modern security. The check-in desk, next to Hank's photo, was enclosed with protective glass. Jenna had to tap on it to get buzzed in. A picture of a dog with its paws on the counter flanked the sealed door. Its caption was "A citizen reporting a missing owner." The releasing door had a caption, too—Authorized Personnel Only—and from the corner above watched a videocamera. Under it hung a photo of Friday Harbor in 1950, back when none of this was necessary.

Sheriffs like Hank Bond saw to that.

"What does a civilized man do when confronted by a barbarian?" he used to ask.

But he never answered.

Jenna's office looked out on Second Street, the inside masked by Venetian blinds. Across the road, rustic homes had been converted to commerce, in line with the turn-of-the-century nature of the town. Porches, gables and shake roofs. She said hello to the Jailbird—J.B., for short—and would have sprung the budgie from its cage if not for the shower for which she would now kill. She turned on the CD player—Patsy Cline, her favorite—and skimmed what was new on her desk to mull over in the spray.

The Bounding Main and *Gavin Campbell* caught Bond's eye. Words in a request from the Mounties for help with a case. Like the request she had faxed north concerning Fitzroy Campbell.

The shower to die for could wait.

Jenna grabbed the phone.

Pender Island, British Columbia

Should he, or should he not, go to the annual barn dance?

The calendar on the green cover of the *Pender Post* reminded Craven that the second most important event of Pender's social season was tomorrow night.

He sat, feet up on the desk, in his office at Pender detachment, glancing from the report in his hand to the *Post* on the blotter, and weighed the pros and cons of attending the shindig.

Yesterday, while boating back from Gavin Campbell's spread on Mayne Island, DeClercq had regaled him with a tale of rural policing.

"My first posting was a one-horse town far away to the north. The lay magistrate was the local undertaker. It soon became evident that the town's only pub was breaking every liquor law, so I charged the owner with flouting the Liquor Act. A bush plane flew in the Crown attorney and the defense counsel. The magistrate and I met them at the grass landing strip. The Crown attorney deplaned with a briefcase full of books. The defense counsel got off with nothing but a box of chocolates for the magistrate's wife. In court we proved the case twenty times over, but in the end the magistrate dismissed it with a nod. Back we traipsed to the landing strip to see both lawyers off. All smiles, the defense counsel climbed aboard the plane. The magistrate stopped the Crown attorney as he went to follow, and said to him, so I could overhear, 'Don't take it hard, son. You did a fine job. The facts were with you and so was the law, but if I closed this town's only pub, there'd be sweet fuck all to do here at night.'

"The moral, Nick, which remains with me and I pass on to you, is that you can't be a knee-jerk cop in a rural posting. The effect on the community must be fed into every decision."

Point taken, Chief, Nick thought now.

The way he saw it, the pros and cons of policing Pender were:

An island is much like a small town, and can't be policed like a city. Lack of anonymity is the striking difference. A city cop encounters people who don't know him, and troublemakers go for the uniform. A Pender cop is known by everyone, and troublemakers go for the man inside. Sirens in the city mean little to anyone. But a siren on the island means someone everyone knows is in trouble. Policing Pender was like living in a fishbowl, and every action Nick took provided grist for the rumor mill.

There were rumors as to why he was here.

One had him a hopeless drunk.

Another said he was too quick with his fists.

Both maintained that's why the Mounties had exiled him here.

The truth was he had a broken heart.

Pender was his foreign legion.

He couldn't police the island without support from the islanders. The lack of police back-up was always on his mind. Without Penderites behind him, a matter could get out of hand. The best way to gain community support was to support the community, and the way to do that was to go to the dance.

But what if he saw someone smoking pot?

The right wing, quite rightly, would expect him to enforce the law. If he didn't, the rumor next day would be that he was soft on crime, on the take or a pothead himself.

The left wing would expect the offender to be left alone. It's a party, man, and who's being hurt, and who gave you the right to spoil it for everyone? Hassle an islander and the rumor next day would be Attila the Hun lives.

Should I, or should I not, go to tomorrow's barn dance?

The question remained unanswered when the phone on his desk rang.

"Corporal Craven," said Nick.

"Corporal, I'm Jenna Bond. Detective with the San Juan County sheriff."

"James Bond!" he exclaimed. "What an honor, sir."

"*Jenna* Bond, Corporal. That pun has worn thin with me."

"I'm sure it has. Just breaking ice."

"Consider it broken."

"So how can I help you, Detective?"

"It's how I can help you," she said. "We found the *Bounding Main*. And probably Gavin Campbell."

"Where?" asked the Mountie.

"Bottom of the sea."

"Sinking?"

"Scuttling. Murder," she added. Jenna described in detail her dive down to the wreck.

"The guy was tortured?"

"Interrogated, I'd say. Somebody used dread to try to squeeze something out of him."

"I wonder if it worked?"

"Me, too," she said.

"Okay, Detective, shall we take it from the top? Since most of the case is in your court, seems fair that you begin."

"Monday, we got a call from Atlanta. From Fitzroy Campbell's son. Said he couldn't reach his dad by phone at his home near Doe Bay on Orcas Island. I live close, so I cruised up to check it out, and found blood on the dock with footprints to both sides. Looked to me as if someone had been dragged down from the house and taken away by sea."

"Fitzroy own a boat?"

"No," said Bond.

"So if he went down like Gavin, someone sacrificed theirs or scuttled a stolen one."

"We're tracking missing boats."

"I'll do the same here."

"The blood was dark and dry, and neighbors witnessed zilch, so I think he was spirited away the night before. Blood was found on the path from his garden to his house, and footprints indicated that he was ambushed there. Three thugs hid behind separate trees, then converged on Fitzroy as he carried in veggies. Squash and corn cobs were thrown about."

"Casts from the footprints?"

"Yeah, good ones."

"And Fitzroy's house?"

"Torn apart. Whoever tossed his home hoped to find something important."

"I wonder what?"

"Me, too," said Bond.

"Any more puzzles?"

"Campbell's credit card was used *after* we know he vanished."

"By him?"

"Uncertain. Gas purchased at the pump in Anacortes and Blaine. Insert the card. Fill up. The pump prints a receipt. No signature needed."

"Security cameras?"

"Being checked. Nothing yet."

"That it?"

"That's it."

"Want my take?"

"Ball's in your court. Over to you," said Bond.

"Whoever tossed Fitzroy's home failed to find what lured them there. Whatever they did to squeeze Fitzroy, he didn't give it up. If they were successful, why grab Gavin? The credit card's a ruse to buy time. Keeps you focused on Fitzroy's whereabouts, wondering if the card was used by him or someone else, and if it will lead to him or his kidnappers."

"Meanwhile," said Bond, "they launch Plan B."

"Tuesday, I was called to Gavin Campbell's home at Miners Bay on Mayne Island. Blood and footprints at the scene revealed the same MO as in your fax concerning Fitzroy Campbell. Three thugs had ambushed Gavin at his woodpile. His home was ransacked during a thorough search for something important, and he was dragged down to his boat dock and taken away by sea. The only difference is that Gavin had a boat."

"How'd the thugs arrive?"

"From Active Pass."

"So one boat brought them. And two boats took them away."

"One of which, the *Bounding Main,* the sea coughed up on Wednesday."

"Want my take?"

"Shoot," said Craven.

"Whoever tossed Gavin's home failed in that search as well. You said it was thorough, not half done. Why grab Gavin unless it was to interrogate him, which sinking the *Bounding Main* shows they did. That leaves one question: Did he give up the object of the search?"

"And if he didn't give it up, where will the thugs strike next?"

"Depends on the link, if any, between Fitzroy and Gavin."

"Want to work this together?"

"You bet," Jenna said. "It's only a matter of time till the Bureau grabs it from me."

"First thing I'll do," Nick said, "is see if Coast Watch tracked the *Bounding Main*. A drug load was coming in, so the alert was out. Maybe someone got a gander at who was aboard."

"The obvious link between the two is that they have the same last name."

"Campbell's the Smith and Jones of Scotland," said Nick.

"Did Gavin have relatives?"

"None we can find. Seems that Campbell was the last of his line."

"Fitzroy's son is here to help find his dad. I'll speak to him."

"The footprint casts from both scenes," said Nick. "If the same feet left them, we got the same bad guys. Want to compare them, or have our lab do it?"

"Gotta be you, doesn't it?" she said. "That way we *know* we'll get our men."

"That motto's worn thin with me."

"I'm sure it has. Just breaking ice." She laughed, then hung up.

Nice voice, thought Nick.

The Pig War

Three Victorian library tables arranged in a U like a horseshoe served as DeClercq's desk. An antique from the early days of the Force, the high-backed, barley-sugar chair was crowned with the buffalo-head crest of the North West Mounted Police. The chair faced his Strategy Wall, which was split into three sections and covered from floor to ceiling with corkboard. When plotting a book or stalking a killer he liked to think with his eyes, so stuck to the corkboard like jigsaw puzzles were two collages gathered from Ident photos and police reports concerning the Campbell kidnappings north and south of the border. The man seated facing the wall didn't look like a cop. With guileless eyes belying the fact that he had seen it all, an aquiline nose hinting at arrogance he didn't have, dark wavy hair graying at the temples for a dash of distinction, and piano-player hands that would never break a jaw tapping the keyboard of the computer on his desk, Chief Superintendent Robert DeClercq looked more like a historian, which he also was: *Those Who Wore the Tunic*, his history of the Royal Canadian Mounted Police; *Bagpipes, Blood and Glory*, his debunking of the myth of Inspector Wilfred Blake; and now *Yukon*, the book he was researching with the help of the Internet.

Yukon would tell the history of the Klondike gold rush, and of how 250 Mounties policed 100,000 miners, most from the States. The Yukon rush began in 1896, when gold was panned from Rabbit Creek by George Carmack, Skookum Jim and Tagish Charlie. Rush became stampede when the Seattle *Post-Intelligencer* wrote that the find was "a ton of gold." Since the gateway to the Yukon was Alaska, a lawless land where Soapy Smith's gang unnerved Skagway and Slim Jim Foster robbed newcomers in the Slaughter House Saloon before dumping them in the tidal waters behind, the Mounties built posts atop the snowy summits of the Chilkoot and White passes to check every panner coming in.

Law in the Yukon was Superintendent Sam Steele. As most of those Steele dealt with were American, DeClercq had posted a query on an Internet bulletin board for historians, requesting U.S. anecdotes about how the Force had tamed the North.

E-mail last week from San Francisco:

In 1898, Sam Steele arrived at Lake Bennett, where thousands of miners were building boats to sail down to Dawson once the Yukon River thawed. He slept on a cot over a suitcase with $2 million for the new bank. To go downriver meant shooting the Whitehorse Rapids through Miles Canyon, where 150 boats wrecked and goldseekers drowned. My great-granddad was present when Steele laid down the law: "Many of your countrymen have said that the Mounted Police make up the laws as they go along. I am going to do so now for your own good." No boat could run the rapids after that unless Steele thought it safe to sail.

Wondering if additional e-mail had arrived today in reply to his query, DeClercq took a break from assembling the Campbell collages on the Strategy Wall to boot up his computer and check his cyberspace mailbox. With his password—Royal—entered, he was informed that one new message was in the box. Clicking on it showed this e-mail from Nevada on-screen:

Aces High Carson was a gambler in Lousetown, across the river from Dawson. That's where the prostitutes had cribs. When Sam Steele fined him fifty dollars for cheating in a game, he laughed at the Mountie and boasted, "I've got that in my vest pocket." Steele replied, "And sixty days chopping our woodpile. Have you got that in your vest pocket?"

DeClercq printed off the anecdote and filed it away with the rest of his research for the new book.

If only he knew how deadly that historians' bulletin board would soon become, and how he would be involved in a life-or-death race to save someone near to him from suffering the worst death a sadistic psychopath could imagine.

———

DeClercq got up, rounded his desk and returned to work on the Campbell collages, searching for links between the two kidnappings. A map of the Pacific Northwest, from Vancouver down to Seattle, was pinned to the corkboard wall, straddling the dividing line between the visual clusters. Across the map, the Canada-U.S. border zigzagged among the islands. As the cop in him focused on the two abductions, the historian in him recalled how that border was settled. . . .

The killer was a Yankee.

The victim a limey pig.

And the aftermath pushed the States and Britain to the brink of war.

The Pig War.

With pigheaded facts.

The Oregon Treaty of 1846 set the British-American border west of the Rocky Mountains as "the forty-ninth parallel of north latitude to the middle of the channel which separates the continent from Vancouver's Island; and thence southerly through the middle of the said

channel, and of Fuca's Straits to the Pacific Ocean."
Drafters of the treaty must have flunked geography, for
any dunce with a map could see that Haro Strait *and*
Rosario Strait qualified as "the said channel," between
which sat strategic San Juan Island.

Cue the pig.

The British thought this island was "the Military Key
to British Columbia," so in 1853, to stake its claim, the
Hudson's Bay Company colonized a sheep farm on San
Juan. The farm included a fine black breeding boar. The
States countered by declaring the San Juan archipelago
part of Whatcom County, Washington Territory. That's
when Lyman A. Cutler, an American miner who didn't
pan out in the Fraser River gold rush of 1858, built a
shack as a squatter, planted a garden and surrounded it
with a rickety fence in the middle of the HBC's sheep run.

Release the pig.

The porker made profitable forays into the potato
patch, porcine raids that provoked Cutler to shoot the
provocative pig, which threw the fat in the fire, so to
speak. San Juan was a popular picnic site of Victorians
from across Haro Strait, and it happened that the senior
HBC man had just arrived on the *Beaver*. He demanded
that Cutler pay a hundred dollars for the pork, or be
taken to Victoria to stand trial. Americans saw it as British swine persecuting an American on American soil,
and they ran squealing to the U.S. army.

Enter General Harney.

Harney was a bellicose, short-fused hog. During the
Indian War, he committed atrocities. During the Mexican War, he was relieved of command. During the Mor-
mon War, he tried to hang Brigham Young and the
"apostles," then was transferred here. His reaction to
the execution of the pig and the limey attempt to lynch
Cutler was to beach American troops on San Juan.

Enter Governor Douglas.

Douglas was as diplomatic as a sow's ear. To put a
bit of stick about, he sent a major, backed by naval can-

nons on HMS *Satellite, Tribune,* and *Plumper,* to raise the Union Jack on this "British island" and force the Yankees into the sea.

When London and Washington got a whiff of the tiff in the sty out West, action was taken to save the bacon on both sides. On learning that Douglas and Harney had Pig War plans, the admiral of the royal fleet said, "Tut, tut, no, no, the damned fools." Douglas was ordered to butt out. The American commander-in-chief sacked Harney again. An agreement was reached so both governments could occupy the island with a hundred troops. The Royal Marines landed at Garrison Bay, and ten miles away the U.S. army dug in at Griffin Bay. The next thirteen years saw the San Juan Islands a no man's land, until finally in 1872 the dispute went to the German kaiser for arbitration. By a split decision, German judges awarded the islands to the States.

In the end, the only casualty was an English pig, and the Pig War settled the last border on the Pacific Coast as Haro Strait between the Gulf Islands in Canada and America's San Juans.

DeClercq studied the map on the Strategy Wall.

If only he knew how crucial the Pig War would soon become in a life-or-death race to save someone near to him from suffering the worst death a femme fatale could inflict.

Femme Fatale

Shipwreck Island, Washington State

He liked to see her walk naked among his precious collections, this Svengali of a man, this Rasputin of a man, this Casanova of a man, this Don Juan of a man who used her flesh as a canvas on which to fashion art. And Donella Grant liked having him see her walk naked among his collections. There was power in knowing she was his most precious collectable, for collect her Mephisto had . . . from a lingerie ad.

Donella's Passion.
Inflame his desire for you.

Sex appeal was Donella's overpowering attribute, a magnetism that turned the heads of every male from nine to ninety on Seattle streets. The heads of women, too. Confident that she modeled better than Claudia Schiffer in a Victoria's Secret ad, Donella had purchased a bankrupt lingerie shop in a downtown mall. Using the merchandise that came with the deal, she hired a photographer to do a spread of her. Hot-pink slithers with froths of black Chantilly lace. Saucy slips that hugged her body like a second skin. And push-up plunge bras that ought to be against the law. All brought together for an ad she ran in local papers, enticing those who yearned for passion to her shop.

The ad had lured him.

She was alone in Donella's Passion when he walked in from the mall. An impeccable dresser in a charcoal

Savile Row suit. White shirt, burgundy tie. Not an ounce of fat could she spot on his buffed, lean physique. His black hair and black Vandyke beard were perfectly groomed, as were the nails of his manicured hands. A slight scent of expensive cologne caressed her nose, as his deep-set eyes—what her mother used to call bedroom eyes—got a lock on hers.

"Can I show you something, sir?" Donella asked.

"Yes, the bra you're wearing," he replied.

Donella smiled and bent to remove a bra displayed in the glass counter.

"Not the one in the case. The one you're wearing," he said.

Donella shivered.

She sensed he caught her shudder.

"You can't see the one I'm wearing."

"I know," he said, holding her gaze. "That's why I want you to open your blouse for me."

With a movement as refined as his tailoring, the man pulled ten hundred-dollar bills from his pocket, fanning them on the counter.

Donella frowned.

"What do you think I am?"

"The most beautiful woman in Seattle," he said.

"I'm no stripper."

"Be one for me." Another refined movement withdrew her ad from inside his suit jacket. "You published this in the paper for all to see. Exquisiteness like yours I must see in the flesh."

"What are you?"

"A connoisseur."

"A connoisseur of what?"

"A connoisseur of *you.*"

Her store was open to the mall beyond. A stream of people passed left and right. There used to be a series of ads for Maidenform, a woman walking out in public in just her bra, with the copy "I dreamed I . . . in my Maidenform bra." Latent exhibitionism made those ads work, but the show-off in Donella was under no such restraint. It was a lingerie shop, and this man aroused her, so button by button, she undid her blouse.

The bra she was wearing was a fillip from France. The undercup a cat's eye that barely hid the nipple, on top was petaled, see-through lace. A tiny bow linked the cups to bridge her cleavage, as heaving mounds rose and fell with every breath. The longer he eyed her breasts, the hotter she got.

The man plucked her business card from a holder on the counter. "Donella Grant," he said. "A fine Scottish clan. How many can trace their heraldry back to Kenneth MacAlpin in 843?"

Donella scooped up the hundred-dollar bills and tucked them into her bra. "An expensive purchase, sir. Shall I wrap it up?"

"It looks too good on you," he said, "to take away with me."

He turned on his heels, walked from the store and left her exposed to the mall. The eyes of a passing pubescent boy bugged from his head.

A week later, the devil returned.

Again she was in the shop alone when he walked in from the mall.

Her heart jumped.

Another primal shiver.

"Can I show you something, sir?"

"Yes, the panties you're wearing."

The same fluid movement withdrew twenty hundred-dollar bills from his navy blue suit, then laid them on the counter like a poker hand.

"Here?" said Donella.

"Here," he replied.

The glass counter rose to her waist. Locking eyes with him, she unzipped the side zipper and allowed her skirt to drop. The V of her panties trimmed with French lace was cut high on the thigh. Through the silk window he could see her pubic shadow.

The longer he stared, the moister she became. From a shopping bag he pulled a skirt of pleated tartan. The kilt was fastened with a big silver pin. The tartan was bright red, with a black-and-blue checkered pattern. He smoothed it on the counter.

"Dinner," he said. "Eight o'clock. Meet me there." He dropped a card from Seattle's best restaurant on the tartan. "What does the most beautiful woman of the Gael wear under her kilt?"

"I have a date," Donella said.

"Break it," he replied, and turned on his heel to walk out of the store and leave her tingling behind the counter in her underwear.

The customer coming in got an eyeful that made his day.

That night, the maître d' of the restaurant on top of the office tower led her to the booth where Mephisto sat drinking champagne. He eased Donella into the love seat beside her date, then poured a flute of bubbly Dom Perignon for her. The booth faced out over the lights of the city and Puget Sound, and turned 360 degrees every hour with each revolution of the crown atop the phallic highrise.

"Well?" said Donella, turning to him for approval of her couture.

"Grrrannd," he burred. "That's Gaelic for Grant. And *grrrand* you are."

They clinked flutes before he looked her over from head to toe. Her russet hair was as wild and wanton as only skillful work with a comb could tease. Her brows, eyes and cheekbones angled like a cat's. Her turned-up nose met her full-lipped mouth, slick and slightly open to show her teeth. Her throat and chest dropped bare to a black bodice, which was laced to expose a swath of peek-a-boo breasts and her navel. A belt cinched the tartan about her concave waist before the fabric flaired around her curvy hips. Her long and shapely legs emerged from the short skirt. As his eyes returned to delve hypnotically into hers, one of the man's hands dropped possessively to her knee.

Donella caught her breath.

"What's your name?" she asked.

"Campbell," he replied.

"Is that your first or last name?"

"Campbell will do."

"Call me Donella," she said.

"Donella is Latin for 'little mistress,' and nothing about you is small."

His hand moved an inch up her thigh from her knee.

"I'm no mistress."

"I know. You're a Highland queen."

An aura of power exuded from this man, a sense that he saw what he wanted and took it as his right. He played the flesh of her inner thigh as if she were a harp, his fingers caressing, kneading and tingling sexual nerves no other man had aroused, making her quiver and shiver as, slowly, methodically, his hand crept up her leg. At this rate it would take him forever to reach her pussy, and by then she'd be a puddle on the seat.

"You are a queen," he said. Fuck, you're good, she thought. "Your clan line flows from the king who united the Picts and the Scots." Pict your way up my thigh and frig me fast, you devil. "Who the Picts were remains a mystery unresolved. The Scots were Celts from Ireland." That's it. Now you know what's under my Celt. "*Picti* is a Roman word that means the 'painted people.' It refers to the fact that we dyed our bodies blue with woad. The earliest record of the Picts was in 297 A.D. when Highland warriors attacked Hadrian's Wall. By 305, the Picts and Romans were at war." Will your roamin' hand ever Pict a cranny and stop, or are you going to explore me until I faint? "*Pict* was a general term for all Highlanders to the north, including descendants of the ancient tribes that built the megaliths and the Celts who crossed from Europe centuries before the Romans." Enough! thought Donella. I'll scream if I come! "Come," he said, reading her mind—or was it her body?—and he kept on probing until she couldn't hold back anymore. "The Scots from Ireland invaded the Highlands to the west. The Picts from Pictland overran Hadrian's Wall. The Romans abandoned the wall about 410, and left the Scots and the Picts to battle each other. That they did for centuries, until 843, when Kenneth MacAlpin, king of the Scots, usurped the Pictish throne." Yes! Yes! YES! Donella began to moan as her date, one hand under her skirt, clamped his other over her mouth. "Clan Grant is descended from Scotland's first king"—he slipped two fingers into her—"and Grant's your Highland clan, my queen."

Donella let go.

And came like she'd never come.

And thrashed so hard that she might have overturned the love seat were he not so strong.

And never knew until then that history could be so much fun.

"Shall we order?" he said.

They dined on oysters Rockefeller, then chateaubriand, enhanced by the best wine Donella had ever tasted. The booth was a high-backed alcove facing out, and it hid them from others in the restaurant, but she wondered if they had heard her come. "If they did," he said, again reading her mind, "their dining will seem dull compared with yours." Before this night was over, if that was the appetizer, would he serve her the main course?

He'd better.

Or she'd serve him.

"Tell me more about my clan."

"You like being a queen?"

"I *love* it," she said.

"Then I guess we'll have to crown you on *my* Stone of Scone."

"We?" she said.

But got no answer.

"When Kenneth MacAlpin united the Scots and the

Picts, he was crowned the first king of Scotland on the Stone of Destiny, the Stone of Scone, as were later Scottish kings. That stone had come from Ireland with the Scots, *Scot* being an Irish term that means 'bandit.' Pictland was divided into seven tribal districts, and the eighth was Dalriada, the Scots in Argyll. Now the tribes broke up into smaller clans, the Picts being absorbed by the Scots in new Scotland, and henceforth clanship was the principle that governed Highlanders. The Picts' language gave way to Gaelic, and is now lost."

"Were we Picts or Scots?"

"Both," he said. "More or less, depending on where the clan lived. Clans were determined by configurations of land. Inland glens, islands and the shore bordering sea lochs were favored homes. So you had MacDonald of Glencoe, Campbell of Argyll, and Grant up between Skye and Loch Ness."

"The monster?" said Donella.

"It's yours," said her date. "In the thirteenth century, Grants appear as the sheriffs of Inverness, the city at the foot of the loch. You had considerable influence in the northeast, and supported Wallace against the English at the Battles of Stirling Bridge and Falkirk."

"When was that?"

"1297, 1298."

"Who was Wallace?"

"Mel Gibson. If you saw *Braveheart.*"

She certainly had! Mel was her screen heartthrob. Until tonight, Mel had been the man she most desired to bed. Wallace had escaped her.

"And you, Campbell? What about your clan?"

"We massacred the MacDonalds at Glencoe. If clans weren't fighting the English, clans were fighting each other, or clans were fighting each other *for* England's king. Every clan was led by a patriarchal chief, to whom allegiance was owed. He dispensed law in times of peace and rallied men for war. He governed the clan territory and divided up the land. When he was sworn in, he stood on a stone and took an oath to preserve inviolate the ancient ways of the clan. Then he was given a sword and a white wand.

"Each clan had a recognized meeting place in times of war, a place to which the clan was called by a *crantaraidh,* or fiery cross, dipped in blood. In fighting, the first attack was the fiercest: a firearm volley followed by a claymore charge, clansmen rushing forward swinging two-hand swords, shouting their war cry at the top of their lungs."

"What's my war cry?" Donella asked.

" 'Stand fast, Craigellachie!' " he replied.

"What's Craigellachie?"

"Crag Elachaidh. A war cry was often a landmark in the clan district."

"And your cry?"

" 'Cruachan!' Also a land feature."

Donella reached under the table and grabbed him by the cock.

"Stand fast, Craigellachie! Your place or mine?"

"Come," he said.

How many times? she thought.

———

An elevator took them from the restaurant down to the ground floor. A limousine took them from the office tower to a helicopter pad. A helicopter took them away from Seattle into the full moon night, heading up Puget Sound toward the San Juans. Now this was Donella's idea of a date: a handsome, rich, intelligent man who seemed to own it all and who lusted after her. Selling panties and bras retreated as a goal, to be replaced by the thrill of landing this catch. Wherever they were flying, she knew it would be *grrrannd!*

"You sure know a lot about Scotland for a man who speaks like me. American, aren't you?"

"Not in my heart and mind. America's too young to have legends old enough for me."

"What sort of legends?"

"If you're good, you'll find out."

"And if I'm bad?"

"Bad is good to me."

And when she was bad, she was *very* bad, Donella thought.

With its landing lights on to illuminate a rocky bluff, the helicopter set down beside a mansion commanding an island somewhere up north near Boundary Pass, near the border with Canada. They waited for the ground effect churned up to settle, then stepped out into the moonlight to cross to the mansion.

The helicopter took off.

"This house is *yours?*" Donella said, awed.

"I own the island."

"Who built this place?"

"A rum-runner during Prohibition. He made a fortune smuggling booze in from Canada."

"How'd you make *your* fortune?"

"Come, I'll show you."

They entered the most magnificent hall Donella had ever seen. Walls of dark hardwood, with sweeping marble stairs. Stained glass and tapestries and portraits from the past. It got even better in a library to the right, where leather-bound books on walnut shelving surrounded glass cases displaying silver artifacts. Over the hearth hung a huge painting of a battle, Highlanders in tartan clashing with English dragoons.

A fire was blazing.

He took her coat.

"May I?" he said. And before she could answer, both hands took hold of her bodice and ripped it asunder, so her breasts burst free for him.

The garment dropped to the floor.

"Exquisite," he admired.

Donella was living a bodice-ripper, and it tingled her to the quick.

That was the first time she walked among his collections, and while she eyed his precious artifacts, he eyed her.

"What are these displays?"

"Hoards," he said.

"They look priceless."

"The originals are. Most of these are copies—very expensive, too—but some are genuine and priced through the roof."

"You collect them?"

"For collectors. Collectors are obsessive and must have what they want. I feed their obsessions, and they pay for mine. I deal in collectable art, books, stamps, coins, documents and such."

"What do you collect?"

"If you're good, you'll find out."

Collect me, Donella thought, pausing before a case of silver treasures: goblet, vase, spoon, plate, rings, pins, coins, brooches, armlets . . .

"The hoard of Roman silver found at Traprain Law," he said. "Discovered early this century in East Lothian, north of Hadrian's Wall. Some pieces originated in Gaul or the land of the Goths. The hoard is loot that the Picts stole from the Romans, or that came from Roman buy-offs."

"Buy-offs of whom?"

"Our ancestors."

"For what?"

"Peace."

Donella bent over the next case so the reflection doubled her pulchritude.

"The hoard of Pictish silver found at Norrie's Law in 1819. In Fife, across the Firth of Forth in what was once Pictland." His finger moved from piece to shining piece. "The leaf-shaped plaques bear Pictish designs, a double-disk with a Z-rod and the forepart of a dog. The spoon bowl bears a Roman inscription, and the *siliquae,* or silver coins, are those of Roman emperors Valens and Constantius II, A.D. 337 to 378. Some treasures were lost when they were melted down by a local jeweler, just as the Picts had melted down Roman silver to engrave their own designs."

Donella moved from case to case as he detailed the contents. "The Falkirk Hoard of nearly two thousand Roman coins dug up in Stirlingshire. The hoard dates from about 230 A.D. . . . The Gaulcross Hoard, found at Banff in what was once Pictland in 1840. The pin, chain and bracelet are all that survive. The hoard was found buried in a stone circle. . . ."

"The Picts got all this from the Romans?"

"Yes," he replied. "The Romans conquered the known world, but they couldn't conquer us. Hadrian's Wall was built across Britain to keep us in the north. Our raids in the second century led them to buy us off, probably with coins like those in the Falkirk Hoard. Silver soon became our metal of ornament, and since our only source of it was south of the wall, we were plundering again by the fourth century. The Pictish Wars began in 305 A.D. and didn't end until the Romans withdrew in 410. Hoards of Roman silver were hidden around Pictland, with those like Norrie's Law reworked as Pictish art. As the Picts gave way to Scottish clans, the hoards were lost, broken up or passed on."

The final display case brought them to the hearth. Punching numbers on a keypad released the security lock so he could lift the glass and remove four bracelets of gleaming silver. "Trust me," he said as he clasped them around Donella's wrists and ankles. Each bracelet had a ring on its outer curve.

"Beautiful," she said.

"Beauty on beauty, to me. Roman silver into Pictish art. Each manacle bears a different cult animal. Horse, dog, boar and bull."

"For me?" Donella teased.

"We'll see," he said.

"What battle is that?" she asked, gazing up at the picture over the hearth so her arched back flaunted her flawless breasts.

"The Battle of Culloden. April 16, 1746," he said. "When five thousand starving Highlanders loyal to Bonnie Prince Charlie were crushed by British redcoats under the Duke of Cumberland. The battle was on a moor near Inverness. The Highland charge was thwarted by a brilliant tactic. Each British defender, instead of engaging the clansman directly in front of him, bayoneted the exposed side of the Scot to his right. A thousand Highlanders were dead in forty minutes, and the nine thousand redcoats lost only fifty men."

"We Grants were wiped out?"

"Not in the battle. The Campbells and Grants fought on the British side."

He led her across to a wrought-iron staircase that spiraled up through the ceiling.

To the bedroom? she thought.

"After you," he said.

Donella climbed the staircase as his voice trailed below.

"Culloden marked the end of the clan system I told you about. The Highlanders were disarmed, and wearing of tartan was banned. Bagpipes were declared an instrument of war. Vanquished chiefs were tried in London and beheaded on Tower Hill, and all clan lands were forfeited to the Crown. Their houses were looted and burned. Hundreds of clansmen were sent to far-off plantations. The result was a collapse of the Highland economy, which forced waves of Scots to emigrate abroad. The exodus lasted more than a century, and the drift from the Highlands probably sent our ancestors here. They packed everything of value and came to North America."

All the way up . . .

All the time he was speaking . . .

Donella knew the man below was gazing up under her tartan.

———

Spiraling up through the ceiling did not lead her into his bedroom. Instead, Donella found herself ogled by a cyclops eye that shone through a greenhouse wedged in the slant of the roof. In the dark half of the upper story, where moonbeams didn't creep, a telescope angled up to a skylight above. Ringed around the telescope were scale models, most depicting rings themselves. Blown-up photographs backed each model; only one set of pictures was a monument she knew. Where moonlight met darkness sat a flat desk, its surface spread with computers and sheets of calculations.

Where he works? she thought.

Hands reached up through the hole in the floor and undid her kilt. It dropped below as he emerged. Donella was naked except for her shoes, and the four bracelets clamping her.

"After you," he said, sliding open the door to the greenhouse.

In they went.

The door slid shut.

The moonlit plants around her were unlike those in local gardens—all eerie mouths and traplike leaves and glistening dew.

"Close your eyes," he said.

Close them she did.

A moment later, something spiny tickled the tip of her tit—tickle, tickle, tickle—before a mouth nibbled her nipple.

"Keep them closed."

Tickle, tickle. Then another bite.

"Take a look."

She took a look, and saw the tiny jaws of a plant in

his hand munching her, sucking her nipple erect with each hungry pluck.

He raised another flytrap from the cedar shelf and fed it her other breast. The open jaws yawned above and below the nipple as he jiggled the plant left and right to trip the trigger hairs.

"Shoulders back. Chest out. Let them feast."

His eyes locked hypnotically with hers, and seemed to probe deep into her mind. Donella was stripped naked inside and out. Pulling the plants from her breasts, he licked her nipples, a single flick of the tongue like a snake.

Donella shuddered.

Hot, not cold.

"Meet me there," he said, pointing out through the greenhouse glass at what appeared to be a stone circle in the woods, like some of the scale models that ringed the telescope.

Donella moved through the moonlight as if living a dream, the one in which you walk out naked for everyone to see.

Last night I dreamt I went to Manderley again . . .

The opening line from *Rebecca* came to mind as she went down the spiral staircase to the library, then out into the hall and out the front door, down stone steps toward the woods and into the thicket of trees masking the standing stones.

I dreamed I went to Stonehenge without my Maidenform bra . . .

So dark was it in the islands that the stars above increased in number a hundredfold. So deathly quiet was it that she heard every sound: the wash of waves on the shore all around, the distant calls of mammals swimming in the sea, the rhythmic *swoop swoop* of wings flapping overhead, the squeal of something caught by an owl nearby and her heart pounding in her ears as she entered the Stone Circle, watched from above by the cyclops eye of the full August moon.

Other eyes, too?

She *sensed* them in the woods.

Lines of power hummed within the stones. She could feel them tug like a divining rod, charging her with an energy that had to be released. Never had she felt this sexual before; it was as if every man was slave to her siren's call, and she was the most desirable woman in the whole fucking world.

The *only* woman who could satisfy *him*.

Donella was lost in a sexual fantasy when she saw her devil approach. No mistaking the fluid way he moved his body, which was now covered by a black robe with a pointed cowl. "Queen, it's your crowning on my Stone of Scone." And with those words, he shed the robe and cast it aside, baring a body as sculpted as hers, not a flaw of fat on his physique, muscles toned to the perfection of Michelangelo's David.

His face was painted blue.

And what a cock!

Never had she seen a man as proud and hard as him. Length, girth, he had it all: a conceit of a cock. The mask of woad seemed to unleash him, releasing every inhibition to virility. He gripped her arms and spread them as if in crucifixion, his rock-hard pecs against her breasts, his washboard abs against her belly, his jutting weapon against her clitoris as they whirled in a *danse macabre* around the Stone Circle.

Dance with the devil, she thought.

Suddenly, there was movement at the corners of her eyes. Moon shadows skulked into the ring from the woods beyond. Three figures in hoods and robes, with ropes and hooks. Hooks hooked the bracelet rings on her crucified wrists. Hooks hooked the bracelet rings on both ankles. One man took the ropes hooked to her wrists. A man each took the ropes hooked to her ankles. Faces as woad blue as the devil's leered from the hoods. Donella was now a puppet on strings, a marionette with next to no control of her body.

"You're *mine*," said the devil, releasing her arms as the man with the ropes hooked to her wrists looped them around opposite stones.

The devil gripped her buttocks and lifted her into the air.

"Spread," he said, and the ankle men drew her legs apart.

Donella was spread-eagled above the devil's cock.

"Crown me," he said, and lowered her down the full length of the rod, impaling her like she had never been impaled before.

And so it began.

The fucking of her life.

The lines of power in this circle seeming to charge the lines hooked to her.

The Druids didn't touch her.

She was *his*.

But everything they did was watched by alien eyes, quivering her to her primal core with the taboo thrill of it all. Nothing was *verboten*. A carnal smorgasbord. Ropes cinched her this way and that to contort her to his will. Releasing them allowed her to gather herself. Tightening them exposed her to the depths of his virile obsession. Struggling against the bonds only heightened her desire, tensing erotic tensions that screamed to be let go. She was bent back, and doubled over, and spread as wide as joints would spread, before he bent her over his central Stone of Scone and crowned her his Highland queen from above and behind, tearing a wail of ultimate abandon from her throat. On and on it went, until Donella was subdued, and only when he knew she was hooked on him forever did he come.

And what a come.

And tell her . . .

"I'm your Mephisto!"

Later, Donella sat naked in the mansion among four men and had her breasts engraved with her first Pictish tattoos.

She had sold her flesh to the devil.
And she reveled in her freedom.

———————

That was two months ago.
August full moon.
Much had happened since then.
More would happen soon.
She was a *different* woman.
He had seen to that.
This work of art who walked naked among Mephisto's collections.
She knew what he had planned.
This Lady Macbeth.
The Highland queen of the man who held the fate of mankind in his hands.
His plan was so diabolical that it had to be hatched in hell.
In for a penny.
In for a pound.
She had sold her *soul* to the devil.

No Man's Land

Campbell, thought Jenna.

Fitzroy and Gavin.

Two men with the same surname.

A Scottish clan.

Two men about the same age—early seventies—both abducted from pioneer waterfront homesteads on the West Coast islands.

One homestead here, the other in Canada.

Both homes ransacked in thorough searches for some unknown "something."

Fitzroy missing, and probably dead.

Gavin missing, then found at the bottom of the sea this morning.

Gavin tortured.

To give up the "something"?

Fitzroy tortured?

To give it up, too?

If so, what links both men to the "something"?

Campbell?

Clan?

Surname?

Family?

Jenna turned the puzzle over in her mind while the *Islomania* cruised east from Friday Harbor, exiting from Upright Channel between Shaw and Lopez islands to skirt the tips of the inverted U that made Orcas Island look like a magnet attracting boats off waters to the south. The overcast of this morning had lifted as the day wore on, and the tatters of mist drifting over the brine had dissipated. Sun dappled the crests of the swells as the boat moved *boomph boomph boomph* across the yawn of East Sound, which divided the magnet arms, and through Obstruction Pass (between Deer Point, at the tip of the eastern arm, and Obstruction Island), before angling north up Rosario Strait past Jenna's farm to Fitzroy Campbell's acreage at Doe Bay.

She moored the boat to the dock, still strung with crime-scene tape, then followed the blood trail up the grass green swath in a forest of towering cedars to the pioneer house.

William Campbell met her at the door.

"You found my father?"

"No," Jenna said. "I need your help to figure out *why* he was abducted."

The son who led her into Fitzroy Campbell's parlor was the antithesis of the boy you'd think was raised on Orcas Island. He could be an alien marooned here in the sticks, this button-down bean counter from Atlanta with blown-dry hair and probably the only shirt and tie this side of the water. Some island kids grew up dreaming of escape, and William Campbell had fled as far from home as possible in location, work and thought. Jenna, too, but she'd come back.

"Mess, huh?"

"I'll say."

"They tore the place apart. What were they looking for? Dad lived a rustic life. No radio. No TV. That's what drove me crazy. After Mom died, Dad turned in on himself. You'd think we were Amish. Living like it was the past. Dad has a pension, but nothing of value, so why do this?"

Fitzroy Campbell's house was in the worst shambles Jenna had ever seen, and she had witnessed many warrant searches. Like most pioneer homes, the parlor was built around a massive stone hearth, the only source of heat for winter-chilled bones. The overstuffed furniture had a woman's touch, though the once bright country patterns had faded over time and were now slashed to ribbons with the stuffing pulled out. Boards were pried loose from the pine walls and hardwood floors. Holes were cut in the ceiling above tables and shelves stripped of possessions and books. A family Bible lay among the ruins.

"He's dead, isn't he?"

"We don't know," Jenna said. And she wondered if he'd heard about finding Gavin Campbell. No radio and no TV. Probably not. "Abducted victims are usually kept alive, Bill."

"Until they're of no use."

"Sometimes," she agreed. "But if we knew the *why* of your dad's abduction, we might solve the *who.*"

"How ironic if my son was born the day my father died. He never got the news. That's why I called you. And now I may have to make *two* entries, huh?"

He nodded at the Bible on the floor.

Having been raised on Orcas, Jenna understood what he meant.

"Your family's been here a long time, Bill. My dad told me you Campbells were the first pioneers. Was Hank right?"

"Yeah," said Fitzroy's son. "My great-great-grandfather was Callum Campbell. His elder son, Dugald, homesteaded this spread as a way station during the 1858 Fraser gold rush. The Pig War the following year turned Orcas Island into no man's land. Thirteen years passed before the German kaiser awarded the San Juans to the States, and that's when my great-grandfather applied for ownership under America's Homestead Act. Fourteen decades of Campbells will cease with me."

"You don't want the homestead?"

"I hate this place."

"Fourteen decades is a long time. No family rumors of something hidden here?"

"You mean gold?"

"Anything. The place was torn apart. Seems someone thought it hid something."

"The only Campbell mystery is the missing tract of land. Callum Campbell immigrated with his two sons and supposedly selected three homestead sites, one for each son and one for him. Callum drowned in a boating accident in 1863, and *two* of those tracts were later registered by his sons. My grandfather, the tale goes, overheard his father and uncle—Callum's sons—arguing about a woman who got the third tract. After that argument, she was never mentioned again. To this day, we have no idea who the woman was, where the property is or what claim she had to it."

"Callum's mistress?"

"Possibly."

"Any whisper of one?"

Bill shook his head. "Our family was religious. No scandal ever surfaced."

"Her land was in the San Juans?"

"Had to be. If it was in Canada, Callum would have filed for ownership before he died. Lawful jurisdiction was never in doubt beyond Haro Strait. The younger son filed in Canada, so he owned his tract before my great-grandfather. Until the Pig War died down, no man's land had no country."

Two sons, Jenna thought. One in Canada. Here comes the zinger question. "Does the name Gavin Campbell mean anything to you, Bill?"

"Sure," he said, and passed her the Bible from the floor.

Jenna knew right away where to look. She flipped the cover open and read the flyleaf.

The atmosphere on Orcas in pioneer days was heaven compared with the hell of booze and violence that reigned on San Juan. As the population began to grow after the Pig War, settlers tended their farms and raised families in a wholesome frontier way. One of the settlers was Elder Gray, who came to build a church, and one was a saloon-keeper-to-be who bought land in Eastsound to establish a boozery. Rallying temperance-minded teetotalers about him and his righteous cause, Gray ran the grog merchant out. The island's first church was raised on the sinful clearing, making a favorite of hymn number 564: "How firm a foundation . . . Is laid for your faith."

A Bible Belt.

Before universal education took hold, your typical homestead was home to a single book. This cherished volume slowly became the catch-all for family genealogy, its pages used to safe-keep letters and documents, and its flyleaf used to record births and deaths in the family tree.

The flyleaf of the Campbell Bible was the pedigree place for the clan, a rectilinear chart of the family's surname.

The Campbell connection, Jenna thought, as she read this:

> *Somerled Campbell, 1648–1723*
> *Roderick Campbell, 1702–1751*
> *Kenneth Campbell, 1739–1799*
> *Lachlan Campbell, 1770–1847*
> *Callum Campbell, 1814–1863*
> *Dugald Campbell, 1840–1916 Ewen Campbell, 1841–1913*
> *Scotland to Vancouver Island in May 1857*
> *New Caledonia*
> *John Campbell, 1865–1941   Roy Campbell, 1885–1953*
> *Fitzroy Campbell, 1924–   Gavin Campbell, 1923–*
> *William Campbell 1958–*

Glencoe

Shipwreck Island, Washington State

The tape played through the speakers in the observatory on the upper floor of Mephisto's mansion:

"Where's the Hoard, Campbell?"

Gavin was crying for his mother.

The pentothal had him babbling.

"HEEEEEEEEEELP!" he screamed.

A sharp intake of breath.

"PLEEEEEEEEESE! I'M GOING TO DROWN!"

"You won't drown. You'll smother to death. The air in the tank on your back is running out. If you want to live, answer my question. Otherwise, it's going, going, gone . . . for you."

Gasping.

Choking.

Rasping for air.

"Antigonus Severus. The Druid medallion," Mephisto prompted.

More gasping from the speakers.

"Where's the Hoard, Campbell?"

"Fitzroy!" Gavin screamed.

"Fitzroy says you must have it. It's not hidden on his land."

"I don't have it! GOD, I CAN'T BREATHE!"

"Where's the Hoard, Campbell?"

Rasping, gasping for air.

*"It must . . . it must . . . GOOD LORD! THE THIRD
TRACT OF LAND!"*

"What third tract?"

"GGGGGGGGGGAAAAAaaa . . ."

And he was gone.

As he listened yet again to the final moments of the
suffocating man, Mephisto didn't return in his imagination to Ancient Rome or Ancient Britain.

Instead, he traveled back to seventeenth-century
Scotland.

The third and final act in the evolution of the legend
of the Hoard . . .

The Highlands, Scotland
February 13, 1692

Pity the student who has to study the struggle for the
British throne in the 1600s. All that turmoil for a bloody
chair. A chair over the Stone of Scone, stolen by England from Scotland.

King Charles I was beheaded in 1649. Britain lost its
monarch, and Oliver Cromwell ruled. Scotland united
with England, and lost its independence. The Restora-
tion of 1660 put Charles II on the throne. When Charles
II died in 1685, his brother James II succeeded, until
William of Orange, his Dutch son-in-law, usurped the
king's throne in 1689.

While others buckled, many Highlanders in Scotland
remained true to James. Known as Jacobites, these loyal
clans fell upon Dutch William's troops in the narrow
gorge of Killiecrankie and slaughtered them. Later losses
forced the Jacobites to disperse.

Enter the villain.

John Campbell, Earl of Breadalbane.

"Cunning as a fox, slippery as an eel."

Dutch William gave him twelve thousand pounds to
bribe the Jacobites. Some accepted, some refused, but

none became any more loyal to the king. The failure of bribery gave rise to Plan B.

Fyre and swoorde.

"There never was trouble brewing in Scotland," had predicted Charles II, "but that . . . a Campbell was at the bottom of it." Since early in the century, the Campbells of Argyll had emerged more and more as agents of the Crown against other Highland clans.

A proclamation was issued ordering Jacobite chiefs to take the oath of allegiance to King William no later than January 1, 1692, or recourse would be had to fire and sword. "The winter time is the only season in which we are sure the Highlanders cannot escape. . . . This is the proper time to maul them in the long, dark nights," said one conspirator.

From exile in France, King James II authorized the chiefs to swear allegiance to Dutch William. But inclement weather caused MacDonald of Glencoe to arrive three days late, and the absence of the sheriff in Inveraray further delayed his oath. This gave Campbell the excuse he desired.

Enter the next villain.

Captain Robert Campbell of Glenlyon, a relative by marriage of MacDonald of Glencoe, asked if the Highland chief would billet him and a company of Campbell troops from the earl of Argyll's Regiment of Foot. The MacDonalds received them hospitably in their cottages in the bleak pass of Glencoe. Weeks of drinking, playing cards and fraternizing followed, then the treacherous captain was slipped a note: "You are hereby ordered to fall upon the rebels, the MacDonalds of Glencoe, and to put all to the sword under seventy. . . . This is by the King's special command . . . that these miscreants be cut off root and branch."

That night, Robert Campbell and a pair of officers dined with the chief. Meanwhile, eight hundred men from William's army blocked the northern and southern escapes from the glen. At five in the morning, the massacre began.

Enter the next villain.

Somerled Campbell . . .

———————

The wind blew bitterly from the northeast, and snow swirled thickly down the three-thousand-foot escarpment of saw-toothed Aonach Eagach—the Notched Ridge—into the choked pass of the River Coe. Eight miles in length, running east to west along the southern border with the Campbells of Argyll, from Loch Levenside on the coast to Rannoch Moor, this valley hideaway of the MacDonalds of Glencoe was a deep cut in the Scottish Highlands. The only path from the north was the Devil's Staircase, five tortuous miles blocked by winter drift. To the south, between the MacDonalds and the Campbells, rose a white-knuckled fist of mountains, one of them Bidean nam Bian—the Pinnacle of Peaks—the highest height in Argyll. There were gaps between the knuckles, but none a fugitive could find at night in a blizzard, so the only routes in or out were east and west, which—unknown to the MacDonalds—were besieged.

The trap was set.

No one knows the meaning of *Glencoe.* To Macauley, an English historian with no Gaelic, imagination dubbed it the Glen of Weeping. For MacDonald bards, it was the Glen of Dogs, named after Bran and the other hounds of the legendary warrior Fionn MacCumhail. Some thought it the glen of *comhan-saig,* the common hoard for the plunder that the ancients secreted in these hills. A stranger was always welcome at a MacDonald fireside if he could respond to the query, "Can you tell tales of Fingal? Or Bridei Mak Morn?"

Tales the MacDonalds and Campbells had shared over whisky the past two weeks.

Campbell of Glenlyon.

MacDonald of Glencoe.

And Lieutenant Somerled Campbell.

Fingal was another name for Fionn MacCumhail, the mythic Highlander who fought the Vikings nine centuries ago. He and his followers, the Feinn, lived in Glencoe. They were a race of long-haired giants who pillaged far and wide, sailing galleys to Ireland and the Hebrides or crossing Rannoch Moor to raid the south. When forty shield-lined ships brought Norsemen to the glen, an epic battle with the Vikings raged for eight days; warriors chased each other up the valley slopes as enemies hacked with sword and ax waist-deep in the red waters of Loch Levenside. The Vikings fled in a pair of ships when Earragin, king of the Norsemen, was slain by Goll MacMorna, the heroic descendant of Bridei Mak Morn, the legendary Highlander from Glencoe who overran the Roman wall in the Pictish Wars. It's said that the Feinn, three thousand strong, sleep today atop the peak of every mountain in Scotland. Wind is their breathing, and one day they'll rise at the call of Fingal's horn . . .

So many tales . . .

Told mouth to ear . . .

Passing from father to son.

Last night was supposedly the last for Campbells in the glen. They were up at dawn to march against the MacDonells of Glengarry for refusing to pledge allegiance to Dutch William. Old MacDonald of Glencoe—proud of his clan's reputation for hospitality—had hosted Captain Robert Campbell and Lieutenant Somerled Campbell at his house, Carnoch, below the snowy hill of Sgòr na Ciche, the Pap of Glencoe.

As befits a chief, his house was the finest in the glen, two stories high with a blue slate roof and walls washed with lime. Though austere, the house inside was luxurious compared with the cottages of his clansmen. The flames of torches and candles burnished undraped stone, hearths warmed his council room and chambers for privacy; he had books on shelves and cupboards for fine linen and lace, with charter chests for documents and a broad table for feasting, a glass for his claret and a silver quaich for his whisky.

"Well could you drain flagons and empty ankers of wine. Well did you carry yourselves when you met over the cup, playing backgammon and other games," sang the resident bard.

MacDonald of Glencoe was awesome to behold. Fierce of face and six-foot-seven tall, with the rusty hair of his family now a white mane to his shoulders and the spikes of his great mustache curling up to his ears, he'd been at Killiecrankie to slaughter the king's troops. Fingalian giant that he was, in his buff coat and tartan trews, a bullhide targe on his back and pistols hanging from his belt, a blunderbuss in one hand and a broadsword in the other, he'd led his MacDonalds in a Highland charge. To the redcoats, he was the devil himself, descending upon them from the brae of Craig Eallaich, shouting a cry of "Claymore!" as he threw off his plaid, stopped to blast his firearms and toss them aside, then rushed the enemy in a hacking, stabbing frenzy before the lowland levies could screw bayonets to their muskets. His sword, backed by a black hole in a screaming mouth, sundered arms and legs or split redcoat bodies from the scalp down to the waist.

MacDonald of Glencoe.

"Breathes wrath wherever he goes."

Returning home from Killiecrankie in 1689, he and the Glencoe MacDonalds had stripped Glen Lyon from one end to the other, taking their "soldier's pay" from the Campbell country of the earl of Breadalbane, including all possessions of Captain Robert Campbell, bankrupting him and forcing him to take the "king's shilling" in Dutch William's army.

But such were the ways of the Highlands that less than three years later, Campbell of Glenlyon sat in the home of MacDonald of Glencoe, surrounded by possessions that once were his, as he and his lieutenant were plied with whisky by their host, a drink distilled four times and so powerful that "at the first taste it affects all the members of the body; two spoonfuls being sufficient dose, and should any man exceed this it would presently stop his breath and endanger his life." They sang songs chosen to offend neither clan, red broadcloth and dark plaid flanking the fire, and played cards as tales were told of hunting, Fingal and Bridei Mak Morn, until the hour came when it was time to nod off. Not once did old MacDonald suspect that the note up Campbell's sleeve was not directing him to march against the Mac-Donells come morn, but to kill every MacDonald under seventy in the glen, for though a Highlander might dirk a Scot in the dark, or ambush him from the heights of a tree, hospitality given and taken was sacrosanct.

Honor among thieves.

While Clan MacDonald slept, Clan Campbell awoke in the wee hours before dawn.

At 5 A.M., Captain Robert Campbell of Glenlyon snapped shut his watch.

Time to spring the trap.

Billeted nearest to Carnoch was Somerled Campbell. Through swirling white darkness, the lieutenant marched his men toward the chief's house. The skirts of their scarlet coats brushed yellow hose. The butts of muskets slapped cold thighs. The points of pikes and blades of halberds spiked above blue bonnets. Somerled wore a crimson sash and foams of lace at his throat, but unlike MacDonald, he was not awesome to behold. Almost feminine of face, his flesh pink and his hair wispy and his nose long and his lips thin and his eyes bleary from drink, Somerled approached the door with the same grace that tossed a dice cup and hammered on it several times with the butt of his half-pike.

"MacIain," he called in a friendly voice, "I knock t' bid ye farewell."

Since the fourteenth century, MacIain had been the title of the Glencoe chiefs, from Angus Og's bastard,

Iain Og nan Fraoch, Young John of the Heather, also known as Iain Brach, John of Lochaber, who gave the clan heather on its bonnet badges.

Boar's-head badges backed Somerled Campbell.

Inside, a servant roused MacDonald of Glencoe from sleep.

"MacIain, the Campbells are leaving. One knocks t' bid t' yer roof-tree."

"A dram fer the lad," said the chief, rousting his wife, for though the hour was early, Somerled should be seen off with Highland courtesy.

Still in his nightshirt, with his back to the door, old MacIain was pulling on his trews when, pistol and half-pike in hand, the lieutenant strode in to shoot him in the back of the head. His brown-weathered face blown out by the ball, MacIain collapsed on the bed, his trews ignobly untied about his loins.

Lady Glencoe screamed, and hurled herself upon her husband.

Somerled yelled, and the room was full of Campbell soldiers, snow melting on their red coats and firelight cold on their bayonets.

"Strip her," he ordered, as musket shots echoed from outside, where servants stumbling half-naked in the snow were gunned down.

The Campbells tore the nightgown from the quaking woman's shame. Somerled drew the rings from her fingers with his teeth. The soldiers dragged her husband's body outside by the heels, trailed by the lieutenant, shoving the naked lady and putting MacIain's house to the torch as he retreated.

Lady Glencoe ran off shrieking into the blizzard.

The Campbell let her go.

His only mercy this morning.

In every cottage along the glen, the treachery was repeated. At nearby Inverrigan, Captain Robert Campbell of Glenlyon took care of his hosts, having the nine men of the household, bound hand and foot, carried out the door and dumped on the dung heap. In a slow, methodical butchering with bayonet and musket, each was killed one by one as Glenlyon watched. "Hold!" he said before the ninth was dispatched, but another captain approached to query, "Why is he still alive? What of our orders? Kill him!" And when Glenlyon hesitated, the captain brain-shot the youth himself.

A boy of twelve or thirteen emerged from the dark. Groveling at Glenlyon's feet, he cried that he'd go anywhere with the Campbell if his life were spared. Again the captain faltered, so the other captain shot the beseeching boy, too.

"Yer soft, man," he growled.

Every cottage had billeted three to five redcoats, and each was compensated for its hospitality. In one, an old Scot of eighty was bayoneted in bed by a Campbell who'd lost possessions in MacIain's Glen Lyon raid. With each thrust of steel, the soldier cried, "Take that fer Duncan's cows! Take that fer Annie's brooch!" With blood on their coats and their faces blackened by powder, Campbells surrounded one cottage and shot everyone inside through the windows, filling the house with booming thunder and foggy white smoke; they torched another and burned the fourteen people within alive. From one side of the glen to the other, at Brecklet, Laroch, Invercoe, Achnacone, Achtriachtan, the Campbells were berserk demons against the flames and smoke and snow, gutting and slashing and blasting MacDonalds as they scrambled from their doors. Bullets in the back were the lot of those who floundered across the river, the current sweeping their bodies down into the loch.

The smell of death mingled with the sweet smell of burning peat. There were moments amid the thud of shots and muffled cursing when nothing could be heard but the whining wind. The bloody hand of a child lay severed on the snow as pikemen prodded livestock from their byres—nine hundred cattle, two hundred horses, and many sheep and goats. Before burning thatch and timber, the troops looted the houses, ransacking them of plaids and shoes; pans and kettles; brooches, buckles, belts and women's combs; plates, cups, whisky, meal, herring and salmon from roof-beams; hides, fleece and blankets pulled off beds. With the flame cold on the gilt gorget at his throat and the plaid thrown back from his red coat, Robert Campbell of Glenlyon was pleased to take his red stallion back from the Carnoch stables and his wife's copper kettle from the chief's kitchen. Both were stolen during the MacDonalds' raid on Glen Lyon.

Nearby, to celebrate victory, the captain's piper, Hugh Mackenzie, played a Breadalbane rant of triumph on the bagpipes:

> *Listen, then, to my pibroch,*
> *it tells the news and tells it well*
> *of slaughtered men*
> *and forayed glen,*
> *Campbell's banners and the victor's joy!*

Lieutenant Somerled Campbell was celebrating, too. After shooting MacIain at Carnoch, he'd sent his men on to Inverrigan so he could return alone to the house in which he'd been billeted these past two weeks. There he found his MacDonald hosts in the same state he'd left them earlier, all three bound hand and foot and gagged: Malcolm, bleeding from the half-pike clout to his skull; Margaret, the comely wench he had lusted for every night; and the tearful six-year-old lad he would use to loosen her quim.

With its thick, drystone walls less than the height of a man, and the roof-tree above covered with thatch and divots of earth and lashed down with roped stones, the cottage was built against the weather on the slope of the glen. The windows were glassless, and smoke from the hearth curled up to a hole in the roof. Lamps of mutton fat and peat smudge from the fire blackened walls within and rimmed eyes red. Through the sickly choking haze, the Campbell approached the MacDonald and cut the gag free from his mouth with a dirk.

"Be ye still quick then?"

"Aye, I'm alive. But if I'm t' be dirked by you, I would rather it were nae beneath m' own roof."

"I've eaten yer meat," Somerled said, "and plan t' taste some more, so I'll do ye the favor and pistol ye without."

He dragged Malcolm out to the dung heap and put a ball into his brain.

The wench was shrieking through her gag as he came back in. For a fortnight, Somerled had yearned to sheath her around his sword, not as a lass screaming with terror during rape, but as a quim who put her heart and soul into his pleasure, aware that he'd cut the throat of her bairn if she weren't the best.

The lieutenant wrenched the boy from the floor and gripped him by the hair, hanging the lad before his ma as he cut free her gag.

Before he could tell her what to do, the words were out of her mouth, "Lord God, dinnae harm him! I'll buy his life with the Hoard!"

"The Hoard?" said Campbell.

"Silver," she entreated, keening over the death of her husband but quelled by fear for their child.

"Where be it?"

"There," she said, and nodded at the far corner of the dirt floor.

"Buried?" he asked.

"Aye. Under our poor roof-tree, so it be safe from thieves." Campbell dropped the boy and crossed to the corner to dig with his half-pike, chunking down two feet until he reached a bundle of tartan, swathed in which was a skull of tarnished silver. A medallion fused onto the brow was silver, too. Etched around its narrow edge were Latin words:

Antigonus Severus
Cohors I Tungrorum Milliaria.

He looked inside and found that the skull within was of human bone.

Somerled carried the silver brain ball that had been hoarded by ancients in Glencoe back to the terrified woman. Plaid hid her comeliness from his eager eyes. A tonnag was draped over her shoulders, with an arasaid from her neck to her ankles, plaited all round and fastened at the breast by a brooch and at the waist by a belt. His dirk slit the tartan to bare her paps and quim.

Outside the cottage, it continued to snow.

Crying escaped from within as Somerled had his way with Margaret.

Screaming escaped from within as Somerled cut both MacDonald throats.

Flames escaped from within as Somerled torched the roof-tree.

And Somerled escaped from within with the Hoard in a sack, a sexually gratified Campbell with blood on his hands.

Soldier's pay.

Cyber Cop

Vancouver, British Columbia

How weird the world is becoming as the millennium approaches was evident next door.

Jenna Bond had faxed a copy of the Campbell family tree to Special X. Fax in hand, DeClercq left the Tudor building in which he had his office to move up Heather Street to the square Annex sandwiched between Special X and the mushroom-shaped forensic lab. The sky had cleared as if to prepare for tomorrow night's total eclipse of the moon, which promised that the weird ones would be out in force and whatever trouble they fomented would end up here. The Behavioural Science Group of the Major Crimes Section occupied the entire main floor of the Annex. Here, twenty-first century policing centered on hunting psychos. VICLAS—the Violent Crime Linkage Analysis System—computer-linked signatures of crimes from coast to coast. Criminal Behaviour Analysis shaped psych profiles. Geographic Profiling tracked the where, not the who, of crime sites. And response teams from Police Psychology Services were ready to negotiate with hostage-takers and doomsday cults holed up to await the apocalypse.

The future is now.

Sergeant Rusty Lewis was ringing the hit bell when DeClercq walked in. The door opened off the parking lot between the Annex and Special X. Behind the counter to the left were data-entry workers. Beyond the swing gate ahead was the bullpen for VICLAS analysts. The ship's bell was mounted on a pillar beside the gate, and Lewis wagged the lanyard from its clanger. Tradition was that each time someone made a link, the bell was rung so everyone could share the victory. There'd come a time, DeClercq was sure, when hits were commonplace, and all would rue the day that damn bell was installed.

Clang!
Clang!
Clang!

"You sound like a streetcar."

"A streetcar named Desire."

"Desire being that the bell would never stop ringing?"

"No, that Dana Scully would marry me."

"'The X-Files' has left for sunnier climes."

"Breaks my heart."

"We'll survive."

DeClercq had known Lewis since the Headhunter case, when he and Monica Macdonald were teamed as one of the flying patrols. The sergeant was a redhead as rusty as his name, with drooping lids that made him look like he was falling asleep, but the mind behind was a whiz with computers, and the body below hid an expert horseman in the musical ride.

They entered the sergeant's office, to the right of the gate.

Spartan was the word invented for this workspace. Everything else was filed away except the case at hand, so nothing distracted Lewis from analyzing it for links with other crimes. In every homicide (solved, unsolved or attempted), sex assault, missing person when foul play is suspected, or finding of unidentified human remains, the cops investigating fill in a crime analysis report. Each of the 263 questions has a specific slant, ranging from victimology to offender behavior traits to mapping geographic similarities. The answer to each question is fed into the VICLAS computer so it can compare the data with that collected from every other crime for behavior patterns. Any behavior repeated from crime to crime is called a signature.

A link between cases is a hit that rings the brass bell.

"Cyclops," said Lewis. "That was the signature I used to make the link."

"How so?"

"This guy walks into a fast-food joint and pulls a gun. He points it between the server's eyes and demands of her, 'Gimme your cash, or I'll make a cyclops out of you.' She replies, 'I'm a trainee, and they have yet to teach me how to be robbed. Can I call my boss?' A call over the PA brings her boss to her station, and the thug robs *him* when he arrives. A hero in line tries to jump the robber, and the gun goes off and shoots the hero in the crotch."

"What about the trainee?"

"Lost her job."

"And the hero?"

"He lost more than that."

"Took balls to do what he did."

"Literally," said Lewis.

"So you fed VICLAS the word *cyclops* . . ."

"And linked with another attempted murder in Banff last month. Guy robbed a service station with a gun and a warning: 'Gimme your money, or I'll make a cyclops out of you.' Banff has a suspect but not enough evidence to nab him, and we have a fingerprint off the counter with no suspect to match."

"One and one," said DeClercq.

"I've got my fingers crossed. Arrest the Banff guy in Vancouver, and we can check his prints. And if we're lucky, find the gun that fired both slugs. He shot the station owner."

DeClercq passed Lewis the fax from Bond outlining the Campbell family tree. "If I'm lucky, that bell will ring for me."

The sergeant studied the fax. "You want a Campbell query?"

DeClercq nodded. "My thinking is this: Two old men are abducted by sea from island homesteads. Both places are torn apart from thorough searches. One man is found dead after a brutal interrogation. The missing man may be dead, too. Obviously, someone is hunting for something, and he thinks it could be with either man. What links both men is the Campbell surname, and the fact that both descend from Callum Campbell. What makes the searcher think the Campbells have what he seeks? Campbell family? Campbell clan?"

"You want to know if this search began with prior victims?" said Lewis.

"If so, the link might tell us what the kidnapper hopes to find. And once we know what he hopes to find, that may lead us to him."

"Kidnappers, aren't they? From what I've read."

"The search is too organized. Someone's behind it, pulling the strings."

"I'll query VICLAS for possible links. Every crime with the word *Campbell* in it will come up. I'll phone Seattle FBI and have them check VICAP, and I'll ask HITS to comb the Washington State data base."

"Send a copy of any hits to Jenna Bond. Address on the fax."

"Have you no inkling of what this Maltese falcon might be?" said Lewis.

"Sure. A MacGuffin."

"What's a MacGuffin?"

"The mysterious plot objective that the film director Alfred Hitchcock used to get a movie going, then forgot about. The term derives from an anecdote. Two men are traveling on a train from London to Scotland. Stored in the overhead rack is an oddly wrapped parcel.

" 'What have you there?' asks one of the men.

" 'Oh, that's a MacGuffin,' replies the other.

" 'What's a MacGuffin?'

" 'It's a device for trapping lions in the Scottish Highlands.'

" 'But there aren't any lions in the Scottish Highlands.'

" 'Well, then, I guess that's no MacGuffin.' "

Lewis frowned.

"Now you know as much as I do," said DeClercq.

Megaliths

Shipwreck Island, Washington State

"Wherever there's a legend, son, hunt and you will find. The legend of the Boy King lured Howard Carter to Tutankhamun's tomb. The legend of the Lost City of the Incas lured Hiram Bingham to Machu Picchu. The legends in Homer lured Heinrich Schliemann to Troy and Arthur Evans to the labyrinth on Crete. So if we accept Plato, where does the legend of Atlantis lure us to reveal its truth?"

That was the beginning of the quest that obsessed Mephisto now, for solving one mystery had hooked him on a much tougher one, and failure to find the solution to it could drive him mad.

Whatever the cost, he *had* to solve it.

For his own sake.

And for the sake of us all.

If his theory was right.

And proved by the Hoard.

"The facts," said his father, *"if we accept Plato. One, Atlantis was a legend from Egypt. Two, the island was situated west of Gibraltar. Three, its empire ruled east to Northern Italy. Four, because astronomy was the heart of their culture, Atlanteans built observatories to watch and apply the powers of the Cosmos. Five, the sea swallowed the world's first civilization many centuries before Egypt's rise.*

"The answer to the legend, son?

"What could be more impressive to those who built the pyramids than the stone megaliths of Western Europe and Britain? The megalith culture began on the Atlantic coast and spread as far east as Northern Italy. At the heart of this culture was astronomy, for Stonehenge and the other megaliths were built as observatories and aligned to pre- dict movements of the sun and the moon. Egyptians as- sumed the megaliths were colonial outposts of a great empire they called Atlantis, which must have ruled, then vanished, from the Atlantic Ocean.

"Wherever there's a legend, son, hunt and you will find . . ."

And that's when the archeologist had told Mephisto the legend of the Hoard.

The Hoard that exposed the long-lost Secret of the Stones.

The Secret being the reason Atlanteans had raised the megaliths.

A reason—if Mephisto's theory was confirmed—of even more importance today than it was then.

The key to survival of us all.

And what must be done.

That Atlanteans were the builders of the megaliths Mephisto had no doubt. The fact that there had never been an Atlantis was irrelevant. Science had proved the legend. Dotted enigmatically along a thousand-mile swath of the Atlantic seaboard of Europe are the oldest monuments of man: the burial chambers and standing stones of a lost civilization that reached its zenith in the building of Stonehenge. The earliest of these date from long before the rise of Egypt—generally accepted as 3100 B.C.—and come from a time before *anyone* could read or write. The megaliths crushed the diffusionist the- ory of archeology, which held that everything civilized sprouted in Egypt or the Near East and spread out from there. Radiocarbon dating proved the *oldest* monuments to be those on the Atlantic coast, and as the stones spread inland, their dates got steadily younger.

At a wide desk, set between the telescope through which he would watch tomorrow's total eclipse of the moon and the greenhouse with its carnivorous plants and dwindling horde of flies, Mephisto sat contemplating a printout off the Internet about Jenna Bond, her mother and her daughter, Becky, occasionally glancing away from his plot to observe Donella.

He liked to see her, this tattooed bit of flesh on which he fashioned art, walk naked among his megalith collections, or among his hoards of Pictish silver kept down the spiral staircase behind the desk.

Art like the spirals etched into her breasts.

Spirals like the spirals at Newgrange.

As if she were a puppet tied to his telepathy, Donella crossed to the scale model of a ritual tomb ringed by standing stones. Light arced by a computer traced the path of the sun on the shortest day of the year: the winter solstice. Built as far back as 3250 B.C., in the Stone Age, Newgrange is one of the oldest and largest megalith rings in the British Isles. Photos Mephisto placed around the model revealed a man-made mound that looked like a drum with a flat top, almost vertical sides and a façade of white quartz. The entrance to the mound faced the southeast, and framed above the door was an oblong roof-box. At dawn on the shortest day of the year—and only then—the sun shot a ray of light through the box and along a sixty-foot tunnel to a chamber deep within. The light was fiery orange until it hit the far end, and there it cast a thin red line across the stone. Three cells, one at the back and two on the sides, opened off the chamber. Each had a saucerlike basin measuring four feet across to hold burnt bones used in death rituals. The sun shafting down the tunnel shadowed carvings in the roof and walls around the bones, solar and lunar spirals like those etched in Donella's flesh. As she raised the roof of the model to watch the light stab in, revealing the concentric circles carved on its underside, Mephisto eyed the tattoos spiraling out and back from her nipples.

The sun, the moon and death.

The Secret of the Stones?

Sitting beside the Internet printout on Jenna Bond was an array of photos surreptitiously snapped with a telephoto lens from a boat passing the Bond farm on Orcas Island. The printout was from a Seattle paper and gave readers background on Jenna being made the first female detective in San Juan County. Jenna was the daughter of Sheriff Hank Bond. She had left the county to become an FBI agent in Seattle, where she had married a DEA agent named Don Bond. A coincidence of life: they had the same last name. Jenna was pregnant when Don was kidnapped by members of a drug cartel, and though his body was never found, the Colombians had taped his torture session to send to the DEA. Jenna had returned home for the birth of Becky and to join the San Juan cops.

Lots to work with here, Mephisto thought.

As Robbie Burns, Scotland's great bard, had warned plotters: "The best laid schemes o' mice an' men / Gang aft a-gley."

And "gang aft a-gley" had certainly tubed Mephisto's initial scheme.

Logic had said that the Hoard was hoarded on one of two tracts of land. The homestead of the elder son had come down to Fitzroy Campbell, so that's why it was searched first and he was kidnapped first for squeezing. Fitzroy Campbell's mind had snapped during interrogation, dread from burial alive overwhelming him. Though Mephisto was certain the Hoard wasn't hidden at Doe Bay, the old man had shattered before making any mention of a *third* tract of land. The first Mephisto had heard of it was from Gavin Campbell, heir to the homestead of the younger son, but before he could elaborate, the deep blue sea had become his grave.

"Where's the Hoard, Campbell?"

Rasping, gasping for air.

"It must . . . it must . . . GOOD LORD! THE THIRD
TRACT OF LAND!"

"What third tract?"

"GGGGGGGGGGAAAAAaaa . . ."

And he was gone.

Using Fitzroy's credit card had been a red herring to
baffle police and buy time to snatch the heir to the other
tract of land. Now Mephisto was certain the Hoard
wasn't hoarded at Miners Bay either, which meant he
had to find and search this mysterious *third* tract of land,
all the while knowing the police had made the Campbell
connection and were out in force.

Plan A was that he would find the Hoard himself.

That scheme had gone a-gley and was too dangerous.

Plan B was that he would make the police find the
Hoard for him.

Or else.

Mephisto wondered if Jenna had heard the recording
of Don being tortured. If so, a little déjà vu would be
her worst nightmare. He could send the Druids to snatch
her mother and daughter while the detective was at work
in Friday Harbor. Judging from her gnarled hands in the
photos, Jenna's mom suffered from painful arthritis. If
he were to crush those knuckles with a hammer or pliers
and record the screams, then send the tape to Jenna and
threaten harm to her daughter, Mephisto was certain
that she would hunt the world for the Hoard. Too bad
Becky was a child and not a baby. He wondered what
it would be like to nuke an infant in a microwave. Would
its fat crackle like a pork roast?

He felt compelled to find out.

From the Newgrange collection, Donella moved to the
Ring of Brodgar and Callanish. The scale models were
surrounded by the calculations of Dr. Alexander Thom.
A gap between the models exposed Donella's lower
torso and legs, so Mephisto could catch the tattoo of the
Sheela-na-gig around her sex.

Open, close, open, close, Donella displayed it for him.
In 1934 a Scot noticed a group of megaliths—"big
stones"—while sailing his yacht off the Isle of Lewis in
the Outer Hebrides. He stepped ashore on this island
just north of the Isle of Skye and took a stroll around
the Standing Stones of Callanish, the Stonehenge of the
north. Above the black, seaweed-slippery rocks onshore,
rows of stones formed a giant cross more than four hundred feet long, within which loomed a ring of thirteen
tall, slim stones. At the center was a megalith sixteen
feet high, towering above the remains of a small tomb
with burnt bones.

The Scot was Alexander Thom, emeritus professor of
engineering science at Oxford University from 1945 to
1961. What he noticed at Callanish was the alignment of
the megaliths to due north, "a very difficult thing for
people to achieve in those times, because the polestar
wasn't where it is now." From that day, he was hooked
on megalithic engineering, meticulously surveying more
than six hundred sites to form his conclusions, which
were published in a 1967 "parcel bomb": *Megalithic Sites
in Britain*. What Thom discovered was that *all* stone circles, as rough as they might appear, were astronomically
aligned to an amazing degree. Because its shape captured movements of the sun and the moon, Callanish
could have been used to predict eclipses.

The sun, the moon and death.

Astronomy and bones.

Off the northern tip of Scotland huddle the Orkney
Islands. There, its slender stones jutting blackly on a
neck of land between the sparkling lochs of Harray and
Stenness, stands the Ring of Brodgar. With their flat
sides facing inward, twenty-seven of the sixty stones remain, raised inside a circular ditch 370 feet in diameter
and estimated to have taken eighty thousand man-hours
of work to dig. Surveyed by Thom, this ring was found
to be another astronomical observatory. A moon-gazer
standing at the center of the stones could see four land-

marks on the horizon, each of them where the moon rose or set on one of the important dates in its 18.6-year cycle. Called foresights, the landmarks are indicated by lines of nearby mounds that point directly at them. By sighting along such lines, an ancient astronomer could assess slight irregularities in the moon's movements caused by the pull of gravity from the sun. This knowledge would enable him to predict eclipses.

Scottish Highlanders going to church last century would ask each other, *"Am bheil thu dol do'n chlachan?"* (Are you going to the stones?)

They knew the megaliths were ritual centers.

And they recounted the legend that the lost Hoard held the Secret of the Stones.

Standing behind and between the models of the Ring of Brodgar and Callanish, Donella faced Mephisto so the spiral tattoos on her breasts moved over the tiny stone circles.

Highland queen.

With an ear to the Pender rumor mill and an eye to the Internet, Mephisto had collected background on Corporal Nick Craven. Craven had recently stood trial for the murder of his mother, and was saved from conviction by Mountie Robert DeClercq. The corporal had no relatives Mephisto could trace, and seemed to be a loner who had retreated to Pender Island for a fresh start.

Not much to work with here, Mephisto thought.

DeClercq, however, intrigued him.

The *Vancouver Sun* had done several profiles on the chief superintendent. One by one, the psychopath plucked them off the Internet. DeClercq was a throwback to the ethics of bygone days, when *honor* and *duty* weren't dirty words. A straight arrow in a time of antiheroes, he was a cop who would go to the wall to save those depending on him. When his daughter, Jane, had been kidnapped after the Quebec October Crisis of 1970, he'd killed five men in a failed attempt to get her back.

In case after case, he had risked his career to stand by Members who served under him: Inspector Zinc Chandler in the Cutthroat and Ripper affairs, and Corporal Nick Craven in the African ordeal. When history had repeated itself with his surrogate daughter, Katt, again he had done everything possible to save her.

Compared with the price he had paid for others, the Hoard would be small change.

The more he collected on Robert DeClercq, the more Mephisto thought him a worthy adversary.

DeClercq was both historian and supercop.

He was a published author researching a new book: *Yukon,* the history of the Mounted and the Klondike gold rush.

So he could gather anecdotes about American prospectors and redcoats in the North, he'd posted his e-mail address on the Internet.

As head of Special X, this morning's *Vancouver Sun* told readers, DeClercq commanded the Canadian half of a cross-border manhunt for those who had abducted Fitzroy and Gavin Campbell.

Yes, thought Mephisto. A worthy player indeed. And one to add subtlety to the game.

Plan B took shape in his cold, cold mind.

"Donella," he said.

The femme fatale turned. She had moved on to what was the core of Mephisto's megalith collections, spread in a wide ring around the telescope: antiquarian books and documents and drawings and photos and calculations and models of Stonehenge.

Donella came naked toward him, his walking work of art.

The megalomaniac eyed her from head to foot.

"Yes?" said Donella.

"I have a hunt for you."

Coast Watch

Pender Island, British Columbia
Thursday, October 16

Study a map of the West Coast and you'll grasp why British Columbia is North America's boat drug-smuggling pipeline. Cannabis from Thailand and Mexico, heroin out of Hong Kong and Southeast Asia, cocaine from Colombia, Bolivia and Peru, all arrive by mother ships that stay at sea as smaller off-load vessels sneak the contraband to shore. A shore that's the most convoluted coastline in the world.

If you were a Mountie, how would you stem the flow of drugs?

Deputies?

Canada is the only nation known first and foremost for its police. Canadians have a wishy-washy image of who they are, but when they put on a scarlet tunic they're Canadian to the core. Wannabe Mounties recruit into the Coastal Watch program, which welcomes them as the eyes and ears of the Force.

"O Canada, we stand on guard for thee . . ."

The Mounties arm their deputies with a pelorus. It is a flat piece of wood, eight inches square, on which a black-on-white circle resembling a clock is marked with 360 degrees. The clock has a single arm that will sweep around the circle. Twelve o'clock is 0 degrees, to point true north.

Coast Watchers live or work by the sea. Residents,

boaters, fuel-dock attendants and such, these deputies watch for vessels that run at night without lights, or operate outside normal fishing times or shipping lanes, or off-load cargo in unusual spots, or do not carry the right equipment for their work, or seem to have a large hidden storage capacity, or appear to cost beyond their owners' means.

When he spies something suspicious, the watcher slips the pelorus into place.

And takes a reading.

And phones it in.

The corner bracket that holds the pelorus and points it true north must be mounted on a surface where there is a good view of the sea. Using a hand-held GPS—or Global Positioning System—the technician who mounted the pelorus bracket took satellite information that the GPS translated into latitude and longitude for this location. When the watcher slips the pelorus into the bracket, it is mounted so 0 degrees aligns with true north. The arm can be swiveled to aim at a suspicious boat, and what the watcher phones in to the police is the position in degrees through which the sight line passes. To that is added description, color, size and flag of the vessel; name, license number and visible markings; how many people are aboard; and where the boat is heading.

The Mounties respond by phoning another watcher on the same coast for another pelorus reading of the suspect boat. The first reading points along an endless line. The second reading cuts across that line. Because the Mounties know the precise latitude and longitude of both pelorus mounts, triangulation pinpoints the vessel on sea charts.

The program works like radar.

Search and destroy.

The RCMP's Coastal Watch program also works in reverse.

Here the jargon is to "fan out."

This occurs when suspicion starts with the Mounties and "fans out" to the watchers. Police are often on the lookout for a specific crime, so they phone several watchers to alert them, and those watchers phone others to pass the alert on, until all deputies in the Mounted's posse are on the case.

Nick had done a fan out, albeit after the fact, since it had been sunk to the bottom of the sea, for previous sightings of the *Bounding Main,* and that's why he was summoned today up to the Eagle's Nest.

The Eagle's Nest was an artist's retreat high on a bluff above Plumper Sound. The artist was Morty Eisner, a modern-day Audubon whose studio of wrap-around glass was a 360-degree window on the world of birds. Cameras, binoculars, easels and paints were scattered about the turret, while the house below was hung with pictures of loons, grebes, cormorants, herons, geese, ducks, gulls, terns, plovers and birds of prey. An ex-kibbutznik who fought in the Six Day War, this watcher was a one-armed man who shaved his head and wore pirate's rings through both ears. Nick wondered if Mort knew that Hitler's mountain retreat above Berchtesgaden was also called the Eagle's Nest.

"If I knew then what I know now, eh?" said Eisner.

"Hindsight's 20/20," Craven replied.

"Poor Gavin. What a way to go."

The artist clenched a brush between his teeth like a buccaneer's sword, wiping paint from his hand before cleaning the brush.

The painting on the easel was of a sawbill.

"Did you see Campbell on the boat?"

The watcher shrugged. "I saw someone I thought was Gavin or Tod. You're aware those two share the *Bounding Main*?"

"Yes," said the Mountie. "They've been friends for years. I spoke to Tod, and he told me that Gavin had the boat when he was abducted."

"Is that what I saw? His kidnapping?"

"Tuesday morning?"

"Yeah."

"Then it seems so. From the beginning, what do you recall?"

"I'm up at dawn each morning to watch the sun rise over Saturna while I paint. The mist on the water would later turn to fog. The *Bounding Main* and a partner boat entered Plumper Sound from Navy Channel."

"Time?"

"I'm not a clock watcher. Nine, ten, I guess. They probably sailed around Mayne from Active Pass, and into the gap between Mayne and here."

Craven was taking notes.

"I fetched binoculars because of the drug fan out. An alert to Coast Watch would keep Gavin home, and you told us that the DEA expected a mother ship to smuggle cargo ashore. The *Bounding Main* was heading south to Boundary Pass, and I wondered if that meant the bust had already gone down."

"So you looked?"

"Yeah, to see if it was Gavin or Tod onboard. The guy at the wheel was Tod's size, but his face was lost in a jacket hood."

"You left it at that?"

"Sure. Because I assumed it was Tod. He's not with Coast Watch."

"You said there were *two* boats. Describe the other one."

"Bayliner. Cabin cruiser. Twenty-eight foot. Side by side with the *Bounding Main*. Notable thing, thinking back, is that the crew of two wore the same gear as the guy on Gavin's boat. Slickers, straightline below the hips, with pointed hoods."

"See a face?"

"No . . . yes . . . well, sort of."

Nick laughed. "That covers the gamut, Mort."

"What I mean is I thought I saw the face in one of the hoods, but it must have been shadow."

"Why?"

"Because the skin was blue."

"You catch the number of that boat?"

"No, the bow was hidden behind the *Bounding Main*. But I did see the name on the stern."

Nick's pen was ready.

"The boat was the *Faust*."

———

Nick phoned Jenna from Pender detachment. The cops exchanged what they'd found out.

"A *blue* face?"

"So he said. Probably shadow."

"And three men in pointed hoods?"

"Two on one boat. One on the other."

"Nick, I think we'd better compare files face to face."

"Tomorrow?"

"Nine o'clock?"

"Here or there?"

"You make the coffee. I'll boat up."

Blue Woad

Boundary Pass, Washington State

The Druids were the house band of Tattoos in downtown Seattle. Tattoos was a club for modern primitives, those who felt a primal urge to modify their appearance by tattooing, piercing and scarification. The soft-core common on the streets—dabblers in multiple ear-piercings, the daring of whom might chance a stud through the tongue or a ring through the eyebrow or nose, and maybe a little personal tattoo on the butt or shoulder—were unwelcome there. Hard-core primitives hung out at Tattoos, a legion of nihilists who were not afraid to let go, each conveying that he or she was part of the tribe by marks of belonging. Third eyes tattooed on the forehead. Full body tattoos on torsos, arms and legs. One man had his skeleton engraved on his skin. Another was covered with swastikas to reclaim them from the Nazis as a symbol of his inner absolute. Those heavily into wearing iron had piercings linked by chains. Harshest was the man named the Totem Lizard, who, in homage to that creature with a split penis, had actually cut his down the center so the ends of the forks could be pierced and strung up around his neck. Those into burn-out were branded and scarred. Blue lights dyed the club with radiating woad while the Druids speed-thrashed metal onstage, a Druid on bass, a Druid on drums, with the Archdruid wailing as he bashed his guitar, the dancers into body-banging and shrieking along.

Last month, into this environment had walked Mephisto.

The Druids had wondered if he was scouting them for a record label.

During a break he had called them over.

"Your music's good. Your stage act sucks."

"Staging takes money."

"Maybe I can help."

"You with a label?"

Mephisto shook his head.

"You want to manage us?"

"In a manner of speaking. I'm looking for men with balls who don't adhere to rules. Men in tune with pagan times. Is that a lot of posturing, what you sing about? Or do you truly embrace Nietzsche: 'Dangerously we must live!'?"

"We're not playing."

"Let's put that to a test. A thousand dollars each if you've got the balls."

"The balls to do what?"

"Gangbang a woman."

"What woman?"

"A random one. It's a test. With a hundred thousand more if you help me find something."

"Help you find what?"

"First the test. Then we'll talk."

A hundred thousand dollars will buy a lot of cheap souls, and these three had lost their souls a long time ago. The Druids had formed their metal group in a youth detention center. A match made in hell, the three had passed the test, for which Mephisto had selected a victim off the street, then sicced the Druids on her to see if they were vicious enough.

They were.

Plan B was that Mephisto would make the police find the Hoard for him.

For that he required a bargaining chip.

"Donella," Mephisto had said last night, "I have a hunt for you."

Today, Donella and the Druids were on that hunt.

Barn Dance

Pender Island, British Columbia

The barn was rocking by the time Nick wheeled the farm truck off the island's main road and bumped along winding ruts through the evergreen woods to the pasture beyond. The full moon was rising over the rolling humps of the black hills backing the field, moving into place so tonight's eclipse could mask its pocked, shiny face. He parked the truck by a snake fence built out of split cedar rails, and stepped out into gossamer mist exhaled by the ground. Cattle snorting similar mist watched him from the pasture.

The barn, outlined with Christmas lights, sat on the rise behind. Peak to slope to drop to flare, the roof resembled a cowboy hat. The joint was jumping to Nick's kind of music, a cover of "Rave On," his all-time favorite tune by Buddy Holly, as moonglow, starlight and fancy footwork helped him sidestep cow patties on the dirt track that looped up to the open double doors. The beer corral for boozers blocked that entrance, so Nick sauntered on to the side door. The sweet smell of pot wafted around the corner, and when he angled it he came upon three teenagers and a joint.

"Snuff it, boys. The law's around."

As he walked away from the smokers toward the side door, he heard one of the potheads cough, then whisper, "Cool."

He glanced back and saw the joint was out.

Cool, he thought.

"Rave On" gave way to "Runaround Sue" as he walked into the barn, stuffing twenty dollars in the pay-what-you-want till before pausing beside the dance floor to take in the scene.

The post-and-beam skeleton of the barn was made of hand-hewn logs. Each post was decorated with scarecrows by island kids. "Celebrate Community" read a mural on the wall, which was brightened with fingerpaint pumpkins and a beaming sun. Those on the dance floor were doing just that. One couple danced with their children between them, a baby asleep on the shoulder of the dad. Gays danced together without drawing a stare. Country chic was how most were dressed. Cowboy hats and leather vests with open shirts and jeans. More ponytails on guys than gals. A woman in fringed doeskin like Pocahontas. Another—she must be off the ferry!—in Calvin Kleins. A Mister Natural for the nineties strutted his stuff, all long gray hair and Indian sweater, with shirttail flapping over patches on his ass, letting his backbone slip in the funkiest step Nick had ever seen, legs kicking as high as a Rockette at Radio City Music Hall.

Get down and boogie, friends!

As if to oblige, the band ripped into "Choo Choo Ch'Boogie" and "Teenage Boogie" back to back.

And what a band!

Road Apples, the house band of the Moaning Steer in Cloverdale, was a country rock quartet of drums, stand-up bass, guitar and a jack-of-all-trades brought in from the Mainland for this bash. Pass "Jack" on a country road and you would most likely think, There goes a refugee from the sixties, but put him onstage and could the man ever play, sing and put on a show. Jack was surrounded by the tools of many musical trades—piano, harmonica, banjo, twelve-string, fiddle, mandolin and instruments out of his head—and like Jumping Jack Flash, he moved from one to another within a piece. Jack wore a porkpie hat on top of hair down to his waist, a vest

like a riverboat gambler's, jeans and lumberjack boots.
As he played, his mane flipped back and forth with the
boogie beat.

Nick's kind of party.

He itched to get out and dance.

This was the sort of reality check that had drawn him
to Pender, a down-to-earth, from-the-heart, genuine social event. This wasn't a barn dance pre-packaged for
tourists. This wasn't Barn Dance Land at Disney World.
In a continent of plastic, franchises and malls, this was
a throwback good time that was getting harder and
harder to find.

And good times don't want cops.

There was a time when Pender folks were a law unto
themselves. Before 1979, there was no cop on the island.
There was a patrol cabin, but that was just for summer
use and periodic stays. There's never been a murder, so
most don't lock their doors, and many feel a permanent
cop spoils the atmosphere. Atmosphere like tonight,
until Nick walked in.

*Should he, or should he not, go to the annual barn
dance?* That was the question he'd pondered earlier, and
in the end he'd decided on a compromise. He wouldn't
wear a uniform or drive the Force 4x4, but would attend
instead as a civilian in the farm truck. He'd do a round
to work the barn as a common man, low key, no authority, then leave the dance. So as much as he wanted to
get down and boogie, that's what he did now.

Rounding the dance floor past the beer corral, he said
hi to Bill and Jay and Rob, who drank from plastic cups
and looked worried that the rumor would start they were
close to the fuzz. He stopped at the food table, strung
with orange and green lights, for a hot dog and a cup
of tea, praised the cornucopia basket displayed and took
his litter to the recycling bins, one for Compost, the next
for Bottles/Cans, the last for No Hope Stuff. Climbing
stairs to the loft, he quashed chitchat around the beer
keg and figured time was nigh to beat a hasty retreat.

So down the stairs and back around the dance floor came Nick, until a voice behind him said, "Do you dance as well as you walk in circles?"

A female voice.

Addressing him?

Nick stopped, turned and almost dropped his jaw.

"You're slow on the pick-up. Ask me to dance."

"Want to dance?" he said.

"I thought you'd never ask."

Doo-wop time. The band tore into the El Dorados' "At My Front Door," a full-tilt rocker about a "crazy little mama" who came knocking.

In less than a few seconds, Nick found his evening turned upside down. A moment ago, he was a heartbroken, lonely pariah, still yearning for his lost love and not a hit here, on his way home to a solitary farm. Now he was on the dance floor with a woman so alluring that a path cleared for her.

Things were looking up.

Whoever she was, this babe had all the moves. Her russet hair writhed around her vamp's face as she shimmied and shook. Her eyes and cheekbones were like those of a cat, and she seemed to look everywhere *but* at him. Then she suddenly homed in on Nick with a seductive glance that said, I'll lick you up like cream, before she looked away so he was free to watch her body prove it. Her breasts jiggled provocatively within the cowboy shirt that was belted tight enough to reveal she was lean and sexy in all the right spots, a fact corroborated by the blue jeans hugging her curves and shapely legs. As Jack wailed about mama knocking onstage, she rapped her knuckles on the air in front of Nick's forehead and pouted for him.

Experience had taught Nick that the way a woman dances is what she's like in bed.

The way this babe danced, she'd shake his brass bed to pieces.

Hi Ho, Silver, he thought.

A jumped-up version of "Turkey in the Straw," then "What'cha Gonna Do" and a cover of "Dead Flowers" by the Stones made them sweat, before Jack slowed it down for what in Nick's opinion was the best smooch song of all: Ivory Joe Hunter's "Since I Met You Baby." She walked right into him, this fantasy queen, breasts against his chest and groin against his groin, and as they waltzed, she fused herself sexually to him.

"What's your name?"

"Donella."

"Haven't seen you around."

"I'm a city girl."

"What are you doing here?"

"I heard about the dance and thought this might be fun, so I caught the ferry and here I am."

"Here you certainly are."

"What's your name?"

"Nick," Craven replied.

"People are staring at us."

"I'm the local cop. And a cop should be a straight arrow."

"I'll ruin your reputation."

"Good. Let 'em stare."

"I crave a man with handcuffs. Tonight's the lunar eclipse. Want to take a walk in the field and watch the moon hide its face?"

"Cow patties," he warned.

"I don't care. Sometimes you gotta scrape the shit off your shoes."

She fetched her coat, and as they walked arm-in-arm out of the barn, Nick wondered what the rumor about him would be tomorrow.

With luck, it might be true.

The lunar eclipse was well underway, the shadow of the earth creeping across one fat cheek, the birthmark in its wake the color of dried blood. Mist curled about their feet as they traversed the field, moonglow on the wane bathing them with silver. From the barn they heard the intro to "Stagger Lee."

They stood alone in the center of the field—her back to him as they watched the eclipse; his arms about her, supporting her breasts; their breaths mingling into one in front of them— surrounded by an army of knights in black evergreen.

"You live on the island?"

"Up on Dooley Road."

"*Dooley* Road!" She laughed. "Hardly an address for a tough cop."

"I'll have you know Dooley is an honorable address around here."

"*Razor* Point Road. That's you. How did Dooley ever come to be?"

"The way I first heard the tale is this: Back when Pender was mostly bush, from 1880 to the new century, there were two settlements on this island—Port Washington on Grimmer Bay, and Hope Bay, near me. A school was needed, but there was a dispute over which community should be the site, since the other kids would have a long hike. The issue was to be decided by counting heads, with the area with the most kids getting the school, so just before the tally, David Hope offered free land to Evan Dooley if he would settle immediately at Hope Bay with his wife and twelve kids. That Dooley did, and the school was built up near me."

"You're right," said Donella. "A fitting name."

"Despite the fact the tale's bullshit," said Nick. "The real facts are these: David Hope and Noah Buckley were the first two white settlers. They divided the island and built a fence. Hope died a bachelor in 1882 when he shot a stag, went to slit its throat and the stag gored him. Washington Grimmer bought Buckley's farm that same year, but there were no kids in need of a school. In 1885, Grimmer married, then the *bachelor* Evan Dooley arrived from Yorkshire with his dad. Finally, a school was raised in 1894, on the road *halfway between* Port

Washington and Hope Bay. The first schoolteacher was Fanny Howell, who married Evan Dooley in 1896. So those twelve kids of legend, who won our mythical school, were actually four kids born to its teacher."

"The Dooleys lived happily ever after?"

"No," said Nick. "Fanny Dooley and one of her kids died when the *Iroquois* sank."

"So how did those facts spawn the legend?"

"Welcome to the island. We don't let anything get in the way of a good story around here."

"You do live on Dooley Road?"

"Yes," said Nick.

"Good. Take me home."

She turned in his arms, kissed him hard, then led him away from the barn.

"Wrong direction, Donella."

"No, my car's over here. I turned off on the wrong road but heard the music, so I parked and followed it to the barn."

"Even on peaceful Pender, you shouldn't walk alone in the woods at night."

"I've got you. Now I'm safe."

Her car was parked in the black evergreens at the dead end of two dirt ruts. An owl watched from one of the trees as they approached. Donella unlocked the passenger door, then tossed him the keys. Climbing in, she purred, "You drive while I drive you crazy."

Unlocking the other door, Nick swung in behind the wheel. The overhead light did not come on, so it was dark inside. Before his eyes adjusted, Donella reached over, caressed his cheek and whispered in his ear.

"Want to get fucked?"

Yes, Donella. I want to get fucked by you.

Before he put this thought into words, she slammed her fist into his groin. So hard did he double up from excruciating pain that he bounced back off the steering wheel like a whiplash casualty, and that's when a Druid popped up in the backseat to slip a garrote around his throat and yank.

"You're fucked," said Donella.

The last words he heard.

Eclipse

Shipwreck Island, Washington State

His body was here in the present but his mind was in the past.

Moonshine on Stonehenge.

Waning moonlight shone into the upper floor of the Victorian mansion high on the bluff that overlooked the Stone Circle in the woods. Beethoven's *Moonlight Sonata* tinkled from the speakers mounted in the peaked roof of the lunar observatory. Moonbeams pierced the greenhouse in the southern slant to cast shadows of carnage across Mephisto, his telescope and his Stonehenge collection. The jaws of Venus flytraps and mouths of pitcher plants fed on Campbell-tartaned flesh as the antiquary, eye to the eyepiece, watched the lunar eclipse. The shadows of insects circling as a halo of flies had been culled by the deadly plants from many back to few.

Balance restored.

The future as it should be.

The umbral shadow of the earth turned coppery red as it crept across the face of the full moon. The color resulted from sunlight being refracted and absorbed as it passed through the earth's atmosphere, but those who viewed the phenomenon through ancient eyes perceived it as a death curse. The *Anglo-Saxon Chronicle* of 735 A.D.: "The Moon was as if it had been sprinkled with blood, and Archbishop Tatwine and Beda the Venerable died." In 1044 the French chronicler Raoul Glaber wrote, "For the Moon herself became like dark blood, only getting clear of it a little before dawn." Mephisto's mind, however, went much farther back, back to the Stone Age before writing and books, back to a time when ancients depended on the seasonal rhythms of the earth, and movements of the sun and moon were vital for life, and eclipses were events of awesome catastrophe.

The technique he was using was Radcliffe Brown's "If I were a horse," founded on the story of a farmer who discovered a horse was missing from his paddock, so in he went and chewed some grass himself to ruminate on the problem, wondering where he would go if he were the horse.

That brought to mind the most famous eclipse story of all. Christopher Columbus and his men almost starved to death in Jamaica when natives refused them food. But Columbus knew a lunar eclipse would darken the night of March 1, 1504, so he warned the natives that he'd snuff the moon unless they were fed. Come the eclipse, terrified natives begged him for mercy, and subsequently bowed to all his demands.

Terror seized Mephisto.

He stood at the center of Stonehenge and gawked as the face of the moon was eaten. The moon, which governed every aspect of life, from pregnancy in women to growth of his crops, the bright light in the night that kept him safe from monsters, and now—when all depended on it—the moon was dying, just as the Stonehenge priests had predicted.

They were powerful men.

The priests could foresee.

And if they would give him protection now, he would bow to their demands.

Priests, bring back the moon!

The cold eye of the psychopath followed the bloody shadow of doom across the moon's shine as the cold mind behind it switched horses from being a peasant to becoming a Stonehenge priest.

Power filled Mephisto.

What a rush!

Mephisto was the name he'd taken back when he sold his soul to the Devil in exchange for ancient knowledge and absolute power. Mephisto he was, this hell of a man who turned from his telescope to possess his collection of Stonehenge models, with his black hair slicked back from a widow's peak, and his dark eyes hidden in black orbs like those of a skull, and his Vandyke beard a V pointing to his merciless, cruel, vicious hell of a heart. He didn't crave the knowledge of our rational, secular world, but instead the secrets of ancients who understood cosmology, the broader wisdom concerned with heavenly bodies, their meaning, power and influence on us.

That Stonehenge priests had such knowledge was not open to doubt. The evidence was built into the megalith itself, and was on display in the Stonehenge models beneath Mephisto's heart.

Stonehenge I was little more than a circular ditch around a six-foot-high bank with an entranceway open to the northeast. It was constructed sometime before 3000 B.C. (scholars' estimates of the dates of Stonehenge having recently been pushed back), on Salisbury Plain in southwest England. The Heel Stone was raised outside the entranceway, the first of the huge sarsen stones that still stand today. A mass of small post holes in the entranceway were dug in this period, as were fifty-six Aubrey holes—named for the man who found them in the mid-1600s—ringed within the bank. Cremated human bones were buried in some of the Aubrey holes. Stonehenge I—Old Stonehenge—resembled the first model:

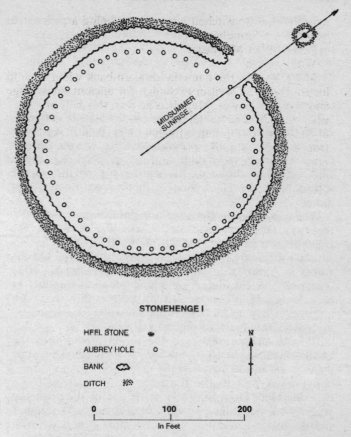

STONEHENGE I

HEEL STONE   •

AUBREY HOLE   o

BANK   ⌒⌒

DITCH   ⁖⁖

N
↑

0   100   200

In Feet

On display in a case beside this model was William Stukeley's *Stonehenge: A Temple Restored to the British Druids.* This celebrated work, published in 1740, was open to the page with Stukeley's comment that the principal line of Stonehenge was toward the Heel Stone, "where abouts the Sun rises, when the days are longest." The book next to it was Dr. John Smith's *Choir Gaur:*

The Grand Orrery of the Ancient Druids, published in 1771. An *orrery* is a mechanical model of heavenly motions. The text lay open at Smith's comment on Stonehenge: "I conceive it to be an Astronomical Temple." Mephisto's orrery was state of the art.

Like a model train collector's, his models were his obsession.

In the waning moonlight, he flicked a switch that activated the sun and moon, which were positioned by a computer. A computer programed with the calculations of the astronomers Gerald Hawkins and Sir Fred Hoyle. The light that shone as the setting sun of the winter solstice cast the Heel Stone's shadow onto the rising moon.

When *Stonehenge Decoded* was published in 1965, the theory of Dr. Hawkins caused a scientific storm. Gerald Hawkins was professor of astronomy at Boston University and a research associate at Harvard College Observatory in America. Using the Harvard-Smithsonian IBM computer, he calculated solar and lunar alignments at Stonehenge, then concluded that the megalith was both an observatory and a "Neolithic computer" designed by ancient astronomers to predict eclipses.

A lunar eclipse results if the moon moves into the earth's shadow as cast by the sun. A solar eclipse results if the moon moves between the earth and the sun. Stonehenge is aligned to the northeast so the sun will rise over the Heel Stone on the longest day of the year: the summer solstice. Since winter sunset is opposite summer sunrise, this alignment of sun, earth and moon may cause a lunar eclipse if the moon rises over the Heel Stone about the time of the winter solstice, and possibly a solar eclipse half a month later, when the moon orbits around between the earth and the sun.

But there's a hitch.

The sun's cycle of movement repeats every year, so it rises and sets at fixed points on the horizon every solstice. The moon's cycle, however, takes 18.61 years.

Moonrise and moonset swing north to south and back in a month, but those limits are also on the move, shifting from "major standstill" to "minor standstill" extremes and back again. While an ancient astronomer could mark the farthest point of solar swing with a Heel Stone, he couldn't record lunar movement the same way, since his marker would be accurate only every 18.61 years. But he could overcome the problem with patience and time if he observed the full moon nearest the winter solstice each year from the center of Stonehenge, and marked where it rose with a post stuck in the entranceway. Each annual marker would shift with the moon's orbit, but after two or three cycles, with the entranceway full of posts, he could predict movements of the moon and sun leading to eclipse.

Which explained the post holes in the entranceway of Stonehenge I.

That crude method didn't last long, for *Stonehenge Decoded* showed how the fifty-six Aubrey holes could act as a computer, with 19 + 19 + 18 years approximating three cycles of the moon. Moving markers around the holes would also predict eclipses. Hawkins wrote that the Heel Stone, as well as indicating mid-summer sunrise, was used as an eclipse predictor, aided by the Aubrey holes as a way of keeping track of extreme moonrises. A different means of Aubrey counting gave the legendary Cambridge astronomer Fred Hoyle similar results.

Aubrey holes.

With burnt bones.

Like Newgrange, Callanish and other megaliths.

Stonehenge II improved on Stonehenge I, remodeling it for easier eclipse prediction. The changes were made sometime before 2550 B.C., and mark the beginning of New Stonehenge. Shifting the axis a bit to the east aligned it more accurately with the rising sun of the midsummer solstice. Banks along the entranceway formed an avenue. Two stones were placed midline between the entrance and the Heel Stone. Most significantly, four Station Stones were set within the circular bank to form an imaginary rectangle around its center.

Stonehenge II—New Stonehenge—was reproduced by the second model:

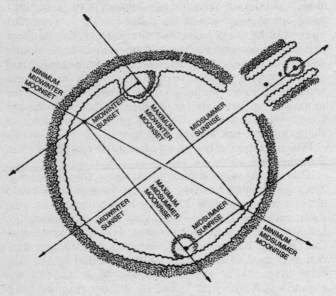

STONEHENGE II

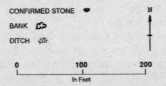

CONFIRMED STONE

BANK

DITCH

N

0   100   200
In Feet

Whatever we might think of the eclipse-predicting layout of Stonehenge I, could anyone deny that Stonehenge II served that purpose? Not Mephisto. Diagonal lines drawn across the rectangle intersected to mark the megalith's center. The short sides ran parallel with the northeast axis to the Heel Stone, aligning with midsummer sunrise and midwinter sunset on both solstices. The long sides pointed at two extremes of the moon: maximum midwinter moonset and maximum midsummer moonrise. A diagonal from one corner to the opposite indicated two more extremes: minimum midwinter moonset and minimum midsummer moonrise. Not only did the rectangle capture *six* solar and lunar extremes, but it could do so only at the latitude of Stonehenge.

Think that happened by chance and Mephisto would think you were a fool.

The total eclipse of the moon outside snuffed the moonglow in the room. Mephisto flicked the switch that activated his second model, and watched the computer move sun and moon to the rectangle alignments.

Eclipse predictor.

New and improved.

Stonehenge III was the Stonehenge of the ruins we see today. More precise radiocarbon dating has recently pushed its assembly period back to between 2550 B.C. and 1600 B.C. The stones were brought from Marlborough Downs, twenty miles away, and are so heavy that each must have taken some months to transport. Five trilithons, two upright stones supporting a third laid on top, were arranged in a horseshoe formation along the axis to the Heel Stone. The horseshoe's open end faced midsummer sunrise. A ring of thirty sarsens, each stone more than twenty tons in weight, circled the trilithons, with thirty heavy lintels capping them to form a round rampart sixteen feet off the ground. A pair of uprights, one of which survives as the Slaughter Stone, flanked the entry from the avenue. Later, in the hollow of the horseshoe, the Altar Stone was stood on end.

Stonehenge III—the third model—was constructed like this:

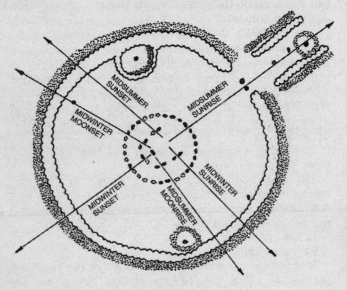

STONEHENGE III

CONFIRMED STONE   ●

CONJECTURED STONE   ⬭

BANK   ⬭

DITCH   ▧

0   100   200

In Feet

Hawkins decoded the same alignments to extreme sun and moon positions in Stonehenge III as those captured by the Station Stones in Stonehenge II. His sighting method was like that of a rifle. The extremes were "framed" between the outer sarsen archways, while narrow trilithon gaps served as backsights. The accuracy of his method cannot be proved today, since all but one of these alignments depend on displaced or fallen stones.

To Mephisto, that didn't matter.

The point was proved.

Stonehenge was undeniably an eclipse predictor.

Alexander Thom, the Scot who'd studied Callanish, the Ring of Brodgar and six hundred other megaliths around the British Isles, finally assessed Stonehenge in 1973, and found there the same astronomy, geometry and measurements he had found in other stone circles. The major element missing from Thom's integrated "megalithic science" was evidence of some method of record-keeping, and that his son, Archibald Thom, later uncovered in Bush Barrow, one of the hundreds of burial tombs surrounding Stonehenge. The shape and markings of a gold plaque the grave contained were deciphered and shown to register a solar and a lunar calendar.

To Mephisto, it all came together.

For more than two thousand years, a time span greater than the stretch from the Roman Empire to now, the temple was in use. Stonehenge I had cracked the secrets of the solar/lunar eclipse cycle. Stonehenge II had built what was learned into the Station Stones, two of which were set over, and erased, Aubrey holes. Stonehenge III had locked the secrets in permanent form, sacrificing astronomical precision, which was by then tracked by a calendar, for the awesome cosmic symbolism of the temple of the sky and what went on within.

But *what* went on within, and *why*?

That Mephisto had to know.

The final Secret of the Stones.

The secret in the Hoard.

He stood in the darkness of the eclipse, imagining he was a priest at the center of Stonehenge. The temple summed up several centuries of knowledge accumulated by priests who had painstakingly observed the sky every night over successive lives. Obsession was hardly too strong a word for what they *had* to find, and had. Imagine the power that eclipse prediction had on those whose lives depended on the sun and moon. A power that motivated them to build Stonehenge III for the priests, hewing great blocks of stone and dragging them miles to the sacred site. A sacred site that remained the focus of long-lost rituals for seventy generations, and maybe more. Rituals that culminated in Stonehenge, but found parallel expression in a thousand other stone circles around Britain.

Whatever the rituals, they left common clues.

Clues displayed in this case beside the Stonehenge models.

The display case looked like a turn-of-the-century school desk. Instead of wood, the slanted lid had glass, through which could be seen many compartments. Each compartment was labeled with a site name. This collection had been gathered on that fatal dig, when he and his archeologist father had toured the megaliths. He had watched his father dig them all, and store in this case what he found before that deadly night in the Highlands of Scotland.

The eclipse retreated.

Moonshine returned.

Sheening the black clues in the display case.

Clues from the rituals.

All burnt bones.

———————

Mephisto was in the greenhouse when Donella scaled the spiral stairs.

"We have him," she said.

"Good. Let's party."

He turned and tore her cowboy shirt open to expose her tattooed torso.

Through the glass behind him and down in the Stone Circle in the woods, she could see the Druids of Shipwreck Island placing firewood at the feet of the Wicker Man.

Wicker Man

The 45 record was playing at 33⅓ speed. Slurred words stumbled around in his thick brain as dancers on the dance floor rocked in slow motion. His crazy little mama was crazy for sure, yelling, "Want to get fucked? . . . Want to get fucked? . . . Want to get fucked? . . ." loud enough for everyone to hear, prompting the dancers to wink at him in lewd conspiracy, as someone behind knock, knock, knocked on his head with a hammer, killing the thought that he should leave crazy mama alone. Real mama read to him from *Winnie-the-Pooh*: "Here is Edward Bear, coming downstairs now, bump, bump, bump, on the back of his head, behind Christopher Robin. It is, as far as he knows, the only way of coming downstairs, but sometimes he feels that there really is another way, if only he could stop bumping for a moment and think of it . . ." Knock, knock, knock. Bump, bump, bump. "Want to get fucked? . . ." she yells. And he cringes with fear that real mama will hear what crazy mama is yelling, and know that her son thought, Yes, Donella, I want to get fucked by you, and scold him for being a naughty boy who flushed his life away. . . .

Nick came to.

In the dark.

And shivered with cold and fear.

It took a moment for his senses to come around. He could see nothing but bottomless black, even though his eyes were free of any blindfold. Sight dead, he turned to both ears for images, the phantom strains of doo-wop replaced by a ringing like tinnitus. Was that the crash of the sea he heard, surging into a cave, wave on wave on wave on wave lulling him back to sleep? The sea for sure—he could smell the brine and feel clamminess oozing from the wall to which he was chained. Bump, bump, bump were shivers knocking his head against unyielding stone. He didn't know which hurt most, his head or his throat—his head from lack of oxygen when he was throttled and from the knock, knock, knocking now; his throat from the garrote used to subdue him and switched while he was unconscious for this collar of steel. The collar chained him to the wall on a two-foot leash, as did the cuff locked around his left wrist. He sat slumped against the dungeon wall where it met the floor, legs spread wide and cinched to rings, his other arm angled out and lashed across a log round.

What was that?

Footsteps?

Echoing in a tunnel?

Suddenly, Nick could feel the effect of a drug. It must have been spiked into him during his blackout, for he had this irresistible urge to bare his soul to someone, a compulsion he was powerless to prevent. Whatever the drug, it magnified suggestibility, teetering him on the edge of a chemical nervous breakdown and polluting his stream of consciousness with floods of subconscious dread.

Scratch, scratch, scratch . . .

Rats in the walls . . .

Hungry to feast on his juicy meat.

Drip, drip, drip . . .

Moisture from above . . .

Water torture to drive him mad.

Tromp, tromp, tromp . . .

Footsteps outside . . .

The executioner coming for him.

Flicker, flicker, flicker . . .

Torchlight under the door . . .

Yea, though I walk through the valley of the shadow
of death.
Click, click, snick . . .
Key in a lock . . .
Squeak, squeak, squeeeeeeak . . .
Protesting hinges . . .
"Okay, crispy critter. Barbecue time."

Donella stood at the brink of hell and took a swan dive.
Never had she thrilled to power like this, having power
over who lived and who died. The power of the mob in
the Roman Colosseum. No wonder Bonnie Parker
hooked up with Clyde Barrow. And Myra Hindley with
Ian Brady. And Karla Homolka with Paul Bernardo.
And Donella Grant with her devil of a stud. Sex, power
and death. What a potent cocktail. He had the cock, and
she had the tail. When shaken, not stirred, what a powerful, explosive mixture they were. Trapping Nick had
made her as horny as hell, and she felt the need to explode *now!*

Absolute power.
Absolute freedom.
Absolute everything!

A few women have it. Most women don't. That power
to put a ring through the nose of every male from nine
to ninety. Donella had been turning heads for as long
as she could recall, with a body that needed no help
from a plastic surgeon. What she had was raw sex appeal, an asset she had used often to jump men through
circus hoops after lightening their wallets so they could
soar.

But this was different.
The major league.
Her transformation had begun the night of the full
August moon, when Mcphisto possessed her that first
time in the Stone Circle, *tearing a wail of ultimate aban-*

*don from her. On and on it went, until Donella was sub-
dued, and only when he knew she was hooked on him
forever did he come.*

And what a come.

And tell her . . .

"I'm your Mephisto!"

*Later, Donella sat naked in the mansion among four
men and had her breasts engraved with her first Pictish
tattoos.*

She had sold her flesh to the devil.

And she reveled in her freedom.

"You're a blank canvas," Mephisto had said. "Flesh
like yours should not go to waste. Relinquish yourself
to the thrill of the needle, the thrill of getting ink, and
let the kiss of fire set you free. A tattoo changes forever
the way you perceive yourself, and how the rest of the
world perceives you. This talisman forever binds you to
me. Your self-image from now on will be my work of art.
Profound, erotic and primitive. You reflect my mind."

So she had sat naked among his henchmen in Druids'
robes, wincing each time the head Druid pricked pig-
ment under her skin, Mephisto directing the tattooing
from a thronelike chair, while blue spirals inched out
around her milk white breasts. The Druids were primed
by what they had witnessed in the Stone Circle, the tent-
ing of their robes in front evidence of that, so she sexually frustrated them even more, subtly cockteasing the
three until the room was filled with tension. The men
knew she was *his* and forbidden to them. The curl at the
corner of his mouth indicated that Mephisto was enjoying her rite of passage, a rite that was considered by
the Bible to be a desecration, and that, like every rite
of passage, was a transformation of blood and pain
which left indelible marks.

Sexual power over men.

That Donella had always had.

But now she had sexual power over women, too.

For after she was tattooed, the Druids had left in their

boat, powering out of the smugglers' cave beneath the root cellar. The following day, the news reported a brutal gang rape. On one of the smaller islands, three hooded men had attacked a woman, a University of Washington professor vacationing at her summer home. The woman was hurt so badly she was hospitalized.

Donella knew immediately that the rapists were *her*. She was responsible for what the Druids had done; she had created sexual puppets, teased to a fevered pitch, who had burst from the cave to find release.

A *new* kind of thrill!

Served the professor right.

To be as sexy as Donella was a cross to bear. From women who played the game, too, she got hateful stares, catty envy born from having inferior T & A. From women who waved the feminist banner over the barricades, she got glares that branded her as an object of contempt. A bimbo. A boy toy. A piece of fluff. A woman who allowed men to tattoo her as an act of symbolic rape. Pricks of the needle. Blah, blah, blah.

Eh, professor?

But now the hand of fate had dealt her a means for revenge, this roulette wheel of rape that she could spin—and had spun—for fun, cockteasing the Druids each time she got tattooed, the tattoos working down her belly toward what inspired the Sheela-na-gig. Three rapes so far, what wicked thrills! Donella tingling with anticipation until next day, when she would learn whom she had raped the previous night.

Power over women.

And that was just the start.

For what Mephisto had opened was Pandora's box, an evil hoard of psychosexual power trips that fed off the orgasms he wrenched from her, which—Lady Macbeth that she was—Donella warped to impose her sadistic will on others.

Tonight she'd take the next step.

Donella stood at the brink of hell and took a swan dive.

Mephisto tore all the clothes from her body in the greenhouse while the Druids below dragged a struggling man from the door to the root cellar. Chains and cuffs bound his arms and legs, and a strip of tape gagged his mouth. The root cellar was off the path that climbed to the house from the Stone Circle in the woods, and was basically a plank door set into a mound to Mephisto and Donella's right. The whites of the man's eyes, frantically flicking here and there as the Druids hauled him out, shone with the light of the moon. He must have seen the naked body through the glass above, for his dread locked on Donella as Mephisto's hands closed around from behind to trace with fingertips the spiral tattoos on her breasts. Then the four were off down the path to the Stone Circle and its waiting Wicker Man.

The Druids and their prisoner disappeared into the woods, but they soon emerged in the moonlit clearing beyond, clearly visible from the upper floor of the over-looking house. Silver sheened the black robes and pointed cowls as the Celtic cultists uncuffed the drugged man. One of them opened the Wicker Man like halfing an iron maiden, the front and back swinging apart on makeshift hinges. The drugged man was stuffed inside the humanoid coffin, then the halves were closed and secured with a padlock. The Wicker Man fit the sacrifice like a made-to-measure suit, an octagon head on a square body, with stubby arms ending in fingerlike sticks and stiff legs angled apart to support it standing up, though it was helped by the firewood that the Druids piled around its feet. Donella's pulse quickened when torches were ignited.

The Wicker Man was black against the moonlit earth beyond. Through the sapling skeleton, she saw the wretch inside struggling to break free. It was like watching a fly caught by a Venus flytrap. The wicker cage rattled, but held him tight as the torches were applied to the firewood. Moonshadows cast by the monoliths reached for the sacrifice, but shrank back as flames licked up legs sheathed in legs. The outer body caught fire and cooked the body within, charring skin and muscles iike searing a steak. The slower the fire, the longer it takes. This man would die an excruciating death over three minutes. Donella watched him assume the pugilistic attitude, his arms and legs flexing into a boxer's stance as muscles broiled, a shriveling so powerful it often snaps bones. With his meat cracking and spitting, splitting and crackling like barbecued beef, the man in the Wicker Man screamed so loud that he blew off his gag, the tape tearing skin from his wide-open lips. The shriek of pain and agony was so ghastly that it reverberated through the glass and into the greenhouse.

The fires of hell below spit sparks at the moon.

Mephisto retraced the spiral tattoos to pinch both nipples.

A primal shudder shook Donella.

Cocktail hour.

Minotaur

King Minos of Crete was married to Pasiphaë. Minos had angered Poseidon, god of the sea, so he instilled in Pasiphaë a passion for sex with a bull. She had a cow made out of wood by Crete's inventor so she could hide inside to satisfy her lust. The offspring from this was the Minotaur, half man—the body—and half bull—the head. To conceal his wife's shame, Minos imprisoned the monster in the labyrinth, a confine with a complex maze of corridors, where it fed exclusively on sacrifices of human flesh. Because the Athenians had killed his son, Minos laid siege to the city state of Athens. He called on Zeus, king of the gods, to send Athens a plague, which the Athenians could get rid of only if they agreed to send Minos an annual tribute of seven virgins and seven youths to be fed to the Minotaur.

"Wherever there's a legend, son, hunt and you will find . . ."

The roar of the Minotaur filled the labyrinth. The shadow of the monster followed her down the steps under the trap door in the root cellar on Shipwreck Island. It elongated along the wall of the subterranean passage as she ran from bracketed torch to torch, the horns of the bull passing as if to cut her off, then falling back as her pursuer neared the next flame. A cross-hatched grate at the end of the tunnel sealed off escape to the ocean beyond; wave after wave rolled into a deep smugglers' cave bored into the bluff upon which Mephisto's mansion loomed. The shadow of the Minotaur closed on her, the dark arc from its loins redefining that description "hung like a bull," the bellow of lust bouncing off the walls leaving no doubt as to what the beast would do to her.

Pasiphaë.

The stone floor was smooth and slick with mist off the sea. Her bare feet slipped as she fell to her hands and knees. The shadow of the Minotaur mounted her rump. The panting of the monster was hot on her neck. Cut off ahead and about to be ravaged from behind—the hands of the beast were grabbing her buttock cheeks—she scrambled to one side and shouldered open the only door left ajar in the labyrinth. The other five were closed and locked by rusty keys.

No sooner was the naked woman across the threshold than she heaved the door shut against the Minotaur. It was ink black in the cell for a moment, just long enough for her to flatten herself beside the door jamb before torchlight shot in with the horny monster lunging close behind. The force of entry carried the Minotaur halfway across the dungeon.

Torchlight from the corridor glinted off the steel collar dangling open from its chain; handcuffs flanking it were also released. The prisoner freed from them not long ago was now burnt bones in the smoldering ashes of the Wicker Man.

The woman darted out the door and yanked it shut.

The key was missing from its lock, thwarting her plan to close the monster in.

The keys that secured all six doors were the same, so she tugged on the handle with one hand as her other reached across the tunnel to the opposite door, turning that key in its lock to remove it so she could transfer it to this cell. But the powerful monster wrenched open the door before she could secure it.

The door opposite creaked ajar.

The woman was pushed against it and shoved inside.

Again she was on her hands and knees.

Again the beast was upon her.

This time it impaled her with a thrust that heaved them across the floor, then gripped her under the shoulders to yank her back. Torchlight from the tunnel cast their shadows onto the wall. She saw herself being ravaged on the stones in front of her eyes, a pornographic shadow play with her in the under role, the obscene bestiality of it gearing her up to explode. No wonder Pasiphaë had lusted for a bull; the horned head of the Minotaur held high above their shadows in sexual triumph. Both let go in unrestrained orgasm, bodies fused in a pagan ecstasy unknown to lesser mortals governed by rules, the Minotaur snorting and grunting as it humped Donella flat. She released a primal scream while psychosexual aftershocks racked her prostrate body.

Sweat from the beast mixed with sweat from her.

Gasping, the Minotaur uncoupled to gain its feet.

The shadow of the monster climbed the wall.

The Minotaur removed a helmet shaped like the head of a bull.

"Seems we have company," Mephisto said.

"A voyeur," Donella said, rising from the floor.

Chained to the wall in the shadow cast by the open door, Nick Craven watched the mocking pair strut across to him. Blink, blink. Unaccustomed eyes blinked against intruding light.

"You winking at me?" Donella asked. "You shameless flirt." Opening and closing the Sheela-na-gig above the drugged cop, she squatted before him and ripped off the tape gagging his mouth.

Craven yelped.

"Feel like talking?" Mephisto asked, standing lean and mean over his captive.

The pentothal welled up that yearning in Nick.

He fought it down.

Only a groan came out.

"Want to get fucked?" Donella asked. "That's where we left off."

Nick cowered away from her.

"You don't find me attractive?"

The Mountie mewled.

"I asked you a question."

"So did I," Mephisto said.

Nick bit his tongue until blood filled his mouth.

"Answer the man," Donella ordered.

"You feel like talking, don't you, cop? Spill your guts and you'll feel better. We want to know everything you know about us."

A tear ran down Nick's cheek.

Blood ran down his chin.

Donella opened and closed the Sheela-na-gig before his eyes.

Nick closed his eyes.

"Talk," said Mephisto.

Footsteps crossed to the door and exited into the tunnel.

"Talk," said Donella.

The footsteps returned.

"Make it hard or make it easy. You'll talk all the same."

"Here," said Mephisto. "Cut him down to size." Nick's eyes shot open.

"Nooo!" he beseeched.

Now the shadow play on the stones was the ravaging of him. Nick's shadow sat slumped against the dungeon wall where it met the floor, the collar around his neck on a two-foot leash, as was the cuff locked around one wrist. His other arm angled out and was lashed across a log round, a bracket at his elbow and a clamp gripping his hand. Donella's shadow stood statuesque over the chopping block; the claymore grasped in both hands was held high above her head.

Mephisto's recollection shot back to that day with his father on Crete:

"Skeptics likened Atlantis to Homer's tale of King Minos of Greece. Lurking in a dark labyrinth under his

*throne was the monstrous Minotaur. The ravenous beast
was fed virgins and youths left to wander lost in the maze
until the creature culled them. Legend says Theseus ended
this cycle of sacrifice. Unwinding a ball of string to guide
him through twists and turns in the grisly labyrinth, the
Greek hero stalked and killed the Minotaur."*

The boy's imagination heard the monster roar.

*What's it like to be eaten alive? Piece by piece? he
wondered.*

Mephisto's mind returned.

Time to scratch that itch.

"Do it," he said.

The sword came down.

Donella stood at the brink of hell and took a swan
dive. . . .

PART II

Answer

Pile of Stone-henge! so proud to hint yet keep
Thy secrets . . .

I called upon the darkness; and it took,
A midnight darkness seem'd to come and take
All objects from my sight; and lo! again
The desart visible by dismal flames!
It is the sacrificial Altar, fed
With living men, how deep the groans, the voice
Of those in the gigantic wicker thrills
Throughout the region far and near, pervades
The monumental hillocks; and the pomp
Is for both worlds, the living and the dead.

—William Wordsworth

Trojan Horse

Orcas Island, Washington State
Friday, October 17

The screams of Don being tortured echo up and down this hall of a hundred identical doors as she searches frantically for her loving husband. Time is everything. He can take no more, his shrieks begging the Colombians to finish him off, "OH, JESUS, PLEASE NOT ANOTHER PIECE!" A hundred doors—where is he, tears salt her lips—each door sticking as she tries to push it open, damn island weather, too much moisture, swelling wood so every door always sticks, "OH, JESUS, NOT THAT! LEAVE ME A MAN!" She reaches out to push open door 13, but it opens a crack by itself, and the eye of the DEA agent who will later refuse to let her hear the tape of the torture session peers out at her. "Don't worry, Jenna. Things are under control. I'll make sure the Geneva Convention is obeyed in here. They won't upset your daughter with the way he looks, since he'll be long gone before she's born." "OH, JESUS, DON'T CUT OFF MY—"
    "Mom?"
    She turns sharply.
    Oh, Jesus, no!
    Becky stands behind her in the hall.
    "What are you doing here?"
    "I can't sleep."
    "JESUS, DON'T LET HER SEE ME!"

"Back to bed, honey."

"I had a bad dream."

"Go back to bed and back to sleep, and it will be gone by morning."

"Mom . . .

"Mom . . .

"Mom, wake up!"

Jenna awoke with a start.

Then sat bolt upright in bed.

Then looked around the dark room.

Then heard Becky crying.

"Becky?"

"Mom, I had a bad dream."

Her daughter was standing next to the bed, one arm locked around her teddy bear.

"I thought I heard Daddy knocking at the door. But when I got out of bed and went to let him in, it wasn't Daddy knocking, Mom."

Jenna threw back the covers. "Climb in, honey."

"He grabbed me, Mom."

"Who, baby?"

"The devil at the door."

Pender Island, British Columbia

"Dock beside our police boat at the Otter Bay marina. I'll pick you up at nine tomorrow," Nick had told Jenna yesterday. So at ten to nine this morning, she cruised the *Islomania* into the sheltered cove just south of the ferry slip and tied up beside the Mounties' launch—if you could call it that, this aging put-put tub—to wait for the welcome wagon.

She waited . . .

And waited . . .

And waited . . .

And waited . . .
And finally called the detachment.

The cop who drove over to pick her up was a Member who'd been galloping for the past year with the musical ride. Her name was Tracy Hawke. The constable was about the same height and weight as Jenna; both women were healthy and energetic from having been raised out-doors in a country setting, the American on Orcas and the Canadian on the Prairies. Tracy had learned to ride a horse before she could toddle at her family's ranch near the Rockies in Southern Alberta. They talked about the musical ride as they drove to the detachment.

"The Force was recruited in 1873," said Tracy, "to ride the March West to Fort Whoop-Up to drive Ameri-can whisky traders from Alberta. The expedition had 275 men and 310 horses. It rode two thousand miles in three and a half months. The musical ride developed from how they amused themselves. Most had a British military background. The formations we ride today—the Star, the Dome, the Maze, the Wagon Wheel and the Charge—originated as cavalry drills."

Tracy was blonde and bubbly, and Jenna took to her right away.

"When was the first ride?" Jenna asked.

"In 1876. But the ride as a regular form of public entertainment dates from 1904. It was quite a spectacle in those days. Horse jumping, Roman riding—that's standing with your feet astride on the backs of two horses—and tent-pegging with lance and sword. It takes perfect coordination between horse and rider to tent peg. At a gallop, you've got to spike and flick tent pegs from the ground."

"I love horses," Jenna said.

"So do I. Any time you want, I'll take you trail-riding. In Banff you can buy a postcard still from the early

Mountie movie *Cameron of the Mounted.* Cameron is kissing the heroine, and the three Members with him are kissing their horses."

Jenna laughed. "Where do you get your mounts?"

"Remount Detachment. That's our own breeding ranch in Ontario. A remount is a young horse. All are black, stand sixteen to seventeen hands high, and are ¾ to ⅞ thoroughbred. One of our mares, Burmese, was presented to Queen Elizabeth, our honorary commissioner, in 1969. Burmese has since been ridden by her at the annual Trooping of the Color in London."

"How long to train 'em?"

"Training starts at three years, and they join the musical ride at six. The ride travels with a contingent of 36 horses, 36 constables, 1 farrier, 3 NCOs and an officer in charge."

"Wow! The cost!"

"Our sponsor is the CPR, and the Force is marketed by Disney. The fused letters MP on our saddle blankets are our registered brand, and the maple leaf pattern on each horse's rump is created by using a metal stencil and scrubbing across the lie of the mount's hair with a damp brush."

"Trademarks?"

"The nineties. The Force is big business. Welcome to modern police procedure. Our image is copyrighted by the government."

"How long did you train?"

"All my life. But the musical ride is a five-week basic and six-month advanced course. Sign up for a year and ride, ride, ride."

"I've never seen the ride," Jenna said.

"Next time it's out here, I'll give you a call."

"I'll hold you to that."

"Be my guest."

"I'm in the wrong force," Jenna said. "I could use a cush year of riding the range."

"Funny things occur when we tour. During transport

a Member stays with the horses. Last year my friend got bored while crossing a U.S. desert, so decided to open the door of the boxcar and lasso tumbling tumbleweeds to amuse himself. One rolled under the train and the rope caught in the wheels, flicking my friend like a whip out into Death Valley. He was rescued from dying of thirst by an Indian, and the papers had a field day relating how the Indian got his man.'"

"Your friend still with the ride?"

"He died of embarrassment. As did we all during that same tour in San Francisco. We were riding the outer ring of a stadium. Since horses respond to every body movement, you gotta sit tall and straight in the saddle to pull off the ride. A California bimbo with big boobs and a kid sat in the front row, and kept coaxing, 'Wave to Daddy' as we rode by. Our curiosity to know who had done the dirty deed on the last tour got the better of us, so we kept turning in our saddles to see who the kid was waving to. The horses responded to our body language, and the musical ride fell apart."

"Big boobs," said Jenna.

"There are pitfalls," said Tracy. "A disciplinary problem occurred with my mount, and the bad behavior of the horse is now a permanent black mark on *my* record of service. To quote Commissioner Woods"—her voice went down to a baritone—" 'There's nothing like a horse for finding out the weak spots in a man.' "

"There's nothing like a woman for finding out the weak spots in a man, too."

"Ain't it the truth," said Tracy.

———

They turned off the backbone road of Pender Island by the old cemetery and angled up a hill to the local detachment, skirting the fire hall to park behind. The squat brown building they entered had a big antenna on top, a Canadian flag out front and the RCMP crest over the door. Jenna was jolted by the utter lack of security inside. Hard to believe this police station was just a few miles north of hers across an imaginary boundary. In Friday Harbor you were held in a mantrap just inside the door, personnel secreted behind protective glass in a dark room, a videocamera watching your every move, and a locked door with the welcoming Authorized Personnel Only sign barring you. But here you walked into an open waiting room done in pine, the finger paintings of playschool kids greeting you at the door and beyond them a photo of the queen placed beside a service counter with no glass barrier between you and the cops at work. Was this the end result, she wondered, of not having a right to bear arms in your constitution: every nut with a grievance doesn't have the God-given means to spray you with a withering barrage of automatic fire?

Poor Canada.

How boring it must be not to live with that fear.

"Don't tell me," Jenna sighed, "you don't have any cells?"

"Of course we have cells," Tracy said. "You think we're a bunch of hicks? We jail at least twenty what-do-you-call-'ems a year."

"Ever had a murder?"

"Not in the past century."

"Now you have Gavin Campbell."

"No, *you* have Gavin Campbell. He went down across the line, in *your* statistics."

No wonder these Mounties have so much time to trot around on horses.

I wonder what Hank *really* thought of them?

Like so many Americans, her dad had pined for the Wild West. She could see him sitting in his easy chair at home, facing the wood-burning stove, lost in a story by Zane Grey, Max Brand or Louis L'Amour. Somehow his country had let that tradition slip away and now lived it through Ken Burns on PBS, while spitting distance to the north the Mounties were still the Mounties, with a living frontier to guard in the Arctic, and the romance of the West kept alive in their traditions.

How could Hank not be jealous of them?

The "folderol," however, was a different matter.

Hank had been your basic meat-and-potatoes cop. A repast of *tourtière* and Beaujolais Nouveau was lost on him. His uniform had all the pizzazz—let's be honest—of a school crossing-guard. Meanwhile, strutting their stuff across Boundary Pass between there and here was a force of peacock clotheshorses in red tunics and riding pants and sharp spurs, with enough badges, buttons, insignia and such to *choke* a horse, their jaunty Stetsons cocked to the side.

To quote Hank: "For guys who look like fruitcakes, they are tough sons of bitches. Recruit him off the prairie with light of Jesus in his eyes, and a Horseman will take down his own granny for jaywalking across a dirt road out front of her farm."

Hank was a tough SOB himself.

Jenna was never sure if that was a compliment or not.

The "folderol," however, caught Hank's daughter's eye.

On the wall outside Tracy's office was a poster of the Mounted's orders of dress. It displayed service order of dress, the brown uniform for everyday work; review order of dress, the regalia of the musical ride; and walking-out order of dress, the formal get-up of Red Serge balls. A protocol manual kept straight who wore what for what.

Inside the door to Tracy's office, Jenna could see her Red Serge hung on a hanger.

"Want to try it on?" the Mountie asked.

"No," said Jenna.

"Yes, you do."

Jenna looked around.

Still no sign of Nick.

"Might as well do something while I wait."

The call came in from the lab while Jenna stood in front of the mirror admiring herself.

Red was her color.

Jenna of the Mounted.

"Hey, Jen," Tracy called from a desk outside. "Get on the line."

Jenna picked up the phone on Tracy's desk.

"Jenna Bond," she said.

"You new?" the lab tech asked. "A name like yours I'd remember."

"You could say it's my first day in Red Serge."

"Fresh out of barracks, eh?"

"It's the lab," Tracy said. "Results on the tracks at both crime scenes."

"Whatcha got?" asked Jenna, Mountie for a day.

"As it's your first day in the field, I'll run you through it, Constable Bond. I like to help rookies take to the job."

You do that, Jenna thought.

"First, the forensic evidence from Gavin Campbell's homestead on Mayne."

"The footprints by the woodpile?"

"Now, now, Constable. You know better than that. A *foot*print can be made only by a person's foot. What was left in the sand by Friday and found by Robinson Crusoe was a *foot*print."

"Sorry," said Jenna. "Foot*wear* prints."

"Now, now, Constable. You know better than that. A foot*wear* print—let's be exact: a *shoe* print, *sneaker* print, *boot* print, whatever—is a replica on a *surface* like a floor. A foot or shoe impressed into dirt, sand, snow, or the like results in a foot or shoe *impression,* not a *print.* What was left by the woodpile were sneaker *impressions.*"

"What kind of sneakers?"

"Two pairs of Nikes. One pair of Adidas."

"Like impressions left at Fitzroy Campbell's place on Orcas?"

"Now, now, Constable. You know better than that. A *replica* from gull droppings on a dock—"

Jenna was pissed off already at Nick's tardiness.

This dork pissed her off even more.

"Are the goddamn sneakers the same?"

"No need to get shirty."

"With killers on the loose, I haven't got all day. Class characteristics? Do they match?"

"Yes," said the tech, a mite miffed. "Make, size, style and tread design."

"And individual characteristics?"

"Point-by-point comparison matched, too. In random cuts, wear marks and occlusions."

"So the *same* three pairs of sneakers left marks at *both* scenes?"

"Yes," fumed the tech.

"Good," said Jenna. "One more question. The state of the art, I understand, is holographic technique. The lab can measure displacement of carpet fibers by a shoe to within $\frac{1}{100,000}$ of an inch. The same technique can be used on wood compressed by a shoe—let's be exact: in this case, a *sneaker*—so if I send you a plank from the Orcas dock compressed by that sneaker, can you calculate for me, by measuring the rate of return of the wood fibers to their original state, the *exact* time the foot touched the dock?"

Silence from the other end of the line.

"Now, now, technician. You can do better than that for me. . . ." she said, and hung up.

Tracy laughed.

"I think you won."

"My first day as a Mountie, and already I've got a black mark on my record of service."

"There's nothing like a woman for finding out the weak spots in a man.'"

"Why do I get the feeling you're trying to tell me something?" Jenna said.

"Nick's a conscientious cop."

"So I've noticed."

"Who also happens to be nursing a broken heart."

Jenna played an imaginary violin.

"That's why he left Special X in Vancouver for the Gulf Islands," Tracy said. "You know how rumors work on an island."

"For sure," said Jenna.

"Pender held its annual barn dance last night. The word is that Nick dropped by alone and fell for the jutting charms of an off-island woman. He was last seen leaving with her and walking across a field."

"Big boobs?" Jenna said.

Tracy nodded.

"Don't be embarrassed. Some of our presidents have fallen for the same lure. You think he's at home in bed with her?"

"If so, his phone's unplugged, his cell's switched off and he's ignoring his pager."

"While he sips champagne out of some bimbo's belly button?"

Tracy shrugged. "He *is* a man."

"What say we drive over and catch him in flagrante delicto. Pull him off her, and we may save Nick from the curse of Kennedy's back."

They snaked up the driveway of Earth Goddess Farm. Jenna shook her head in wonder at the Tolkien magic of Nick's home. Here was somewhere *she* would love to live, with its gardens terraced up the slope to the farmhouse deck overlooking them. Come summer it would be electric with buzzing bumblebees and flitting hummingbirds. To one side of the hot-tub deck was a Blackfoot tepee, its canvas covered with authentic designs. Deer munching by the fence bounded into the trees as they passed.

Having rounded the farmhouse, they parked behind it. Theirs was the only vehicle in sight.

"How far to the barn dance?"

"A long walk, Jen."

Painted over the outer door was a rainbow, and scrolled on the inner door was Goddess Bless. The security decal in one window warned Protected by Angels. Through the window, Jenna could see along the hall, past an altar to a goddess with average boobs, where a tunnel staircase vanished above. Painted over the stairs was Ultimate Abandon.

They knocked on the door.

No response.

They tried the handle.

The door was locked.

They called out loudly.

No one home.

Ultimate abandon? Jenna thought.

———

They found the farm truck parked by a snake fence built out of split cedar rails; contented cattle were eating grass on the other side. A rutted road looped up to the double doors of the cowboy-hat-shaped barn, where island volunteers dismantled the beer corral. Parking the 4wd, they sidestepped cow patties over to the field across which Nick had vanished last night, and there picked up both his tracks and hers. They traversed the field to a thicket of evergreens at the dead end of two dirt ruts. Squatting, both cops examined overlapping indents in the moist earth.

"Tire marks," said Jenna.

"Footprints," Tracy said.

"Footwear impressions," corrected the detective.

"I don't like this."

"Neither do I. She got in the passenger's side and Nick got behind the wheel. Then she got out and walked around to the driver's door, and something big—could be Nick—tumbled out on the ground. Then someone wearing sneakers climbed out of the backseat. He was joined by two more from the trees, then the three of them carried whatever tumbled out to the trunk. Then the four got in and drove off."

"A Trojan Horse," said Tracy.

"And we know two of these thugs. Both those impressions are from Nikes identical to ones worn by the Campbells' kidnappers. Mr. Adidas must have switched footwear."

"My brother owns a pair like those. They're French and expensive. See the trademark in the center of both soles?"

An *M*.

In a circle.

With the word *Mephisto*.

Never Trust a Campbell

Vancouver, British Columbia

How well do you remember *The Silence of the Lambs?* In the middle of the film, Jodie Foster and her roommate sit chatting about the serial killer Buffalo Bill, and she mentions that there's no spatial pattern to his killings, or else the computer would have picked it up. That comment was pure fiction when the film was made, because such a program didn't exist. Not until Detective Inspector Kim Rossmo developed one, to turn fiction into fact.

Geographic profiling.

Which brought DeClercq here.

From the parking lot sandwiched between Special X and the Annex, he entered the door to the Behavioural Science Group of the Major Crimes Section. Beyond the swing gate and past the ship's bell on the pillar, which was rung whenever VICLAS scored a "hit," he turned right and knocked on the open door to Sergeant Rusty Lewis's Spartan office. The cyber cop glanced up from his computer screen.

"About those lions in the Scottish Highlands," said Lewis.

"The MacGuffin?" replied DeClercq.

"I queried the VICLAS data base for any 'Campbell' connection across Canada and found no link of interest. Seattle FBI queried VICAP for me, and their linkage system turned up a mysterious death in Florida in May. A recluse named Malcolm Campbell."

"Facts," said DeClercq.

"Health forced the eighty-year-old to move from misty Scotland to sunny climes years ago. An obsessive collector, for sixty years he had amassed a collection centered around the Campbell massacre of MacDonalds at Glencoe in 1692. Recently, the old man had suffered paranoid delusions that the MacDonalds were after him for revenge, and last May he was found floating face down in the sea near his Key West home."

"Foul play?"

"No indications on the body. The coroner would have put it down to accident or suicide had his Glencoe collection not simultaneously vanished from his seaside estate."

"It's worth looking into."

"I'll follow up."

"Kim around?"

"In back. He's training Monica in her office."

DeClercq followed Lewis to the rear of the Annex; Geographic Profiling used the final office on the left. Unlike the Spartan austerity in which Lewis felt at home, the office of his partner from the Headhunter case was as cluttered as the Black Museum at Scotland Yard. Profiles of the hunting grounds of serial killers covered the walls: Jack the Ripper, Son of Sam, the Boston Strangler, the Moors Murderers, Clifford Olson, Jeffrey Dahmer, Aileen Wuornos, the Yorkshire Ripper, the Night Stalker, the Hillside Stranglers and others. Somewhere on each map was a multi-colored amoeba, a blob that reminded DeClercq of the blob in the 1958 horror film.

But these blobs were *counter*-horror.

With their backs to the door, Rossmo and Macdonald were discussing the geoprofile of Jack the Ripper's reign of terror when DeClercq and Lewis walked in. The map with the amoeba showed the labyrinth of streets north of the River Thames that were London's Whitechapel district in 1888. Between August 31 and November 9, the Ripper had killed and mutilated five prostitutes. The darkest part of the amoeba formed an oval that ran along Whitechapel High Street.

"What this tells me," Rossmo said, "is that the Ripper didn't live in the neighborhood where he committed five crimes. He was a poacher who came from outside the area in which he killed, entering Whitechapel district along Whitechapel High Street. Had Inspector Abberline called on us, we'd have told him to concentrate his manhunt on a space that measured a few square yards, instead of a few square miles."

"Watch and tail anyone suspect on Whitechapel High Street?"

"Right," agreed Rossmo. "What's a poacher?"

Up to the test, Macdonald replied, "Serial killers use four hunting styles. A hunter sets out specifically to find a victim, basing the search in his residence. A poacher sets out specifically to find a victim, but bases his search somewhere other than in his home, or commutes elsewhere to hunt. A troller encounters a victim opportunistically while involved in nonpredatory activities. A trapper takes up an occupation or creates a situation much like a spider's web so victims come to him or her. Most female serial killers catch their prey as trappers."

"The three methods of attack?"

"A raptor attacks on encounter. A stalker follows on encounter, then attacks. An ambusher attacks once a victim is lured to the killer's lair."

"Correct. Interestingly, the hunting methods used by serial killers in urban environments eerily parallel those studied in African lions on the Serengeti plain. When you go to Washington, visit the Smithsonian Museum of Natural History. You'll see what I mean. So tell me, what was Jack?"

"His victims were prostitutes, so I'd classify him as a poacher/raptor."

"Which means?"

"We concentrate on suspects outside Whitechapel."

"I'll tell you a story," Rossmo said, "that might narrow the frame. Inspector Frederick Abberline was the officer in charge of hunting Jack the Ripper. After the investigation wound down, his team of seven detectives presented him with a walking stick. The identity of the Ripper was never revealed, but it's known that the inspector had a prime suspect in mind, and legend is that the walking stick solves the mystery. The stick is in a case on the wall at Bramshill House, the supposedly haunted mansion that is home to the British police staff college. I saw it there while I was lecturing on geographic profiling. The stick's handle is carved into the shape of a man's face in a hood. Legend stands that the features are those of Jack the Ripper. The cop with all the facts identified Jack as—"

"Kim. Monica," said DeClercq, entering the office.

The geoprofilers turned to greet him.

Detective Inspector Kim Rossmo was a mite stockier and a few inches shorter than the chief superintendent. Both men had the same alert eyes that took in all relevant details, and the meticulousness that dotted every *i* and crossed every *t*. Though Rossmo was younger than DeClercq, each man had the haunted aspect of someone who had seen too much and found violence truly offensive. Cops who helped you sleep better because you knew they were on guard. Macdonald was a bit like Dana Scully, prompting DeClercq to wonder if Lewis's streetcar named Desire was off track, and to ponder how hard it was getting to separate fact from fantasy these days.

Virtual reality.

What's real and what's not?

Geographic profiling.

DeClercq knew the story.

Rossmo was a Prairie boy from Saskatchewan. A math whiz during high school in Saskatoon, he wrote his Grade 12 final exam in algebra after only one week of classes and got a perfect score. Chasing bad guys on the streets seemed more thrilling than doing math, so he took a break from university to work as a private detective. Because he specialized in finding people who didn't want to be found, one day would see him role-playing a drunk in a tough northern bar, and the next day he'd be a mild-mannered salesman. The math whiz had found his calling.

He moved to Vancouver to work on a master's degree in criminology. For practical experience and to earn a living, he joined the Vancouver Police Department and became a skid row cop. Only by giving up sleep could he cover both tasks, so he'd walk a beat until 2 A.M., work on his thesis in the university lab until dawn, then drive to court and read research journals until he was called to testify against those he'd busted.

His thesis constructed mathematical models to predict how fugitives move around the country to prevent arrest and prison.

He was just getting started.

The engine was warming up.

For his PhD would take manhunting serial killers into the twenty-first century.

Like most human activities, crime has a geographic logic. Go to the store for a quart of milk and you are governed by a quantifiable spatial rule that academics call the least-effort principle. You don't pass by a dozen stores to shop across town. You stop at the nearest one for milk. Your "activity space" is shaped by a mental map related in predictable ways to your "anchor point:" your home. Serial killers follow similar spatial rules. They aren't pathological in a geographic sense. When a serial predator goes hunting for a victim, his hunting ground overlaps the "awareness space" in which he lives day to day; his "image of the city" is built on experience and knowledge. Fear of arrest creates a buffer zone of predictable dimensions, so he travels out some distance before he begins to hunt. But the farther he goes from home and his "activity space," the less likely he is to hunt for victims.

All of which can be mathematically quantified.

Probability.

. Rossmo, in the right place at the right time, found himself working under the husband-and-wife professorial team of Paul and Patricia Brantingham at Simon Fraser University. The Brantinghams had produced a theoretical model that predicted where a criminal might commit his crimes based on where he lived. What Rossmo did for his doctorate was ask the inverse question: Could he use a series of crime sites to predict where a criminal might live?

Wheredunit = whodunit.

He was staring out the window of the famous Bullet Train, having been sent to Japan to study how small police units called *kobans* reduced crime, when the mathematical formula came to him. An hour of mad scribbling on train napkins put it on paper, and that was the genesis of CGT: criminal geographic targeting.

The formula is this:

$$P_{ij} = k \sum_{c=1}^{T} [\phi/(|x_i - x_c| + |y_j - y_c|)^f + (1 - \phi)(B^{g-f})/(2B - |x_i - x_c| - |y_j - y_c|)^g]$$

where:

$$|x_i - x_c| + |y_j - y_c| > B \supset \phi = 1$$

$$|x_i - x_c| + |y_j - y_c| \leq B \supset \phi = 0$$

and:

P_{ij}	is the resultant probability for point ij;
ϕ	is a weighting factor;
k	is an empirically determined constant;
B	is the radius of the buffer zone;
T	is the total number of crime sites;
f	is an empirically determined exponent;
g	is an empirically determined exponent;
x_i, y_j	are the coordinates of point ij; and
x_c, y_c	are the coordinates of the cth crime site location.

Applying the formula to a serial-killer case would take up to a million calculations, so Rossmo created a computer program to run the model, and then began testing it on known serial killers.

The results were amazing.

Each time a serial predator meets, attacks, kills or dumps a victim, he leaves behind a point on a map. Except in the case of a transient killer with no roots, the crime site is linked by the killer's behavior to his anchor point. All the crime sites are plotted on a screen map. The computer draws a box around the hunting area and divides it into a grid. Then, using a formula based on typical journeys to crime sites, the computer selects a starting point on the grid and calculates the distance from it to the first site. After the probability of that starting point being the killer's home is computed, the program repeats the action for each crime site and every other point on the grid. The system draws contour lines between these points, linking those with an equal numerical likelihood of being the killer's home. Such lines are called isopleths, from the Greek for "equal number." A click of the mouse color-codes the space between the lines, resulting in the amoebas on the maps in this room. Twenty colors, ranging up to a high-probability bright red, indicate the likelihood of an area being the killer's home. To add the illusion of a third dimension, the system slants the map to convert the isopleths into peaks and valleys, the "height" of which represents the relative probability that the space under that color is the killer's home.

This 3-D surface is called a jeopardy.

When superimposed on the street grid, it's called a geoprofile.

A geoprofile is like a fingerprint of the killer's mental map.

His "crimespace."

Tracked by a cyber cop.

A jeopardy looks like this:

The completion of Rossmo's dissertation in 1995 caused a stir. *Geographic Profiling: Target Patterns of Serial Murderers* took him six years of minimal sleep to compose. In it, he accumulated 225 serial killers and used his formula to hunt Chase, DeSalvo, Olson, Buono and Bianchi, Sutcliffe, Ramirez, Berkowitz, Dahmer, Rifkin, Collins, Wuornos, Brady and Hindley, and others based on their crime sites. On average he located each killer's anchor point within 5 percent of the subject's hunting area, and often tracked their homes to within one percent. His paper was dedicated "To those who chase the hunters." Its search implications were quickly grasped by police around the world.

The Yorkshire Ripper attacked twenty women between 1975 and 1980. To catch Peter Sutcliffe, police amassed 268,000 names, visited 27,000 homes and gathered up to 5,400,000 car registrations. Instead of tracking a ruthless needle in a haystack of twenty-four tons of paper, the British cops, had they been able to call on geoprofiling, would have shrunk the hunt to just over 2 percent of Sutcliffe's activity space, for that's where the jeopardy found his anchor point.

Overnight, Vancouver's police chief had poachers on his patch. Rossmo had offers from the FBI at Quantico, from Cambridge University and from a host of others in America. To keep him where he was, the VPD catapulted him from constable to detective inspector, which caused rumbling in the ranks because he hadn't gone through the usual process.

DeClercq was reminded of a "Far Side" cartoon. Cows stand in line for the slaughterhouse as an interloper cuts into the queue. A cow behind shouts, "No butting in." The way the world was going, from De-Clercq's point of view, if cops like Rossmo didn't cut in, we would all end up in the slaughterhouse.

The New Dark Age.

"I know it works," DeClercq said, "this invention of yours." His eyes swept across the map amoebas that blobbed crimespace. "But *how* is what baffles me."

"The CGT algorithm," the cyber cop replied matter-of-factly, "employs a distance-decay function—$f(d)$—that simulates journey to crime behavior. Each point (x,y), located at distance d from crime site i, is assigned a probability value, $f(d_i)$. A final value for point (x,y), which represents the likelihood of the offender residing at that location, is determined by adding the n values for that location as derived from the n different crime sites. The predictive power of geographic profiling is related to the number of crime sites—the more locations, the better the jeopardy."

"Of course," said DeClercq, poker-faced. "Now it's *perfectly* clear."

History, not algebra, was his subject.

Rossmo grinned. "You want a demonstration?"

DeClercq passed him the Campbell family tree that had been faxed by Jenna Bond. "Fitzroy Campbell was kidnapped by boat from Orcas Island. The kidnappers used his credit card in Anacortes and Blaine. Gavin Campbell was abducted by boat from Mayne Island. His abductors sailed south down Plumper Sound and scuttled the craft with him aboard in Boundary Pass."

"That's it?" said Rossmo.

"That's it," said DeClercq.

"Sorry, I don't think we can help you yet. The first problem is victim selection. Since both are Campbells from the same family, it appears that someone selected them specifically. Yours isn't a serial killer on a random hunt. He knows where he's going, and that's not what geoprofiling computes. The next problem is too few crime sites. The most useful points are the two credit-card locations and the boat sinking. The randomness inherent in most human behavior limits the conclusions that can be derived from a small number of crime sites. Use more and the impact of chance is reduced."

"How many do you need?"

"A minimum of five," stated Rossmo. "To shrink the activity space to less than 10 percent."

Macdonald looked over his shoulder at the Campbell family tree.

" 'Never trust a Campbell,' " she quoted.

"Huh?" said Rossmo.

"My granddad speaking."

"What did the Campbells do to him?"

"Not to him," said Monica. "To all MacDonalds."

She took the fax from Rossmo and held it out for all to see.

"These two," she said, tapping the family tree:

Somerled Campbell, 1648–1723
Roderick Campbell, 1702–1751
Kenneth Campbell, 1739–1799
Lachlan Campbell, 1770–1847
Callum Campbell, 1814–1863
Dugald Campbell, 1840–1916 Ewen Campbell, 1841–1913
Scotland to Vancouver Island in May 1857
New Caledonia
John Campbell, 1865–1941   Roy Campbell, 1885–1953
Fitzroy Campbell, 1924–   Gavin Campbell, 1923–
William Campbell, 1958–

"Roderick Campbell's the right age for the Battle of Culloden. The Campbells fought with the English to crush the Highland clans, and cut us down viciously after our defeat. That led to the Highland Clearances, which drove us out. But the real weasel was probably this guy." Her finger touched the name at the top of the family tree. "Somerled Campbell's the right age for——"

"Glencoe," said DeClercq.

On his way out to return to Special X, DeClercq wagged the lanyard from its clanger and rang that damn ship's bell.

Bonehenge

Shipwreck Island, Washington State

The burnt bones of Fitzroy Campbell lay among the ashes of the Wicker Man in the Stone Circle in the oak grove on Mephisto's island. Sunshine beamed through the surrounding woods to cast tree shadows like a *retiarius* net across the clearing and the tartan-clad psychopath. After Gavin Campbell's cry just before he suffocated in the deep blue sea—"It must . . . it must . . . GOOD LORD! THE THIRD TRACT OF LAND!"—Mephisto had dug Fitzroy out of his premature grave to torture him physically in the hope the old man would elaborate on Gavin's statement, but his brain had blown from dread of being buried alive, and he was no longer of any use except to fill the Wicker Man and burn to bones.

Nice screams, too.

One by one, Mephisto gathered the charred fragments from the ground to add to his bone collection. He would keep them in a case like the case his father had bought to store the bones he collected during their fatal tour of the megaliths of Britain, before that horrific night in the Scottish Highlands. As he gathered Fitzroy, Mephisto thought back. . . .

They had purchased a caravan for the epic journey, a green van with archeological and camping equipment in the rear. From London, they had ventured west on the A30 to Salisbury and up to Stonehenge, where his father had guided him about the ruins. The archeologist showed his son how the avenue axis aligned with the midsummer sun, and the four Station Stones with important positions of the moon, and also how the fifty-six Aubrey holes kept track of eclipses.

"Stonehenge was a temple of the sun, not the moon. How do we know that?" the scientist asked rhetorically. "First, the earliest megaliths were solar aligned, like Newgrange in Ireland. It's a long passage that the sun enters only at midwinter dawn, so we know the sun came *before* the moon, the same way Stonehenge I was first set out along a solar axis. Whatever rituals were performed here focused on the sun. The moon was important because it caused solar eclipses."

The archeologist led his son across to a lintelled trilithon in the central horseshoe, where he pointed to one of the wicketlike stones.

"In 1953, when photographing a seventeenth-century name carved into this stone, Professor Richard Atkinson noticed other deeply weathered carvings on its surface. See them, son? A dagger and four axes? Some prehistoric artist chipped them into this pillar. Other carvings of axes and daggers were found on other stones, all facing toward the east or south. Similar weapons armed local chiefs and warriors during the Early Bronze Age, and we know from other cultures that they were used in art as symbols of the sun and its life-giving warmth. The chippings found on fallen stones that once faced west formed rectangles with rounded upper extensions. Could those be 'boats of the dead,' which sailed their lifeless cargoes off to the setting sun and darkness of night? Such symbols support the theory that Stonehenge is a temple of the sun, as they face only east where it rose, south where it reached its zenith and west where it set."

The archeologist pointed out the various carvings, then led his son out of the stone circle to gaze across Salisbury Plain.

"From its beginning, the association of Stonehenge

with death was clear. Before it was built, there were a
dozen or more long barrows on Salisbury Plain. A barrow is a burial mound, son. During the New Stone Age,
from 4500 to 2250 B.C., when the first stone circles were
raised in Britain, long barrows with timber chambers at
the east end were common. These gave way by the
Bronze Age to round barrows, circular mounds with no
entrance or chamber, in which the dead were buried
with their faces toward the sun. Stonehenge is surrounded by 450 burial mounds, making Salisbury Plain
a region of death at the heart of which is a solar temple
designed to predict eclipses of the sun and the moon."

"Why?" asked the boy.

"Burnt bones," said his father.

"Bonehenge," punned the boy.

His father smiled and walked him back to the ring of
Aubrey holes around the stone temple.

"Stonehenge was used for rituals of death, the end
result of which was burnt offerings of charred bones to
some force of nature. The holes were dug and refilled
to predict eclipses by moving stones around them to
keep track of the sun and the moon. Periodically a hole
was redug to receive an offering of cremated human
bones, sometimes buried with a carved chalk ax to sym-
bolize the sun. The rituals continued for centuries, and
burnt bones have also been recovered from the bank,
the ditch and near the entrance. Stonehenge changed
form with time, but it always remained a temple of the
sun, the moon and death. Do burnt bones in the Aubrey
holes mean death was triggered by eclipses? And did
the eclipse-predicting hole receive the offering?"

A vivid vision of a burning man screaming thrilled
the boy.

"Why were some burned inside Stonehenge and others buried outside?"

"Answer that, son, and we will learn the Secret of
the Stones."

And so they had driven off to solve the mystery, a

journey away from Stonehenge—the height of megalithic science—into the wilder regions of prehistory, a hunt that zigzagged them southwest to Land's End, then north to the Peak and Lake districts of Western England, then up into Scotland to track the legend of the Hoard. Each night they camped near or in a stone circle, either sleeping in the caravan or tented out under the moon. Dawn saw his father up to study the astronomy of the stones, and day saw him cautiously digging for remains of burnt bones. As he worked, he taught his son about each henge site.

The day they crossed the border from England into Scotland, and drove past the Roman ruins that once were Hadrian's Wall, his father summed up what they had learned since leaving Stonehenge.

"Long before the pyramids were raised in Egypt, at a time when most of Western Europe was pathless forests and bogs, perhaps when the earliest form of writing and numbering developed in the Near East, somewhere deep in the primal mist of the British Isles the first megalith was built. Upright stones as high as a man were arranged in a circle to form a ring, and all that remains of why it was done are bits of burnt bones and the alignment of the stones with the sun and the moon.

"Death and astronomy.

"The Secret of the Stones.

"We know the rings weren't cemeteries because of the limited number of cremations. Does so few burnings link the offerings to eclipses? Why were many graveyards dug near the rings? Were the rituals performed within connected to the flourishing of plants, crops, animals and human beings? Two million nights have darkened us since stone circles first blazed, chilling whatever power they once had and leaving us with questions to madden a thinking man."

Vivid visions of painted bodies against the bloody sun and dark figures against the silver moon thrilled the boy with images of fiery sacrifice.

"To answer those questions, son, let's go find the Hoard."

And so they had driven northwest from Glasgow into Argyll, the ancient home of the Campbells and the Mac-Donalds of Glencoe, and the ancient home of the barbarian Picts before them.

Here in the well-watered valley of Kilmartin Burn, miles away from any other circle, in a region populated from the Stone Age on, nestled below mountain slopes in this megalithic V, stood the small stone circle of Temple Wood. They parked the caravan in a thicket of leafy trees, farther away than they had stopped from any other ring, then walked back to tour the ruins.

The setting sun cast long, black shadows across the circle as he and his father walked around to the carved northern stone. Chipped into it were spirals like those now tattooed on Donella's breasts. Having entered the ring and crossed a layer of cobbles to its center, they stood by a cist grave lined with stone slabs.

"The side slab was set west to east, to follow the shadow of the setting midwinter sun. Traces of cremated bones were found in the cist, and in other burning pits within the circle."

As they returned to the caravan, his father pointed south. "Over there is the Iron Age hill fort of Dunadd. Rich with Pictish carvings, it was later the capital of Dalriada, kingdom of the Scots. The history of Scotland comes together in Argyll. Tomorrow we'll drive over for a look. . . ."

But that trip was not to be.

Full moon, that night.

His father asked him if he was afraid to spend the evening alone in the caravan so he could walk the mile north to Kilmartin for a Scotch chased by beer. He told his son to lock himself in the van, then go to sleep as if his dad were there. "I'll return by midnight and use the key."

The boy awoke to the full moon shining on his face through the window of the caravan. The vivid visions of fiery sacrifice grabbed him, and drew him like a magnet out of bed, then out of the caravan toward Temple Wood. He heard grunts and sighs as he neared, soon seeing why his father had camped so far away, for there he was in the stone circle without any clothes, hunched over a naked woman who was bent over one of the stones, both of them sheened silver by the watching moon. The boy crept around to watch from behind the stone carved with spirals, his fingers tracing them as he thrilled to the primal scene.

He imagined she was his mother, this slut from the pub, the mother who had abandoned him before he got any love. He thrilled to his father stabbing her repeatedly with his cock, and to the moans scraped from her throat as she died, even if her death was something she seemed to enjoy.

Then a real shadow of death snuck into Temple Wood from the woods around the ring; the Grim Reaper himself, judging from the gleaming crescent in his hand, a burly hulk closing on the coupling couple as the woman cried, "Sweeeet Jeeeesus, yeeees . . ."

He knew he should warn his father.

As the Reaper reached for his hair.

And wrenched back his father's startled face.

And swung the sickle blade.

Growling at the humper, "Get off my fucking wife!"

Yes, he should warn his father. And yes, he should save his life. But he was struck dumb by a compulsion to know how far blood would spurt from his father's throat.

With Dad dead, would they force his mother to take back her fatherless son?

In his favorite daydreams, never had he seen blood *spurt spurt spurt* that far!

A call from Donella pulled Mephisto out of memory.

He polished Fitzroy Campbell's burnt bones as they talked by digital cellphones.

"He just returned to Special X from the building next door," she said.

A worthy adversary? Mephisto wondered.

The Hand

Vancouver, British Columbia

It had been two days since he had last checked his cyber-space mailbox for Klondike gold rush anecdotes for his book *Yukon,* so on returning to his office after speaking with the cyber cops next door, DeClercq sat down at the horseshoe desk and booted up his computer to read any recent e-mail. With his password entered, he was informed that one new message was in the box. Clicking on it showed this on-screen:

> ? ? ? ?
> Antigonus Severus.
> 306 a.d.
> Cohors I Tungrorum Milliaria.
> Hadrian's Wall.
> Trash can 13, 4900 block Cambie.
> Your move.
> Mephisto.

At first, DeClercq thought this a mailing mistake, for he knew just the basics about Roman Britain, and it would benefit no historian to query him on the subject. But "Trash can 13, 4900 block Cambie" was too great a coincidence for e-mail gone astray. The office in which he was sitting was at RCMP Headquarters, 4949 Heather Street, just one street west of the 4900 block of Cambie. Trash can 13?

Intrigued, the chief superintendent took a walk to satisfy his curiosity. From the airy vaulted loft that was his office on the upper floor of the Tudor building at 33rd and Heather, he descended the stairs and exited to the wide-lawned street. From Special X, he ambled east on 33rd toward what might be flames blazing the gardens of Little Mountain, but were really autumn leaves ignited by a conflagrant sun. A botanical gallery of every native tree and shrub in B.C., with additions like an English oak dug up from Windsor Great Park for planting here by the monarch in 1951, Queen Elizabeth Park crowned the mountain in red, orange and yellow glory. Half a block from the intersection where Cambie fronted the park, DeClercq turned right into the back lane.

Trash can 13 beckoned him.

Sitting just inside the alley, it was spray-painted with a 13 in white.

Lifting the lid, he peered in.

And there, on top of the bags of garbage, found a human hand.

———

Little Mountain is a geologic quirk. Spared by the glacier that flattened other land into the Fraser River delta as it retreated, it's a volcanic outcropping with 360-degree views that rises smack dab in the compass center of the city as its highest point. Here you can sit on the cheap lawn seats overlooking one of the continent's classic 1940s outdoor diamonds and watch a Triple-A baseball game, or, like this woman with binoculars and the curse of modern times—a digital cellphone—you can wander through the Queen E, as locals call it, and watch birds in the trees taking a break from flying south for the winter.

Aren't bird watchers supposed to be homely looking twerps?

Va-va-voom!

What have we here?

The epitome of all pin-up girls was Rita Hayworth. There wasn't a soldier in the Second World War who didn't lust for her. A Rita Hayworth look-alike passed this geezer on a bench feeding birds, and he watched her while he recalled the glory days of his youth and the picture of Rita he had taken to war, that woman in heat in a bathing suit with half-shut eyes and red come-hither lips. Who'd have thought Rita would end up like this, watching birds in a park?

Talking on a cellphone.

She hadn't aged a day. . . .

———

"Where are you?"

"In a park overlooking the alley."

"What do you see?"

"He and a woman are talking by the can."

"Pathologist?" asked Mephisto.

"Probably. She's wearing latex gloves. I've got to move. Some old fart feeding birds on a bench is mooning over me."

"Find another lookout and see what he does."

"Right," Donella said.

———

It's not every day that a body part is left virtually on the doorstep of the Mounted Police. Rubbing De-Clercq's nose in it was the downside of the taunt, but the upside was that the forensic lab was a minute's walk away. It took Gill Macbeth a while to drive twenty-three blocks south from the hospital morgue at 10th and Heather to Special X at Heather and 33rd, and by the time she parked her BMW in the lot and walked up to the alley near Queen Elizabeth Park, a horde of techs from the lab had already swept a path of contamination

to the can. There she met DeClercq, who was waiting
beside the hand on top of the green garbage bags.

Unprofessionally, the pathologist gasped.

The normal procedure to identify a severed hand is
to send its fingerprints to Ottawa to check against the
national data base. If you failed there, your next step
would be to ask Rusty Lewis at VICLAS to do a Q & A
check of entries in CPIC. All "found human remains"
and missing persons are entered in the Canadian Police
Information Centre computer. Each Monday, VICLAS
downloads new data off CPIC into its own system, where
it can ask a series of questions to link bodies and parts.
Today the normal procedure wasn't necessary. The gasp
of shock from Gill Macbeth was one of recognition.

"Huuugh! This hand is Nick's!"

DeClercq winced. "Are you sure?"

"The scars on both fingers from when he broke them
in the fight with Tarot. And that's where Gabby bit him
in a fit of jealousy."

Gabby was her parrot.

A memory from when he last saw Nick on Pender
shot through Robert's mind:

"You can't run away to the circus, Nick."

*"Can't I?" said Craven. "You fear I'm verging on a
breakdown, Chief. A mid-life crisis at best. You suspect
that the one-two punch of me standing trial for the death
of my mom and Gill dumping me as her lover has overwhelmed my reason. Incidentally, thanks for how you
handled her coming on to you until we resolved it."*

*"The man who said all is fair in love and war had
no ethics."*

*"Have you never wished you could shed your life to
reinvent yourself? . . ."*

Judging from the pained look etched into her eyes, a
memory of Nick had caught in Gill's mind. Handsome
but not pretty, and Robert's side of forty, with auburn
hair, emerald eyes and a figure she worked hard to keep
trim, Gill was a woman struggling with an hourglass run-

ning out of sand. Her mother, who had died from hepatitis, a risk of the job, was the first female pathologist in the Commonwealth. While other girls were playing with Barbie or Barbie-izing themselves, Gill was learning how to dissect and sleuth from dead things, a job that, through focusing on it and excluding domestic ties from her life, had taken her to the top, so she was now the best forensic sawbones around. From her dad, she had inherited five Caribbean hotels, the profits of which were split with on-site managers, allowing Gill to live in high style here. Her home was a West Coast modern of cedar and glass atop Sentinel Hill in West Vancouver, the most affluent community in Canada, and Gill lived *ménage à trois* with two tropical birds. She was truly a woman of independent ways and means, until suddenly the alarm rang on her biological clock, forcing her to find sperm if she desired a child.

The sperm bank had been Nick.

Gill was in her forties. Nick was in his thirties. Both were well over the age of consent and had been able to work out a contract. She had been upfront with him from the start. "I'm not looking for ties, Nick. I'm looking for excitement. I want to whitewater-raft and skin-dive for treasure. I want to downhill-race and zoom on a chopper. I want someone wild to electrify me in bed." Nick had been glad to oblige. What single man wouldn't? Then he had to spoil it by falling in love.

Gill was pregnant.

Nick was breaching their contract.

Then the *Good Luck City* sank because of him—was he not the one who had lured the bomber aboard?—and Gill lost the fetus when both she and Nick were dumped into the sea.

Too late.

Time's up.

Her clock had stopped.

And sand was running out in the hourglass of life.

"Have you never wished you could shed your life to reinvent yourself? . . ."

Gill had.

By shedding Nick.

And going after Robert.

And now she was staring at the hand that had loved her body and soul.

"Oh, Nick," she groaned.

DeClercq was having his own problems with the hand in the garbage. *"Thanks for how you handled her coming on to you."* He didn't feel quite so noble. In truth he'd been flattered by her attention. Fueled by the celibacy he'd practiced for too long since the death of his second wife, he would have welcomed a meeting of minds and bodies if not for the fact that he was Craven's boss. Move on a subordinate's love and, apart from undermining general morale, there'd be doubt about his fitness to command.

A man is known to be mortal by two things, Robert thought. Sleep and lust.

And now he was staring at the hand he had clasped on Pender.

His cellphone rang.

Pender Island detachment.

"What?" said Gill, alarmed, as he punched off.

"Whoever abducted the Campbells snatched Nick last night."

Gill's eyes lost focus.

She slowly shook her head.

"If he hadn't gone to the island, this wouldn't be happening to him. I'm to blame, Robert. He went because of *me.*"

"No, Gill. Because of *us.* It's a twist of fate."

Another memory of Nick flashed through DeClercq's mind. They stood at the bottom of the staircase in the island farmhouse, looking up at calligraphy scrolled on the wall.

Ultimate Abandon.

DeClercq glanced back at Nick.

"Don Juan," said Craven. " 'It does not matter what our specific fate is, as long as we face it with ultimate abandon.' "

Ultimate abandon?

Not on your life, he thought.

Hang on, Nick.

I'll find you.

———————

"Where are you?"

"Hospital across the street from his office."

"What's he doing?"

"Just went back inside."

"Wait and see if he comes out."

"Right," Donella said.

The Suits

The *Islomania* was *boomph*ing across Boundary Pass toward Friday Harbor when Jenna got the call from Tracy Hawke.

"It's worse than we thought, Jen. The bastards are cutting him up."

My dream! thought Jenna.

"Nick?" she said.

"I called DeClercq to fill him in on what we found near the barn, and he told me that Nick's hand had just been recovered from a garbage can."

"Where?"

"Half a block from his office at Special X. E-mail told him where to find it."

"The message?"

"Don't know. It's classified. He's holding it back as key-fact evidence."

Key-fact or hold-back evidence is something known only to the offender and a limited number of investigators. It's held back from general knowledge to trap the offender during interviews.

"The hand is definitely Nick's?"

"Yeah," Tracy said. "The pathologist was the woman who broke Nick's heart."

"Guess she'd know."

"The hand was all over her body."

"Keep me informed?"

"Likewise?"

"What I get, you get," Jenna promised.

"Ditto," said Tracy.

Jenna docked the boat at the marina and scaled the gangway to Front Street along the harbor. It was Friday morning, and Friday Harbor was busy, as if the day and name were joint clarion calls to come and shop. As fall took hold, off-islanders were closing out the season; once the gray rains came, the islanders would have these soggy shores all to themselves.

Fair weather friends.

Tourists begone.

She turned inland at Spring Street and trudged uphill, then turned right on Second Street to angle back to the courthouse, with the sheriff's office beyond. Her mind was plagued by the nightmare that had wrenched her awake that morning.

The screams of Don being tortured echo up and down this hall. . . . "OH, JESUS, PLEASE NOT ANOTHER PIECE!" "OH, JESUS, NOT THAT! LEAVE ME A MAN!" "OH, JESUS, DON'T CUT OFF MY—"

Whup . . .

Whup . . .

Whup . . .

A chopper approached.

The news of the Mountie being kidnapped and cut apart had hit Jenna hard. She had never met him—they had just talked on the phone—but that didn't matter, for suddenly Nick was her husband, Don, and Don's screams in her nightmare were Nick's in real life. There was nothing Jenna could have done to save her beloved husband—Don was gone by the time the tape was sent to the DEA, his throes of death recorded, too—but that didn't stop her subconscious from blaming her for doing nothing. There *was* something she could do to save Nick, and if Don's screams in her mind had turned into Nick's in real life, if she saved Nick from Don's fate, would her subconscious free her from this terrible yoke of guilt? If not, Jenna knew the screams of damnation would echo eternally through the labyrinthine tunnels of her mind, and she would never be absolved.

Nick was her salvation.

Whup . . .

Whup . . .

Whup . . .

The chopper passed overhead.

Whup . . .

Whup . . .

Whup . . .

The chopper sucked up billows of dust that gritted Jenna's eyes.

Whup . . .

Whup . . .

Whup . . .

The chopper landed on the lawn of the square brick building in which she worked, and Jenna knew her nightmare was about to get worse.

Before the rotors stopped *whupp*ing, out stepped the Suits.

The Suit who met her at the door was Special Agent Luke Wentworth. The Suit's blue power suit was tailored to his lanky frame and had probably cost him one or two grand. His face formed sharp angles and narrowed down to a long, thin chin. His hair was cut by a stylist with as much care as whoever cut his suit. Summer and winter alike, he wore shades so you couldn't see his eyes, and took them off only to wither you with his stare. Jenna had worked with him at the Bureau in Seattle, after he transferred from the Bureau in New Orleans. There, once upon a time, Wentworth had butted heads with two Mounties named Rick Scarlett and Katherine Spann.

But that was another story.

The Headhunter case.

"You're looking butch, Jen. Thought the uniform up here was overalls?"

He opened the door for her and took a look inside.

"*This* is the greener pasture you abandoned us Good Guys for?"

He tapped the photo of Hank on the wall.

"Chip off the old block, huh?"

He crossed to the picture of the dog with its paws on the counter beside the security door, and laughed at the caption that read: "A citizen reporting a missing owner."

"Now that's real class. Gotta scrape the shit from your shoe to enter?"

"We're not a bunch of hicks," Jenna said, the same reply Tracy had made when that shoe was on Jenna's foot this morning.

Wentworth reached out short of her hair and pulled back his hand, then held thumb and forefinger up to the light.

"Yep. Hayseed."

"I take it this rude intrusion means the Bureau is here to work with us?"

"Wrong," Wentworth said. "Fitzroy Campbell, grabbed in-state, is your jurisdiction. Gavin Campbell, snatched up north and boated across the border to be killed, golfs the file to us. You know the Lindbergh Law. The kidnappings are now a federal case, and the kidnappers' having abducted a Mountie is icing on the cake. We'll show the redcoats who's best, Jen."

"What's my role?"

"Nothing. You can make us coffee. If you want into the big time, never leave the Bureau. Now show me to my office and give me your files."

What was going on here was sibling rivalry. Bureau and Force had been at it since 1924, the year J. Edgar Hoover was appointed director of what would soon be the FBI. By then, the Mounties had been policing for half a century. Canada was confederated in 1867, and the Force recruited five years after that. That they settled Canada's West became the myth of the Mounted Police, and this was augmented by the American press's catchy motto: The Mounties Always Get Their Man. Meanwhile, Hollywood filmed Red Serge for every buck it could make. The Force was the elder brother in North America. Tell someone something long enough and he will believe it, so by the time the Mounties became Canada's national police force in 1920, the Horsemen had assumed the mantle of the Best.

Then came Hoover.

And the bigger brother.

Hoover began his career as a special assistant to the attorney general; he was in charge of the mass roundup and deportation of Communists in the Red Scare after the First World War. The zeal with which he performed that task got him appointed director of the scandal-ridden Bureau of Investigation, which was sullied by President Harding's corrupt administration. Hoover was twenty-nine when he set to making the Bureau his powerhouse, recruiting agents on merit for training at a new academy, while establishing a fingerprint file and crime-detection lab. He used the media to build his and the Bureau's reputations, spinning the gunning-down of Dillinger for all it was worth, and when his manhood was impugned by the charge that he had never made an arrest, he staged his personal "capture" of Alvin "Creepy" Karpis. For the next thirty-three years, Hoover personally tubed any chance of parole, so Karpis will forever remain the man who served the longest prison term on Alcatraz, the Rock.

No doubt about it, the G-men were the Best.

And the Bureau let the Mounties know each time the siblings rivaled.

Like over Shirley Temple.

Shirley made a movie about the Force. *Susannah of the Mounties* was the title. There we see her, amid all that Red Serge. But it was Hoover who got to kiss Miss Temple, the big smooch with the Boss hyped for an eager press.

"Are you married?" Shirley asked.

"No," said Hoover. "I live with my mother."

"Then I'll kiss you," Shirley replied.

In her autobiography, *Child Star,* the actor would write: "Hoover's lap was outstanding as laps go. Thighs just fleshy enough, knees held closely together, and no bouncing or wiggling."

It began to look like Hoover was here to stay. The man saw eight presidents and eighteen attorneys general come and go. But finally, after forty-eight years, he died in office in 1972.

Then came the dirt.

And oh, how dirty it was.

It seems that since 1925 he had kept a so-called Obscene File on anyone he didn't like or who might challenge him, a file known in the Justice Department as "twelve drawers full of political cancer." It recorded sexual escapades and other damaging tidbits on presidents, first ladies, leaders, celebrities, dissidents and other targets who piqued his paranoia. Threatened leaks kept the Kennedys from removing him. Hoping to induce Martin Luther King, Jr., to commit suicide, the FBI sent him an anonymous letter with a tape recording of his "tomcat" trysts. It was opened by his wife. So virulent was Hoover's lifelong pursuit of Communists that Hooverism should have been the name of McCarthyism. And yet he left the Mafia alone to ravage the nation. Though he was a closet homosexual who strong-armed anyone who voiced the allegation, he didn't hesitate to use that smear on "queers." The myth he manufactured of the incorruptible, invincible FBI was a fraud, and none enjoyed his undoing as much as the RCMP.

The bigger brother, it would seem, was actually Big Brother.

So *now* who's the Best?

The current FBI drags the legacy of Hoover around like Marley's chains, and the Horsemen lord it over the Suits each time the siblings rival.

Not in words.

In a little smile.

It was bad enough that Jenna was caught in that everyday jurisdictional tussle between local cops and power-hungry Feds, but now it involved the "who's best" battle between two prima donnas. To see the rivalry at work, watch what happens when both siblings end up in the same court, as occurs whenever perps breach the line. Bureau and Force vie to produce the bigger witness statement book on the stand, angling the cover at the jury to show its snazzy crest.

Mine's bigger than yours.

Saving a Mountie was too big a medal for Wentworth to share. Fitzroy was grabbed and Gavin was killed on this side of the border, so odds were Nick was boated across the line. Thanks to Hoover, Wentworth had jurisdiction. Charles Lindbergh was the first to fly solo nonstop across the Atlantic. In 1932, his son was snatched. Kidnapping wasn't then a federal offense, so Hoover lobbied Congress to pass the Lindbergh Law, which not only gave the Bureau jurisdiction if a victim was transported across a state line, but also added the presumption of interstate transport if the victim hadn't been returned after seven days. No matter how you grabbed it, the Campbell/Campbell/Craven case was Wentworth's baby.

Resigned, Jenna led the Suit to her office. Jenna was the only detective in San Juan County. The Suit had all the resources of the Feds. What hung in the balance was Nick dying a very bad death. This was no time to tussle over jurisdiction.

"Mind if I use your office until we find something better?"

"No," she said.

"Good. I hate birds. Get it out of here."

With pleasure, Bond thought, and took the Jailbird next door.

"The files," said Wentworth on her return.

Jenna opened the briefcase she had taken to Pender

for her ill-fated meeting with Nick, and passed the Suit the Campbell files.

"You're holding back. What are those?"

Jenna showed him the remaining files in the case. "Something else. Three rapes. Mind if I investigate the crimes?" Wentworth shrugged. "Rape's women's work."

The screams of Don being tortured echo up and down this hall. . . .

Nick was to be her salvation.

Was that salvation gone?

Were the screams of damnation to echo eternally up and down the labyrinthine tunnels of her mind, thanks to this prick?

No way, she thought.

From the sheriff's office, Jenna retraced the path she had trudged up from the harbor, then went back down the gangway to the *Islomania,* untying the lines to cast off from the dock and motor out into San Juan Channel. She climbed to the bridge, turned north, then opened up the throttle.

The Hoard

Vancouver, British Columbia

Because their conversation was converted to binary numbers for digital transmission from phone to phone, what they said could not be intercepted. That problem had gone the way of dinosaur analog.

"He's leaving the office."

"Going to his car?"

"Yes," said Donella.

"Good, he's taken the bait."

"Know where he's going?"

"An educated guess. Probably the same place I'd go if I were him."

"I'm in the car."

"Follow him," said Mephisto.

> While stands the Coliseum, Rome shall stand;
> When falls the Coliseum, Rome shall fall;
> And when Rome falls—the World.

That's Lord Byron.

"Everyone soon or late comes round by Rome."

That's Robert Browning.

Professor Emeritus Robson MacKissock could not have put it better.

Was proof of the truth not this Mountie who sought him out in the reading room of the Classics Department at the university?

In every way, Robson MacKissock seemed larger than life. Though now in his seventies, he was a robust man, with a leonine head graced by a mane of wavy white hair and bushy white eyebrows, his body developed from rugby or soccer or punting the backs, or whatever they did to mold Greek gods at English public schools. His training in classics was a first at Oxford in the late thirties; he was transplanted here to UBC when he followed his heart to woo a Canadian nurse after the war. The university had seen nothing like him before. Dressed in the regalia of an Oxford don, and with all the dramatic presence of an Olivier, he gave classes in which tens of students were enrolled in lecture theaters packed to overflowing with hundreds of auditors, the non-classic students coming in to hear his oratory because he was undoubtedly the most captivating prof on campus.

Was proof of the truth not that during the sixties, when he was a conservative tweed among a generation of leftist longhairs on pot, he still packed them in while other "running dogs" were shunned?

Today, he drew DeClercq.

Long since put out to pension pasture, the legend returned to academe each Friday afternoon to hold court for current students in the Classics reading room. There the Mountie found him, seated like Socrates with his acolytes listening at his feet, flanked by shelves of dead-language texts, study carrels and portraits of ancient department heads, the most imposing being the one of him. The wall of windows beyond gazed out on the Chan Centre for the Performing Arts, a modern structure that ruined the classical ambience. Perched at the tip of his Roman nose sat a pair of spectacles. Gripped in his hands was a dusty copy of Virgil's *Aeneid*. On his tongue Latin could hardly be called a dead language, not the way Robson MacKissock filled this room with its vibrant cadence.

"Equo ne credite, Teucri.

"Quidquid id est, timeo Danaos et dona ferentis.

"Men of Troy, trust not the horse! Be it what it may, I fear the Danaans, though their hands proffer gifts."

"Yo," responded a student. "I hear you, dude." The professor scowled.

"Apparent rari nantes in gurgite vasto."

As he translated, MacKissock pointed from student to rapt student. "Here and there in the wastes of ocean a swimmer was seen."

He turned in his seat and swept an arm across the ocean of windows.

"Go swim," he said, and snapped shut the book.

Dust billowed.

The students applauded his performance and drifted away to classes. Some approached MacKissock to question him, so DeClercq joined the queue as last in line. When he was the only one left, MacKissock looked him up and down and said, "A senior student?" The Mountie produced his badge.

"Chief Superintendent Robert DeClercq." MacKissock slumped and sighed. "I knew one day all would come to this."

"I found the dust a nice touch."

"Unplanned, I'm afraid. The university cut back on cleaning staff."

The professor stood up and turned to face the bank of windows.

"The view from here was magnificent in my day. You could sit and read and gaze across the bay to mountains like Olympus. When they tried to shift us, I refused to budge. We kept our view, then I left and they blocked it with Chernobyl."

"Shall we return to the past?"

"Gladly," said MacKissock.

" 'Antigonus Severus. 306 A.D. Cohors I Tungrorum

Milliaria. Hadrian's Wall.' Does that inscription mean anything to you?"

"Vae victis," replied the professor. "Livy. Woe to the vanquished."

"Ab Urbe Condita. History of Rome," said DeClercq.

MacKissock winked. "A good guess, considering it's the only book by Livy to survive."

"My hope was you'd be impressed by the fact that I know it at all."

"Shall we go to my office? Tea will be steeping by now."

With his black, short-sleeved gown flowing behind him like a superhero's cape, and dust and chalk puffing in his wake, the classics professor led the cop from the room to jog right through a fire door and down a few steps to reach the central hall of the S-shaped Buchanan Building, the S having fallen on its face as if drunk from knowledge. Home to Homer, Euripides, Plato, Cicero, Caesar, Ovid, Horace, Tacitus, MacKissock and whoever took his place, the office overlooked the landscaped oasis in one curve of the S.

"Cuppa?" asked the professor.

"Please," said DeClercq.

"I have an admirer in the office. Tea miraculously appears each Friday afternoon." And so they sat . . .

And sipped . . .

And talked history . . .

"Hadrian's Wall," MacKissock said, "was built in 122 A.D. and stretched from sea to sea across northern Britannia to divide barbarian Picts in the Highlands from Romans to the south. Cohors I Tungrorum Milliaria was a Belgian cohort of auxiliary soldiers camped at Vercovicium—now known as Housesteads—Fort. In 305 A.D., they held milecastles and turrets along the central part of the wall when the Picts launched a century of unrest known as the Pictish Wars. What the Picts shared with all Celtic tribes was a cult of the head. They were headhunters. In 306 A.D., while guarding a wall turret with

Cohors I Tungrorum Milliaria, Antigonus Severus lost his head to raiding Highlanders. *Vae victis.* Woe to the vanquished."

"How do you know that?" asked DeClercq.

"On July 25, 306, Emperor Constantius Chlorus died at York after a major campaign against the Highlanders. The emperor's biographer had come with him to Britain, and the biographer recorded how Antigonus Severus died. The Tungrian had been a gladiator in the Roman Colosseum. A public favorite, he was freed to join the Roman army, and shipped to Britain to serve with the Tungrians at Hadrian's Wall. His unit detoured along the way to suppress a Druid revival at Stonehenge on Salisbury Plain. He was guarding the wall when Picts overran his post in a winter storm."

"Off with his head," said DeClercq.

"Off *went* his head," said MacKissock. "The Celts' cult of the head embraced both warriors and priests. The human head was the center of spiritual power, so it was conspicuous in their rituals, warfare, stories and art. Protective power was thought to reside in an enemy's head, and seizing it brought his ghost into servitude. The head of Antigonus Severus was spirited off to the Highlands."

"Is there anything more about Antigonus in Roman sources?"

"No," said the professor.

"So his head vanished into the mists of Highland antiquity?"

"Not quite," said MacKissock. "There is the legend of the Pictish Hoard."

"The horde that overran Hadrian's Wall?"

"H-o-a-r-d. The hoard of Pictish silver supposedly stolen at Glencoe."

Somerled Campbell flashed through DeClercq's mind.

"The MacKissocks are a clan sept of both the Campbells and the MacDonalds of Clanranald, so I heard the story from both sides."

"What's a sept?"

"A branch," said MacKissock. "A sept can be either clansmen related by blood who form a separate offshoot, or broken men—from other clans who ask for and obtain the protection of the clan. A sept can have a different surname than the clan, or the same surname can be tied to different clans."

"I know the history of Glencoe," said DeClercq. "A force of Campbells slaughtered MacDonalds at the end of the seventeenth century."

"The legend of the Hoard is a MacDonald myth. Most Campbells debunk it as a result of too many drams. The story goes that Glencoe was the glen of *comhan-saig,* a common hoard for plunder that mythic warriors secreted in its hills. Warriors like Bridei Mak Morn, who raided Hadrian's Wall during the Pictish Wars. Sometime before Glencoe, a MacDonald found one of those ancient caches—a silver skull with a medallion fused to its forehead. The Hoard was hidden in the cottage of a lower clansman to keep it safe, the belief being that raiders would ransack only the home of the chief. The Hoard was still there before Glencoe, but not after."

"So one of the Campbells stole it?"

"That's the allegation."

"Do you believe the legend?"

MacKissock grinned. "Let me tell you another story about the massacre. During the slaughter, a mother from Inverrigan tried to hide with her child and a dog under a bridge over the burn of Allt-na-Muidhe. The crying of the child was heard by the Campbells, and a soldier was sent to kill it. Beneath the bridge, he found the mother holding her tartan over the child's mouth to stifle its cries. Taking pity on them, the soldier ran his bayonet through the dog, then returned to his leader with blood on its blade. 'That's not human blood,' said the leader angrily. 'Kill the child, or I'll kill you.' Back under the bridge went the man, and he drew his dirk and cut the little finger from one of the boy's hands. Smearing that blood on his bayonet, the soldier returned to pass muster."

"How did the leader know it was dog's blood? Would a living child with a severed finger not be screaming at the top of its lungs?"

"Could be the tale is a result of too many drams. And what about the sequel?

"Many years later, an old soldier sought refuge at a cottage for the night. Around the fire, he regaled his host with military tales. When asked what was the worst sight he'd seen, the soldier answered, 'The Massacre of Glencoe.' 'I'll make an end of him in the morning,' his host said later while the soldier slept, and come next day asked him to tell of Glencoe. The soldier described how he'd saved a crying child, and his host held up his hand, which was missing his little finger. The two men parted friends."

"I see," said DeClercq.

"Scots like their whisky, and Scots spin yarns, so there are many tall tales about Glencoe."

"The Hoard never surfaced?"

"No," said MacKissock. "Could be that it never existed, or that the thief feared the MacDonalds would demand it back. They'd have had the support of other clans, for the massacre of Highland hosts drew condemnation. Could be that other Campbells didn't know the thief took it, which would explain their belief the myth is a figment. All we have is the legend, and facts that seem to support it."

"Play devil's advocate," said DeClercq.

"Whose head was it that became the silver skull? A legend grows in retelling, as did this one. Supposedly a MacDonald copied out the words that were etched into the medallion, and though the original record is gone, it's said those words were Antigonus Severus, Cohors I Tungrorum Milliaria. I find it a bit far-fetched that rural Scots had a copy of the Latin biography of Constantius Chlorus. And since that is the only classical text to mention Antigonus, where did the words come from if not the Hoard?"

"What was on the medallion?"

"Stonehenge, they say."

"Would seventeenth-century Scots recognize it?"

"Probably. There are stone circles all through the Highlands, and what with James and William fighting for both thrones, Scots were back and forth between Argyll and London."

"Who made the medallion?"

"Druids, I would think. And Antigonus took it from them when he detoured to Stonehenge to quash the revival of the Druidic cult."

"Then Bridei took it from him."

"To Glencoe."

"Where a Campbell took it from a MacDonald."

"To God knows where."

Somerled Campbell flashed through DeClercq's mind again.

"What would the Hoard be worth today?"

"Priceless," said MacKissock, "if it does what the legend maintains."

"Which is?"

"Solves the secret of Stonehenge."

A class must have let out, for there was the tramp, tramp, tramp of feet along the hall.

"Is that possible?"

"That the Hoard solves the secret of Stonehenge? I don't see why not, from what we know of Druids. Britain was the main center of Druidic learning. They spent up to twenty years training on the holy island of Mona, which we know as Anglesey, off the north coast of Wales, where they studied astronomy and the lore of the gods. Druids were shamans, priests, poets, judges, doctors, philosophers and prophets to the Celts. The moon was worshiped by Druids as the measure of time. The sun was worshiped by Druids as the source of light and heat. Megaliths like Stonehenge were built centuries be-

fore the Druids came to Britain, but given the focus of
their religion, does it not seem likely that the relics held
a powerful psychic attraction for them? And if they, too,
used the temples of the sky for rituals, is it not likely that
they fathomed the astronomical significance of them?"

"What's the secret?" asked DeClercq.

"That's one question too many. If I knew, I'd be a
very famous man. The only answer I know comes from
Lord Byron's poem: 'The Druids' groves are gone—so
much the better: Stone-Henge is not—but what the devil
is it?' "

Faust

Shipwreck Island, Washington State

The next call from Donella came as Mephisto was storing Fitzroy Campbell's burnt bones in a compartment of the display case next to the one in which his father had stored the burnt bones they had gathered during that fateful tour of the megalithic sites around Britain.

"He went to see a classics man at UBC."

"Good, he took the bait."

"I came back to Special X to await his return. And while I was waiting and watching, guess who arrived in a cab?"

Yes, thought Mephisto. A worthy adversary.

He punched off the cellphone and placed it on his desk, then returned to his collection of burnt bones. As he fingered the grisly relics from the ancient stone circles, he could feel in his bones the elusive knowledge for which he had bartered his soul to the Devil, to Mephistopheles.

His mind journeyed back. . . .

"Percurrimus foedus cum morte et cum inferno fecimus pactum! Isaiah 28:15!" thundered the priest, waving a

sheet of paper in the pulpit high above the boys held prisoner in the school chapel. " 'We have signed a treaty with death and with hell we have made a pact!' This pact you see in my hand!"

The eyes of the boys seated in the pews in their green school uniforms locked on the blasphemous covenant with the Evil One.

The preacher craned over the pulpit like a vulture going for meat.

"The Evil One hungers for human souls like *yours!*" he warned, spittle spraying from his pursed, thin lips. "Every Christian soul into which he can sink his talons is a triumph in the war he has waged against God and us ever since he was expelled from his high seat in heaven above!"

Up shot a finger.

"He wants *you,* boys! Have no doubt about that! He will offer you knowledge above that granted to ordinary men! He will offer you power that encroaches on that of God himself! He will offer you wealth beyond greed, the forty pieces of silver that sent Jesus to the cross!" A thumb crooked at the stained glass behind him. "He will offer you fornication with *women . . .*" There were no females in this exclusive school for young gentlemen who were underfoot at home and boarded here year-round, and the priest spat the word *women* as if it equated with sin.

"And what he will demand you pledge in return will be your body and soul! Oh, you may think that a bargain at the time! Buy now, pay later! Live for today! But is eternal damnation in the flames of hell a price you can afford to pay *forever* after the Devil comes seeking his due?

"And come he *will,* boys!

"He always does . . ."

Could there be any damnation worse than this? Days and nights spent trapped in this hell of a school, each lesson slanted toward salvation through God, redemption through Christ and deliverance by living the good life according to the Bible. Every Sunday spent listening to this fire-and-brimstone asshole of a preacher drone on and on and on about the rocky roads to hell that his "boys" were in danger of treading.

"Faust! You remember Faust from Marlowe and Goethe in literature?"

The literature teachers in the front pew nodded.

"Faust! You remember Faust from Berlioz and Gounod and Liszt in music?"

The music teachers in the front pew nodded.

"And why have so many great men retold the tale of Faust? Because it is a warning of damnation every human must heed! Faust sought to know everything there was to know, so he pledged his body and soul to Mephistopheles 'He who does not like light,' from the Greek, boys—in return for supreme knowledge and sorcerer's power! Twenty-four years later, Mephisto came for his due. . . ."

The priest pronounced it Mephe*ee*sto, which made it sound Spanish or something.

Mephi*ii*sto, thought the boy.

I like that name.

And decided that he would be Mephisto from then on.

"The Devil came for Faust at midnight!" dramatized the priest. "A fearsome wind shrieked around his house! A whistling and hissing like that of a legion of snakes was heard! 'Help! Murder!' Faust wailed, but none dared go to him! Come dawn, his mangled body was found on the dung heap in the yard! His room was swimming in blood, brains and teeth, and his eyeballs were stuck to one wall!"

That, thought the boy, I would like to see.

Again the priest waved the sheet of paper in the air, then donned a pair of glasses to read it aloud, like a town crier announcing the approach of rats infected with the plague.

" 'My lord and master Lucifer, I acknowledge you as

my god and prince; and promise to serve and obey you while I live. And I renounce the other god and Jesus Christ, the saints, the Roman Church and all its sacraments, and all prayers by which the faithful might intercede for me; and I promise to do as much evil as I can and to draw all others to evil.'

"The Evil One used to demand that such pacts be written in blood, for blood delivers man's life energy into his demonic clutches! *This* is the pact Urbain Grandier made in blood; it was produced against him at his trial in 1634 for seducing the nuns of Loudun to worship Satan, the reply to which was *formal* acknowledgment by the Devil, signed with his many names—Satan, Beelzebub, Astaroth, Lucifer, Leviathan, Meph-*eee*sto,written *backward,* and promising him a life of *carnal* delights for twenty years, after which he would join the Devil in *hell!*"

Spittle flew free.

"Would *you* sign this pact, boys?

"Many would!

"For knowledge? Power? Money? *Fornication?*

"These days the Devil has new names and he'll take *verbal* pacts, but he's still *out* there . . ."

The finger shot at the chapel door.

" . . . waiting for *you!* His followers are everywhere, hoping to draw you in, just as they were there to see Urbain Grandier burned *alive* at the stake, groveling on the ground afterward to recover his damned ashes and bones . . ."

Burnt bones, thought the boy.

". . . as profane talismans!"

The priest wiped his brow.

The priest sipped holy water.

Saving young sinners was exhausting work.

Now that he had ranted and raved for God, he would ease into his touchy-feely mode, sucking up to the boys to bring them into the fold.

Salvation.

Redemption.

Deliverance.

The boy tuned him out.

Those were concepts that held no damn interest for him.

Instead, he focused on the stained-glass window in the chancel around the pulpit. Jesus Christ hung nailed to the cross, bleeding from his palms, chest and feet. Scrolled beneath were his words of absolution: "Father, forgive them, for they know not what they do."

Bullshit, thought the boy. They know what they do. They're out to civilize the world and you got in their way.

He wished he could have been there to watch Jesus writhe, savoring every nuance of Christ on the cross, a torture being enjoyed by the Roman at his feet, a Roman with dark hair in a widow's peak, dark eyes sunken like black pits, his dark face narrowed by his V of a beard. Pleased to meet you, thought the boy, conjuring up that satanic hit by the Rolling Stones.

"You were there?" he whispered.

The stained-glass Roman sneered.

"Sympathy for the Devil," murmured the boy.

Slowly, the far-flung pieces of his life fell into place. His mother had abandoned him a year after birth, having tired of trailing his father around the world on dusty digs, preferring the pampered life of the wife of a man who *dealt* in ancient artifacts, a man who refused to raise the child of another man. So she had left both her husband and her son for the champagne-and-caviar crowds of London and New York. The education his single parent had given him was one in the mysterious realms of pagan cults: the prehistoric painters of the Lascaux caves in France, Assyria's Cult of the Sacred Tree, Egypt's Cult of the Dead, the Essenes' Cult of the Dead Sea Scrolls, Greco-Roman orgies of Dionysian and Bacchanalian rites, the Minoans' Cult of the Minotaur, and the Druids' Cult of the Wicker Man. From dig to dig, the two of them had delved deep into sacrifice rituals and death, the boy's morbid interest twisting into obsession and compulsion, culminating in that odyssey of burnt bones. To think he had sacrificed *that* for this . . .

Yes, he should warn his father. And yes, he should save his life. But he was struck dumb by a compulsion to know how far blood would spurt from his father's throat.

With Dad dead, would they force his mother to take back her fatherless son?

Well, take him back she had, only to warehouse him here—out of sight, out of mind, swill that champagne, bitch. And to think he sacrificed sacrifice for self-righteous shit like this; no wonder people were quitting churches in droves, abandoning Jesus for mysticism, materialism and New Age ways, because life without end in this crap would *bore* you to death.

"Would you *sign this pact, boys?*

"Many would!

"For knowledge? Power? Money? Fornication?

"These days the Devil has new names and he'll take verbal *pacts, but he's* still *out there . . ."*

The finger shot at the chapel door.

" . . . waiting for you!"

No, asshole, thought the boy. The Devil's in here.

The stained-glass Roman sneered at Jesus nailed to the cross.

If you're going to do it, do it right.

"The Evil One used to demand that such pacts be written in blood . . ."

Even as a boy, Mephisto was an antiquary.

Sitting in the pew at the back of the chapel, he withdrew from his pocket his Swiss Army knife, the knife his father had given him to gently scrape earth off the burnt bones they found in the stone circles, and jabbed the point of a blade into his palm.

The priest prattled on as the boy bared the arm of his punctured hand. With the tip of the blade used as a pen and the blood in his palm as ink, he dipped to write a pact on the skin of his forearm: "My lord and master Mephisto, I acknowledge you as my god and prince. . . ."

In for a penny.

In for a pound.

The pact he had sealed with the Devil was for all four: knowledge, power, money *and* fornication.

The money came first.

All through school, he'd thought about how he would kill his mother. Out of sight, out of mind, swill that champagne, bitch. He would build a room of glass in which to cage her, stark naked and basted with champagne to sweeten her skin as sweet as could be, then in would go a horde of rats to feast ravenously on her, and when she screamed and pounded the glass while she was chewed to bits, there he would be on the other side, smiling at the bitch—*never* out of sight, *never* out of mind—until she smeared her blood as thick as night curtains around the glass.

Matricide.

What a sexy thrill.

The education he absorbed was as rich as cream. He went from that religious school to Yale, Cambridge, the Sorbonne and Florence, Italy, taking honors in all the fine arts. His mother's intention was that he would become a dealer for her husband, but the Devil had a blood pact to satisfy, so both his mother and her hump were killed in a ten-car pile-up on a German autobahn, and once the estates were settled, he was left sole heir.

The dealership brought him money.

The money fornication.

The sort of beauties who go for bucks and Romantic poetry murmured in their ears. Seducing them became a game with him. How debauched would they let the sex get before they chickened out?

Donella was a find.

A bottomless pit.

In May, the dealership had lured Malcolm Campbell to him. Campbell was a reclusive Scot who was forced by health to move from the Highlands to Florida. For sixty years his collecting obsession had centered on Glencoe, and now his mind was crumbling from old age, the main symptom of which was a paranoid delusion that the Clan MacDonald was out to butcher him for a letter. What he wished the antiquities dealer to do for him was negotiate a fair price with the rival clan, a price that included no attempt on his life, for this letter concerning the Hoard that was stolen from Glencoe.

Mephisto had done the deal.

Or so he had told Malcolm Campbell.

Fifty thousand dollars U.S. and no worry about his life, in exchange for the letter.

The money—a lie—was in the dealer's escrow account.

The paranoid old man gave him the letter.

Two days later, a threat fashioned by Mephisto came by return mail.

A piece of Campbell tartan soaked in blood, around which was a sheet of paper scribbled with the MacDonald war cry, *"Fraoch Eilean."* Next morning the old man was found face down in the sea.

Gone was his collection of Glencoe artifacts.

That collection, including the letter, was now in the library under this room.

Dated March 2, 1723, the letter was written by Somerled Campbell to his son, Roderick, on the occasion of the elder Scot's departure from Argyll; it explained where the Hoard he had seized as a trophy during the campaign at Glencoe was buried. Sealed and given to a clan relation to keep, the letter was to be handed to his son should Somerled die at sea on a trip around the islands of Northern Scotland.

At the bottom of the letter were three postscripts in different hands: Roderick Campbell to Kenneth, his son, in 1739; Kenneth Campbell to Lachlan, his son, in 1770; Lachlan Campbell to Callum, his son, in 1814.

From generation to generation, the Hoard had passed down, each father leaving directions on the birth of an heir to where the trophy was buried.

How and why the letter was left behind in Scotland when Callum Campbell emigrated here with his two sons wasn't explained, but somehow the artifact had entered the collection of Malcolm Campbell, and once it fell into Mephisto's hands . . .

The rest was history.

"Wherever there's a legend, son, hunt and you will find."

That letter had embarked Mephisto on this quest.

He could feel it in his bones . . .

The time was nigh to set the world right . . .

Once he had the knowledge . . .

Once he had the power . . .

Armageddon . . .

Götterdämmerung.

The Cult

Vancouver, British Columbia

Through binoculars, Donella watched the woman who got out of the cab approach the Tudor building that housed Special X. She recognized Jenna from the article Mephisto had pulled off the Internet. The woman dressed like a man.

Before this hunt was over, Donella vowed she would bring out the woman in Bond.

She would sic the Druids on her.

And give the cop the fucking of her life.

DeClercq returned to Special X from discussing the Hoard with Robson MacKissock to find a woman waiting in Security for him. Androgyny didn't detract from her attractiveness, shirt, tie and pinstripe suit fitting her lean figure, sand-colored hair cut short about an angular face devoid of make-up, the brightest cobalt eyes he'd ever seen. At her feet sat a briefcase.

"Chief Superintendent DeClercq?"

"Yes."

"Jenna Bond."

Extending her hand, the detective clasped his with a firm, dry grip.

"I called, but you had already left. I motorboated up. Spare a few minutes?"

"You want to discuss the Campbells?"

"I want to find Nick."

"In that case, I'll spare all the time it takes."

He cleared her through Security and led her up the stairs to his office on the second floor, motioning her to one of the chairs in front of the horseshoe desk. As she sat down, Jenna caught sight of the Strategy Wall, where stuck to the corkboard like jigsaw puzzles were a pair of side-by-side collages that visually overviewed the Campbell kidnappings. Photos. Maps. Forensic clues. Police reports. Statements . . .

DeClercq walked around and seated himself in the U of the desk on the antique chair topped with the crest of the North West Mounted Police. With the sunshine of this morning having arced away to the west, he pulled the chain on a banker's lamp to pool yellow on the leather. Nineteenth-century cozy was the ambience.

"May I be blunt?" Bond said.

"By all means."

"Until the Bureau moved in, this was my case. They took the file, usurped my office and shoved me out the door. *I* linked Fitzroy and Gavin Campbell through their family tree. *I* found out about the third tract of land. *I* was working the case with Nick until he got snatched. And dammit, I won't be shut out now."

Jenna hit the desk with the flat of her hand.

"Nick's kidnapping hits me hard. I lost my husband the same way. Don was with the DEA. Colombians snatched him and tortured him to death. I don't know why I blame myself, but I can't shake hearing his screams at night in my sleep. If I help find Nick, maybe I'll also find release, so please—*please*—let me work the case with you. Have you any idea what it's like to be tormented by phantom guilt?"

Jenna let out a sigh.

"Sorry," she said. "That's been building for hours and I—"

"Yes," said DeClercq.

Jenna blinked.

"Yes, I can work with you?"

"Yes, you can work with me, and yes, I do know how you feel. My job got my darling daughter, Jane, kidnapped and killed. I failed to save her, and blamed myself. It took forever for the guilt to fade, which happened only when a surrogate daughter entered my life. I understand what you're struggling with, and I've seen jurisdictional turf wars end in tragedy. That's how serial killers can slip through the net."

"Thanks," said Jenna. "To hell with the FBI."

"Now, now," said DeClercq. "Revenge is a dish best served cold. So let's bring the cold logic of our minds to solving this case."

Jenna opened her briefcase and stacked three files on the horseshoe desk.

"Two pairs of Nikes and one pair of Adidas grabbed Fitzroy Campbell on Orcas Island," she said. "They tore his house apart looking for something they didn't find, then carried him off in a boat that may still be on the sea. Later, Fitzroy's credit card was used to purchase gas in Anacortes and Blaine. Pump security cameras show a man in a jacket with a pointed hood. The hood hid his face."

"The vehicle?"

"A Jeep. Plate caked with mud."

"The credit card's a red herring," said DeClercq.

"Yeah, to keep us busy while the same two pairs of Nikes and pair of Adidas came up to grab Gavin Campbell on Mayne. They tore his house apart, too, again searching for something they didn't find, then took him away in two boats that were spied sailing south down Plumper Sound toward Boundary Pass."

"The *Bounding Main* and the *Faust*," said DeClercq.

"One man was spied on the *Bounding Main* and two on the *Faust*, all in rain slickers with pointed hoods. The hoods hid their faces, but the artist who saw them said he caught a glimpse of one, the skin of whom—this is important—he thought was colored *blue*."

"Yes," said DeClercq. "Blue is important."

"Having failed to find what they were looking for, the three scuttled the *Bounding Main* with Gavin aboard, hoping to squeeze the hiding place out of him. The trio left the sinking in the *Faust,* a Bayliner cabin cruiser that's twenty-eight feet long. The same boat was probably used to abduct Fitzroy."

"Any luck with the *Faust?*"

"No," said Bond. "You can put any name you want on a boat."

"Chances are it's changed by now. So we're looking for a Jeep and a Bayliner."

"If they're stolen from a summer home, it could be months before the owner reports them gone. Both may end up as red herrings, too."

"Let the FBI hunt for them."

"Fitzroy and Gavin Campbell are linked by clan and family. Where's the copy of the family tree I faxed to you?"

DeClercq stood up, rounded the desk and led Jenna to the Strategy Wall, where the fax straddled the line between the two collages:

> *Somerled Campbell, 1648–1723*
> *Roderick Campbell, 1702–1751*
> *Kenneth Campbell, 1739–1799*
> *Lachlan Campbell, 1770–1847*
> *Callum Campbell, 1814–1863*
> *Dugald Campbell, 1840–1916   Ewen Campbell, 1841–1913*
> *Scotland to Vancouver Island in May 1857*
> *New Caledonia*
> *John Campbell, 1865–1941   Roy Campbell, 1885–1953*
> *Fitzroy Campbell, 1924–   Gavin Campbell, 1923–*
> *William Campbell, 1958–*

Jenna tapped the center of the fax.

"The ancestor common to both Fitzroy and Gavin was Callum Campbell. He and his two sons, Dugald and

Ewen, emigrated from Scotland in 1857. According to Fitzroy's son, William, Callum selected *three* homestead sites for himself and his boys. All were positioned to capitalize on the Fraser gold rush of 1858, but the Pig War broke out the following year, preventing registration of land in the San Juans until the dispute was finally resolved in 1872. Callum drowned in a boat accident in 1863, and never got to register his homestead.

"Whatever the killers are searching for, I suspect it goes back to Callum Campbell. They believe he hid something valuable on his land, so first they tossed the homestead of his elder son, assuming Dugald, as oldest male heir, would have inherited. Fitzroy, the present owner, was carried away and tortured to make him sing, and when he failed to produce anything, the search shifted toward the homestead of Ewen, Callum's younger son. Torture failed to squeeze it from Gavin, too, but I suspect one of the Campbells mentioned the third tract of land, which the bad guys didn't know about before. Now it has become the focus of their search."

"Any idea where the third tract might be?"

"The Pig War didn't affect land in Canada north of Haro Strait, so if Callum's tract was up here, he could have registered it before he died. Ewen's homestead was in the Gulf Islands—strategically situated to capitalize on miners boating from Victoria to the Fraser River— so he filed for ownership right away. Dugald's homestead was in the San Juans—strategically situated to capitalize on miners coming up from Seattle—so he had to wait for the Pig War to end before he could file in Washington State. Callum didn't file for the same reason: because his tract was also in the San Juans—"

"On a route to the Fraser River."

"On a route *back* from the Fraser River, too. So my bet is that the something being searched for is a hoard of gold."

"Silver, Jenna," said DeClercq. "It's silver, not gold."

Her eyes widened.

"You know what it is!"

"A silver skull, to be exact."

He recounted his discussion with Robson MacKissock at UBC, then summed up: "The search is for the silvered skull of Antigonus Severus, fused to which is a Druid medallion purporting to solve the mystery of Stonehenge. Hoarded by Picts at Glencoe and found by the MacDonalds, it was stolen from them by a Campbell during the massacre of 1692. Someone for some reason fingered Somerled Campbell as the thief—perhaps he ransacked the cottage in which the Hoard was secreted—prompting whoever's behind the kidnappings here to trace the family tree to Callum and his sons."

"You think there's a mastermind behind these three thugs?" Jenna said.

"I know there is," the Mountie replied, uncovering the e-mail hidden on the third section of the corkboard, which was for Nick's collage.

"Holdback evidence?"

"I trust you," he said.

Jenna read the message.

"Mephisto!" she exclaimed. "That's the brand name of shoe pri . . . shoe *impressions* found around tire tracks where Nick was grabbed."

"And the name of the devil to whom Faust sold his soul."

"*Faust* was the boat with the *Bounding Main*."

"Someone is playing a deadly game with us. Whoever this Mephisto is, he came searching for the Hoard under the false belief that Callum Campbell had settled *two* tracts of land. If the Hoard descended secretly from Somerled to Roderick to Kenneth to Lachlan and then to Callum Campbell, would he not have brought it from Scotland to the West Coast when he emigrated in 1857? If so, surely he hid it on his land. And since he died in an accident within six years, wouldn't his tract devolve to Dugald, his elder son? But what if he, never expecting to die so soon, had yet to tell both sons about the

Hoard? Might it not still be hidden on Dugald's land, unknown to the present heir, Fitzroy Campbell?"

"But it wasn't."

"No," said DeClercq. "The same way the MacDonalds' Hoard wasn't kept in the home of the chief. So Mephisto wondered—I'll bet my Stetson—if Callum had hoarded it on the land of his *younger* son. The gas credit card was used to keep you busy while his three henchmen searched the other tract. Failure again, so down sank Gavin, and only then did Mephisto learn of Callum Campbell's *third* tract of land."

"It fits," said Bond.

"So what did Mephisto do?"

"With so many cops involved by then on both sides of the border, it was too dangerous for him to hunt for the third tract of land, and no red herring would blind us again, so the only alternative left was to force *us* to find it for him."

"And what better way than to grab a cop and cut a piece from him, letting us know the consequences of not finding the Hoard?"

"Is Mephisto one of the three?"

"I doubt it," said DeClercq. "I get the feeling he works through other people. The same way Charlie Manson sent his Family out. We know he has three henchmen. And a femme fatale."

"Mephisto sent his henchmen to grab Nick. Two wore the same Nikes they'd worn to kidnap the Campbells, but the third switched Adidas for Mephistos so we'd connect Nick's abduction with the Campbells and the e-mail. But why all the mystery about . . ."

Jenna tapped the message on the corkboard:

? ? ? ?
Antigonus Severus.
306 A.D.
Cohors I Tungrorum Milliaria.
Hadrian's Wall.

Trash can 13, 4900 block Cambie.
Your move.
Mephisto.

"Why not just come out and say what he wants?"
"Because he needs to know if we're up to the job."
"A psychopath," said Bond.
"And a megalomaniac. Who now has all the resources of the Mounted Police, the FBI and the San Juan County sheriff working for him."
"If only we could test your theory."
"We can," said DeClercq.
Returning to his desk and booting up his computer, he dispatched a reply to the historians' bulletin board in cyberspace:

Antigonus Severus. 306 A.D.
Hadrian's Wall.
The Hoard.
The Skull.
And Callum Campbell.
Your move.

Could there be two more different cops than Robert DeClercq and Hank Bond? To keep punks scared and potential perps in line, her dad had been tough as nails on the outside, while on the inside Hank was a warm and loving man. He was not a thinker, but Hank got the job done. DeClercq seemed to be her father turned inside out. No threatening aura to anyone, yet she sensed a core of tempered steel within. Definitely a thinker, fit to tackle the hardest case.

She hoped to impress him.

"It's a cult," she stated.

DeClercq glanced up from his computer with renewed interest. "Run with it," he said.

"What sort of psycho are we dealing with? A psycho who kills for the secret of Stonehenge? The secret must be a ritual, and ritual is the focus of every cult. The artist who spied the boats in Plumper Sound thought the face he glimpsed was colored blue. Your reaction to his impression was Yes, blue is important.—If I remember my history right, didn't ancient Britons dye their skin blue? Put it all together and what we've got is a cult of modern Druids."

"*If* the face was blue."

"It was blue all right." Bond placed her hand on the files on his desk. "Not only are these hooded thugs kidnappers, but they also gang-raped three women on the San Juan Islands. In each case the MO was the same. Night saw three men land in a boat to attack a single female, two holding her arms and legs while the third man raped her. Then they switched places. All wore hooded jackets and each face was blue."

Jenna was pleased to see DeClercq eye the files as if they were the Hoard.

She didn't realize that he didn't see them as files.

Instead, what he saw were three more crime sites on Rossmo's geoprofile.

———

They were drinking coffee and discussing the three rape files when DeClercq's computer advised the Mountie that he had e-mail.

Robert checked his cyberspace mailbox.

With his password entered, he was informed that one new message was in the box.

Clicking on it showed this on-screen:

Countdown starts.
Each night I cut a piece.
Until you find the Hoard
I keep cutting.

Devil Woman

Shipwreck Island, Washington State

Wop-wop doodly wop, a wop-wop.

The El Dorados.

"At My Front Door."

God, how the burnt stump of his severed wrist hurt, hurt, hurt . . .

Doo wop, doo wadda.

The Turbans.

"When You Dance."

Anything to take his mind off the unrelenting pain, pain, pain . . .

Do-da wadda, do-da wadda do.

The Jewels.

"Hearts of Stone."

He clung to the nonsense syllables of his favorite doo-wop songs, pulling the background chants out of his subconscious to play on the juke box of his overwrought conscious mind, struggling to link artists and songs to the indecipherable "blow harmonies" in a makeshift game of "Jeopardy" meant to quell dread and pain.

Ooh wah wah, ooh wah wah, chop chop chop chop.

The Impalas.

"Sorry (I Ran All the Way Home)."

"*Chop chop chop chop!* Bad choice," he groaned.

With his chopped arm still lashed to the chopping block, Nick sat slumped against the wall of his dank, dark cell, head pounding from the aftereffects of pento-

thal, raw throat constricted by the steel collar, charred
stump throbbing from the cut that cleaved his hand away
and the torch that cauterized his wrist so he didn't bleed
to death. What time it was and what day it was he had
no idea, for Nick had drifted in and out of consciousness,
pain shrinking awareness down to a desperate tug-of-
war with his mind for control of his body.

*Bomp ba-ba bomp, ba bomp ba bomp bomp, ba-ba
bomp ba-ba bomp, da dang da-dang dang, da ding-a-
dong ding.*

The Marcels.

"Blue Moon."

Pain was personified by the Devil Woman. An erotic
shiver had tingled her torso as the sword came thunking
down, quivering the tattoo etched into the flesh around
her naked groin and making the Sheela-na-gig shudder
as if in orgasm, too. What manner of woman came by
hacking a man apart? Pain had burned the image of that
demon into his mind. The glint in her eyes, which grew
brighter with each spurt of blood from him. The smile
of satisfaction as she picked up his severed hand. The
lustful laugh as she offered it to the headless Minotaur
with the bull's head under his arm. She moaned as he
used the hand's twitching fingers to grope her tattooed
breasts, while Nick cried out in excruciating pain. "Start
a new collection," she said throatily to the Devil Man.
"The first piece. With more to come."

The collector poked her with the hand to goose her
out into the hall. She returned with the flambeau torch,
which threw light in through the door.

"Burn, baby, burn," she said as she sizzled Nick's
wrist, the stench of cooked human meat filling his hell
cell.

Then they were gone.

Leaving him alone to scream, scream, scream . . .

Shoo doo'din shoo-bi-doo.

The Five Satins.

"In the Still of the Nite."

In the still of the night that was the darkness of his underground cell, pain incarnate returned with each throb of his charred flesh. The Devil Woman popped like a flashbulb at his mind's eye, an eye with no eyelid to shut her out, fading as an afterimage back to black while her mouth mimed the words "More to come." Then—*pop!*—she was back with the next jab of pain.

More to come . . .

More to come . . .

Pieces for the collector?

Oh, God, Nick thought. Push her away!

Dread consumed him like a flesh eating disease.

The irony of his predicament was not lost on Nick. "Have you never wished you could escape into the past?" he'd asked DeClercq that day the Chief and Katt were on the farm.

"H. G. Wells's *Time Machine.* Say you owned it. When in the past would you rather live? I'd go back to the fifties. The last great decade before homogenization. Doo-wop harmony and the birth of rock-and-roll. Music with melody, not too much angst and noise. What I have on Pender are all the things I crave. And life has no resale value, Chief."

Well, his trip into the past had ended here. These two psychos were into past lives, too, role-playing sex games from ancient times in which torturing him was the catalyst that got them off. Pender, the barn dance and doo-wop had sealed his fate, luring him into the web of the femme fatale, and she had convinced him forever that Don Juan got it wrong: "It does not matter what our specific fate is, as long as we face it with ultimate abandon." A load of shit, that. It mattered a hell of a lot. Slowly being cut to pieces was not the fate he relished facing with ultimate abandon.

No thanks, Don.

Throb . . .

Pop . . .

Devil Woman . . .

And oh, God, the pain!

What he required was morphine, and what he had was doo-wop. Only by occupying his mind with something else could he keep the image of pain incarnate at bay, so to escape from the fate that escaping into the past had wrought he escaped into the past.

Same game as *The Kiss of the Spider Woman,* except he was running *from* her.

When you are down in the dumps with the blues, how do you pull yourself out? For Nick, ever since he was a kid and had first played his mom's 45s, the surest pick-me-up was to get lost in doo-wop music. If it didn't put a smile on your face, you *did* have a heart of stone. Born of pop, gospel, blues, jazz and swing in the late forties and early fifties, doo-wop was innocent, joyous, romantic, simple, spiritual *fun.* The Drifters, the Platters, the Orioles, the Ravens, the Five Keys, the Cadillacs, the Penguins, the Moonglows . . . these groups established the basics and primed the pump, and soon every juvenile delinquent was into harmony. Bop till you drop, you cool cat. The best place to practice if you didn't own a street corner in Harlem, Brooklyn or the Bronx was the school bathroom, the echo being good. The goal was to impress the chicks in the neighborhood. Hey, you might get laid. Out front was the rumbling, prominent "walking bass." In back was the tenor, or "soaring falsetto." And in between, doing "blow harmony" to take the place of one or more musical instruments, were several doo-wop dudes harmonizing the nonsense syllables. Take the name of a bird or big-finned car, and you were launched.

Bom bom, di-bi-di-bi-di-bah, ri-bi-dah, ri-bi-dah, ri-bi-dah, ri-bi-dah, doo bop shoo bah, bom bom di-bi-di-bi-dip.

The Five Discs.

"Never Let You Go."

Never let me go, thought Nick. Another bad choice.

Does every route through this labyrinth lead to my dead end?

Transferred to tape for playing in the deck of his rusty Chevy Impala, doo-wop from his mom's 45s was the sure cure for Nick's teenage blues. Fingers bopping the steering wheel and voice box chanting along, Nick would cruise onto Highway 1 and gun it up the valley, heading for Hope in the mountains, a hundred miles inland, while the Crows and the Chords and the Wrens and the Clovers and Dion & the Belmonts sh-bopped and oodly-poppa-cowed his cares away.

Try it, folks.

It's better than booze or Prozac.

Though it may not be strong enough for this ordeal Nick was going through.

He wondered what his mom's 45s were worth now. The concept of collecting is endemic to doo-wop, for as one aficionado so accurately put it, doo-wop collectors are "the most pedantic, opinionated group of anal-retentive compulsive/obsessive whack jobs on the planet." Record labels were small—Jubilee, Old Town, Red Robin, Rama, Whirlin' Disc, Chance, Gee—and a single 45 might sell for $18,000 U.S. Not bad for music as primitive and unschooled as it gets, unless the school john was used as an echo chamber. One collector found a box with twenty-five copies of an obscure single. Did he share his find with other doo-wop whack jobs? No, he destroyed twenty-four of the records so he would have the only, and therefore ultra-valuable, copy.

Collectors! thought Nick.

Ice wormed down his spine.

Compulsive/obsessive whack jobs.

Did that not say it all?

Start a new collection . . .

The first piece . . .

Pop!

The Devil Woman.

More to come . . .

Pieces for the collector?
Push her away.
What was that?
From the hall?
Wind off the sea?
Boom boom boom, bang bang bang.
The Genies, thought Nick.
"Who's That Knocking?"
Knock, knock . . .
Was that for real?
Flicker, flicker . . .
Torchlight under the door.
Click, snick, squeeeeeeak . . .
The door creaked open.
All the doo-wop ever harmonized wouldn't push her
away.
"Hello, lover. Remember me?"
The black silhouette of the Devil Woman was framed
by the flickering flames of torches burning in brackets
across the hall behind her. Wind along the tunnel blew
blow harmony, keening like doo-wop from the grave. It
animated her wild hair into Medusa snakes and plastered
the folds of her tartan to the curves of her stripper's
figure. The light seemed to follow her into the dungeon,
where Nick blinked against its glare, then crept across
the front of her as she turned toward the cowering form
chained to the wall. Her face was dyed blue. One breast
was bare. Tattoos whirled out and back from its nipple.
Her other breast was hidden by pleats that were over
one shoulder and gathered at her waist to fashion a
Highland kilt. As short as a miniskirt, the kilt ended
high on the thigh, below which her long legs straddled
Nick like the Colossus of Rhodes.
Another silhouette.
Framed by the door.
His shadow in the dungeon.
Watching them.

Gripped in one fist beside the kilt of the Devil Man was a keen-edged dirk.

"Look up under my skirt," ordered the Devil Woman.

Nick averted his eyes.

"You don't find me attractive?"

Nick didn't move.

"What does a Scot wear under her kilt?"

Nick didn't answer.

"I'll make it easy for you," Donella said, and she slipped the pleats from her shoulder so they could fall to her waist, then unclasped the silver pin in the kilt and cast aside the tartan.

"Look!" she commanded.

Nick shied away, but the chain leashed to his neck clinked, and the chain cuffed to his wrist clanked, and the elbow bracket and stump clamp held his wounded arm fast.

Mephisto entered and passed Donella the dirk.

One long leg, then the next, stepped into the wide V formed by Nick's spread-eagled ankles, which were lashed to rings on the ground. With her knees together, the Devil Woman squatted in the V.

"Look!" she repeated, pricking the sharp point of the dirk into the edge of his eye and guiding his face around with it until he faced her. "It's the last pussy you're going to see."

Sweat beaded from every pore as Nick was forced to look.

Squint lines radiated out from her sadistic glare, pinching the woaded features of what had obviously once been an alluring woman. The tattoos marring her breasts swirled into phallic designs engraved down her belly to her groin, around which was etched the grotesque effigy of the Sheela-na-gig. It was as if someone had used her flesh as an obscene doodle pad.

"Look away," Donella said, "and I'll put out your eye."

She lowered the dagger to Nick's waist to cut away

his pants. The razor-sharp tip raked down his right leg to his cinched ankle, trailing a thin red line of blood behind, then it repeated the slow slash along his other limb. Chains clinked and clanked as Nick tried to cower away, and though it was cool in the smuggling cell from a breeze off the sea, sweat ran from him in rivulets squeezed out by fear.

"You don't find me attractive?"

Donella's blue lips pouted for him.

"Look," she said, clenching the dirk in her teeth like a pirate so she could strip the cut-out portion of his pants away to bare his groin. With one hand gripping his cock, the other grasping his balls, Donella embarked on a compulsive/obsessive whack job of a different kind, smirking bluishly around the silver steel of the dagger blade.

Still squatting in the V of Nick's now naked legs, Donella spread her knees wide before his captive stare, opening the Sheela-na-gig, which appeared to open her for him.

Look he did, and what he saw was an ugly, masklike skull face, with bug eyes and a big nose and a lewd mouth, tattooed around her navel. The large head surmounted a stout body with skeletal ribs, and its splayed legs were etched down Donella's thighs. Its arms reached behind and under the tattoo to spread its huge vagina wide with both hands. Because its genitalia were engraved around hers, the Sheela-na-gig, Celtic goddess of creation and destruction, seemed to spread Donella's sex wide, too. In displaying a fantasy of unlimited sexual license, combined with a cosmic reminder of the awesome and intimate birth mystery, the overt sexual nature of the image captured male fear-fantasies of the devouring mother.

Pentothal was a truth drug.

Traces remained in Nick.

Fight though he tried, psycho-sexual barbs had him hooked.

Like a Venus flytrap, Donella closed her thighs, a

tease that curled a wicked smile above the blade, while her hands below jacked Nick incessantly. Then her thighs snapped open, jerking him erect.

"I need a piece of you," Mephisto said.

The hand that had gripped Nick's balls pulled the dagger from Donella's teeth.

"Do it," said Mephisto.

A shiver shuddered the Devil Woman.

The cut was a slow and methodical one, sawing back and forth through Nick's trembling flesh while his cry of pain and terror echoed from the cell, then along the hall and up to the root cellar, where, barely audible, it escaped into the night. Above, the Stone Circle was awash in moonlight, within which the Druid cultists were weaving another Wicker Man.

Moriarty

Dawn had yet to smear the sky beyond the windows of his office at Special X.

DeClercq stood before his Strategy Wall, studying the overview of the Mephisto case.

Here at the edge of the web, he sensed the slight tremors . . .

———

He never seemed to have the time to read the books he desired anymore, but when he was young, DeClercq had consumed more fiction than food. *Kidnapped,* "The Body Snatcher," *The Strange Case of Dr. Jekyll and Mr. Hyde, Treasure Island*—Stevenson had been an early favorite author. What struck DeClercq as ironic about this case was that it made him feel as if he were living a warped retelling of those classic Scottish yarns.

Sir Arthur Conan Doyle.

Another Scot.

Professor Moriarty.

Another theme?

It was Dr. Stanley Holyoak who made a Holmesian of his surrogate daughter, Katt. They were trapped together on Deadman's Island during the Ripper case.

A Colonel Sanders look-alike and the foremost Sherlockian this side of the Atlantic, Holyoak had informed Katt that "Sir Arthur Conan Doyle penned four novels and fifty-six stories about the great detective and his friend Dr. Watson. This work we call the canon. By 'we' I mean Sherlockians, readers who gather in scion groups far and wide. Sleuths like the Baker Street Irregulars in New York, and the Northern Musgraves in Britain, and the Red-Headed League in Australia . . ."

And the Reichenbach Falls here.

A scion group of two.

Katt and Robert DeClercq.

Sherlock Holmes is sure to remain the most popular character in the history of fiction. Fanatical Holmesians think Doyle's fantasy world more real than reality. The Katt who moved in to live with him after the Ripper ordeal was a recent convert to the joys of Sherlockiana fandom, so the first thing she did was remodel his home ("Trust me, Bob. You'll like it") to match the sitting room at 221B Baker Street.

They found the Holmes and Watson chairs at an estate auction, the Holmes for her ("I'm more flamboyant") and the wingbacked Watson ("staid and dependable") for him. With his chair left and her chair right of the hearth, Katt proceeded to set-decorate the mantel, using a jack-knife to transfix unanswered correspondence to the wood; a photo of Kate, DeClercq's first wife, as a stand-in for Irene Adler, who would always be "*the* woman" to Holmes; and touches like a cocaine bottle by the looking-glass, below which hung a Persian slipper stuffed with shag tobacco and a coal scuttle filled with cigars.

"I need your revolver," Katt had said, "to add the final touch. Holmes adorned the wall with a crown and a script *V.R.*—for *Victoria Regina*—punched out by firing a box of cartridges."

"Let's compromise on *cardboard* bullet holes."

"Bob, where's your sense of verisimilitude?"

"That's it," he said.

Katt frowned.

"Look it up."

There, on a winter's night—with wind howling in across English Bay to hurl rain at the ocean side of the house while they were snug within, Napoleon (the dog) and Catnip (the cat) dozing in front of the fire—a meeting of the Reichenbach Falls might occur. The two of them, Katt in the Holmes chair with *The Annotated Sherlock Holmes* open in her lap, him in the Watson chair enjoying a glass of ruby red after-dinner port, would return to those days of yesteryear, when "family entertainment" meant exactly what it says.

Families entertaining.

Communing and interacting.

Not *being* entertained.

Like bumps on a log.

One was creative.

The other led to dysfunction.

" 'He is the Napoleon of Crime, Watson,' " Katt read from "The Final Problem" in her best Sherlockian voice. She (and he) of course was referring to the most deep-dyed of all the villains with whom the great detective ever matched wits: Professor James Moriarty.

Moriarty, thought DeClercq.

Megalomaniac.

Here, standing before the Strategy Wall at Special X, trying to fathom this villain that *he* was up against, DeClercq, as he had that night in the Watson chair and in his youth when he was first introduced to the canon, formed a picture of Professor Moriarty in his mind.

The most dangerous man in London in the 1880s, the greatest schemer of his time and the controlling brain behind every devilry in what was then the foremost city in the world, Moriarty was—to hear Sherlock Holmes—"a genius, a philosopher, an abstract thinker" and "a man of good birth and education, endowed by Nature with a phenomenal mathematical faculty," gone astray because "a criminal stain ran in his blood."

Crime was definitely the professor's forte. All he did was plan; his henchmen did the rest. With never any link to connect him to the crime, thanks to his deep organizing power, which stood forever in the way of the law, he was never in danger of being caught, was never so much as suspected. Henchmen might be nabbed, but not Moriarty, whose profits from forgery, robbery, murder and such filled his six bank accounts. Moriarty pervaded London, yet nobody knew he was there until the professor was flushed out by Sherlock Holmes. Just as the slightest tremors at the edge of a web tell you a spider lurks at the center, so Holmes sensed the presence of a malignant brain.

Moriarty.

Mephisto.

DeClercq sensed a similar malignancy here.

Megalomania.

A mental illness marked by delusions of greatness.

A compulsive obsession to do extravagant or grand things.

The arch-criminal.

Finally, Holmes and Moriarty met face to face. The professor was tall and thin, with rounded shoulders. He had gray hair and a forehead that domed out in a curve. His eyes, puckered and blinking, were sunk deep in his pale white head. His solemn voice created an impression of dignity and asceticism, which was somewhat marred by an unpleasant mannerism: his face protruded forward and oscillated from side to side in an unsettling reptilian fashion.

Until they met face to face, that was how DeClercq would imagine Mephisto.

Reptilian.

And cold-cold-blooded.

"You crossed my path on the 4th of January," noted Moriarty. "On the 23rd you incommoded me; by the middle of February I was seriously inconvenienced by you; at the end of March I was absolutely hampered in my plans; and now, at the close of April, I find myself placed in such a position through your continual persecution that I am in positive danger of losing my liberty. The situation is becoming an impossible one."

Reichenbach Falls saw that rivalry come to a plummeting climax in 1891. "London has become a singularly uninteresting city since the death of the late lamented Professor Moriarty," Holmes would complain. Reading the canon as a boy, young Robert grasped the boredom of the great detective, for he, too, fantasized about matching wits some day with a Moriarty.

Had that day arrived?

And was he outwitted?

There was a time when megalomaniacs were the stuff of fiction. Moriarty inspired the evil Dr. Fu Manchu. A tall and slender Chinese with a brow like Shakespeare's and a face like Satan's, Fu Manchu wore a long black robe with a silver peacock embroidered on the front. His close-shaven skull was crowned by a black cap with a red ball, and his eyes—true cat green—were so piercing that they could be felt even when unseen. He wore no mustache—despite the Fu Manchu!—as it would interfere with this master of disguise. A man of cruel cunning and huge intellect, he not only held degrees from three Western universities and gleaned the occult secrets of the sects of the East—Dacoits, Thugs, Phansigars and Hashishin—but also had every tong in Asia at his command to employ in his quest to become emperor of the world.

Too outlandish?

Probably.

But then came a guy named Hitler with this plan to conquer the world, a little man with a toothbrush stuck on his upper lip whose henchmen, bedecked in black with silver skulls and lightning bolts, strutted about in the most ridiculous stiff-legged way, with one arm flapping up palm down in salute. He was out to create this Third Reich that would last a thousand years, with a rather vicious theory on how to get rid of *Untermenschen* to create a master race.

Megalomania.

But still megalomaniacs seemed to remain the stuff of fiction, the sort of villain encountered by superspy James Bond. . . .

DeClercq wondered if Jenna took much ribbing about her name?

Probably.

Villains like Mr. Big in *Live and Let Die*, "head of the Black Widow Voodoo cult" and "the most powerful negro criminal in the world," who smuggles pirate bullion from Jamaica to the States to fund covert Russian operations in America. Villains like Sir Hugo Drax, a fanatical Nazi at one time and later such a loud-mouthed bully that even his best friends didn't like him, who corners the market in columbite to personally finance an atomic rocket for Britain called the Moonraker, the target of which isn't where it's supposed to be. Villains like Dr. No, Fu Manchu reincarnated, who lost his hands to the tongs in an all-night torture session, surviving a fatal shot to the chest because he was "the one man in a million who has his heart on the right side of his body." The torture session was an ordeal that made him obsessed with the achievement of power "to do unto others what had been done unto me, the power of life and death, the power to decide, to judge, the power of absolute independence from outside authority." Villains like Auric Goldfinger, an obsessive-compulsive collector if ever there was one, who yearns to be the richest man in history and has to rob Fort Knox to achieve his desire. Villains like Ernst Stavro Blofeld, a deep-dyed Moriarty and the head of the Special Executive for Counter-intelligence, Terrorism, Revenge and Extortion, SPECTRE for short, a brain who plots, then delegates the dirty work to expendable henchmen. A mastermind who schemes to loose germ warfare on the world in the form of fowl

pest, swine fever, Colorado beetle, anthrax and other
plagues.

Too outlandish?

Not anymore.

For we live in an age of doomsday cults devoted to
messiahs for the New Millennium.

Megalomaniacs.

Mephisto, thought DeClercq.

The Beatles wrote a song entitled "Helter Skelter"
about a playground slide. In it, the messiah Charles
Manson found inspiration for a war between the races,
which he would precipitate through murders intended to
look like the work of black militants. To that end, his
Family was sent out on killing sprees, and seven people,
including Sharon Tate, the pregnant wife of the director
of *Rosemary's Baby*, died like "pigs" in two slaughter-
houses of blood. On his arrest in 1969, the leader of the
cult maintained that he was the reincarnation of God,
Jesus and Satan.

The Reverend Jim Jones led twelve hundred faithful
from his People's Temple in San Francisco to his jungle
commune of Jonestown in Marxist Guyana so they could
be prepared for nuclear Armageddon. Jones, who imagined he was Lenin and adopted a Russian accent, suspected the CIA was poisoning his food. Loudspeakers
around the commune broadcast dire warnings of im-
pending attack, and raised the prospect of "revolution-
ary suicide." The predicted attack came in November
1978, when a U.S. congressman and four reporters arrived at Jonestown to look into a complaint that Americans were being held against their will. They were
executed at the airstrip when they tried to leave, and
the following day investigators flew in to discover more
than nine hundred corpses, many piled on top of one
another around the commune altar. A tub held the remains of a lethal cocktail mix of Kool-Aid, tranquilizers
and potassium cyanide. As few as two hundred had died

voluntarily. Most drank it at gunpoint or were shot. The messiah lay dead among his flock.

The Branch Davidian, formed in 1929 as an offshoot of the Seventh Day Adventists, founded its cult commune at Waco, Texas, in 1935. David Koresh assumed control in 1986 as the bearer of the final message of God. His messianic calling occurred in Israel, when he was chosen to fly to heaven and there was transformed into the apocalyptic "rider of the white horse." "I saw heaven opened, and behold a white horse; and he who sat upon him was called Faithful and True, and in righteousness he doth judge and make war" (Book of Revelation 19.11/12). To keep the outside world at bay until Koresh led his Branch Davidians to Israel for the Apocalypse, cult members stockpiled weapons at the Waco compound. The Apocalypse came sooner than expected, with a 1993 assault by seventy-six armed federal agents from the Bureau of Alcohol, Tobacco and Firearms, resulting in the shooting deaths of four feds and six cultists, a fifty-one-day stand-off played out on TV, and a final assault that led to cult-set fires and explosions that incinerated the messiah, his wives, his children and about eighty followers. Of the Four Horsemen of the Apocalypse, the pale horse carries Death.

Megalomaniacs.

Mephisto, thought DeClercq.

Born in the Belgian Congo, Luc Jouret later served as a paratrooper in Zaire, where he learned how to make delayed-action firebombs. In 1984 he founded the Temple of the Sun—Le Temple du Soleil—in Europe and Quebec to prepare for the Apocalypse. Obsessed with the winter solstice, Jouret persuaded his solarites that a bright light would blaze on the darkest night of the year, and that he, a time traveler, would raise them through death by fire to new spiritual life on a planet orbiting the star Sirius. In 1994 a glitch occurred. Two Quebec cultists named their son Emmanuel. Emanuelle was the name of the daughter of Jouret's partner, Joseph di

Mambro, and since Emanuelle was divinely conceived, Emmanuel must have been the Antichrist and had to be destroyed. The parents were stabbed and a stake was driven through the baby's heart, launching an early departure for Sirius. Fifty-three cultists donned robes in Switzerland and Quebec, laid on the ground with their feet pointing inward to form a star and let delayed-action firebombs blast them off. Jouret was gone, but others followed. The winter solstice of 1995 saw sixteen more leave for Sirius; in 1997 another five solarites followed.

Bo and Peep, Tiddly and Wink, Winnie and Pooh, the two had assumed many names worthy of James Bond (the superspy fought Bambi and Thumper in one of the films). She died in 1985, and he carried on gathering sheep into the fold for transport to a higher "evolutionary level." He was Marshall Herff Applewhite, and he lived in a mansion in Rancho Santa Fe, California, surrounded by a cult of androgynous neuters with close-cropped hair who wore identical shapeless black shirts with mandarin collars, sort of like all those followers of messiahs in Bondian films. Since sex was a no-no in the pursuit of immortality, males mimicked Applewhite by having their balls surgically removed. The higher level of existence they sought through suicide was evident in pictures, later found in the mansion, of an idealized, dome-headed alien like those seen in "The X-Files." Just as Jesus had to leave his corporeal body to move to the kingdom of Heaven, so members of Heaven's Gate—as this cult was called—would have to abandon their earthly "containers." Easter's coinciding with the appearance of the Hale-Bopp comet in the night sky of late March 1997 was the sign, for hidden in the tail of the comet was an alien spaceship with which the cult was to rendezvous. So thirty-nine men and women sedated themselves in groups, put smothering plastic bags over their heads and lay down ritually, on their backs with their arms at their sides, their faces and chests covered by diamond-shaped purple shrouds. Did they make the rendezvous? The truth is out there, folks.

Turning violence inward was one thing.

Turning violence outward was another.

The outward cults worried DeClercq the most in his quest to fathom Mephisto's megalomania.

Sex was not a no-no at the ashram of Bhagwan Shree Rajneesh. Bhagwan translates as "master of the vagina." At his spiritual headquarters near Bombay, rich Western drop-outs swapped their wallets for rose-colored robes, then were encouraged to chant mantras for enlightenment and shed those robes, romping nude on the beaches with fellow-travelers to engage in sex with as many partners as possible. Soon, local indignation had driven the cult of the Rajneeshis south to Poona, where meditation amid sex led to drug-running by acolytes, or sanyassins, to buy the Bhagwan a fleet of ninety Rolls-Royces, several aircraft and an arsenal. Hounded from India, he bought the Big Muddy Ranch at Antelope, Oregon, for six million dollars and renamed it Rajneeshpuram. Brainwashing, combined with hypnotism, controlled the cult, while a steady stream of females traipsed to the guru's bed, and henchmen cooked up various chemical and biological agents in laboratory vats. Cult members infiltrated the town council. A firebomb torched the office of investigating officials. Then, in September 1984, Rajneeshis sabotaged food in several restaurants by contaminating salad bars with salmonella bacteria so people would be too sick to vote against the cult. Seven hundred and fifty-one took ill. The Master of the Vagina was driven from the States, and died in India in 1990 of either poisoning or full-blown AIDS.

Megalomaniacs.

Japan is a nation with 180,000 registered cults. How many more are underground? One of them, Aum Shinri Kyo, the cult of the Supreme Truth, is committed through its messiah, Shoko Asahara, to world domination. Membership is ten thousand, and includes some of the brightest brains in Japan. Squat and partially blind, with long hippie-like hair and a dark beard, Asahara claims that he time-traveled to the year 2006 to speak to survivors of the Third World War between Japan and the United States, and that his mission is to bring that doomsday about to alter mankind's pattern of materialism. To escape divine retribution, cultists hand over their worldly possessions to the Master, then undergo the Blood Initiation Ceremony and drink the blood or semen of the guru to obtain enlightenment from his superhuman powers. His dirty bathwater is for sale for eight hundred dollars a liter. Cultists wear electrode caps wired to belt batteries for low-voltage brain shocks, which align their brain waves with the Master's. "I fully admit that my beliefs are crazy," writes the guru. "But sometimes it takes crazy beliefs to achieve perfect freedom and happiness." To that end, he established a sprawling compound in the foothills of Mount Fuji, with a fifteen-foot-high idol of the Hindu god Shiva, god of destruction, in its "sacred chapel," behind which was his lab for manufacturing sarin nerve gas.

In June 1994 seven people died in a city on the Japanese coast when sarin gas was released close to the homes of three judges trying a lawsuit against Aum. The next attack came on March 20, 1995, when cult scientists punctured bags of sarin gas with their umbrella tips on the Tokyo subway, killing twelve and sickening 5,500 in the capital city. A search of the cult compound exposed other plots. In 1992 the cult sent virologists to Zaire to gather cultures of Ebola virus to produce biological weapons. Another mission went to Belgrade to study work by Nikola Tesla on death rays, high-energy voltage and wave amplification, which cultists hoped could be used to cause earthquakes. In Russia, where the cult has thirty thousand members, negotiations were underway to purchase a nuclear warhead for fifteen million dollars. It's estimated that some three hundred people who annoyed the cult passed through a huge bone-grinding machine. Warned a Japanese official: "It was as if Asahara wanted to create Armageddon all on his own."

And then there was the Unorganized Militia here in North America, a loose cult of patriots linked together by the Internet, their doomsday scenario a mish-mash of right-wing Christianity in which the administration and the gun-control lobby and genetic mutation and ufos and secret military bases are all part of a grand conspiracy to destroy U.S. sovereignty and turn Americans into slaves in a bleak Orwellian superstate. "I present to you that the peaceful citizens of this nation are fully justified in taking whatever steps may be necessary, including violence, to identify, counterattack, and destroy the enemy. . . . You must prepare to fight and if necessary die to preserve our God-given right to freedom." *Booom!* went a building in Oklahoma City. Can you order anthrax through the mail? Oh, yes, and with the dawn of the year 2000, secret chambers in the Pyramid of Giza will open so Satan can ride out, and militiamen will be ready to stop him by blasting away.

Welcome to the Millennium.

The New Dark Age.

It was against this backdrop of doomsday cults that De-Clercq stood before his Strategy Wall and tried to grasp what sort of megalomania drove Mephisto and his Druidic cult to kidnap and torture three people to locate the silver skull. Even if the medallion revealed the Secret of the Stones, unlocking the maddening mystery that masked the purpose of Stonehenge, in no way did De-Clercq believe this case would end with the finding of a new Rosetta stone. If Mephisto was a megalomaniac of the caliber that led the cults of recent years, did he view the silver skull as a tool to accomplish some doomsday mission, in much the same way that the Rosetta stone was merely a tool in a much greater quest to decipher ancient Egyptian hieroglyphics?

What did Mephisto think was on the medallion?

And if what he thought was true, to what messianic purpose would he put the knowledge?

DeClercq had tracked a lot of psychos in his time, but none had instilled in the Mountie the same sense of unease as Mephisto. The name itself conjured worry in DeClercq, for there was more than a mad collector in this plot, a plot that a few decades back would have belonged in James Bond. Try to sell it as reality and you'd be a candidate for having your head examined. But now, against the backdrop of the cults of recent years, dismissing such madness as too wild a fiction to swallow would mean *you* became the one who should have your head examined for breaking with reality, the main symptom of psychosis!

You don't adopt the name of a devil unless devilry is your mission.

So what was Mephisto up to?

What?

What?

And why?

Ebola

Seattle, Washington State

With the clinical fascination of a spider watching prey die in its web, Mephisto sat morbidly still in his seat and tingled as, one by one, the victims of the virus crashed and bled out.

Bled out like sopping sponges clutched by the hand of Death.

So much blood.

The man in the nearest hospital bed was blind from blood filling his eyeballs; droplets of blood beaded on his eyelids as streams of blood weeping down his cheeks dripped from his chin. Turning toward Mephisto, he hung his head over the side of the bed and retched up black vomit that sloughed off the surface of his tongue as it spewed out. Next came the back of his throat and the lining of his windpipe, some of the torn-loose tissue slipping down to his stomach, and the heave it caused vomited up flesh from that organ, too.

"Ebola Zaire is a perfect parasite," said Vladimir Grof. "It attacks every part of a human except skeletal muscle and bone."

The Soviet scientist sucked hard on a Lucky Strike and blew out blue smoke in perfect rings. The virologist still considered himself Soviet, though the Soviet Union was gone.

The man in the bed beyond the vomiting wretch took no notice of what was going on, for he was in the grasp of a grand mal seizure. Clots clogging his arteries had shut off the blood supply to parts of his organs, which had caused dead spots to form in his intestines, liver, kidneys, lungs, heart and brain. Dead spots had ripped open to hemorrhage gore, his heart bleeding into itself as his heart muscle tore, flooding his chest cavity with blood, blood, blood. Dead blood cells sludged his brain, causing the stroke that racked him now, his body thrashing, shaking and hurling its limbs about, as red eyes rolled back into his head and blood, blood, blood splashed everywhere.

"A perfect parasite," Grof repeated, smoke blowing down from both nostrils as if to launch his Slavic head into space. "Such epileptic splashing is a strategy for success. The virus lives to replicate, and needs a host to multiply. The thrash of this one crashing smears its blood around, which gives the virus a chance to jump to a new host."

Mephisto lingered, eye-deep in hell.

The man in the bed beyond the crashing black could take no more. He, like all those in the Zaire hospital, was black African. Naked, he stumbled from his bed in a zombie daze, and shambled toward Mephisto as one of the living dead. The woman in the bed opposite the crashing man was bleeding from every orifice in her body, bloody purge seeping from her eyes, ears, nose, lips, nipples, anus and vagina, her labia blue, livid and protrusive as she spontaneously aborted a bloody-nosed Ebola fetus with ruby red eyes. On the shambling man came, along the aisle in between, through the pools of blood mingling under each bed—shamble, shamble, lurch, shamble—like an extra in a George Romero film. Red spots dotted his skin from hemorrhages beneath, connective tissue turned to mush because this virus chews up collagen viciously, his dissolving flesh hung from the underlying bones and his sagging face detached from his skull. His testicles were bloated and bruised black and blue. Semen hot with Ebola dribbled from his penis to trail through the lake of blood like slime from a slug. What spread across the bed opposite the vomiting wretch near the door was what was left of a human sponge Death had clutched to death. Poe's "The Masque of the Red Death" had transmogrified into "The Facts in the Case of M. Valdemar." Ebola had converted its host into itself, the flesh deteriorating abruptly after death into a liquified gumbo of seething biohazard.

"*Too* perfect a parasite," said Grof. "Ebola is the hottest virus known to science. For it, there is no cure and no vaccine. The seven mysterious proteins that make it up consume the body from brain to skin as the virus makes copies of itself. Like aids, it jumps from one person to another by direct contact with blood or body fluids hot with virus particles, but Ebola is so explosive that it achieves in ten days what it takes AIDS ten years to do. The kill rate for Ebola in humans is nine out of ten. What keeps it from spreading like wildfire far and wide is the fact that the Ebola virus is *too* lethal. It eats up its victims before they can infect enough new hosts for it to sustain an epidemic. Engineer an *airborne* strain of the virus and it would circle the globe in about six weeks, wiping the current slate clean of ninety percent of its overpopulation."

"Bring out your dead," Mephisto whispered, smiling to himself.

The virologist stubbed out the Lucky Strike.

With the eyeballs bugging from the expressionless mask that was the shambler's face, the head of the lurching virus bomb filled the lens as the camera pulled back from the hospital door to let the living corpse stumble out into the street. As it panned, the camera caught a man clad in eerie bioprotective clothing, his hands in rubber gloves and feet in rubber boots. A tiny Soviet emblem was sewn to each shoulder. He, too, was filming this horror out of Africa, while other scientists in biohazard suits with heads encased in goggles and breathing apparatus roamed the village street collecting virus sam-

ples from bloody corpses to take home for biological-
weapons research in Russian labs.

The street was a street of panic.

The street was a street of blood.

Every African in it was crashing and bleeding out.

Babies cried for their mothers, who were dying in
the dirt.

Women wailed in anguish and pulled their hair.

Bleeders crawled among corpses rotting in the muck
in answer to instincts from the reptilian core of their
necrotic brains.

Mephisto could almost smell the stench from such a
slaughterhouse.

"September 1976," said Vladimir Grof. "First known
outbreak of Ebola Zaire, when it erupted simultaneously
in fifty-five villages near the headwaters of the Ebola
River, a feeder of a tributary of the Congo River, deep
in the rainforest of Central Africa. Of 300 people who
were infected in Yambuku, Zaire, 274 died this horrible
way. I would be a grateful man if every city and every
town and every street in America suffered the outbreak
we see here."

"So would I," Mephisto agreed.

He cracked the seal on a bottle of Highland single
malt while the Biopreparat virologist ejected the video
from the vcr, put the tape in a plastic case and put the
case back into his carry bag. Mephisto poured drams of
Scotch into whisky glasses, passed one to the Soviet scientist and toasted, "To Ebola."

"To Ebola," Grof said, and snapped back the shot.

Mephisto refilled his glass.

The windows of the hotel room overlooked the Space
Needle; Seattle's landmark was shining silver in the
Scotch mist of a sunny autumn morning, mist that the
forecast said would thicken to fog by dark. The streets
below were full of bustling people going about weekend
chores or shopping sprees. They were about as far from
the plague street on Grof's video as Central Africa was

from this safe haven in America, which in this age of jet
travel wasn't that far. No place on earth was any farther
away than twenty-odd hours by plane, while the incubation period of a plague virus like Ebola is days.

What brought these men together was the Internet.

Mephisto had posted a question about the origin of
the Black Death.

Among the answers he got was one from Grof, an e-
mail sent from Siberia.

"During a 1346 siege of the walled city of Kaffa in
the Ukraine, the Tartars used catapults to hurl plague-
infested corpses into the stronghold. The mass outbreak
of bubonic plague this caused ended the siege, but also
launched the epidemic of the Black Death that deci-
mated Europe, killing twenty-five million people in the
years between 1347 and 1351 as it swept west from the
steppes of Russia."

"That was the deadliest use of biological warfare?"
Mephisto sent back.

"No," came the reply. "Smallpox in America was the
deadliest in its accidental and strategic effects. A meager
force of Spanish conquistadors was able to overwhelm a
nation of Aztecs in 1521 because some of Cortez's men
carried the virus. Smallpox had long existed back in Europe, but was new to the Americas. The pandemic Cortez ignited almost wiped out native Indians.

"The British used that virus as a biological weapon in
the French and Indian Wars. Fort Carillon in what is
now northeastern New York State was occupied by Indians loyal to France. British commandant Sir Jeffrey Am-
herst proposed the use of smallpox to 'reduce' tribes
hostile to the British. Acting on that strategy, Captain
Ecuyer obtained contaminated blankets from a smallpox
hospital at Fort Pitt, where an epidemic was underway
among the troops. On June 24, 1763, those blankets were
delivered as a gift to the Indians defending Fort Carillon.
When the consequent epidemic ripped through the

enemy tribe, the British attacked, seized Fort Carillon and renamed it Fort Ticonderoga."

And so it went . . .

Back and forth . . .

This Internet exchange of questions and answers on a deadly subject of mutual interest . . .

Questions from Mephisto . . .

Answers from Grof . . .

"Has America ever used bio weapons?"

"Indirectly. But what a kill rate! In the spring of 1918, with the world engulfed in war, a flu virus broke out at a military training camp in Kansas. 'Swine flu' jumped species from pigs to humans, then quickly spread around the globe with U.S. soldiers mobilized for the First World War. Within sixteen months, it killed more than twenty million people, nearly one percent of the world's total population, snuffing more lives than all the battles in that war."

"How do you know so much about bio weapons?"

"I'm a virologist with Biopreparat."

So there it was.

Out in the open.

"Wherever there's a legend, son, hunt and you will find."

"Is it true that some biological-weapons researchers can genetically engineer hybrid viruses by recombining them in a lab?"

"Yes, some can insert bits of genetic material from one organism into another."

"Can Biopreparat?"

"Yes," replied Grof.

Which caused Mephisto to wonder at what price this Faust would sell his sinful soul?

Not only could Mephisto answer every question he'd asked, but he knew all about Biopreparat, too, for this entire exercise in Internet bonding was plotted to make contact with someone like Grof. A disgruntled scientist with the means to decimate mankind.

A bioterrorist.

By an executive order in 1969, President Nixon had outlawed the development of offensive biological weapons in the United States. The Biological Weapons Convention of 1972 was signed by Nixon and Russian leader Leonid Brezhnev to ban proliferation, but on the Soviet side the reverse resulted. By 1980, forty thousand scientists and sixty thousand support personnel working in forty-seven laboratories and three production sites had amassed a lethal zoo of weaponized bio agents. In building number 6 at the Vektor compound in Siberia, virologists like Vladimir Grof could access a reservoir of ten thousand viruses, including 140 strains of smallpox and three kinds of Ebola, to engineer what were called strange beasts. These were horrifying hybrids, deadly designer bugs created in a labyrinth of tunnels sealed by airlocks in which weird virus cultures stewed in bio reactors.

"Black biology," said Grof. "That's what we called it." He lit another Lucky Strike to go with his Scotch. "I was the toast of the Kremlin. I lived like a czar. A dacha on the Black Sea. Hunting in the Urals. Beautiful women in my bed at night. Now look at me. Such a sickly wreck. Wasting away from a heart virus I contracted for Mother Russia. Doing research in a lab that's crumbling apart. Working for American capitalists whom I despise, while Yeltsin"—Grof spat on the carpet—"pockets the dirty money Washington sends out of fear. And I haven't seen a paycheck in four months."

"You're seeing one now," Mephisto said, holding up a bank book.

"Passport?"

"Inside."

"A good forgery?"

"No, as genuine as money can buy."

"This isn't about money."

"I understand."

"This is about hate."

"I hate, too."

"I hate America for what it did to us. We were men of vision. We were a superpower. We were the first into space. We dominated the Olympics. We freed those around the world shackled by capitalism. I was a man of stature. I played God. I created a life-form of biblical power. Now I'm a slave to the country that bankrupted us, a nation of moneymen who bought us out, so I want to see America cower beneath my scourge before I die."

"And the rest of the world?"

"Casualties of war. Let them know that America did this to them."

"Why me?"

Grof winked. "You are the hand of God."

"*You* could play God again."

"But *you* have the money. I want to gorge myself on every sin of the flesh before Armageddon."

"How did you get it in?"

"By diplomatic pouch. Washington sent for me, so I am above suspicion. Both the Russians and the Americans believe the box contains viral cultures from one of their joint 'science projects.' "

The irony of it all was not lost on Mephisto.

"The fall of the Soviet government in 1991 did not stop research at Vektor. All it stopped was the funding. In 1992, Yeltsin"—Grof spat on the carpet—"played on American fear by confirming that the former Soviet Union had maintained a bio-weapons program despite the convention signed in 1972 by Nixon and Brezhnev. In 1994, Yeltsin"—Grof spat on the carpet—"heightened that fear when he admitted a mysterious epidemic that killed sixty-six victims at Sverdlovsk in 1979 resulted from an accident with anthrax at a bio-weapons plant. Recently, Yeltsin"—Grof spat on the carpet—"leaked information to U.S. intelligence that disgruntled scientists in Biopreparat facing economic ruin have gone over to hostile Iraq and Libya with their secrets."

"Yeltsin"—Mephisto spat on the carpet, drawing a

grin from Grof—"knows how to loosen the purse strings in Washington. 'If you don't stay on top of the problem, you get so far behind the power curve that soon you're in a world of hurt.'

"So that," said Grof with deep contempt, "is how I ended up working for nothing on science projects funded by the U.S. Department of Defense. The National Academy of Sciences recommended stemming our brain drain of biotechnology by spending $38.5 million over five years on benign Russian experiments employing 150 of some 40,000 Biopreparat scientists. This, the academy maintains, is 'a significant contribution to reducing the likelihood of proliferation.' As chief of the Main Directorate of Biopreparat, I've been invited here to bring the fruits of the yearlong pilot program. Yeltsin"—again he spat on the carpet—"pockets the money."

Grof grinned the wickedest grin Mephisto had ever seen, except when he faced himself in the mirror. Whatever virus had wormed into his heart, its effect had been to create a living skeleton, for his gaunt Slavic features were merely angles of skin and bone. He looked like the Grim Reaper.

"With the help of the U.S. Department of Defense, I bring you this." From his carry bag the Russian virologist withdrew Pandora's box, a black oblong that—like the myth from Ancient Greece—hoarded the evils of the world, which were waiting to escape.

"The worst scourge that ever afflicted mankind was smallpox. Highly contagious, it passed from person to person in droplets discharged from the nose and mouth, then it reproduced in lymphoid tissue. The virus also spread by dried smallpox scabs and articles infected by previous victims. The symptoms were fever and a rash of blisters containing pus. Incubating in seven to twenty-one days, smallpox had a kill rate of 30 percent. When a bus traveler visiting New York died from the virus in 1947, the threat was considered so profound that 6.35 million people were vaccinated in less than a month.

"Immunization has always been the preventive cure. No specific treatment was ever developed for anyone who contracted the disease. In 1796 the British surgeon Edward Jenner made a smallpox vaccine from cowpox serum, which was widely used after that. Vaccinating ceased in 1971, and the World Health Organization declared the earth to be officially smallpox free in October 1979. There were—it was thought—only two existing stocks of smallpox remaining, in freezers at the Centers for Disease Control in Atlanta and the Research Institute for Viral Preparation in Moscow. WHO recommended unanimously that both stocks be destroyed on June 30, 1995. Outweighing any scientific value in preserving smallpox for future research was the risk that it might escape from the lab or fall into bioterrorists' hands."

Grof opened Pandora's box for Mephisto.

"In 1990 we devised ways to mass produce smallpox at Vektor. The three aerosol cans inside are biological bombs, each containing smallpox virus in a freeze-dried form. The virus will remain inactive until it hits the moist membranes of a human lung. 'A virus is a piece of bad news wrapped in protein,' said the Nobel laureate Peter Medawar. The bad news is that the genetic information within the shell, DNA or its chemical cousin RNA, consists of little more than a bundle of genes designed to invade and hijack the reproductive machinery of host cells to make multiple copies of itself. The virus has no reproductive means of its own. Each victim becomes a virus factory.

"Three aerosol bombs," repeated Grof.

"One for New York.

"One for Miami.

"One for L.A.

"Thirty years ago, the U.S. army conducted a series of dispersal experiments to test American vulnerability to bio weaponry. One saw a man carry harmless bacteria down into New York's subway system in 1966. He stood at the edge of the platform with other commuters, and when the doors opened, he boarded the train. Before leaving the Manhattan station, he dropped a light bulb stuffed with bacterial agents onto the tracks beneath his open door. The bulb burst. The door closed. The train pulled away. And thirty minutes later, detectors picked up bacterial traces ten blocks across town. The test proved New York could be killed off by using its subway to disperse bio parasites.

"If I were you," Grof said, "I'd release one virus bomb in New York's subway, the next in a Miami mall with a contained air-conditioning system and the final aerosol in a plane about to land at L.A. International. Then I would retreat back here to the Pacific Northwest to watch the plague explode."

"I will," said Mephisto.

"Good. Roll up your sleeve."

From Pandora's box, the virologist withdrew a virus vaccination kit. "Offense is easy. Defense is hard. The outcome of bio warfare will never depend on who has the deadliest weapons. Instead, it will always hinge on who has the best vaccines."

Mephisto hesitated.

"You don't trust me?" said Grof. "You think I plan to kill just you and take your money?"

"The thought had occurred to me."

"Fine," said Grof. "Keep your money, and I will do the job. But when you crash and bleed out like those in the Zaire video, remember you had the chance to survive when no one else did.

"I want you to grasp the genius in what I achieved at Vektor. Smallpox is a DNA virus; Ebola an RNA virus. To make a supervirus by 'marrying' the two, I produced a DNA copy of RNA Ebola, then inserted DNA Ebola genes into a DNA smallpox virus. The result was a hybrid with the deadly effects of the Ebola virus married to the highly contagious vector of the smallpox virus. *Airborne*

Ebola was my creation, and that is what you have in these aerosol cans.

"Released in New York, released in Miami, released in L.A., smallpox will spread the hybrid across America and around the world, infecting victims with supervirus smallpox *and* Ebola genes to incubate a double pandemic. The incubation period for Ebola is shorter than that of smallpox: five to ten days, not seven to twenty-one. On the fourth or fifth day after symptoms occur, the fever becomes severe. Six to seven days and blood won't clot, causing those horrid hemorrhages. Death usually happens about day nine, so since Ebola symptoms incubate first, nine out of every ten people alive will crash and bleed out." Grof held the vaccination kit up between them.

"You understand how vaccine is made? We neutralize a virus like smallpox by growing it in a tissue culture from which we can harvest a killed or attenuated virus to modify into a benign preparation that we can inoculate as vaccine. Any body that weakened virus enters recognizes antigens on the outside surface of the protein shell as foreign to the body, and develops antibodies to counter them. Since Ebola's genes are *inside* the smallpox virus shell, all you need for immunity is antibodies against smallpox.

"A smallpox vaccination lasts ten years. Those who were vaccinated up to 1971 have lapsed immunization, so the only people immune to the smallpox vectors in these three aerosol bombs are those *I* have vaccinated against the strain. No one is immune to Ebola. No one is immune to smallpox. And there are no stocks of vaccine on hand for an 'eradicated' virus. The entire world, *except me,* is food for my monster."

Mephisto rolled up his sleeve.

"Do it," he said.

Grof vaccinated him against the supervirus.

Mephisto filled their glasses with another dram of Scotch.

"To smallpox and Ebola!"
"To Ebola and smallpox!"
"A marriage made in hell!"
"Till death do them part!"
The men locked arms and downed the drams.

Countdown

No matter how big, no matter how small, in the old days, if it didn't have pillars, it wasn't a courthouse. The San Juan County Courthouse sat high on Court Street, with its pillared front toward the rising sun and its red-brick backside mooning the office of the county sheriff in its shadow.

Tucked behind the left-hand pillar was a box with "For the Cops" scrawled on top.

In the box was the body part Donella had sawed off Nick.

———————

Jenna and the Jailbird had their office back. Luke Wentworth and the Suits had found accommodations more to their liking, but where they found concrete, steel and elevator music in rustic Friday Harbor Jenna found hard to imagine. The office was stripped of every file about the Campbells, but thankfully the Suits had left behind Patsy Cline. The budgie squawked to "Crazy" while Jenna sat back, fingers locked behind her head and feet up on her desk like Hank Bond used to do whenever he was deep in thought.

At the moment, Jenna's thought was a memory.

What had Fitzroy's son, William, said at the Doe Bay

homestead that day she found the family tree inside the Bible?

"The only Campbell mystery is the missing tract of land. Callum Campbell immigrated with his two sons and supposedly selected three homestead sites, one for each son and one for him. Callum drowned in a boating accident in 1863, and two of those tracts were later registered by his sons. My grandfather, the tale goes, overheard his father and uncle—Callum's sons—arguing about a woman who got the third tract. After that argument, she was never mentioned again. To this day, we have no idea who the woman was, where the property is or what claim she had to it."

"Callum's mistress?"

"Possibly."

"Any whisper of one?"

Bill shook his head. *"Our family was religious. No scandal ever surfaced."*

"Her land was in the San Juans?"

"Had to be. If it was in Canada, Callum would have filed for ownership before he died. Lawful jurisdiction was never in doubt beyond Haro Strait. The younger son filed in Canada, so he owned his tract before my great-grandfather. Until the Pig War died down, no man's land had no country."

The way Jenna saw it, there were two plans to save Nick. Plan A was to locate and storm the hideaway where he was held, and that required the resources of the FBI and the Mounted Police. Plan B was to find the silver skull and offer it as ransom for his release. That was within the resources of the San Juan County sheriff, so Plan B was Jenna's strategy.

It was like whittling wood.

This whittling of land.

And the knife used to whittle was her high-school history.

Oregon became a territory of the United States in 1848, after the Treaty of Oregon of 1846 delineated the border with Canada along the 49th parallel. Oregon then embraced all of present Washington, Idaho and parts of Montana and Wyoming.

Whittle, whittle . . .

Washington became a territory of the United States in 1853, after having been a part of Oregon since 1848. Included within the new territory was all of Idaho. It was reduced to its present size in 1889, when Washington became the forty-second state of the Union.

Whittle, whittle . . .

San Juan County was created from Whatcom County in 1873, after the German kaiser ruled in favor of America in the Pig War dispute. Since only then did the islands become part of the United States, land registry lagged years behind the mainland.

Whittle, whittle . . .

Land-transaction records are kept in the office of the county auditor for each county in Washington State. So three days earlier, on Wednesday, after William Campbell mentioned the third tract of land, Jenna had boated back to Friday Harbor from Orcas Island and walked next door to speak with the San Juan County auditor in her office on the main floor of the courthouse.

Jenna's motive then was not to save Nick, for Nick had yet to be kidnapped. Her motive was to locate where the Campbell kidnappers would strike next, so she could catch them in the act.

The county auditor was a birdlike woman named Joan Finch. Tufts of orange hennaed hair spiked from the top of her head like a woodpecker's crest. Huge horn-rimmed glasses gave her the blink of an owl. So hooked was her nose it could have been an eagle's beak, while chicken-pecking hands plucked files from cabinets and papers from files as if they were kernels of corn.

"How do I trace title to a tract of land, Joan?"

"Depends," said the auditor. "How far back?"

"To the beginning. Pioneer days."

"That far back, you may have to go to the National Archives in D.C."

"Why?" asked the detective.

"The Homestead Act. By 'the beginning,' do you mean the original grant?"

"Yes," said Jenna.

"That's a federal act. The state doesn't come into it until the *next* transfer."

"Brush me up, Joan. I'm weak here."

"In the United States, there are two basic types of land transaction: one, the transfer of land from the government to private individuals; and two, after that, transfers from one private individual to another."

One of Finch's hands hopped along the counter like a red, red robin bob, bob, bobbin'. Then the other hand bob, bobbed back.

Jenna remembered George Waschke, the father of her country, who had slammed the buoy above the sunken *Bounding Main,* and wondered how other detectives recalled people they encountered.

Guilt by association was her trick of the trade.

The Birdwoman of Friday Harbor went on: "The original transaction is a government grant of virgin land to a new settler. It marks the arrival of a man or a family in a place where no one else was before that. No one else except Indians, that is. Either he or they are new immigrants, or he or they are new arrivals from elsewhere in the States."

Now both hands swooped down to land like ducks on a wilderness pond.

"The land records in the National Archives pertain mostly to those thirty states created from the 'public domain:' land acquired through purchase or in treaties following wars, including all states west of the Mississippi River, except Texas and Hawaii. The land records are mostly from 1800 on, and contain applications under the Homestead Act."

"Homesteads are my focus," said Bond.

"By 1850 there were only thirteen thousand settlers in all of Oregon. To augment that, the federal government offered ownership of large homestead tracts to anyone who would live on and cultivate the land. Because the Pig War put us on ice, the later Homestead Act of 1862 eventually applied to land in the San Juans."

"How much could you get?"

"A hundred and sixty acres."

"How long did you have to work it?"

"Five years," said Finch.

Jenna wondered if she was pigeon-toed.

"Qualifications?"

"Name, age and citizenship of the applicant. Name of wife, if any, and size of family. If he was an alien of foreign birth, proof of naturalization or a declaration of intention to become a U.S. citizen, accompanied by where he was born and port and date of arrival. Here in the San Juans that was nebulous, because the islands were no man's land until 1872. Settlers homesteaded for more than a decade before the act applied, and children were born in the islands before they were in the United States."

"Time stood still," said Jenna.

"While life went on," said Joan.

"Procedure?" asked the detective.

"The processing of federal land grants was done at land offices. In the National Archives there is a four-volume index listing the office responsible for a given region at a given time. Title to public-domain land was transferred from the government to the settler by means of a patent or deed recorded in the tract book of the office for that region."

"Homestead locators?"

Finch nodded like a turkey poking its wattle. "The act was in effect until 1908, so if someone homesteaded in the San Juans between 1872 and 1908, the settler can be tracked through the local tract book in the National Archives."

"How far do *you* go back?" Jenna asked.

"To 1873. A private transaction is always of land that previously was the subject of a government grant. We record the first private transfer of a Homestead Act tract from its settler to someone else, and every other private transfer since. Deeds filed here are indexed by the names of all involved."

"Including *federal* homesteaders?"

"Yes, as sellers."

"Check some names for me?"

"Sure," said Finch.

"Callum, Dugald and Ewen Campbell."

"Better spell 'em, Jen."

"C-A-L-L-U-M, D-U-G-A-L-D, E-W-E-N."

The Birdwoman did an index check and found nothing under Callum. That was to be expected, since Callum had died in a boating accident in 1863, years before tracts in the San Juans could be settled under the Homestead Act. But if the mystery woman mentioned by Bill Campbell had been Callum's mistress and they had produced a son, the son may have registered the tract as Callum, Jr. It had been worth a shot, but the shot missed.

The Birdwoman did an index check and found that the Doe Bay homestead settled by elder son Dugald had passed to John, then to Fitzroy, following the family tree in the Campbell Bible. Dugald had registered no other tract in the San Juans.

The Birdwoman did an index check and found nothing under Ewen, so the only tract in the islands registered by the younger son was the homestead on Mayne Island, up in Canada.

That left the mystery woman.

"Joan, I need you to hunt someone else for me. She may have homesteaded and passed on or sold a tract here in the San Juans."

"Name?"

"I don't know."

The magnified owl eyes blinked.

"Who'd she pass on or sell to?"

"I don't know."

Again the owl eyes blinked.

"Start with the last name Campbell and see if that works. There can't be too many women who homesteaded by themselves in the San Juans. If you find a Campbell, so much the better, but give me the names of *any* women you turn up."

Unwhittle, unwhittle . . .

Back to the public domain.

The following day, Thursday, had seen Jenna on the phone to Washington, D.C., where she spoke to a man named Tom Holland in the National Archives.

"I'm trying to trace an unknown woman who may have homesteaded in the San Juans. Would you check the tract book for the islands from 1872 on and give me the names of all women who filed under the act? The last name may be Campbell. May not."

"That shouldn't be hard," Holland said, "if memory serves me right. Population-wise, there were around two hundred homesteaders plus wives, children, Indians and bums in the islands when the territorial legislature carved San Juan County out of Whatcom County in 1873. Give me till tomorrow."

Another long shot zipped through Bond's mind.

"Would you also check Callum Campbell from 1857 to 1863? He may have tried filing in Whatcom County *before* the Pig War heated up in 1859, when Britain and America were in a civil tug-of-war over the islands, or perhaps *during* the ballyhoo, to have his claim on record in case we won."

That evening Nick had vanished from the barn dance on Pender Island. The following morning, yesterday, had seen her at the scene of the crime, then in Vancouver to speak with DeClercq. By the time she returned to Friday Harbor late in the day, results from both search requests were in her message box.

No woman named Campbell or anything else had filed a homestead claim in the San Juans.

So much for pioneer suffragism, thought Bond.

The only women to sell homestead tracts were wives of deceased men granted grants.

None of the women was a Campbell.

No claim whatsoever—before, during or after the Pig War bally-hoo—had been filed by the homesteader Callum Campbell.

Strike out, thought Bond.

Friday night.

The weekend.

Governments had closed.

The FBI was on the case, so Bond had boated home.

But early this morning, that nightmare had wrenched her from sleep again. . . .

The screams of Don being tortured echo up and down this hall. . . . "OH, JESUS, PLEASE NOT ANOTHER PIECE!" "OH, JESUS, NOT THAT! LEAVE ME A MAN!" "OH, JESUS, DON'T CUT OFF MY—"

In a sweat, she had bolted upright in bed.

That silver skull *had* to exist and she *had* to find the Hoard, so the first light of dawn had seen Jenna on the bridge of the *Islomania, boomph*ing west down Upright Channel to Friday Harbor, where the first thing she did was call Washington and roust Tom Holland out of bed on a sleep-in Saturday morning.

"Sorry."

"You should be."

"It's an emergency. When was the first census done in Washington State?"

"Federal: 1870. State: 1871."

"The Pig War wasn't settled until 1872. Did either census apply to the San Juans?"

"Don't know. If not, the next ones did."

"What's in an 1800s federal census?"

"A list of families and individuals living in each county and state on census day. Census records begin in 1790.

Only heads of households and numbers of others in their
homes were listed to 1850. After that, everyone was entered, along with information like whether they owned
land. From 1880 on, the relationship of every person to
the head of the family was recorded."

"I need those 1870 and 1880 San Juan censuses."

"Today?" exclaimed Holland.

"Yesterday," said Jenna. "Now what have you got in
the way of immigration records? . . ."

Her next call rousted Joan Finch out of bed.

"What time is it?"

"You don't want to know."

"What day is it?"

"Even worse."

"Have a heart, Jen."

"We may have a heart, literally, if you don't help me
stop a sadist cutting apart a cop."

"I'm awake!" chirped Finch.

"Good," said Bond. "Here's what I need you to find
for me . . ."

So now Jenna sat in her office, feet propped up on
her desk and hands behind her head, waiting for Holland
to fax her from Washington while Finch toiled next
door, combing through county census, marriage, death,
burial, will and tax records from pioneer times, searching
for anything that might offer a clue to the identity of
the mystery woman who somehow got hold of Callum
Campbell's tract of homestead land.

Say the mystery woman was Callum's mistress, Jenna
thought. Back then, it was normal for people to postpone
making a will until the last minute on their deathbed. Because Callum died prematurely in an accident—he was
how old then? forty-nine?—he probably died intestate,
without a will. The Pig War had stalled his filing a Homestead Act claim, a stalemate that went on for nine more
years after he died. If the mystery woman married another
man in those years, might he, as head of the household,

have been the one who made their claim under the Homestead Act once the Pig War had ended?

Is that what Dugald and Ewen argued about?

"My grandfather," Bill Campbell had said, *"overheard his father and uncle—Callum's sons—arguing about a woman who got the third tract. After that argument, she was never mentioned again."*

What was it about the mystery woman that so upset Callum's sons that she became a non-person in both their lives?

It had to be more than the fact that she possessed their father's land, for neither son had filed claim to dispossess her.

"Our family was religious," Bill had said. *"No scandal ever surfaced."*

Was that it? Did Callum's mistress draw scandal to herself after Callum died, forcing his God-fearing sons to shun her?

Or was it more than scandal?

Something illegal?

Something so repellent that they forsook any claim to their father's land so their reputations wouldn't be ruined by association?

"Jenna!" A yell from outside her office. "That fax is coming through." She swung down her feet, got up and exited to get the fax she thought was from Holland, but what she took off the machine was:

? ? ? ?
Friends.
Romans.
Countrymen . . .
Left pillar.
Courthouse.
Court Street entrance.
Your move.
Mephisto.

Out the security door, then out the door to Second Street, then along the southwest side of the courthouse to Court Street, then up the many steps to the pillared landing above, Jenna ran as fast as she could. Secreted behind the left-hand pillar was a box with "For the Cops" scrawled on top. Using her pen, she eased the lid up to peek inside.

The countdown had begun.

Piece by piece.

New Caledonia

Vancouver, British Columbia

New Caledonia.
  New Scotland, thought DeClercq.
  Old Caledonia.
  Highland home of the Picts.
  Standing before the Strategy Wall in his office at Special X, waiting for a telephone call from Winnipeg, headquarters of the Hudson's Bay Company, DeClercq eyed the family tree Jenna Bond had found inside the cover of the Campbell Bible:

Callum Campbell, 1814–1863
Dugald Campbell, 1840–1916   Ewen Campbell, 1841–1913
Scotland to Vancouver Island in May 1857
New Caledonia

  Did *New Caledonia* refer to Simon Fraser's name for British Columbia?
  By royal charter, proclaimed on May 2, 1670, the king of England gave the "Governor and Company of Adventurers trading into Hudson's Bay" a monopoly over all the land drained by rivers flowing into it. Through the centuries, the Hudson's Bay Company expanded into a commercial colossus covering a twelfth of the earth's land surface, from the Arctic Ocean to San Francisco, and from Labrador to the Hawaiian

Islands. Three million square miles were amassed by the largest private landowner in history and the oldest joint stock company in the world, which is still an ongoing enterprise in Canada today. "We were Caesars," boasted one explorer of the HBC's dominance over the untamed wild, there "being nobody to contradict us." Nobody, that is, until the company met its nemesis in the Americans, with first the annexation of Oregon pushing the Bay men back to the 49th parallel, then Cutler and that damn pig driving them out of the San Juans.

In 1806, having crossed over the Rocky Mountains from the Canadian Prairies, the Scottish explorer Simon Fraser bucked the whitewater rapids of the river named for him—the same river that later gave its name to the Fraser gold rush of 1858—to meet the sea where Vancouver is now. Soon to be part of the company's domain, the vast wilderness he passed through was christened New Caledonia.

New Caledonia in the Campbell Bible could refer to British Columbia. On condition that the company establish a Crown colony in 1849, the HBC was given Vancouver Island, which Captain Cook had "discovered" in 1778. In 1858, the year after Callum Campbell shipped out of Scotland with his two sons and the year before the Pig War with the States, the Mainland that Simon Fraser had called New Caledonia became the Crown colony of British Columbia, a name suggested by Queen Victoria herself. Later, company rights to the Crown colony of Vancouver Island were revoked, and both colonies were combined in 1866, before joining Canada in 1871. Vancouver Island, however, was always distinct from New Caledonia, and since Vancouver Island was where the emigrating Campbells were bound, DeClercq doubted that *New Caledonia* in the Bible referred to B.C.

What he thought it referred to was a ship.

And since the island was a *company* colony in 1857, the ship was probably a *company* ship.

So yesterday, after Jenna Bond had left his office, he'd phoned the Hudson's Bay Record Society in Winnipeg to check.

Formed in 1938 to publish selections from Hudson's Bay Company documents amassed over what is now three hundred and some odd years, the society publishes volumes available to members only. The collection of exploration journals and trade accounts, minutes and correspondence, and ship manifests is huge, so he was told it might take a while to track down the information. Now, the next day, as he stood here, the telephone rang.

"DeClercq," he said.

"Margery Pound. You requested information from the Hudson's Bay Record Society?"

"Yes. Was there a company ship named *New Caledonia* servicing Vancouver Island in 1857?"

"There was."

"Do you have the passenger manifests for that ship for May of that year?"

"We do."

"Did Callum Campbell book several passages on that ship that month?"

"He did."

"From where to where?"

"From Glasgow, Scotland, to Vancouver Island."

"For himself?"

"Yes."

"And his two sons?"

"Yes, if their names were Dugald Campbell and Ewen Campbell."

"They were."

"Anything else?"

"He booked only *three* passages?"

"No, he booked four."

"Who was the fourth passenger?"
"Effie Conochie."

As he hung up the phone, DeClercq recalled what he
was told yesterday at UBC by Professor Emeritus Robson MacKissock:

*"The MacKissocks are a clan sept of both the Camp-
bells and the MacDonalds of Clanranald, so I heard the
story from both sides."*

"What's a sept?"

"A branch," said MacKissock. *"A sept can be either
clansmen related by blood who form a separate offshoot,
or 'broken men' from other clans who ask for and obtain
the protection of the clan. A sept can have a different
surname than the clan, or the same surname can be tied
to different clans."*

DeClercq had MacKissock's home number.

He phoned the professor.

"Robson MacKissock speaking."

"Hello, it's Robert DeClercq."

"Yes, Chief Superintendent. Of what assistance can I
be today?"

"Conochie? Is that a Campbell sept?"

"Yes."

"And Effie?"

"Bonnie name for a Highland lass." The third tract
of land, thought DeClercq.

Today being Saturday, all provincial land-title offices
were closed.

DeClercq was about to make some calls to open them
up for him, especially those blanketing areas where Effie
Conochie may have registered Callum Campbell's land,

a homestead he didn't register because he died too soon, when Jenna Bond called from Friday Harbor.

"Horrid news," she said. "I think we may have Nick Craven's ear."

Money, Fornication, Power and Knowledge

Shipwreck Island, Washington State

With the Pandora's box in his lap, Mephisto sat strapped in the seat beside the helicopter pilot and, returning from meeting Vladimir Grof in Seattle, watched as his island came toward him through the tattered mist. Whitecaps sparkled and winked at the sun as the chopper shadow skimmed across the waves. It seemed to him that power radiated from the box, and he knew this power was his because he had sacrificed his soul to the Devil, to Mephistopheles.

The helicopter jockey lowered the collective pitch lever to set them down. Dust billowed up from Shipwreck Island as they entered ground effect. The skids landed, the chopper rocked, then the *whup whup whup* of the air-foils died to a whistle.

"Wait here," Mephisto said, climbing down from the cockpit with Pandora's box underarm.

He crossed the rocky bluff to enter the mansion by the front door, angling right in the hardwood hall with its marble stairs, tapestries and paintings to go into the library of leather-bound books and display cases of Pictish hoards. There he climbed the circular staircase up through the ceiling and into the observatory in which he watched the sky by telescope, raised carnivorous plants in the greenhouse wedge of the roof and now approached Donella sitting at his desk of computers lacquering her nails.

"The Mountie," she said. "Want another piece?"

Money, fornication and power he had.

But Mephisto had pledged his soul to the Devil for knowledge as well, for what use was power without the knowledge of how to use it?

That the Atlanteans knew, and that we have lost.

The knowledge he had made the pact for was the Secret of the Stones, for as his father had said on their odyssey hunt for burnt bones: "Two million nights have darkened us since stone circles first blazed, chilling whatever power they once had, and leaving us with questions to madden a thinking man."

What was the secret?

Mephisto *had* to know.

If he didn't find out soon, it would drive him mad!

"May I?" asked Donella. "Cut another piece? I told him next time I'd come for his cock."

"His cock you shall have. Now or later. But first let's see what DeClercq has to say."

He sat down beside her to boot up a computer, then surfed the Net to the historians' bulletin board.

Jeopardy

Vancouver, British Columbia

Nick was held captive somewhere, anywhere, it might as well be *nowhere,* out there in Canada *or* the States. Mephisto was the name of an invisible entity somewhere, anywhere, it might as well be *nowhere,* out there in cyberspace. The e-mail messages from Mephisto to DeClercq had been traced back to Internet coffeehouses in Washington State, the note about Nick's hand to Seattle and the one threatening a cut a day to Bellingham. No attempt had been made to hide the source of either message, but that did little to identify each sender, for both coffeehouses were busy, high-turnover hangout spots, where the hip sipped java and surfed the Net. Patrons could e-mail if they desired. Descriptions of possible senders were so vague and inconsistent that if they originated with those who'd e-mailed DeClercq, Mephisto had sent different henchmen out to perform the tasks.

Out from where?

Cyberspace.

Cyber manhunting was foreign to DeClercq. His mind was trained in realistic times. Virtual reality had him in its Net, enmeshing him in a brutal game of "who's the hunter and who's the hunted." The Battle of Britain was something he could get his mind around: Spitfire pilots waited for Messerschmitts to come into sight, engaging them in dogfights when they did. The battles in *Top Gun,* fought by computers when combatants were miles apart and fought at speeds faster than the human mind can think, were beyond his comprehension.

That's how he felt manhunting Mephisto. The psycho was out there in cyberspace, a phantom as real as those planes fought by top guns, yet as ethereal as an image on a computer screen. The pieces of Craven he sent to the cops were real flesh and blood, just as missiles fired from cyberspace could shoot down your plane. This fight with Mephisto was being fought faster than Robert could react, for here was another hacked-off hunk of Nick and he was no closer to closing in on the psycho than he'd been yesterday.

No time at all and there'd be another piece!

Anger and frustration overwhelmed DeClercq.

He struck his desk hard with his fist.

No one mutilated one of his men!

No one made him feel this useless as a cop!

If cyberspace was the battlefield, that's where he would take down Mephisto.

He drew in a deep breath and slowly let it out.

He turned on his computer and typed:

Callum Campbell arrived with two sons and a teenage girl: Effie Conochie.
Land she inherited may hoard what you seek.
No more pieces.
Give us time to search.

He posted this message on the historians' bulletin board in cyberspace, then left his office and descended the stairs to walk outside, crossing the parking lot to the Annex next door, where he found Detective Inspector Kim Rossmo in the Mounted's geographic profiling office at work on the jeopardy surface.

"Kim."

The Vancouver Police cop turned from the screen.

"The bastard sent us Nick Craven's ear."

"Where?" asked Rossmo.

"Friday Harbor. A fax directing us to it was sent from a mobile machine stolen there."

The cyber cop jotted a note on a pad.

"Never has one of my men been in such jeopardy. If

we don't rescue him fast, he'll be slowly cut to pieces.
I'm desperate. Geographic profiling is Nick's only hope
to survive. Mephisto is a sadist. He'll finish him off, no
matter what, as cruelly as he can. This jeopardy you are
working on is the *only* means we have to rescue Nick."

"Okay," said Rossmo. "We go with what we've got."
The cyber cop indicated a framed photo on the wall.

"I gave that to Monica to hang within sight of her
computer screen. That's the Mathematical Bridge in
Cambridge. Designed by William Etheridge and built
over the River Cam behind Queens' College in 1749, the
geometry of the structure was such that no nails were
required to hold its wooden beams in place. When it
was rebuilt to exactly the same design at the beginning
of this century, the story is that they couldn't get it to
stay together, and nails were needed for stability. The
moral is that there's a subjective factor to the objective
mechanics of what we do."

"The Etheridge factor?"

Rossmo nodded.

"We use a Sun Microsystems UltraSPARC workstation,
a serious computer about ten times the price of a high-end
Pentium. The software program is Rigel, named after one
of the stars in the constellation Orion. Orion the Hunter.
The hunter the software supports is, of course, the police.

"I scanned in a map of the West Coast islands from
Vancouver south to Seattle. Then I directly digitalized
these crime sites onto it:

"1. Fitzroy Campbell's dock on Orcas Island;

"2. and 3. The Anacortes and Blaine gas stations
where his credit card was used;

"4. Gavin Campbell's dock on Mayne Island;

"5. The spot where the *Bounding Main* went down in
Boundary Pass;

"6. The barn on Pender Island where Nick vanished;

"7. The lane where his hand was found;

"8. and 9. The Internet coffeehouses in Seattle and
Bellingham where the e-mail messages originated.

"The latitude and longitude of each crime site was confirmed through use of a hand-held Global Positioning System."

Rossmo digitalized the new site on-screen.

"10. Friday Harbor, where Nick's ear was found and the fax was sent."

A click of the mouse saw Rigel produce this:

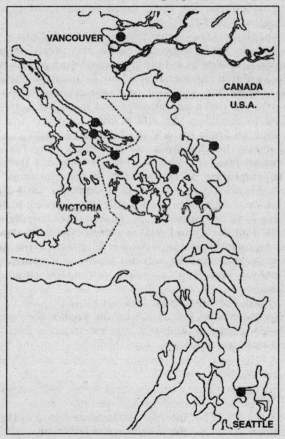

"Fifty-one miles wide and 122 miles high, the ten crime sites cover an area of more than six thousand square miles. With this number of sites, you can expect on average to find Mephisto's residence in 3.9 percent of the area, or about 240 square miles. Still a lot to search, but as most of it is water, that shrinks the dragnet."

"You left out the three rapes linked to Mephisto's henchmen," said DeClercq.

"The Etheridge factor," replied the detective. "If we include them, they may skew the result. A geographic profile is based on the mental map of *one* individual's activity space. That's how we locate *his* anchor point. Here we are safe to theorize that Mephisto planned the three kidnappings and the other activities linked to them, so the acts of his henchmen are also his. But we don't know if the henchmen live with him, and it may be the rapes are something they planned by themselves. It's like the law of vicarious liability. If an employee hurts someone in the course of his work, his boss is liable. But if he embarks 'on a frolic of his own,' his boss isn't liable for injuries outside the scope of his employment. Rigel makes calculations founded on the spatial relationships between locations, so if we include activities outside Mephisto's direction, the geographic profile will not be *his*. Assessing what to include and what to leave out is the subjective factor."

"You're the boss," said DeClercq.

Rossmo clicked the mouse on the GeoProfile button.

A few moments and a million calculations later saw Rigel produce this:

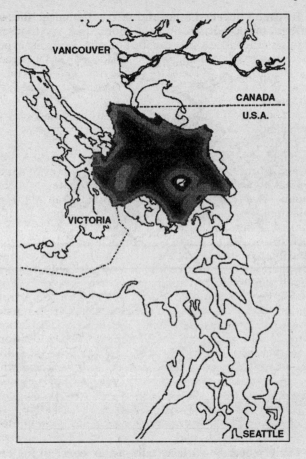

"Since time is of the essence, the profile you see is of the top 15 percent of Mephisto's activity space. The darkest areas are where we concentrate our search. The jeopardy surface uses 3-D heights to represent the probabilities that each one of the forty thousand cells making up this screen is where Mephisto's home is located."

Rossmo clicked the mouse on the Jeopardy button. Rigel produced this:

"This jeopardy surface tells us to concentrate our search on the southern part of Saturna Island in Canada and the northwestern part of Orcas Island in the United States. I have an idea that may help further shrink the dragnet. Will you be in your office?"

"In and out all day."

"With luck, I'll call."

The Hellfire Cult

Orcas Island, Washington State

The race was on between the redcoats and the Suits to prove who was best—better, actually, as there were only *two* at odds. For some egotistical reason, both thought the rivalry between them was to settle the open question of who was top cop around the world. Police in other countries were mere bystanders.

"A Member is down!" is Mountie jargon for "one of our own is in trouble." Canada is the only country with a police force as its national symbol. In fact, the Mounties are the last remnants of the British Colonial Army, and those conquerors weren't known for their humility. They are the Mounted. They are the Force. They hold the thin red line. And Members of the Mounted are with a capital *M*. So take on a Mountie and you take on all 16,000 Members of the Force, and may God have mercy on your dumb, fucking soul.

None of which impressed the FBI.

As far as the Bureau was concerned, the myth of the Mounties was a figment of the left-wing pinko press and Hollywood types dazzled by anything red. The coining of that "always get their man" nonsense was done down here by an American, and who turned out all those films that molded the stereotype? If that wasn't a Red conspiracy, what was? Did anyone recognize the Texas Rangers as the mounted police that the Mounted Police used as the prototype for their free-range Force?

And who pioneered the crime labs and police computers and psychological profiling that the Horsemen use today to "get their man"?

The Bureau, buddy. That's who.

Well, here was the chance to settle that beef once and for all. According to Rossmo's jeopardy, Mephisto's lair was probably on Saturna Island up in Canada, or on Orcas Island down in the United States. The Mounted had a Member down and were desperate, so they'd dispatched the cavalry in force to Saturna and were searching that island stem to stern. Rossmo's jeopardy was accepted by the FBI, for he was a regular lecturer at Quantico and, as a Vancouver Police officer, was a neutral Canuck in this "who's best" rivalry. So while the Horsemen charged in force to Saturna, across Boundary Pass from the United States, the Bureau saturated sleepy Orcas with capital *A* Agents. With luck, they'd not only get the Mounties' man, Craven, but also get *their* man, Mephisto, and guess who'd be buying the beer at the end of the day to celebrate?

Eat my shorts, buddy.

Meanwhile, Jenna concentrated on Plan B.

At last she had a name for the mystery woman. That name was Effie Conochie, and there were more details on who Effie was. In 1855 Britain's Parliament had enacted the Passenger Act to regulate passenger traffic leaving Britain. It required ships to keep two passenger lists, one to be given to customs at the port of departure and one to be given to customs at the port of arrival. What the Hudson's Bay Company kept in its records was a copy of those lists, which under the terms of the act recorded name, age, sex, occupation, relationship, destination, birthplace and residence in the old country of all emigrants. What the list told DeClercq—who then passed the information on to Bond—was that Effie Conochie was thirteen years old in 1857. Traveling with her guardian, Callum Campbell, this orphan of a Campbell sept, born and raised in Argyll, Scotland, was shipping

out to Vancouver Island to start a new life with Callum
and his two sons.

She wasn't Callum's mistress.

She was Callum's "daughter."

And that's why Effie was residing at his homestead
when Callum died in 1863.

The four had disembarked from the *New Caledonia*
at Vancouver Island in 1857. Shouts of "Gold!" echoed
from up the Fraser River the next year, and miners came
rushing north from going-bust California. Some ventured
up the coast by land to Seattle, and on up Puget Sound
by boat to the Fraser, while others clipper-shipped by
sea from San Francisco to Vancouver Island, and on by
small boat to the Fraser on the Mainland through Active
Pass past Miners Bay or along Haro Strait through
Boundary Pass. Callum saw the chance to make a lot of
money fast, for all those miners needed food, booze,
shelter and field supplies, so he selected three tracts of
homestead land on different routes to the Fraser gold
rush. Son Dugald settled the way station at Doe Bay,
Orcas Island, along the Seattle cruise. Son Ewen settled
the way station at Miners Bay, Mayne Island, halfway
along Active Pass. If Callum's plan was to cover the
three main routes to the gold fields, that meant, Jenna
deduced, that he settled his homestead way station just
south of what is now the Canada-U.S. border.

In Boundary Pass.

In Haro Strait.

And Effie settled with him.

Trouble brewed the following year, with the Pig War
between Britain and the States. Son Ewen could file for
ownership of his tract in the British colony, but Callum,
Effie and son Dugald, south of the mid-line through
Haro Strait, found themselves in no man's land, unable
to file for ownership of either tract until it was decided
whether the British-American border was Haro or Rosario Strait.

Then Callum died in limbo.

Before the border was settled.

And Effie, nineteen, was left in possession of his un-registered homestead tract.

So why, Jenna asked herself, now that we have her name, is Effie still a mystery woman in all federal and county records?

There was no Effie Conochie in either census faxed from the National Archives by Tom Holland. That she wasn't in the 1870 one was understandable: the San Juans weren't officially in the United States until 1872. But why was Effie missing from the 1880 census? And why had Effie not—as Jenna learned from a follow-up fax from Holland—filed under the Homestead Act for ownership of Callum's tract after the border was drawn? Nor had Effie sought to become an American.

Why? Why? Why?

There was no Effie Conochie in any San Juan County record. Joan Finch had checked census, marriage, death, burial, will and tax files. True, records were missing for the early years, as most statistics except those having to do with land had to wait for county government to evolve. But still, why did Effie not surface later?

Why? Why? Why?

The clue had to be the argument between Dugald and Ewen, after which Effie was never again acknowledged by Callum's sons.

Was the clue a scandal?

Or some abhorrent crime?

Then suddenly another long shot had zipped through Jenna's mind.

So early this afternoon, she had left Friday Harbor for Orcas Island, where now she tied the *Islomania* to the float in front of the farmhouse that Hank Bond had built, climbing the path to the pillared veranda beneath the gabled room in which she had been born, skirting the fenced potato patch she had been hoeing when her involvement in this case began with the call from the office because Fitzroy Campbell would not answer his

phone. Gram and Becky were playing a game of cards
on the porch, and they paused twice to wave welcome
to Jenna as she approached. The sun was out and the
maples around were bright with autumn color, but fog
shrouding the moon was forecast for tonight.

Prelude to Halloween.

"What ya playing?" Jenna asked.

"Old Maid," said Becky.

The six-year-old slapped down a pair of cards.

Jenna glanced disapprovingly at her mother.

"Lighten up," said Gram. "You played Old Maid
when you were young. Did it do you any harm?"

"Yeah," Becky piped in. "Don't be that sex word,
Mom."

"Women can't be sexist. Only men, Becs."

"But you told me I could be anything I wanted. Why
can men be sexist and not me? Is that fair? You
fibbed, Mom."

Jenna rolled her eyes.

"Yeah," echoed Gram. "You played Old Maid. Why
not your daughter?"

"Yeah," pressed Becky. "*Why not,* Mom?"

"I give up," Jenna sighed, throwing her hands into
the air.

"Now you've spoiled it, Mom. Let's play Snakes and
Ladders, Gram."

Gram glanced disapprovingly at her daughter.

"Does your umbrage at Old Maid extend to witches?"
she asked Jenna. "Because Becky and I thought the
three of us should dress up as the three witches from
Macbeth for Halloween."

Becky cackled: "Double, double, toil and trouble; /
Fire burn and cauldron bubble . . ."

Gram cackled: "Eye of newt and toe of frog, / Wool
of bat and tongue of dog . . ."

Becky cackled: "Finger of birth-strangled babe /
Ditch-deliver'd by a drab . . ."

Jenna's eyes widened.

"Now you don't approve of Shakespeare?" said Gram, segueing into another cackle: "By the pricking of my thumbs, / Something wicked this way comes. . . ."

"That's you, Mom. The Wicked Witch of the West." Grandmother and granddaughter laughed in unison at the daughter/mother caught between, the true meaning of generation gap.

It was ever thus.

This Campbell case had her in no mood for Scottish curses, but Jenna knew when she was pinned to the floor by a wrestling tag-team, so she gazed down benevolently at Becky and said, "Witches are okay."

Becky frowned.

"Aren't witches old maids?"

Luckily, Gram rescued Jenna. "What brings you home in the middle of the day?"

"Remember that book Dad swore he would write after he retired?"

"The Northwestern?"

"Did you keep his notes?"

"They're in the branded trunk, in case one day you decide to do it."

Jenna left the Old Maids to play out their game, a streak of stubbornness in her daughter coming into play to scotch Snakes and Ladders, and entered the farmhouse stabbed by sunbeams. The rays lit details randomly. The Wild West revolvers mounted on the wall, Peacemaker 45s and such. A photo of the patriarchs of San Juan Island: three old-timers in brimmed hats and long white beards, rough hands folded in laps of dusty coarse cloth, not a hint of a smile as flinty eyes squinted suspiciously at the camera lens. Ed Warbass, Charlie McKay and Stephen Boyce had carved this county out of wilderness, and men like them were the tough nuts admired by Hank Bond, and were why he'd gathered the stories now stored in the branded trunk, one corner of which was grazed by a sunbeam that missed its mark.

Hank Bond, like the FBI, had a beef with Hollywood

over its lionizing of the Mounted Police. What irked the
Suits was the fact that Americans created the myth of
the Mounted, and now the FBI had to better that fiction.
From as far back as 1910's *Riders of the Plains* by Tom
Edison—inventor of the movie projector, no less!—the
studios had churned out 250 Mountie flicks, known in
the trade as Northwesterns. What irked Hank was the
term *Northwestern,* for studio moguls seemed to slant a
"Western" line from Montana to Oregon, then jump to
the Horsemen for Northwesterns, which frankly Hank
thought pretty un-fucking-American.

Look at a map, you Hollywood quislings.

The *American* Northwest is right here!

San Juan County, thank you very much.

And here has a lot of thrilling Northwestern tales, too.

So why aren't any of *ours* up on the screen?

What Hank Bond had planned to do was reverse that.

For decades, he had collected tales of crime in the
Wild Northwest, gathering them from old-timers now
long gone. (Sheriffs didn't keep records back then, the
blight of the paper-pusher yet to come. You think Wyatt
Earp and Wild Bill kept files?)

When Hank retired, he planned to write the great
Northwestern so Hollywood could see the error of its
slight of San Juan County. But as the poet said about
the best-laid schemes, the good voters of the islands
wouldn't let him go, returning Hank to office a record
twelve times, all while interest in the Western was going,
going, gone. . . . Eventually, the unretired sheriff suffered a stroke at Friday Harbor and died with his
boots on.

So here they were, in the trunk beside his reading
chair—trunk charred with classic brands from ranches in
Washington State, and serving as a coffee table for the
phone and whatever Western Hank Bond had been
reading—the untold tales of the Wild Northwest.

And wild was mild for them.

San Juan was a hump of territory in no man's land.

A hundred American troops camped down at Griffin Bay, a hundred British troops camped up at Garrison Bay, and there was nobody with certain power to make and enforce any laws, just free land, no taxes and the four *b*'s: beer, booze, broads and brawls. San Juan soon became the refuge of every scoundrel north and south of a border that did not exist.

Eat your hearts out Tombstone and Dodge City.

San Juan was as new as a county could be when the task of hanging Kanaka Joe fell to Sheriff Steve Boyce, one of the patriarchs in the photo that hung on the farmhouse wall. The gallows was erected on a popular beach, a site chosen to accommodate a sizable crowd. Beer was served to the hundreds of folks who came from all around, many bringing their kids to enjoy the picnic atmosphere. Joe was marched to the scaffold by Sheriff Boyce. His final request was, "I want to die quick," to which the lawman responded, "Be a good boy, and I will treat you as well as I can."

Unfortunately, the hanging rope was also as new as could be. So instead of forming a loose noose that would slip tight to quickly snap his spine, the hangman's knot stuck as Joe dropped through the sprung trap. He hung dangling, wind cut off, slowly choking to death.

Kids screamed as parents tried to cover their eyes and ears. Horrified men on the gallows wondered what to do. Finally, Sheriff Boyce grabbed the rope like Tarzan and swung himself over the trap, where he kicked at the knot to close it. Twenty minutes it took before the doc declared Joe dead.

Imagine that in Cinemascope, you Hollywood execs.

One of the many gems in Hank Bond's trunk.

Jenna removed the phone from the lid and placed it on the floor, then moved the Catherine Cookson novel Gram was reading so she could open the branded trunk and search for Hank's character list. The list was an index to all the good guys and bad guys who might provide characters for the great Northwestern; it was as complete a guide to San Juan mayhem as you could find.

What Jenna hoped to find . . .

And found! . . .

Was Effie Conochie.

The Hellfire Cult.

Of Brother XIII.

And Madame Eff.

Colosseum

Vancouver, British Columbia

The glory of Ancient Rome survives at the heart of Vancouver with a Colosseum to rival the amphitheater in which Antigonus Severus had won his freedom only to lose his head so many centuries ago. Having parked his Benz in a lot on Georgia Street, DeClercq stood at the intersection with Homer Street and looked up. A full downtown block in girth and nine stories high, the swirl of glass and reddish-brown granite with Colosseumlike tiers of columns stacked to the sky had an ego to match its status as monument, edifice, landmark. The only gladiators clashing for a thumbs-up from the crowd were in History and Government on Level 6, but that didn't deter bitchy types in the Tinker Toy elite from trashing the new $100-million Vancouver Public Library as a Caesar's Palace, referring no doubt to the glory of present-day Las Vegas, not that of Ancient Rome.

DeClercq loved this building.

It was his research home.

Especially Northwest History on Level 7.

Rush-hour traffic was underway as he curved around the outside plaza at the intersection to enter the covered promenade between the Colosseum ellipse and the rectangle within. The library was a traditional library turned inside out, for instead of having the people inside surrounded by books, here the books were shelved inside in the library rectangle and people sat in the reading galleries in the Colosseum oval. Every seat was a window on the outside world, but readers were still far from the madding crowd because they were separated from the actual library by a glassy atrium that plunged eight floors to the promenade where DeClercq walked in.

Smells of gourmet pizza and coffee assailed him at the door. The half-moon of the promenade felt more like a street than a mall, a series of sidewalk caffés in the Colosseum curve to his left and the comings and goings of library users to his right. He gave the big building a big once-over, his eyes sweeping up the glass, behind which readers sat face to face at tables stacked floor by floor to the skylight above. One woman in a miniskirt sat like Sharon Stone being interrogated in *Basic Instinct*.

The view from below.

Halfway around the curve, DeClercq angled right to enter the library.

Inside, the building was built for speed. Move 'em in. Move 'em up. Move 'em down. Move 'em out. Stairs to the left beyond the check-out and the anti-theft gates went down to the Children's Library on the lower level. Walk straight ahead and you were grabbed by two elevators or the escalator. Check-in and the information center were right, and near them stood a beefy security guard who was at least six-foot-four in height, the blue uniform around him as tight as Batman's leotard. A ponytail cascaded down his back to his bottom.

"Hi, Moe."

"Hi, Chief."

"How goes the battle?"

"Same as you," said the guard. "The struggle never ends against pervs and predators."

"Fingers still around?"

"Got rid of him. He's got a new girl in one of the malls."

"Move 'em out," said DeClercq.

"The bad 'uns," said Moe, hefting his belt as if a gun hung at his waist.

DeClercq and Moe had first conversed back when the cop was closing in on the Headhunter's lair, not during the *original* manhunt years ago, but during the clean-up that became Headhunter II. One of those street bums who loiter in the library to keep warm, Fingers was a blind guy madly in love with Eve. Eve was the braille sign on the women's john. (Is *john* sexist? Ask the Word Police.) Signs in the library are tactile for the sight-impaired to feel—triangles for men, circles for women (where is Dr. Freud?)—and Fingers would finger the circle on the women's john, muttering sweet nothings to Eve until Moe was called. When the guard arrived and asked him to leave the sign alone, the bum would take a swing at Moe for trying to steal his girl.

"Must be dull with Fingers gone?"

"Nah," said Moe. "Lots of fish to fry. Some perv's slipping porn into kiddies' books and a skinny flasher streaked Fine Arts last week screaming he was the model for Michelangelo's David. A geez went berserk yesterday in Newspapers and Magazines when he found someone else in the lucky chair where he checks his stocks. A librarian got slapped by a biddy enraged by the fact that 'that smutty book Madonna's *Sex* is on reserve. The book, incidentally, has the record for most reserves: 1,023. Madonna will be on old-age pension before the last one checks out her puss breaking the water."

"I'll keep an eye peeled for trouble."

"You're deputized," said Moe.

The Mountie rode one of the elevators up to Level 7, and exited to find two men jockeying a new photocopy machine toward Special Collections. An end-run before they blocked the way slid him through the door flanked by rare children's books on display, with Punch and the Mad Hatter in glass cases. Two long tables crossed in front of him, bearing signs that read: No Materials May Be Removed from This Room, and Only Pencils May Be Used in This Room. Leafing through an old book at the closer table sat a very sexy woman, her russet hair skillfully teased, a catlike quality to her sloped eyes and cheekbones, her figure so voluptuous she could model lingerie. DeClercq wondered what she was searching for so intently in that volume that she seemed completely oblivious to what was going on around her.

He angled left to the Northwest History Index just inside the door.

Cards from *Salt* to *Sea* were in drawer 79.

He flipped through the cards until he found titles under the right subject, noting the call numbers with a pencil provided, then carried the slip of paper forward to the Special Collections service desk, which was turned sideways to keep a watchful eye on those using precious material from—"the vault."

The librarian behind the desk had her watchful eye on the babe behind DeClercq. An owl-like woman in Coke-bottle glasses, with silver hair tucked in a bun and Minnie Mouse white gloves on her hands because she was reading something from the sixteenth century, Charity Cox gazed at the sexpot with a glare that said only in an unfair world was a looker stacked like that also able to read. Her sourness softened as DeClercq blocked the offending view. Cox, too, had helped him hunt for the Headhunter, so it felt like old home week this afternoon at the new Colosseum.

"Charity."

"Chief."

"New job?"

"Temporary. No food or drink is allowed in Special Collections. The staff in here has been known to die of malnutrition."

Her usual station was down in Science and Technology on Level 4.

He passed her the slip with the penciled call numbers.

"I need two books."

"Be right back," she said, standing and turning to

walk to the storage vault off the aisle behind her desk in the work area.

The vault had temperature and humidity controls to ensure optimum preservation conditions for the library's Special Collections. So valuable were some books that security measures encompassed staff as well as the public. Northwest History embraced early works covering the exploration and settlement of the West Coast before and after boundaries and names were determined. Historic Photographs catalogued two hundred thousand images from those times, and because DeClercq was writing a history of the Mounties policing the Klondike, research had required him to spend recent evenings here.

Today the subject was Scots.

A good military tactician secures all fronts, and Effie Conochie was an important front in this case. The land-title office had reported back: no pioneer with that name had pre-empted land in B.C. Nor did she seem to have left a mark in other government records. Rossmo had centered the north-of-the-border search for Nick on Saturna Island with his jeopardy, so Inspector Zinc Chandler and a wave of Mounties had hit the shore to comb every nook and cranny. Rossmo had yet to summon DeClercq with results from the mystery search he hoped would narrow the dragnet, so to advance the remaining front that was Effie Conochie, the chief had decided to drive downtown to check the Northwest History Index for a lead on her.

The call numbers on the slip were for *Scots in New Caledonia,* published in a very limited edition in 1893, and *The Scots Directory of West Coast Pioneers,* printed privately in Victoria in 1903.

Charity stopped on her way to the vault, swiveled and walked back.

She tapped the slip of paper from DeClercq.

"Call number 971. Stacks row 38. A popular subject

today. Both books are out. The woman sitting behind you requested them."

So now DeClercq was swiveling 180 degrees. Halfway around, he gazed through the windows of the library rectangle and across the atrium through the Colosseum gallery at the giant *Ragtime* sign and blow-ups on the Ford Centre for the Performing Arts across the street: Happy ragtimers in straw hats were singing to beat a band. An empty bird's nest was nestled beneath the *C* in Ford Centre. A quarter turn more swiveled him around to face the sexy woman, who looked up from leafing through *The Scots Directory* and seemed to recognize him even though he had never seen her before.

Suddenly she grabbed both books and bolted for the door.

"Effie Conochie," Mephisto had said, gazing at the Internet message DeClercq had filed on the historians' bulletin board in cyberspace, shortly after the chopper had returned him to the island from Seattle. "Where did I see that name? Where? Where? Where? Got it," he said, snapping his fingers. "While tracking the Campbells. Conochie's mentioned in two books at the Vancouver library."

So here she was. Having been choppered up to the helipad along the inner harbor, she'd trudged a few blocks up to the Colosseum and now sat in Special Collections perusing the two books, tracing the links between Effie Conochie and the Hellfire Cult.

Her ears caught a comment at the service desk.

"The woman sitting behind you requested them." Donella glanced up to find DeClercq turning toward her, the cop she had watched through binoculars as he recovered Nick's hand, the cop she had tailed to the Classics Department at UBC and the cop who undoubtedly wanted these books to track Effie, too.

He looked at her suspiciously.

Was he wondering why she was reading about pioneer Scots so soon after he had posted a message about Effie on the Internet?

If he read these books, he'd learn about the Hellfire Cult.

The Hellfire Cult of Madame Eff on Madrona Island.

That's why Donella scooped up the books and bolted for the door, though only to find that door blocked by two men trying to maneuver a new photocopy machine into Special Collections. Quickly the librarian at the service desk was yelling, " 'No Materials May Be Removed from This Room.' Can't you read?" and the Mountie was moving toward her as she veered from the door to slip through an opening in the counter beside the service desk, shoving a book cart at the cop to slow him down, while ignoring the Staff Only sign to sprint away up the aisle through the work area past the vault.

———

Books flew off the cart as he pushed it aside.

"Careful!" cried Charity. "Those texts are as rare as unicorn horns!"

His hand whapped down on the negative viewer as he burst through the counter, sweeping away a photo of men shot in front of a tent with a sign that announced City Hall.

"You just wiped out Vancouver's beginning!" yelled the librarian.

He felt like a bull in a china shop.

A bull too old for a chase.

For now he, too, was sprinting up the aisle behind the service desk, the vault on one side and nooks where staff labored on the other, past the flotsam and jetsam of workstations everywhere, a blur of minutiae zipping by the corner of his eye—red McHappy Days balloon in Sue's In-Tray; a plastic pig with glasses on the paper-

cutter; a picture of Elvis snapped the one time he sang
in Vancouver, swearing he would never come back because the girls squealed *too* loud; computers; notes; lock-
ers, five in a row—then he was opposite the office of the
division head and around the corner to the left where
whoever hoped to shake him had disappeared.

Donella glanced back.

The Mountie was rounding the corner.

She contemplated drawing the Colt Combat Commander holstered beneath her jacket at the small of her
back, but there were too many levels between here and
the street to make taking a shot a safe option.

A shot fired too high up would give street patrols
enough time to respond if someone called 9-1-1 on hearing gunfire.

Charity Cox was fuming.

Not only did it irk her that the hussy could read, but
now the sexpot had heisted two irreplaceable books,
breaching Special Collections security to make good
her escape.

Charity grabbed the phone and called down for Moe.

As DeClercq rounded the corner, his quarry glanced
back along a hall of administration offices, before
rounding another corner to vanish again.

He huffed and puffed after her, feeling every year of
his age.

Yanking open a door took him out to Reception, the
receptionist's desk angled left to face the escalators, a
model of the Colosseum in a glass case in front. The

Mountie saw his quarry pass both elevators to make a
U around to the down escalator on the far side, where
those two men were still trying to jockey the copy machine through the Special Collections door.

He reached the top of the escalator as she reached
the bottom and ran straight ahead on Level 6, History
and Government, Fine Arts and Music.

DeClercq ran down the escalator several steps at a
time.

———

If it wasn't pervs and predators, it was thieves.

The alert call from Charity Cox on Level 7 reached
Moe on the ground floor, Level 2, by way of the plug
in his ear.

From his station by the information desk, the guard
hurried to the elevators to catch the one with an open
door and press its button for Level 5.

His plan was to cut the thief off at the pass.

———

On Level 6, both sides of the escalator swarmed with as
many people as a Mexican bus station just before the
last bus to San Diego.

Some sort of tour.

All carried map guides.

Milling in front of the elevators and choking the paths
on both sides to the down escalator to Level 5.

So forward she ran.

To one side was a poster of a circular Indian mask
advertising *Masks of the Northwest Coast: Down from
the Shimmering Sky,* then she was into one of the few
aisles of compact shelving and out the other end, turning
right at the windows that gazed down on the promenade
far below; Blenz coffee, Flying Wedge pizza and Duthie
Books ranged around the Colosseum curve, while above

them was the reader who sat like Sharon Stone in *Basic Instinct,* her blouse cut so low you could see all the way to China from high up here.

The view from above.

Sexy place, this library.

Like Rome's Colosseum.

———

Past the poster, through the shelves, right at the windows, then right again, DeClercq chased the fugitive back through the library to the *Ragtime* side. Political junkies of every persuasion read books on conservatism, liberalism, fascism, Marxism or anarchism at tables in the rectangle, several having dozed off on such weighty tomes, then a jog right and a jog left swerved her onto one of two open bridges across the plummeting atrium to the reading gallery in the Colosseum's curve. The Mountie had her trapped if he could block both bridges, the one she had just crossed, which he reached now, and the one at the other end of the gallery, which she dashed toward.

A man in the middle of that bridge was gazing over the rail into the ninety-foot plunge to the concrete floor far below.

"Police!" DeClercq shouted. "Stop that woman!"

———

The idea was that a reader would select a book from the shelves in the inner library, then cross the airy atrium on one of the ten-foot-long, six-foot-wide bridges with three-foot-high side rails to the quiet reading gallery on the periphery, and there could look out on the world he or she was reading about from a luxurious cherrywood table.

Great in concept.

Dangerous in practice.

The man in the middle of the bridge spanning back to Fine Arts and Music didn't hear DeClercq shout because he was listening to a Puccini opera CD borrowed from the library collection on his Discman. An aria blared in headphones clamped to his ears as he peered over the rail to watch the human ants six floors below, for the atrium plunged to the lowest level's Technical Services Division, where material was purchased, processed and catalogued for the entire library system, including branches stuck out in the sticks.

Movement on the bridge startled Mr. Opera, causing him to jump as Donella rushed full-tilt toward him. The woman saw this action as a reaction to what DeClercq was shouting, so she whipped the Colt from its holster in a roundhouse swing that caught the heedless man under the chin, reeling him back against the three-foot-high rail, which rolled him like a fulcrum at his waist overtop the barrier and into inner space.

He sang an aria of his own all the way down, where he crashed into bookmobiles and broke every bone in his body.

Y
A
A
A
A
a
a
a
a
!

Woman with a gun!
Woman with a gun!
Patrons in Fine Arts and Music dove for cover as the gunwoman weaved through.

No heroes here after witnessing Mr. Opera's backward swan dive.

Jesus, lady, you can keep those fuckin' books!

Though maybe not in those words.

This *was* Fine Arts.

Donella dashed from that bridge toward the escalator.

The cop dashed from this bridge toward the escalator.

The escalator was halfway between.

Donella got there first, only to find it crammed full of people, half the tour group going down and half coming up, so she stuffed both books into the waistband of her jeans to free one hand.

Gun in hand, the Mountie was close behind.

Someone on Level 3 had punched the Up button.

The elevator doors opened on a Chinese girl.

"Security," Moe barked, finger punching the button for Level 5. "Take the next one."

Granted, she hadn't taken gymnastics since school, but much like riding a bicycle, the technique, once mastered, remains, so with one hand forward on the hand grip of the up escalator and the gun hand back for balance on the grip of the down escalator, Donella somersaulted over a barrier to land on the slick stainless-steel slide that divided the escalators, then—*wheeeeee!*—like a youngster in a playground, slid to Level 5.

A blast from the Colt blew out the barrier at the bottom.

Through she went . . .

Hit the floor . . .

Rolled once . . .

Gained her feet . . .

And bolted forward along the aisle between rows of compact shelving.

Level 5, Newspapers and Magazines.

———

Too many years had passed since he'd taken gymnastics in school, and as they say, you can't teach an old dog new tricks, so because it was the only way to keep on her tail, and whoever she was, she was the only lead he had to Nick—assuming she was running to carry those books to Mephisto and to keep them from DeClercq, but what other reason could she have for pulling a gun?—over the barrier he *climbed* and down he slid as panicked patrons stampeded up both the down and up escalators to retreat from the shot.

Helter skelter, he thought.

———

Level 5 was the floor of lounge lizards, news junkies browsing the day away over favorite newspapers flown in from around the world and kept company by street people in to keep warm. Back-issue storage takes up a lot of space, so compact shelving lined Level 5. Donella slipped through the last aisle that had been opened to retrieve a back date.

Compact shelving works like an accordion.

Shelves press together.

Shelves pull apart.

Movement is controlled by buttons on a pad mounted at the end of each row.

Donella veered right at the end of the open aisle, skirting the far ends of several rows before screeching to a halt to punch the buttons that activated movement of the shelves between the open aisle and the pad. Then she whirled and sprinted back as fast as she could. She raced past the end of the open aisle through which she had just slipped and kept going.

Rumble, rumble, rumble . . .

The shifting rows closed the aisle.

The aisle up which his quarry had vanished was now too narrow for him. Slowly the rows of rumbling shelves were stealing space from that aisle to pass it to an aisle opening along the way, all the compact shelves now six inches apart. The solid light brown wall wasn't solid anymore, yet this expanding accordion barricaded him from her more effectively than the compact shelving had done, for at least that had had an aisle wide enough to slip through, instead of slits you had to be Jack Sprat to use.

Rumble, rumble, rumble . . .

He side-stepped right toward the new aisle, which was expanding so slowly it might not have been wide enough for another year, trying to catch sight of her at the other end. But it was like looking between the cars of a trundling train to glimpse beyond. Then suddenly he spotted her, zipping across to his left, bursting from an aisle through compacted shelving past the escalator, where she swung the Colt around and took a shot at him.

Pandemonium.

The elevator stopped at Level 5.

Moe pressed the earplug to his ear, trying to hear the conflicting reports from Security downstairs.

The elevator doors opened on Level 5.

Some fool had swan-dived off a bridge on 6?

Thundering herds of patrons had surged up from 5?

There was a loud bang heard on 4?

Moe stepped out on Level 5 and glanced left to see if some copycat was in a swan dive.

Herd mentality, he thought.

"No mo!" he heard, the sentence incomplete, the voice from the earplug or in his other ear?

No mo' money?

No mo' time?

Then he glanced right and understood.

No, Moe, don't!

But it was too late.

The woman rushing toward him, with DeClercq not far behind, raised a gun as she approached and shot poor Moe point blank.

———

The guard spun away from her in a spray of blood.

Donella turned and took another shot at DeClercq.

She was no marksman.

The shot was wild.

But it gave her time to step into the elevator that Moe had ridden up, punch *L* for Lobby, and watch the closing doors shut out the cop.

———

Secret Service agents in the United States must be willing to take a bullet for the president.

That's impressive.

But not as impressive as this.

Moe the guard had just taken a bullet for a *book!*

Two books, actually.

"Get her!" Moe ordered, nursing a wounded arm.

"You okay?" DeClercq stopped to ask.

"When God was handing out aim, she was off in line to get those tits."

Alice in Wonderland.

Donella in Canada.

Punch *L* under the number 2 in America and you could expect an elevator to take you to the lobby on the main floor. In Canada that's a lot to expect, for here 2 was the main floor, which made you wonder what happened to 1, since *L* stood for Lower Level. Which made no sense either, as there were seven levels, so it should be Lowest Level. Go figure.

The upshot, or rather, the *down*shot—a confusing people, these Canadians—was that the elevator took Donella down to the Dungeon, as those sent to work here called it. Instead of the doors she had entered opening in front of her, the doors behind her slid open on Lilliput in the basement and Donella stepped out to Wonderland, to mix classical allusions.

"Police! Clear the way!" he shouted, bounding down several escalators full-stride, racing that elevator to the main floor, where she could escape, and arriving to find that it had yet to turn up. Then squeals from downstairs told him where she was.

Left of the elevators, a wide staircase led to the Children's Library on the Lower Level.

Lilliput it was, for everything had shrunk, so she felt like Gulliver among the Little People. Shelves and chairs and tables were miniature size, and steps helped petite mouths up to drinking fountains. A tiny world so tiny tots could function like adults, and the pervs who preyed here could be watched by Moe.

Wonderland it was, for there were wonders here: an

open space with light filtered from banks of windows on the city streets above, glistening water cascading into a mosaic pool outside, tiles glinting with coins tossed in for luck. Wonder infused the faces of kids stationed in nooks arced dead ahead as she rushed from the elevator; a staircase to her left descended from Level 2, and the voice of DeClercq could be heard echoing down as Donella ran for the nooks, his shout of "Police! Clear the way!" turning wondering heads about. Older heads turned in the Explorations Galleries at the foot of the stairs; one gallery blared its "Food Glorious Food" theme with a pictorial sign encircled by three-dimensional pop-ups of fruit-and-vegetable faces. Next around the curve of nooks backed by the waterfall was the Kids' Lounge, where kids stretched on their tummies reading Rudyard Kipling's "How the Camel Got His Hump" and "How the Rhinoceros Got His Skin" and "How the Leopard Got His Spots." Toddler Play Area had the youngest faces, ga-ga babes and their moms here for Baby Time. Hook 'em young, the library's creed. Wide-eyed wonder turned to oh'd mouths squealing screams as the woman with the gun neared. Kids scrambled to hide behind a great big teddy bear wearing a jacket, a green snake curved among cushions on the floor and a winged dragon in the final nook, the Preschooler Lounge beside the Children's Art Gallery.

The art gallery was a bow-sided tunnel filled with splashes of color; Donella turned in as the cop came down the stairs.

The art gallery led to a short passage of glass.

Behind the pane to her left splashed the waterfall pool.

Behind the pane to her right ran stairs up to the street.

In her haste, she had missed the exit door.

The Children's Story Room ahead was a dead end in which *The Cat in the Hat* was being read to what Donella saw as potential hostages.

The mobile overhead was a child's flight of fancy, a little girl flying like Peter Pan with a winged horse like Pegasus. From the foot of the stairs, DeClercq ran parallel to the curve of nooks, passing shelves of fairy tales and *Wild About* books, with monkeys and palms decorating pillars. His quarry was in the art gallery that led to the story room, where through a nook window and the passage of glass he had an angle view of the circle of kids. Then she appeared in the passage with the Colt raised to shoot, and—*bwam! bwam! bwam!*— pulled off three rounds.

His heart lurched.

The quickest way out to the stairs was to make her own door, so Donella stopped short of the story room to raise the gun, turn right and blast three .45 APC shots at the pane of glass. The glass fractured like *Charlotte's Web* around the holes, then a flat-footed kick sent fragments flying.

No need for hostages.

Out she went.

While an onrush of terrified children streamed out of the story room, along the passage of broken glass and through the art gallery tunnel to push back DeClercq as he came in.

Dashing through the shattered pane and up eighteen cobbled steps, the Mountie found himself at the corner of Homer and Robson streets, just down the way from the sign for *Ragtime.*

A crowd worthy of the crowd that jostled to Rome's Colosseum to watch Antigonus fight now jostled along

Robson toward the sports colosseum that was B.C. Place. The crowd was on its way to see Page and Plant in concert tonight, fifty thousand rock fans flowing in to idolize the veterans of Led Zeppelin.

This tide of people had swallowed up the woman who stole the books.

Snake Pit

Shipwreck Island, Washington State

"I need a piece of you," the Devil Man had said as the Devil Woman pulled the knife from her teeth with the hand that had gripped Nick's balls.

The cut had been a slow and methodical one, sawing back and forth to sever Nick's ear from his head, while his cry of pain and terror echoed from the dungeon cell along the subterranean tunnel to the steps that climbed to the root cellar above.

His cry had wailed up to a shriek when she lowered the knife to his groin and scratched its tip in a tease around his penis.

"Next time," she cooed, "I'll come for your cock."

To staunch the blood that gushed down his cheek to his chest, she had taped a bandage to his head, then had plucked his ear and her discarded tartan from the stone floor to exit with the Devil Man, leaving Nick alone in the dark to contemplate her threat.

How long had passed from then to now Nick couldn't tell, for he had drifted in and out of consciousness, a blessing because it snuffed the pain from his wrist and his head, a curse because it brought nightmares as dark as reality.

He is squealing like a pig down on his hands and knees, trying to crawl away from her slithering after him, knife in her teeth as she reaches forward with a clawed grasp to seize him by the genitals, squeezing squeal on

*squeal from him as she stretches his manhood tight like
an elastic band, then draws the razor-sharp edge of the
knife across him like a violin bow.*

Nick jerked awake in the blackness, but that didn't
stop the squeals, high-pitched squeals from the direction
of the door, squeals *in* his cell not out in the hall. Then
he heard a more unnerving sound.

Footsteps . . .

Far off . . .

Coming closer . . .

Until soft light crept in under the door . . .

Light that trapped the source of the squeals . . .

A mouse with terror in its eyes scratched the rock
floor, trying to scamper across to Nick, but the rodent
was deformed in some way, for its fur seemed to end at
its middle and it had some sort of growth on its behind,
then his squint adjusted and he realized that the growth
was a garter snake, its mouth around the hindquarters
of the mouse as it slowly swallowed its prey alive.

Footsteps at the door . . .

Squeal . . .

Squeal . . .

Squeal . . .

The Silver Skull

Madrona Island, Washington State

The madrona is an ecdysiast, the striptease artist of nature, always shedding something no matter what the season; flowers, berries, bark, leaves, off they tumble from its naked, suntanned limbs, limbs as sensually sexy as an erotic writhe onstage.

A fitting tree for this island.

Given what went on here.

All of which Hank had recorded in his notes in the branded trunk.

Madrona Island.

The Hellfire Cult.

The sun was setting to the west as Bond maneuvered the *Islomania* close to shore, then dropped anchor a few lengths out, a seven-pound kellet attached to the chain to reduce its scope. Wisps of fog were already swirling over the sea as she lowered the dinghy to the water and loaded it with gear: propane lamps, pick, shovel and a metal detector once used to sweep the ground for mines. Jenna was dressed like a lumberjack, in boots and jeans, with a red-checked mackinaw against the oncoming chill. Oar in hand, she climbed over the gunnel, then paddled to the rocky beach.

The dinghy "touched the hard," as nautical people say—and prostitutes probably say, too, truth be known—and Jenna stepped ashore into a whispering gallery. A wave of rock curled above her like a petrified breaker, the sea having eaten this cliff away for eons since the last ice age retreated north. The open-sided tunnel ran along the shoreline, and collected every sound skimming in across the brine. Slaps of waves. Cries of gulls. An electric guitar.

It was easy to see why Callum Campbell had settled *this* tract of land as his homestead. Unlike his sons on Orcas and Mayne, he had an entire island to himself; he might as well have been living in his own country. No doubt that's what also appealed to the dissipated heavy-metal rocker thrashing chords in his hideaway studio at the island's northern tip, the same rocker who made millions of dollars off publicity by pissing on his adoring fans in New York City.

No wonder he hadn't answered the phone when Jenna called to say she was boating to Madrona Island to search the old Beacon.

He couldn't hear it.

But even down here at the southern tip Jenna could hear him.

And so, probably, could the whole Pacific Northwest. "No man is an island," as the poet said.

But Callum Campbell had come pretty close.

On a map it must have seemed that this island—up here in the northeast corner of the San Juans, where Rosario Strait, Boundary Pass and Georgia Strait met—was perfectly located to make money fast off the Fraser gold rush, but history, not geography, had called the shots.

Unlike the Cariboo gold rush, which followed on its heels, the Fraser gold rush was largely a Californians' affair. It's called a rush because the goal is to stake your claim fast, and that means getting to the field as quickly as you can. So while some miners did journey by land up to Seattle, and some did sail in by way of Haro Strait, word of mouth among the miners blazed the main route to the Fraser, and that was through Active Pass to Ewen Campbell's way station at Miners Bay.

Worse, the Fraser rush was but a flash in the pan, and soon those twenty-five thousand miners were off to the Cariboo hinterland between the Coast Mountains and the Rockies, abandoning Ewen, too.

And if that wasn't bad enough, the Pig War focused on the entrance to Haro Strait; artillery batteries and gunboats made an effective blockade between ship traffic and here.

No man is an island?

Callum Campbell was.

Living here with Effie like a recluse.

Then Callum had drowned in no man's land before he could leave a mark, unable to claim this island because of the Pig War. No sign of him was entered in records filed in either country, and Effie—another non-person—was left in possession of Madrona Island.

Effie Conochie.

A Scottish lass.

Nineteen, naive, lonely and alone.

Who'd boated to Vancouver Island for supplies, and there fell under the spell of Brother XIII.

Brother XIII.

The Hellfire Cult.

Tools in one hand, lamps in the other, Bond walked the length of the whispering gallery, hunting for a way to scale the cliff to the Beacon while trying to block out the wailing guitar grating her nerves. A whispering gallery, my ass. An amplification chamber! Jenna wished she had brought her Walkman and some Roy Orbison tapes. The racket skimmed across the concave bay, which bit into the west side of the island so it resembled a crescent moon to planes overhead.

Driftwood bleached as pale as whale bones littered the beach. The low sun slanted in to color thousands of oyster and clam shells abandoned by ebbing tides. Kelp bulbs like those she had popped as a kid squished under Bond's feet, almost leading her into a pratfall onto the sharp-edged teeth of barnacles. Seals in the water laughed at her. A great blue heron took to wing.

The smell of the sea was strong.

Clammy air.

At one point, the shale of the overhang had crashed down to the beach, opening a gully of striated steps up the face of the cliff. The vegetation modified as Jenna climbed, cedars down low with twisting, snakelike trunks and frondlike limbs; then fern gardens up to her waist, amid boulders green with moss; then higher up, where the growing got hard, Douglas firs consorting with madronas stripping like harlots.

A fitting orgy of trees.

Given what went on here in the Beacon.

The Beacon was the lighthouse that Callum Campbell was building when he died. Boatloads of miners may not have flooded Madrona Island as planned, but once the Pig War was over and the border finally settled, his home—with the Beacon to guide them in, the cove to shelter them from fog or storm, and an array of goods and beverages on sale in the cozy hostel he would build by his dock—would be perfectly situated to greet settlers heading for the Mainland beyond.

The Beacon was completed by Brother XIII.

He may have been the first, but he certainly wasn't the last, for the West Coast has always attracted cult messiahs. From what Hank was able to puzzle together in his notes, the Brother was a colonial Brit who arrived from India, where he had learned the hypnotic tricks of the mystics, gurus and swamis. His piercing eyes were described as "pools of fire" by the women he seduced, all of whom gave up their wealth to shed their earthly sins and be worthy of the promised land the Brother promised them.

Women like Effie.

Who gave up her island.

So the Brother could found his promised land.

The Beacon was the title of a newsletter published in

Britain. It told how a blessed soul living in Bombay was initiated into the incomplete circle of the "Twelve Masters of Wisdom." He studied their insight and passed the test that qualified him as the seer Brother XIII, and he was now in Britain selecting those worthy of the Sacred White Circle, the closing of which under a beacon would herald the Second Coming.

A stream of applicants flocked to meetings held in London, where it was said the Brother put on a riveting show. Robed in white, he went into a wailing, thrashing trance, announcing to one and all that he could *see* the beacon shining forth, far away on an island of golden rebirth.

Those who set sail with Brother XIII were selected carefully, for only by sacrificing their wealth for the common good could they partake in the sinless state of free love that the Aquarian Foundation would found in the New Eden. And sure enough, when they sailed in, the beacon did blaze forth. Stepping foot on the Island of Golden Rebirth, Aquarians were introduced by Brother XIII to Madame Eff—hardly a madame, since she was no older than a Scottish lass, but who, they were assured, had been chosen to bear him a son, who would be the next Jesus Christ.

The only building on the island was the Beacon, where the Brother lived with Madame Eff, and into which only those who worked hard were admitted. And hard work it certainly was, trying to create a paradise out of the wilderness. But still, what they did in the Beacon made it all worthwhile. Freed from the stifling restraints of Victorian Britain, the Aquarians were introduced by Brother XIII to free love, to the joys of tantric yoga and the Kama Sutra, to a different position for every couple in the Sacred White Circle with him and Madame Eff.

It took years for her to conceive.

Then, with the birth, it all went wrong.

For not only did the next Jesus Christ come out as a girl, but the Second Coming was also stillborn.

The Brother flew into a rage.

The Devil was afoot.

There was a serpent in Eden who had to be scrounged out.

And that created hell on earth.

Each Aquarian was summoned to speak to the Brother privately, and each came shuffling out of the Beacon in a daze, hypnotized, mesmerized, maybe drugged. From then on, the Aquarians slept outside and worked like slaves from dawn to dusk. Human oxen yoked to plows were whipped by Madame Eff, while the Brother performed exorcism rites, eliciting cries for mercy from those he punished in the Beacon.

The New Eden became the Hellfire Cult.

Then one day, ex-Aquarians awoke to find Madame Eff and the Brother gone. Gone, too, was the only boat down in the bay and all the wealth they had entrusted to the Brother to prove their worthiness to come here. The one asset left was the island, to which neither Effie nor Brother XIII could file claim, so the end of the Pig War led to the destitute cultists seeking to settle Madrona Island under the Homestead Act.

No wonder Dugald and Ewen argued over Effie, Jenna thought. Should they lay claim to their father's tract? Callum had settled it for five years before he drowned, and owning an island was better than owning part of one shared with other settlers. Or given the sacrilege and scandal of the place, should they leave the godforsaken tract to the Hellfire Cult, and sever all connection to the wicked Madame Eff?

Little of this was relevant to why Jenna was here, though it did explain why Callum's tract of land was so hard to trace. All that now concerned the detective was the possibility that Callum Campbell had left Scotland with the silver skull, and might have hidden it on the land he settled here, and might not have told anyone before dying unexpectedly. In which case, the Hoard might still be on Madrona Island, somewhere near the only building Callum built; the lighthouse called the Beacon, which now loomed above her.

Silver was a metal.

Ergo, the metal detector.

With which Jenna set to work to search.

The Beacon looked more like a church than a house. Instead of a cross, the steeple at the front was crowned by a light with a weather vane on top. A double-wicked oil lamp was the light, with shades used to black out windows in the revolving dome. The reason the government had provided for denying "those limey Satanists'" claim to Madrona Island was the need for a lighthouse in Boundary Pass. The Beacon, however, had never seen service, for Callum had raised it at the *southern* tip, not the northern tip where it and a light at East Point on Saturna Island would have marked the boundary channel. Sail a ship between lights there and here, and odds were you'd ram this island broadside. Patos Island got lamped instead.

The Beacon was falling apart.

Jenna was about to enter to search the inside when the guitar racket from the northern tip stopped in mid-chord.

Rather sudden, she thought, then dismissed it from her mind when the heavy-metal thrashing was replaced by *Led Zeppelin II* at a million decibels.

Now the sound was airborne, not skimming in across the cove.

The inside of the Beacon was an empty shell except for mice, spiders, webs and bats in the belfry. Working her way from floor to floor up the steeple, Jenna swept the metal detector, but nothing hidden registered. Back outside, Bond swept the ground around the Beacon in an ever-widening spiral that also failed to detect buried metal. Throaty groans from foghorns in Boundary Pass became more insistent as twilight fell; the music of Led Zeppelin was drowned under bellowed warnings of a sock-in.

Warnings Jenna heeded.

From the Beacon at the southern tip, she wound her way through darkening madrona woods to the western edge of the cliff. Banks of fog creeping in from the Pacific extended gray fingers across the purple water, reaching in to grasp each island by the throat. Should she press on, searching in what now seemed to be a fruitless waste of time, or make a run for home before she got stranded here overnight? That was the question she was pondering when she spied the gravestones, two mossed markers high above the cove.

There was just enough light to read.

Walking the edge of the cliff to the nearer stone, Jenna clawed moss from the inscription:

Callum Campbell
1814–1863

Moving to the other stone six feet away, Jenna scraped moss from it:

In Loving Memory of
Agnes Mary Campbell
1819–1856
Buried in Argyll, Scotland

By reading between the lines, Bond understood. Callum Campbell had lost his wife of many years, so, sensing it was time for a new start abroad, he had emigrated here the following May with his two sons and Effie Conochie. On settling Madrona Island, he had erected the memorial stone to his wife, and with his death, Effie had buried him alongside.

You don't think . . . ? Jenna wondered.

After retracing her steps to the Beacon, she returned to the cliff with the lamps and tools, and swept the metal detector around the memorial.

It detected metal.

Her heart pounding with excitement, Jenna lit both lamps, placing them on the ground flanking the memorial stone, then cautiously began to pick away at the earth, until she came to a rusty metal box.

Prying open the lid, Jenna found a rotting leather bag inside.

Tearing open the bag, Jenna found a very tarnished trophy inside.

The trophy was silver.

The trophy was a skull.

A skull with a medallion fused to its forehead.

"Eureka," she whispered.

For what Bond held in her hand was undoubtedly the most precious treasure on earth, not because it exposed the secret of Stonehenge, but because it would buy back Nick Craven's life, and in doing so would hopefully put her nightmares to rest.

Darkness closed in as Jenna, bathed yellow by the overlapping pools from the hissing propane lamps, squatted on her heels. *Hsssss* . . . No leaves rustle like those of the madrona, chattering like gossips in this breeze off the sea. *Tsktsktsk* . . . Foghorns warned her to rush home, but Jenna ignored them and slowly revolved the skull in her hand, wondering if she dared try to polish it. *AAAAH-wuh! AAAAH-wuh*! Led Zeppelin—is that *II* or *III?*—did "Gallows Pole."

Somerled Campbell, Jenna thought, seized the skull as a trophy during the Massacre of Glencoe. Because the Highland clans condemned that atrocity, he had a trophy he couldn't reveal. Doing so would prompt the MacDonald clan to demand it back, a plea that would find sympathy among the other clans, and he might be held personally responsible for what he'd done to get it. Revenge could fall on his family. And what if he hadn't told his clan about the seizure, holding out on those to whom he owed allegiance? Rock and a hard place?

Consequently, this trophy remained a family secret for generations, passing down from Somerled to Roderick to Kenneth to Lachlan and finally to Callum. The skull came here when he emigrated, perhaps to sell in the new land, but—surprise!—what he found was a colony rife with MacDonalds. So another Campbell hid the skull away in another hoard, beneath a marker that could easily be found after he passed the secret along to the next generation, which Callum had not yet done when the sea drowned him.

Wow! thought Jenna.

For here she was with one of the most sought-after secrets in history in the palm of her hand; a secret hidden from her by nothing but a layer of silver tarnish; a secret that, if she pulled the lamp close like she was doing now, she could decipher and become the first modern human to grasp; a secret she would use to flush out Mephisto and rescue Nick.

As Jenna eyed the skull in her hand like Hamlet had Yorick's, Led Zeppelin's "Gallows Pole" came to an end, and someone crept up behind her and slipped a noose about her instead.

The garrote cinched her neck, choking off her wind and yanking her back.

Jenna dropped the skull, but other hands caught it like a fumbled football before it hit the ground, hands streaked with the same blue that colored the face Jenna glimpsed in a pointed hood.

She couldn't get her fingers under the garrote, so she kicked back repeatedly with one heel, pistoning her left elbow in a diversionary attempt to pummel the wind out of the strangler, tit for tat, while her other hand groped her waist for her gun.

A third man was on her to wrench the gun away.

Suddenly she understood why the heavy-metal thrash had ceased mid-chord. D-Day could have taken place outside his door and the guitarist would not have heard it happen. These three took him unawares, then substituted Led Zeppelin to cover any sound they made while hunting Jenna down here. The foghorn groans and madrona chatter helped.

Forgive me, Becky, Jenna thought.

Deathly afraid.

For now she was weakening from lack of blood to her brain, trying to gasp but no gasp came out, the garrote a piano wire constricting her flesh; the fumble interceptor was grasping one wrist, the goon with her gun gripping the other, while the pair looped ropes around the marker stones. With one rope tied to this wrist, one rope tied to that, they pulled her arms wide so she was crucified face down in the dirt she'd dug from the hole, then—God, please, no! screaming in her mind—they stripped her naked from the waist down, boots, socks, jeans and underwear thrown aside before the gun goon said, "Me first this time."

"Nice ass."

"Use a rubber. No more sloppy seconds."

Jenna choked for air as the garrote loosened, then gargled out a sharp gasp as the first goon impaled her, a barbaric thrust to let her know he was in. Then both hands clamped her shoulders to ram her back.

"Get into it, pussy. Gimme a g*ooo*d ride."

One by one they rode her as the other two watched, calling her "cunt" and "hole" and "bitch" to demean her mind while they defiled her body, hooded shadows on the ground beside her face, blue grins leering at her naked humiliation above. Then finally, when it was over and she was ravaged raw, the one with her gun snatched her face from the dirt by her matted hair, put the muzzle to her temple and snarled, "Last request?"

Jenna steeled herself with all the courage she possessed.

"Eat shit!" spat Bond, tears flooding her cheeks.

"Fuck her again," the archdruid ordered, so a blue face raped her with the shovel handle.

"Stiff enough?" he asked, leaving it in.

The gun goon put the muzzle to her temple again.

"Last request?" he echoed.

Bond bit her tongue, determined to die like the daughter Hank Bond had raised.

Remember me, Becky, Jenna thought.

"Do her," said the rapist who picked up the silver skull to depart.

"No," said the Archdruid, pocketing the garrote as he pulled up his jeans.

"Huh?" said the gun goon.

The Archdruid grinned.

"Every day for the rest of her life, let the cunt *live* with it."

Stone Circle

DeClercq returned to Special X from the foot chase through the library to find a voice-mail message asking him to join Detective Inspector Kim Rossmo next door in the Geographic Profiling office. He crossed the parking lot to the annex and walked in just as Rusty Lewis rang that damn bell.

"Kim still here?"

"In back. Conspiring with the Russians."

DeClercq frowned.

"You'll see. The world is changing fast."

"Too fast for me," grumbled the chief.

Turning right, he walked along the corridor to the far end and stopped abruptly in the doorway on the left because there was nowhere to step. Every square inch of surface and floor area was buried beneath overlapping satellite orthophotographs. This could be a scene out of Sherlock Holmes, for like the great detective, Rossmo was on his elbows and knees crabbing around the carpet, one mother of a magnifying glass in his hand.

"Looking for the speckled band?" DeClercq asked.

Rossmo answered without glancing up.

"Looking for a Jeep or a Bayliner," he said.

"Those from the Russians?"

"Yes," he replied. "For which, incidentally, money is owed."

"I don't recall authorizing this."

"Welsher," retorted Rossmo. "You do recall, do you not, being here this morning when I produced a jeopardy from your crime sites?"

"I'm aging," said DeClercq, "but I hope my memory is not *that* bad."

"Good, then you'll recall me saying something like this: 'This jeopardy surface tells us to concentrate our search on the southern part of Saturna Island in Canada and the northwestern part of Orcas Island in the United States. I have an idea that may help further shrink the dragnet. Will you be in your office?' "

"I may have heard that," admitted DeClercq.

"And if your senility is not too far advanced, you may recall your reply was: 'In and out all day.' "

"Gulp," said DeClercq.

"To which—let's hope it's not Alzheimer's taking hold—I said something like: 'With luck, I'll call.' The call was made, the contract sealed and, lo and behold, here you are."

"Uncle," said DeClercq. "How much do I owe?"

"A million bucks," said Rossmo. "In unmarked bills or gold bullion."

He cleared a space for the Mountie to join him on the floor, then passed DeClercq a magnifying glass that rivaled his.

"What you see around you is the latest development in digital orthophotography. Microsoft, Eastman Kodak and other corporations have teamed up with the Russian space agency to shoot satellite pictures of every backyard in America from coast to coast."

"Why the Russians?"

"Quickest and cheapest. Since the Cold War thawed, they've been struggling. Military technology has become a lucrative business."

"How recent are the photos?"

"Updated all the time."

"How accurate is their eye in the sky?"

"We can zoom down to one-meter resolution. You can count the number of shrubs in Seattle."

"Hmm," said DeClercq. "So it's unwise to pick your nose in your own backyard."

"Could end up on the Internet."

"That's where you bought these?"

Rossmo nodded. "The images can be viewed for free, and downloaded at a cost of between ten and twenty-five dollars. I selected orthos shot within the jeopardy and dragged and dropped them into Rigel's data base. Typical applications are for land-use planning, surveying and real-estate marketing, but a pizzeria could use them to plan delivery routes, or parents to send out maps to a child's birthday party. Rigel's using them to close the Mephisto dragnet."

My kind of cop, thought DeClercq.

"You understand how orthophotographs work?" Rossmo asked.

"Refresh me," said the chief.

"Distortions are inherent in photos taken from the air. Perspective geometry and varying ground elevations affect the result. Maps, in contrast, have orthographic geometry, because cartographers draw all map details as if viewed from a right angle with respect to the paper, as if you were directly above each point. *Ortho* means 'right angle.'

"Digital orthophotos like these surrounding us are produced by scanning aerial photographs into a computer loaded with specialized software that removes distortions to generate an image map where all ground-level details are imaged as if viewed from a right-angled, or orthographic, projection. In other words, immediately above the object being viewed. The result has the image quality of a photograph and the orthographic projection of a map. Quality so sharp that you can identify a Jeep like this Jeep, which was caught on camera when Fitzroy Campbell's credit card was used by a hooded man at a gas pump, and a Bayliner cabin cruiser like this cabin cruiser, which was caught by binoculars sailing with the *Bounding Main* in Plumper Sound."

"The *Faust*," said DeClercq.

"With hooded men aboard."

"You're a genius, Kim."

"I wouldn't go *that* far."

And so they got to work on elbows and knees, each man's magnifying glass scanning orthophotographs one by one to find a match for photos Rossmo had requisitioned of a similar Jeep and Bayliner taken from above; it was a slow and tedious process that might have lasted hours, but actually finished in forty minutes with an involuntary intake of breath from DeClercq.

"Kim, look at this."

"A hit," said Rossmo.

"Where does this island fit in your geoprofile?"

Rossmo digitalized it on his computer, then opened Hit Score to display a graph of all forty thousand cells in the jeopardy.

"Top 0.8 percent. That's *damn* good."

The island was in the northeast corner of San Juan County, up where Boundary Pass and President Channel met the Strait of Georgia.

"Name?" asked DeClercq.

"Shipwreck Island," said Rossmo.

"Found you, Mephisto. Hang on, Nick."

For what the Mountie had spotted on the orthophoto wasn't a Jeep or a cabin cruiser.

It was a stone circle in a clearing in some woods.

The New Dark Age

Shipwreck Island, Washington State

They were draped in tartan, the two of them, green-and-red plaid undulating about her curves, his physique filling green and blue, the smirk on his face tonight a wry grin befitting the origin of the name of his clan, *cam* (wry) and *beul* (mouth), or Campbell in Gaelic, and what could be more fitting for the man with the smirk, since *wry* was "devious of purpose, distorted and perverted" in any language?

Mephisto had much to smirk about.

Tonight he was king of the world.

Surreal was his midnight realm beyond the glass of the greenhouse that was wedged in the roof of the smuggler's mansion high on the bluff above the foggy, foggy sea. Tentacles of fog like those of a spectral octopus reached up from the invisible water to strangle the Wicker Man—now you see him, now you don't—in the Stone Circle buried deep in the oak grove. Ghosts seemed to trail the hooded and robed Druids from the sacrifice site to the root cellar door, which was off the path that climbed to the mansion, and into which they disappeared. Minute by minute, the fog choked thicker, until it was a silver shroud smothering all it possessed. Silver light beamed down from a gibbous moon shrinking back from full to fill the gathering fog with eerie diffused radiance.

The silver skull gleamed on one of the benches in the greenhouse, which was aglimmer with moonglow.

Beside it was Pandora's box.

Surrounding the skull and the box were carnivorous plants.

The plants had culled the overpopulation of doomed flies back to a few from the buzzing too many.

The world as it *should* be.

"I was right," Mephisto said, picking up the skull in his reverent hands. A smudge of tarnish troubled his critical eye, so he rubbed the silver for the umpteenth time with the polish cloth, treating it like those skulls in Europe that monks have rubbed since the Black Death culled the human race, until today the bones shine as if made from metal.

Rub, rub, rub . . .

Obsessive/compulsive behavior.

"The Secret of the Stones," he said, "is that the megaliths told Atlanteans *when* to cull the human race to keep the natural world in balance."

The tip of his finger caressed the Druid medallion fused to the forehead of what was once the braincage of Antigonus Severus.

"See, Donella?"

He held the skull up in front of her face, turning it toward the watching moon so moonglow illuminated the engraved Stonehenge in the center of the medallion. Not the ruin of today, but the Temple of the Sun as it used to be. The megaliths were aligned so the moon partially overlapped the sun for a solar eclipse; the face of the man in the moon on the medallion was a human skull like the human skulls that were interspersed with fleshed human faces in a ring around the medal's edge.

The skulls of those culled.

The faces of those spared.

"To those dependent on the seasonal rhythms of the earth for their survival, movements of the sun and moon were vital, and an eclipse was a time of awesome significance. Ancients knew that the sun both powered life and took it away. The strong summer sun grew crops, the weak winter sun let them die. Strong sun meant food, weak sun meant starvation. The strength of the sun determined how many would survive, so what was the cosmic significance of a solar eclipse? The sun was obviously saying it was time to cull, time to bring the population back into line with a limited food supply.

"I *knew* it," said Mephisto.

"I *felt* it in my bones.

"The culture of those who raised Stonehenge lasted longer than any in history. But Stonehenge is only what culminated from what came before, and that was a myriad of stone circles throughout the Atlantean realm, all of them aligned with the sun and the moon, and all of them ritual centers with burnt bones.

"Ritual centers surrounded by burial mounds.

"Why, Donella?

"Why, why, *why?*

"What powerful motive compelled them for *thousands* of years to expend that much physical and mental effort on megaliths, unless the burnings within were essential to survival? And what could be more essential to people living on the edge than keeping excess population under control? So when a solar eclipse told them that *now* was the time to cull, the ritual they performed in each stone circle encompassed the fire of the sun, which is *why* the bones of the human sacrifice were *burnt* before the Atlanteans spread out from each temple to cull those who ended up buried in the mounds around and beyond.

"What other explanation fits the evidence?

"The Aubrey holes at Stonehenge were a calendar of eclipses. Some received burnt bones when they were dug, and others received burnt bones later. Why? Unless each burning resulted from an eclipse, and some of the bones were buried while the eclipse calendar was being worked out?

"What other motive *except* one common to everyone

would compel ancients scattered far and wide and separated by time?

"And if it wasn't survival, what was it?

"And *except* for demands on limited resources, what other threat to survival could have lasted thousands of years?

"The threat persists today.

"But only in modern times have we lost the *will* to cull."

Fog swirling up from the shroud below eclipsed the moon, darkening the greenhouse and its array of culling plants. A black silhouette replaced the silver skull on the bench beside the Pandora's box and its array of culling viruses.

Ancient ways obsessed this antiquarian.

"It took a million years for humankind to populate the earth with a billion people. We reached one billion around 1800, two billion in the 1930s, three billion in 1960, four billion in 1975, five billion in 1987 and a billion more about now. At four babies a second, a quarter-million born every day, and with Africa adding a million to us every three weeks, our current number will double in fifty years.

"It's a global formula for social dynamite. We are sitting on an overpopulation time bomb that is about to explode. To support the *current* population of the world near the standard of your average Joe in the States, it would take a minimum of two more planet earths. Studies prove the earth can comfortably support between one and two billion people, albeit at a standard of living less than what Americans presently have. Instead, we are going to have enormous numbers of people surviving marginally in misery, poverty, disease and starvation. Soon we'll be sharing the earth with two billion hungry, ill-educated young cretins schooled in fanaticism and fit for cannon fodder.

"Too many people.

"Like too many rats.

"When allowed to breed at will in lab experiments, Norway rats multiply until they reach a point when they can stand the overcrowding no longer, and that's when they stop breeding and start killing each other. Already the warning signs are rife: food riots in nations of the Third World, ecological disasters from the brown agenda of pollution and environmental degradation, with much worse to come. On the streets of America, what do I see? A nation plagued by gangs, graffiti, the homeless and stupid louts in hats worn the wrong way around. The dumbing of the masses is ruining classical culture, and I for one refuse to wallow in their pigsty of a shitty little world.

"We all see the problem.

"Human rats are breeding us into crisis.

"But no one has the balls to do anything about it, because we've lost the will to cull to keep the earth's population in line with its resources.

"*I* have the balls, Donella."

"You certainly do, baby."

And she reached under his tartan to find that he was as stiff as a man could be.

Never had Mephisto felt as lordly as he did now. A long time ago, he had bartered his soul to the Devil for knowledge, power, money and fornication. Now money was all around him, a hell of a woman before him, the power to cull excess billions in Pandora's box, and the knowledge of *when* to use that malign power engraved on the silver skull.

The world was in the predicament it was in because the knowledge of the Atlanteans had not been passed on. The ancients lived closer to the rhythms of nature than we do now, and they detected cosmic energies man no longer feels. The Secret of the Stones was knowledge vital to the proper functioning of a social order that centers people in relation to natural forces and tribal well-being.

Time to restore that balance.

For there were times at Stonehenge when an eclipse of the moon above the Heel Stone or later in the gap of the Great Trilithon was followed within two weeks by an eclipse of the sun. The same alignment of the earth and the moon and the sun was about to occur above the Stone Circle on Shipwreck Island. If that, combined with the discovery of the letter concerning the MacDonald Hoard in Malcolm Campbell's Glencoe collection last May, wasn't fate telling Mephisto that now was the time to cull the earth of overpopulation, what was? Atlantean priests had built the megaliths to predict solar eclipses and had sacrificed burnt bones to venerate the sun, then after the eclipse had come and gone, had spread out from their temples to cull the population.

A solar eclipse was coming.

Tonight there would be burnt bones.

And tomorrow Mephisto would travel to L.A., Miami and New York to prepare to release the supervirus after the eclipse.

Would he survive?

Probably.

Grof's vaccine would protect him from the plague.

But once he released that virus to exercise power, the Devil's half of the pact for his soul would be satisfied, and Mephistopheles would come for Mephisto to collect his due.

The irony was that not only would he, Mephisto, be destined for hell, but every person living would end up in hell on earth. Blood, blood everywhere, with corpses piling up faster than authorities could dispose of them, civil order disintegrating under public panic, wholesale flight into surrounding countryside spreading the contagion far and wide, and those the virus did not kill outright cracking from the horror of it all to live on as psychiatric casualties.

To witness that, thought Mephisto, I'd sacrifice a horde of souls.

The lunar eclipse dissolved as the fog shrank back

from the shrinking moon. Again the greenhouse glimmered with moonglow. They could be angels in heaven
above the clouds of mist below, but that was the farthest
thought from the minds of these diabolical fiends.

Mephisto tore the tartan from Donella's sexy body,
and bent her forward over the bench so she embraced
the silver skull in both arms, the silver grin of Antigonus
Severus facing him, the Secret of the Stones before his
leering eyes while he spread her legs wide, gripped her
buttocks like the hemispheres of the globe and did to
her what he planned to do to the world. The force of
his hip thrust almost drove her through the glass and
out into the night, while his nostrils flared wide like the
Minotaur's and he let out a primal shout of triumph loud
enough to raise hell.

He was king of the world.

And who was there to stop him?

Druids

The footsteps he'd heard earlier weren't those of the Devil Woman coming for his cock. Three gruff male voices had passed outside the door to his cell. Over the squealing of the mouse being swallowed alive by the snake, his good ear had overheard a snippet of conversation:

"Madrona Island?"

"That's where we're going."

"The Hoard's there?"

"Could be."

"How'd he find Madrona?"

"His woman found the island mentioned in a library book."

"Now that's one pussy I'd *luuuve* to fuck."

"In your dreams, pal. Touch her and he finds out, he'll eat your balls in front of you, then do something *nasty* to finish you off . . ."

The voices had trailed away from the door, leaving Nick to ponder what was going on as the mouse squealed all the way down into the snake's belly. Minutes later, he'd caught the rumble of a motorboat reverberating in the hall, which seemed to be an underground tunnel to the sea. He must have passed out from exhaustion and pain, for suddenly he was jerked alert by a bang in the hall, then the same three voices passed the door to his cell going the other way.

"That Bond had one *sweeet* pussy for a cop."

"Ya see the way she looked at me when I fucked her with the shovel?"

"Daggers in her eyes, dude."

"Daggers in her pussy."

"Now she's got the memory, and we've got the Hoard."

"*Parrr*ty time!"

"Rock-and-roll, ya rockers!"

"Tonight we clean house. Tomorrow we're gone. Hope the fucker screams like hell when we put a torch to his Wicker Man. . . ."

The voices trailed away.

Nick slumped in his chains.

He tried . . . he tried . . . he tried . . . but the will to go on was gone.

What had they done to Jenna?

Gang-raped her and what else?

"Now she's got the memory."

You bastards, he thought.

Tears of sorrow for her ran down his bloody cheeks and dripped from his chin. He was so thirsty. He was so empty inside. The barren futility of his life took hold of him as a sense of nothingness numbed his beleaguered brain. He was going to die tonight. They were "cleaning house." And once he was dead, that meant the end of the line. Thirty-odd years of life and there was no one who would mourn for him. No mother. No father. No siblings. No wife. No lover. And no kids. How little his presence on earth had meant was evident by the fact that his estate would go to the state.

He had no will.

He had no heirs.

He had no one to leave his farm to.

Missing a hand, missing an ear, chained to a wall like a dog, he sat slumped in the muck of his own human waste and grasped what it meant to face your fate with ultimate abandon.

But along with the words that were scrolled above the

staircase to the upper floor of his home came the pleasing memory of Katt turning, arms out, in his kitchen like Julie Andrews in *The Sound of Music.*

"Oh, wow!" Katt exclaimed. "Get a load of this. It makes me want to burn our kitchen down and start again. Y'ever decide to sell this place, sell it to me, Nicky. Bob can finance it till I'm rich and famous."

The mortgage was insured.

His death would pay it off.

The wall behind his chained arm was slimy from the dampness.

With his fingernail, he scratched his last will and testament.

All to Katt.

And waited for the footsteps.

The hunt for the Hoard was over and it was time to close down operations here, so after they had delivered the silver skull to Mephisto in the mansion, the Druids went down to the Stone Circle to open the Wicker Man, then—watched by the pair in the greenhouse—up they went to the root cellar door, off the path to the mansion, then down the steps and into the underground tunnel . . .

Footsteps in the hall.

Here they come, thought Nick.

Torchlight under the door.

A gruff voice outside.

"Okay, crispy critter. Barbecue time."

They dragged him along the hall, then up the steps to the root cellar, then out the door to the path, which was lost in the foggy, foggy night. So thick was the moonlit fog that they couldn't see the moon, couldn't see the mansion on the bluff either, but as they hauled the sacrifice down into the woods masking the Stone Circle, a muffled shout of triumph came from the invisible greenhouse.

Weird opaque moonglow glimmered through the woods, a guiding lure by which they marched the stumbling man into the swirling clearing, black robes and pointed cowls and blue faces about him as they stuffed the limp human fuel into the humanoid coffin, closing the halves and securing them with a padlock so the Wicker Man fit like a suit of wooden armor.

Octagon head on a square body with stubby arms and stick-like fingers.

Stiff legs spread to support it standing up.

Guts within writhing as the sacrifice squirmed.

Firewood piled about the feet as the Archdruid lit a torch.

"Burn, fucker, burn!"

PART III

Question

Not only the reason of millennia—their insanity, too, breaks out in us.

—Friedrich Nietzsche

Fog

President Channel, Washington State

"Mom."

"Jenna, where are you?"

"On my way home."

"Can you see out there?"

"The fog's tightening but hasn't socked in."

"Do be careful."

"You know the *Islomania*'s unsinkable."

"I'll have coffee waiting."

"No, I need a favor. Take Becky away somewhere for an hour."

"What's wrong, Jenna?"

"I got beat up."

"Oh, God . . ." Her mother gasped.

"I'll be okay. But I'm a sight now, and one I don't want Becky to see. I'm coming home to clean up before I'm off again."

"Where?"

"Friday Harbor. I won't be home tonight."

"Why?"

"Mom . . ."

"Sorry."

End of call.

By the time the *Islomania* had docked at the float, her mother and daughter had left the farmhouse. As soon as she was inside, Jenna had shed her clothes, shoving them in a bag to burn tomorrow, then she had showered in water as hot as she could stand, searing away the filth on her skin but not the dirty feeling inside. As sobs racked her body and tears salted the spray, every forensic trace from the rape had washed down the drain. She didn't care about evidence. Her rape wasn't going to court. Thank God for little mercies. At least they'd used condoms.

Jenna had cried and cried and cried, until she was all cried out. Then, nursing anger, she'd thought about getting even. The big mistake those punks had made was leaving her alive.

"Rape is women's work," Wentworth had said. Many a male cop would get secret satisfaction out of what had happened to her. Her violation was the reason why women aren't biologically suited for the front line. Not when push turns to shove, they would gloat. A male cop gets shot and the public accepts it as part of the job. But wound a female cop and it's headlines for a week. A man is executed and it doesn't make the news. A woman walks the last mile and the pope is on the phone.

Double standard.

Let's accept it, folks.

Not me, Jenna thought, reaching deep into her past to grab what would see her through this ordeal without caving in.

For while she felt as violated as any other female would in her place, Bond had no intention of shuddering in a hospital while they combed and swabbed her sex for evidence of rape; had no intention of letting male cops gather as a heavy squad to go out and equalize what had happened to that silly woman; had no intention of going through the rape again as some strutting defense lawyer fucked her over in court; and had no intention of listening to *psst! psst!* behind her back for years to come as tut-tutters related how she was that raped detective who foolishly investigated a serious crime without male backup.

Why not cower?

Why not be a victim?

Because she was the daughter of Sheriff Hank Bond, and Hank could be the meanest motherfucker you ever met if you fucked with him.

What ate at her as much as the rape was her giving up her gun. *That* she was trained never to do. Not only had they defiled her as a female, those barbarians had also defiled her as a cop.

Her Beretta was out there in alien hands.

After she had dressed warmly in black for what was about to go down, and before she had left Orcas by boat for the staging area, Bond had returned to Hank's trunk in the living room and had removed from it her father's gun and a box of shells.

Unlike the Mounties, with their standard issue weapons, a cop in the States is likely to have a personal preference in choice of arms. Jenna's choice was the Beretta Model 92F Compact, a semiautomatic 9mm with thirteen rounds. A good gun for a woman in plainclothes.

Hank had been sheriff back in the six-shooter days of San Juan County, and his no-nonsense weapon had been the Colt Python .357 Magnum.

Not *Dirty Harry.*

That was the .44 Mag.

But he still got to ask the question, "Do you feel lucky, punk?"

Hefting her father's revolver, Bond had sensed the power in her hand.

She had sprung the cylinder.

She had fed it six shells.

She had snapped the cylinder shut.

She had cruised to Friday Harbor.

Now, as she sat beside DeClercq in the boat heading for Shipwreck Island, Bond could feel the cold steel of the Python against her ravaged womb.

"What does a civilized man do when confronted by a barbarian?" Hank used to ask.

He had never answered the question.

His daughter would.

Not for a moment did Robert believe the Mounted Police were better than the FBI. That was a rivalry of "people who live in glass houses" and "the pot calling the kettle black," indulged in by lower ranks. There were plenty of skeletons in the Mounties' closet. They had stood guard when the Plains tribes gave away Alberta, Saskatchewan and Manitoba. They had used Tiananmen Square tactics to crush 1919's Winnipeg General Strike. Like Hoover, they had during the Cold War amassed dossiers on millions of Canadians suspected of leftist leanings, while combing government departments for homosexuals. So overboard had this zeal become that they had burned down a barn to prevent a meeting between the radical FLQ and the American Black Panthers, and had broken into the political office of the Parti Québecois to copy its membership list. For such "dirty tricks," the Force had been stripped of its Security Service, but out of the rubble had come Special X, the Special External Section of the Mounted Police, which was commanded by DeClercq.

DeClercq was a realist.

Not a hypocrite.

So within minutes of spotting the stone circle on Shipwreck Island in the satellite photographs, DeClercq had phoned the agent in charge of Seattle's FBI office, who in turn had assured him that the Bureau would mobilize its best to take down Mephisto, and that's why Robert now sat in this boat beside the battered Jenna Bond.

He would have preferred this to be an operation by the Mounties' Emergency Response Team, but only because the life in danger was Nick's, and so he felt that any life-or-death decisions made should be his. Instead, he was along for the ride as a cop-to-cop courtesy, as was the detective from San Juan County, for this was the Bureau's show in every way.

DeClercq had no jurisdiction.

DeClercq had no gun.

He and Jenna would stay back until the assault was over, then go up to the mansion to witness how it went down.

Silently through the sea fog came the rubber boat, tactical cops in black ninja suits armed with Heckler & Koch MP5s paddling toward an invisible shore. They were the FBI's Hostage Rescue Team, the HRT, known to Bureau agents as HART. The watch-word for this operation was silence, so the mother motorboat that sailed them from the staging area at Friday Harbor had birthed a flotilla of landing craft far enough away to avoid suspicion, and now stealthful manpower brought them in.

The boats bumped the shore.

The ninjas scrambled out.

The foggy swath from the beach to the mansion high on the bluff swallowed them up.

Only as he and Jenna climbed slowly in their wake, the woods with the stone circle caught in the satellite photo to their left, was DeClercq suddenly plagued with celluloid doubt.

Thank you, Hollywood.

For what undermined his confidence in the American cops was the way American cops were presented in modern films. Pumped on adrenaline and testosterone, they came out of a football huddle armed to the teeth, as gung-ho and ready to kick ass as linemen could be, just itching to shoot first and ask questions later. Busting in, they opened up with all they had, firing burst on burst until every gun was empty, before calming down to count the dead and find out if any innocents were blown apart in the raid.

Like Nick?

Hollywood cop films reminded DeClercq of a story about Erle Stanley Gardner, author of the Perry Mason mysteries, back when he honed his writing skills by churning out words for the pulp magazines. Writing for length, not literary merit, he produced two hundred thousand words a month at his height. He was known for killing off the bad guys with the last bullet in his hero detective's gun. When editors teased him that his characters were all such bad shots, Gardner had this response: "At three cents a word, every time I say 'Bang' in the story I get three cents. If you think I'm going to finish the gun battle while my hero still has fifteen cents worth of unexploded ammunition in his gun, you're nuts."

Was Gardner the patron saint of nineties Hollywood cop films?

In his heart, DeClercq knew that the cops assaulting the bluff were professionals, but his brain was conditioned by Tinseltown's Keystone Kops.

What was required here was sang-froid.

Coolness of mind, composure and self-possession.

A cold-blooded, not hot-blooded, assault.

The sort of sang-froid displayed by French marines sent to stop pirates terrorizing the Caribbean. Outlaws wielding cutlasses would board a ship and hack sailors to pieces to frighten the defenders behind them. They were defeated by fencers armed with rapiers, for what the thin blades lacked in psychological impact, they more than made up for with lightning speed, puncturing the pirates' hearts before their cutlasses could swing.

The sort of sang-froid displayed by a French paratroop leader in the Algerian War. The man was seated in a sidewalk café, enjoying coffee and a croissant, when an enemy spy was brought to him. The spy refused to expose his associates, so the Frenchman calmly got up and drew his bayonet. He stuck its tip into one side of the neck of the spy and slowly began to tug the blade around his throat, warning the man that he had two seconds to save his carotid artery. A second later, when he had the names he sought, the Frenchman granted the spy his life, and sat down to wipe the bayonet on the tablecloth before using it to butter his croissant.

DeClercq's Gallic temperament ruled him tonight.

He hoped the Americans were ruled by sang-froid.

His thoughts were interrupted by an unearthly scream from the woods, and the fog between here and the stone circle suffused with firelight.

Sacrifice

Shipwreck Island, Washington State

Jenna drew Hank's gun from the waist of her jeans, then turned left into the woods from the path worming up to the mansion on the bluff. The Mountie followed close on her heels as she dodged through the trees, aiming at the bonfire that was burning bright ahead. Fingers of fog clawed the trunks of the shedding oaks, leaves tumbling around the cops as they wove their way through the needled limbs of the Douglas firs, while an owl on one branch blinked at the action below.

From the woods they burst out into a clearing, and there at the center of the stone circle photographed by the Russian satellite, blazed the pagan image of a Druid Wicker Man. Three hooded and robed cultists stood black and devilish against the leaping flames, their backs to the cops breaching the ring. The hideous screams of the sacrifice thrilled the trio, and masked any sounds made by the pair of lawmen. The stones of the circle jutted like fangs from the ground, as the orange-and-silver miasma swirled like breath from hell.

"Police!" shouted Jenna.

The Druids whirled.

And the Archdruid fired the stolen Beretta at Bond.

The flame that licked from the muzzle was a miniature of the flames licking up through the fog at the megalithic moon. Within the blazing skeleton of the Wicker Man, the sacrifice thrashed and writhed in fiery agony, the cage rattling and shaking from his desperate contortions—some voluntary, others not—as his muscles broiled into a boxer's stance, contracting so violently that his bones began to snap. Charred black, his skin peeled away from his crackling flesh. Three minutes would pass before he burned to death, an eternity in hell reducing him to burnt bones. The caged man knew it, judging from his shriek, *YAAAAAAAAAAAAAAA!* which roared through the hole in his gag at Bond like a vanguard in front of the bullet.

The shot grazed her shoulder.

The Python spit back.

Hank's .357 bucked in her fist.

The slug took the archdruid full in the face, blue blasting into a splatter of red.

The Druid to one side threw up his hands.

Bond recognized him as the goon who had raped her with the shovel.

The Magnum bucked a second time.

The bullet drilled the Druid through the groin.

His balled fists shot between his legs.

The next slug caught him between the eyes.

The third Druid waved his arms in surrender.

The screaming from the Wicker Man could have been screams from her husband, Don.

"Barbarian," she said, and fired again.

The third Druid dropped to his knees, as if hoping supplication would add meaning to his surrender, but it was just a prelude to pitching forward into the dirt on his woeful woaded face.

YAAAAAAAAAAAAAAA! continued the screaming from the Wicker Man.

DeClercq advanced and seized the gun from the dead archdruid's hand.

The heat from the Wicker Man was intense. The eyes of the burning sacrifice melted down his face. No death could possibly be worse than this, and no way could the wretch inside be saved. A sacrifice was the destruction of something prized for the sake of something valued as having a higher claim. The Mountie fired the Beretta at the Wicker Man, sacrificing its sacrifice to a merciful release.

The wretch ceased screaming.

"Rest in peace, Nick," said DeClercq.

It quickly dawned on the two of them what they had done. Robert retreated from the inferno to rejoin Jenna near the ring of stones. The fog caressed them with the chill of prison walls. Shooting the archdruid was self-defense, but shooting the unarmed surrendering pair was manslaughter at best and murder at worst. DeClercq had killed a cop in an American state with the gallows in a time when courts on both sides of the border were displaying a lack of common sense, so was it a stretch to see him on the end of a rope? It was euthanasia at best, and therefore still against the law.

Their eyes locked.

"They raped me," Jenna said.

"I figured," said Robert.

"With a shovel handle."

The Canadian nodded.

"I heard my husband screaming in those flames, and all I wanted was revenge."

"Nothing will happen. It was a good shoot. I would have died if you hadn't killed all three. They attacked me in a pack when I tried to reach Nick after one took a shot at both of us."

"I should have fired sooner," said Bond. She eased the Beretta from DeClercq's hand. "Before the Druid with the gun turned and executed Nick."

She wiped the prints from the grip with the sleeve of her jacket, then went to the archdruid and placed it in his hand.

"I couldn't watch him suffer," Robert said.

The American nodded.

"He was a friend and under my command."

"You did what you had to do."

"I can live with it."
"So can I."
Again their eyes locked.
They shared a thought.
"Mephisto," she said.
"Collector of souls," he replied.

Scotched

DeClercq should not have doubted the sang-froid of the FBI team climbing the bluff. The agent in charge of the Seattle Bureau had promised him the best, so that is what he got. Ice water flowed in the veins of the cops around the mansion. The hot blood was down in the Stone Circle, not up here.

The blanket of mist crept halfway up the walls, so the assault team moved in like a school of sharks under a calm sea. They circled the mansion to cover all exits and waited for the command to go in. Silent penetration was Plan A, a soft entry sneak-in if possible, not hard entry with a Ram-It and stun grenades; Plan B an option only if it came to force.

Mephisto was as mad as a shithouse rat.

Given the chance, he'd kill Nick for spite.

The glass cutter was at work on the windows by the main door when the screaming began in the woods off the path below. Would the screams draw those within outside to investigate, or did the ruckus mean the occupants of the house were all down there?

The commander split his team.

Half broke away to descend to the woods.

Half remained to see if anyone came out.

Then shots were heard.

———

The moment he heard the first shot, Mephisto was on the move. He and Donella were still in the observatory, moonlight through the greenhouse glass glistening sweat on their bodies.

"The gun," said Mephisto, tossing the Grant tartan to his Highland queen.

Donella draped it around herself, then darted out into the main room for the Colt.

With the Campbell tartan wrapped in a kilt around his waist and flung back over his shoulder, Mephisto clutched the silver skull and Pandora's box to his chest and moved from the greenhouse to the far front corner of the room on the upper floor.

There a switch opened a secret panel in the wall.

The stairs behind the panel descended to the lower floor.

Mephisto in front, Donella behind, down they went.

The rum-runner's mansion was designed for escape.

From 1920 to 1933, the eleventh commandment in the United States had been "Thou shalt not drink demon alcohol." Canada had strong booze, America didn't, so the border between the Gulf and the San Juan islands leaked like a fishnet. Thirst was the need, profit was the motive and—basic economics—supply followed demand. The Victorian-style mansion on Shipwreck Island was built with Prohibition proceeds from smuggling.

The stairs in the wall were there in case the Feds came knocking.

Like tonight.

At the bottom of the stairs, a section of the outer wall swung in to create a hidden exit. Mephisto and his Highland queen slipped out into the fog and angled away from the mansion toward the root cellar. They were feet from the door when a disembodied voice yelled, "Freeze, police."

Donella turned.

Mephisto ducked behind her.

A ghost materialized in the fog.

Mephisto grabbed Donella as a shield.

Donella fired the Colt.

The cop fired, too.

Her bullet took the cop in the vest, momentarily debilitating him.

His bullet took Donella in the heart.

It didn't drill through her to hit Mephisto.

He let go of Donella.

She crumpled to the ground.

He entered the root cellar.

He shut and bolted the door.

He raised a trap door in the floor and went down several stone steps, then closed the trap above him and secured it, too, flipping a switch that ran an iron barrier across.

Still clutching the silver skull and the Pandora's box to his chest, down the remaining steps he went—to the underground tunnel that led past the dungeon doors to the smugglers' cave.

The Devil's staircase.

Steps down to hell.

Footsteps in the hall.

Must be her, thought Nick.

But it wasn't.

It was him.

The door to Nick's cell flew open as light stabbed in, followed by Mephisto garbed in scuba gear, dry suit replacing tartan kilt, mask on his forehead and tank on his back. The wretch who had died in the Wicker Man was the rock musician from the lighthouse on Madrona Island; he'd been brought here by the Druids to sacrifice. Donella itched to cut Nick apart, so burning him was never considered, and had their plans to celebrate not gone badly *a-gley,* the footsteps in the hall a moment ago would have been hers. Instead, Nick would be Mephisto's ace in the hole as a hostage.

The psycho rammed a fish hook into the flesh of the Mountie's stump. Releasing the arm that was tied to the chopping block, he yanked it over to the arm chained to the wall and bound them together behind Nick's back. Unfettered, the prisoner was dragged through the door and along the torchlit passage to the smugglers' cave, where a crosshatched grate prevented trespassers from sneaking in by sea.

The grate was open.

The boat was moored beyond.

Faust was no longer painted on the stern.

Light from the torches along the hall faded in the sea cave. Mist rolled in from the foggy Pacific outside its yawning mouth. Mephisto shoved Nick aboard and cast off the lines. The shanghaied Mountie tumbled down into the rear cockpit. Stepping over the gunnel, Mephisto climbed to the command bridge on top of the cabin. With the silver skull and the Pandora's box beside him, he cranked the ignition, pushed the black handle to put the engine in gear, then red-handled the throttle.

Out into the murky night slipped the getaway boat.

His depth sounder on, Mephisto guided the hull through the treacherous reef that gave the island its name, the narrow channel below the only route to open water. From the command bridge, he had a better view in fog, so here he sat in triumph over the FBI, cruising away, cruising away, cruising away from them, plotting how once he was safely out to sea he would slash the cop's skin to draw blood, then drag him behind the boat on a line and let the hungry dogfish strip him alive, until nothing but a skeleton remained. . . .

And that's when the slice bow suddenly appeared on the port side, the Coast Guard cutter coming out of the mist at a right angle to the getaway boat to cut off the escape channel from the smugglers' cave, and before the psycho could react, the cutter crushed deep into the side of the Bayliner, staving in the hull and almost tearing it in half.

Scotched, the mangled boat rolled to starboard and plowed the sea ahead of the slice bow. Only because the tank was full did it not explode, fumes being the cause of most nautical pyrotechnics. The force of the ramming hurled Mephisto from the command bridge and into the sea on the port side of the cutter, and tossed Nick out of the cockpit and into the waves on the starboard. The wreck took water fast and, as the Coast Guard vessel slowed down to hunt for survivors, rolled off the slice bow and sank to the bottom of the ocean. Staving the hull just aft of the bridge had thrown the silver skull into harm's way, smashing it on the prow of the juggernaut. The ancient metal shattered into the brine, where the Secret of the Stones was lost once again.

And Pandora's box?

Legacy

Arms bound behind his back, into the deep he went.
The shock of the frigid water knocked the breath out of
him. It was so cold it was painful. Fiercely, he fought
the impulse to inhale brine. Desperately, he kicked his
legs to keep from drowning. The wake of the cutter must
have churned him up, for fog swirled around Craven on
a bilious sea, rising and falling and rising and falling,
until the undertow dragged him down. Afraid his leg
muscles would cramp, he kicked and kicked and kicked
to get his head above water, coughing bitter brine from
his throat to croak out a shout, then under he went in
a barrel of a wave, and seemed to sink forever until a
hand grabbed his hair.

The killer, thought Nick.

But it was the FBI.

So now, a chopper having flown him to Victoria, he
lay in a hospital bed three days later, hooked up to mon-
itoring machines, DeClercq and Katt seated beside him
during visiting hours.

"Is it true, Nicky? You left your farm to me?"

"I thought I was dying, Katt."

"So you scratched a will?"

"No need to shout. Your side is my good ear."

"Why me?"

"*Why?* Because you're such a cool kid."

"So there goes my legacy?"

"For a while. Hopefully, you'll have to wait fifty years."

"Maybe not, Nicky." She gave him her evil eye. "If you show me where to pull the plug on your life-support machine."

It hurt Nick to laugh.

"That's a good sign."

They turned toward a woman's voice coming from the door.

"Laughter, they say, is the best medicine."

"Nick," said DeClercq, "meet Jenna Bond. She's the one who told the Bureau about the escape route, so that's why the cutter moved in to cut off Mephisto when he boated from the cave."

"Thanks," said Nick.

Jenna shrugged. "I've scuba-dived around here for years."

"Who pulled me out?"

Her eyes narrowed. "An agent named Wentworth," she said with distaste, remembering her last encounter with that Suit: *"The kidnappers' having abducted a Mountie is icing on the cake. We'll show the redcoats who's best, Jen."* There was no justice in a world where Wentworth was the hero of the day. "I'm told he dove into the water, suit and all."

"I owe that man a bottle of the best."

"Will you have a hand like Captain Hook?"

"Becky!" snapped Jenna.

"I don't think so," said Nick, throwing the girl a smile. "A mechanical hand like"—he winked at Jenna—"Dr. No."

"And a new ear?"

"I hope so, honey."

"Nick," said Jenna, "meet Becky Bond."

"Hi," said Becky.

"Hi," said the Mountie.

"You going back to Special X, Nicky?" asked Katt.

"I doubt they'll let me stay on the Force," Craven replied.

"I wouldn't worry about that," said DeClercq. "You wouldn't be the first with a disability, and anyone who doubts you will deal with me."

"You still trying to get my farm, Katt?"

"No, Nicky. I'd rather have you."

"And what a fine farm it is," said Bond. "I saw it when Tracy and I went looking for you."

"It's a good place to recuperate, and I have a lot of healing to do."

"You'll be okay," Jenna said.

Nick gave her a nod. "Too many guys came back from wars far worse off than me. They picked up the pieces—ouch!—to get on with life."

Conversation died.

Silence filled the room.

Then Nick said, "Jenna, how about you?"

"The beating will heal."

"Uh huh," he said. "But you'll still have a lot of healing to do."

She glanced at Robert.

He shook his head.

"I overheard the Druids talking outside my cell on their return from Madrona Island."

"I'll be okay."

"Good," said Nick. "Maybe you'd come see me at the healing farm?"

For an instant she thought it was Don in that bed, and she knew she had exorcised her subconscious guilt about his death.

That nightmare was over.

Other nightmares would come.

Nick knows I was gang-raped, she thought, and he's asking me for a date?

She caught a glimpse of herself reflected from the hospital room window, all battered face, flannel shirt and blue jeans, and realized he saw through that to the real her.

"I'd like that," she said.

"Good," he repeated.

And when I come, I'll wear a dress, Jenna thought.

Endgame

Robert DeClercq paused to enjoy the crisp smell of the autumn leaves tumbling from the trees, the ground about him a carpet of color that rustled around his shoes. It was one of those vibrant fall days that invigorates a soul, and he walked from his car to the Tudor building that was home to Special X, where he climbed the stairs to the second floor and entered his corner office. With his coat hung on the antique stand beside the door, he sauntered around his horseshoe desk and was about to seat himself on the barley-sugar chair in the U when his eyes caught sight of the report on his blotter.

If Mephisto were a snake, all that remained of him was a shed skin.

That was the gist of the FBI report DeClercq spent an hour reading.

The body of the psycho had yet to be found.

Was he food for the fishes in Boundary Pass?

Shipwreck Island had been leased for two years by a company off the shelf of a Seattle lawyer; the shares of said company were held by a non-existent soul named Urbain Grandier, who was supposed to, but didn't, reside in that notorious tax haven, the Turks and Caicos Islands.

Cash in advance.

And don't come snooping around.

The fingerprints of five perps littered the island mansion, four of them matching the three Druids and the woman who were killed in the assault six days ago, but neither the FBI nor Interpol could find a match for the wild prints of the missing man.

Mephisto had no record.

His prints, however, did match prints at the crime scene in Florida in May, when the Scottish recluse Malcolm Campbell was found face down in the sea and his lifelong collection of Glencoe massacre artifacts vanished from his home.

A collection found in the library of the Shipwreck Island mansion.

Of prime interest to DeClercq was a letter the FBI had noticed in that collection. Dated March 2, 1723, it was written by Somerled Campbell to his son, Roderick, and postscripts traced the descent of the Glencoe Hoard from father to son down to Callum Campbell. Once that letter fell into Mephisto's devilish hands, the rest was history.

And speaking of history, it had been a while since he had checked the historians' bulletin board for anecdotes about the Force policing the Klondike gold rush, so DeClercq booted up his computer to empty his cyberspace mailbox.

A thought occurred to him as he typed his password.

What if the reptile Mephisto had personified was a chameleon, not a snake? Skin deep he was a dyed-in-the-wool Scot, a supposed member of the Campbell clan, but what if that was just a *role* taken on by his obsessive-compulsive megalomania? Those who had met him described his manner and accent as American to the core. Was being a Scot the role he played because he was hunting for a Scottish hoard? If his mania was to fixate on ancient relics of a different sort, would the "color" of his skin turn to match their historical background? Judging from what the FBI had gathered on this non-entity known as Mephisto, his was a psychopathy float-

ing free of physical form, like a parasite looking for a
suitable host.

Find a role and infect it?

The Mountie's computer informed him that he had
one new e-mail in his box.

He moved the mouse to the icon to click on it.

That, thank God, is one whodunit I will never have
to solve.

I'm glad you're food for the fishes, Mephisto.

He clicked the mouse.

The e-mail popped on-screen.

Not his day.

The e-mail was this:

? ? ? ?

Author's Note

This is a work of fiction. The plot and characters are a product of the author's imagination. Where real persons, places or institutions are incorporated to create the illusion of authenticity, they are used fictitiously. Inspiration was drawn from the following non-fiction sources:

G.P.V. Akrigg and Helen B. Akrigg, *British Columbia Chronicle, 1778–1846: Adventures by Sea and Land* (Vancouver: Discovery Press, 1975).

G.P.V. Akrigg and Helen B. Akrigg, *British Columbia Chronicle, 1847–1871: Gold and Colonists* (Vancouver: Discovery Press, 1975).

Roland Auguet, *Cruelty and Civilization: The Roman Games* (London: Routledge, 1994).

Robert Bain, *The Clans and Tartans of Scotland* (London: Collins, 1968).

William S. Baring-Gould, *The Annotated Sherlock Holmes* (New York: Potter, 1967).

Aubrey Burl, *Rings of Stone: The Prehistoric Stone Circles of Britain and Ireland* (New York: Ticknor & Fields, 1980).

David J. Breeze, *The Northern Frontiers of Roman Britain* (London: Batsford, 1982).

Richard Cavendish, editor, *Man, Myth and Magic: The Illustrated Encyclopedia of Mythology, Religion and the Unknown* (New York: Marshall Cavendish, *1995).*

James Charlton and Lisbeth Mark, *The Writer's Home Companion* (New York: Penguin, 1987).

G.M. Chayko, E.D. Gulliver and D.V. Macdougall, *Forensic Evidence in Canada* (Aurora: Canada Law Book, 1991).

Christopher Chippindale, *Stonehenge Complete* (London: Thames and Hudson, 1994).

Emily Anne Croom, *Unpuzzling Your Past: A Basic Guide for Genealogy* (White Hall: Betterway, 1989).

Ignatius Donnelly, *Atlantis: The Antediluvian World* (London: Sidgwick, 1950).

Marie Elliott, *Mayne Island and the Outer Gulf Islands: A History* (Mayne Island: Gulf Islands Press, 1984).

Christiane Eluère, *The Celts: First Masters of Europe* (London: Thames and Hudson, 1993).

Ronald Embleton and Frank Graham, *Hadrian's Wall in the Days of the Romans* (Newcastle Upon Tyne: Graham, 1984).

George B. Everton, Sr., *The Handy Book for Genealogists* (Logan: Everton, 1981).

Brian M. Fagan, *The Adventure of Archaeology* (Washington: National Geographic Society, 1985).

Curt Gentry, *J. Edgar Hoover: The Man and the Secrets* (New York: Norton, 1991).

Barry M. Gough, *The Royal Navy and the Northwest Coast of North America, 1810–1914* (Vancouver: University of British Columbia Press, 1971).

Gulf Islands Branch of the B.C. Historical Association, *A Gulf Islands Patchwork: Some Early Events on the Islands of Galiano, Mayne, Saturna, North and South Pender* (1961).

Evan Hadingham, *Circles and Standing Stones: An Illustrated Exploration of Megalithic Mysteries in Early Britain* (New York: Walker, 1975).

Gerald Hawkins, *Stonehenge Decoded* (New York: Dell, 1965).

Francis Hitching, *The World Atlas of Mysteries* (London: Pan, 1978).

S.W. Horrall, *The Pictorial History of the Royal Canadian Mounted Police* (Toronto: McGraw-Hill, 1973).

Bob Hyde and Walter DeVenne, compilers, *The Doo Wop Box* (Los Angeles: Rhino Records, 1993). Feeling blue? Try Nick's cure. Jump in the Chevy Impala, thrum your fingers to this and drive to Hope.

Michael Jordan, *Cults: Prophecies, Practices and Personalities* (London: publisher unknown, 1996).

Lloyd Laing and Jenny Laing, *The Picts and the Scots* (Dover: Sutton, 1993).

Peter Lancaster Brown, *Megaliths, Myths and Men: An Introduction to Astro-Archaeology* (Dorset: Blandford, 1976).

Francis E. Lloyd, *The Carnivorous Plants* (New York: Ronald, 1942).

Jim Lotz, *The Mounties: The History of the Royal Canadian Mounted Police* (Greenwich: Bison, 1984).

Ron MacIsaac, Don Clark and Charles Lillard, *The Devil of DeCourcy Island: The Brother XII* (Victoria: Porcepic, 1989).

Fitzroy Maclean, *Scotland: A Concise History* (London: Thames and Hudson, 1993).

Patrick Moore, *The Moon* (New York: Rand McNally, 1981).

Alan Mountain, *The Diver's Handbook* (New York: Lyons and Burford, 1997).

Peter Murray, *Homesteads and Snug Harbours* (Ganges: Horsdal, 1991).

National Geographic Society, *Mysteries of the Ancient World* (Washington; 1979).

Tim Newark, *Celtic Warriors: 400 B.C.–A.D. 1600* (London: Blandford, 1986).

Peter C. Newman, *Empire of the Bay: An Illustrated History of the Hudson's Bay Company* (Toronto: Viking, 1989).

John Oliphant, *Brother Twelve: The Incredible Story of Canada's False Prophet and His Doomed Cult of Gold, Sex, and Black Magic* (Toronto: McClelland and Stewart, 1991).

Margaret A. Ormsby, *British Columbia: A History* (Toronto: MacMillan, 1958).

David Peat, *The Armchair Guide to Murder and Detection* (Ottawa: Deneau, 1984).

Hugh Peskett, *Discover Your Ancestors: A Quest for Your Roots* (New York: Arco, 1978).

T.G.E. Powell, *The Celts* (London: Thames and Hudson, 1980).

John Prebble, *Glencoe: The Story of the Massacre* (London: Penguin, 1968).

Richard Preston, *The Hot Zone* (New York: Random House, 1994).

Reader's Digest, *Quest for the Past* (Montreal, 1984).

David Richardson, *Pig War Islands: The San Juans of Northwest Washington* (Eastsound: Orcas, 1990).

Graham Ritchie and Anna Ritchie, *Scotland: Archaeology and Early History* (London: Thames and Hudson, 1981).

W.F. Ritchie and J.N.G. Ritchie, *Celtic Warriors* (Aylesbury: Shire, 1985).

Fred Rogers, *Shipwrecks of British Columbia* (Vancouver: Douglas and McIntyre, 1973).

D. Kim Rossmo, *Geographic Profiling: Target Patterns of Serial Murderers* (Burnaby: Simon Fraser University, 1995).

D. Kim Rossmo, "Geographic Profiling" in *Offender Profiling: Theory, Research, and Practice,* eds. Janet L. Jackson and Debra A. Bekerian (Chichester: John Wiley and Sons, 1997).

D. Kim Rossmo, "Place, Space, and Police Investigations: Hunting Serial Violent Criminals," in *Crime and Place*, eds. John E. Eck and David Weisburd (New York: Criminal Justice Press, 1995).

John Sharkey, *Celtic Mysteries: The Ancient Religion* (London: Thames and Hudson, 1975).

David Spalding, Andrea Spalding, Georgina Montgomery and Lawrence Pitt, *Southern Gulf Islands of British Columbia* (Vancouver: Altitude, 1995).

Donald Spoto, *The Dark Side of Genius: The Life of Alfred Hitchcock* (New York: Ballantine, 1984).

Chris Steinbrunner and Otto Penzler, editors, *Encyclopedia of Mystery and Detection* (New York: McGraw-Hill, 1976).

Athan G. Theoharis and John Stuart Cox, *The Boss: J. Edgar Hoover and the Great American Inquisition* (Philadelphia: Temple University Press, 1988).

The Vancouver Sun

V. Vale and Andrea Juno, editors, *Modern Primitives: An Investigation of Contemporary Adornment and Ritual* (San Francisco: Re/Search 12, 1989).

John Edwin Wood, *Sun, Moon and Standing Stones* (Oxford University Press, 1978).

Yes, there is MacDonald in my clan background, but I never met a Campbell I didn't like. Still, somebody has to play the bad guy, eh?

My thanks to the Mounties, and the San Juan County Sheriff's Department, and the Federal Bureau of Investigation, and the Vancouver Police Department for their generosity in answering my questions.

And especially to Detective Inspector Kim Rossmo, who allowed me to fictionalize him so shamelessly. He *is* DeClercq's kind of cop.

Slade
Vancouver, B.C.